By Christopher Dow

Fiction
Effigy
>Book I: Stroud
>Book II: Oakdale

The Books of Bob
>Devil of a Time
>Jumping Jehovah

The Clay Guthrie Mysteries
>The Dead Detective
>Landscape with Beast
>The Texas Troll Unlimited
>Darkness Insatiable

Roadkill
The Werewolf and Tide, and Other Compulsions

Nonfiction
Lord of the Loincloth (nonfiction novel)
Book of Curiosities: Adventures in the Paranormal
Occasional Pilgrimage: Essays on Film, Literature, and Other Matters
Living the Story: The Meandering, True, and Sometimes Strange
>Adventures of an Unknown Writer
>Vol.I: Growing Up Takes a Long Time
>Vol. II: Growing Old Takes Longer

Martial Arts
The Wellspring: An Inquiry into the Nature of Chi
Circling the Square: Observations on the Dynamics of Tai Chi Chuan
Elements of Power: Essays on the Art and Practice of Tai Chi Chuan
Alchemy of Breath: An Introduction to Chi Kung
Leaves on the Wind: A Survey of Martial Arts Literature (Vol. I–VI)

Poetry
City of Dreams
The Trip Out
Texas White Line Fever
Networks
A Dilapidation of Machinery
Puzzle Pieces: Selected Poems

Editor
The Abby Stone: The Poetry of Bartholo Dias
The Best of Phosphene
The Best of Dialog

LANDSCAPE WITH BEAST

LANDSCAPE WITH BEAST

CHRISTOPHER DOW

Phosphene Publishing Company
Temple, Texas

Landscape with Beast
© 2016 by Christopher Dow
ISBN 10: 0-9851477-5-X
ISBN 13: 978-0-9851477-5-4

Published by
Phosphene Publishing Company
Houston, Texas, USA phosphenepublishing.com

2.1

For Shannon

Our wisdom comes usually from experience, and our experience comes largely from our experience.

—Unknown

LANDSCAPE WITH

BEAST

1

THE FIST WENT BY HIS face with an audible whoosh. Guthrie launched a back fist at the side of his opponent's head, but the man's arm snaked around Guthrie's, trapping it in a movement almost too quick to follow. He twisted suddenly to his left, locking Guthrie's elbow, and thrust forward, releasing Guthrie at the last instant. Guthrie felt himself lifted off his feet, and he fell backward and landed on his butt on the cement floor.

He scrambled to his feet and warily approached his opponent. The man's dark eyes, twinkling with amusement, watched him calmly.

"I'm going to get you," Guthrie said. "Eventually, I'm going to get you."

"Not until you learn to relax and go with the flow," Li Wu replied, shifting his stance slightly as Guthrie neared. "Tension is a handle your enemy can use against you."

"Yeah, well, handle this...."

Guthrie planned to feint to Wu's head with his right, rabbit punch him in the gut with his left, then use a right palm strike to his sternum but he never got past the feint. Wu's right hand snared Guthrie's right wrist, then he stepped behind Guthrie's forward leg, lifted his left bicep into Guthrie's armpit, and twisted to the left, levering Guthrie over his leg.

Guthrie fell backward with a woof. He and Wu were in the gym in Guthrie's new garage, and the cement floor would have been harder on his back and head than it had been on his butt, but thankfully, Wu broke his fall just before Guthrie hit.

"I just don't get it," Guthrie said as he rose. "You seem to know what I'm going to do before I do it. A year of this, and I still can't touch you."

"Listening and sensing energies, Clay. They allow you to perceive incoming force and give you ample opportunity to divert it to your best advantage." Wu put a hand on Guthrie's shoulder. He was an inch or so shorter than Guthrie, and leaner, but infinitely more deadly. "You've learned how to do the tai chi movements, but using them properly requires letting go of your preconceptions and expanding your sphere of awareness to include your opponent."

"I don't know if I'll ever get that."

"Tai chi isn't simple, but you've come a long way since we started. Next lesson, we'll work on sensitivity training."

"Why not now? We've only been at it for an hour. It's not even ten."

"We'll have to cut it short today." Wu gestured through the open garage door toward the back of Guthrie's house. "You have a visitor."

"Oh." Guthrie had a sinking sensation in the pit of his stomach.

A smile creased Wu's handsome face.

"Do I detect a note of trepidation in your voice?"

"I barely seen him for the last three three years, and I'm not sure I want to now. He's too damn scary. And since he's visiting me, he probably want me to do something for him."

"Yes. He is scary. But remember, I have to see him a lot more often than you do. And, yes, he probably wants you to do something. That's the way it is with him"

"I don't know how you take it," Guthrie said, shaking his head.

"Listening and sensing energies," Wu said, and they both laughed.

"Okay," Guthrie said. "Next Tuesday, then?"

"We'll see. Call me when you're free, and we'll resume your training."

So, Guthrie thought. It's going to be like that.

Wu retrieved his wallet, car keys, and cell phone from where he'd left them on the clothes dryer and went out of the garage, into the early June sunshine. Guthrie punched the button to roll down the garage door and followed him.

Thank goodness the year had been unseasonably cool so far, he thought as he watched Wu walk to the wooden fence across the driveway and push through the gate. But as the gate shut behind Wu,

Guthrie stared at the back door, thinking that the heat had finally arrived, unannounced. Maybe he should follow Wu, get in his own car, and drive away from here. But Wu didn't start his engine, and he'd parked behind Guthrie's Xterra. Apparently, he was waiting to give the old man a ride home. Or at least somewhere.

Guthrie briefly wondered if the old man had been waiting the whole time or if someone had brought him while Wu was throwing Guthrie around in the garage. Did it matter? He was in there now.

Sighing, Guthrie went up the back steps and into the house.

He found his visitor sitting on the sofa in the living room, reading Guthrie's copy of James Howard Kunstler's *The Geography of Nowhere*.

"Hello, Master Tereba." Guthrie gestured toward the book. "I thought you already had that kind of geography figured out."

He didn't ask why the old man was here; he'd learn soon enough. As he sat in the easy chair across the coffee table from the sofa, Tereba set the book on the table, turned his unfathomably deep eyes on Guthrie, and smiled. He didn't look any different than the last time Guthrie had seen him: his short bush of white hair contrasting sharply with his mahogany skin and the liveliness of his lithe body and sure movements. He was dressed in a white cambric shirt and khaki pants, and white sneakers clad his feet. Guthrie couldn't help but smile himself at how deceptively innocuous the old man looked—like just another African-American gentleman of indeterminate older age.

"It is a most interesting book," Tereba said. "When I visited the Columbian Exposition, America's future was depicted in such clean, sweeping lines. As Mr. Kunstler point out," he tapped the book, "it's just become cluttered, noisy, and dehumanizing."

Indeterminate older age was right, Guthrie thought.

"I guess we've gotten pretty good at messing things up," he responded a bit sourly. He wasn't thinking of his own circumstances, which hadn't been so bad lately, but society everywhere seemed to be in generally rotten shape, which was bound to affect his livelihood. And everybody's peace of mind.

"These days, people take fantasy as fact," Tereba said. "Worse, they take fact as fantasy."

"Strange words coming from you. But I guess you'd know better than anyone."

"Of all people, you understand how to cut to the true heart of the matter."

Guthrie passed off the compliment, if it was one, mostly because he didn't believe he had any greater insight into reality than the next person. Tereba excepted.

"What brings you here?" Guthrie asked, tiring of the cryptic remarks that passed for Tereba's small talk.

"Perhaps I just wanted to check on you."

"Li could have told you anything you wanted to know."

"Some things one must discover for oneself."

Guthrie had to admit that was true.

"You appear to be well and fit. Wu reports that you have been receptive to his training."

"Yeah, I'm pretty much always on the receiving end."

Tereba chuckled then waved around the room.

"I see you've repaired your house."

"New roof, a little carpentry, paint, new garage."

"All necessary. But what about beauty? Your walls remain barren."

"You mean art?" Guthrie shrugged. "I guess I've been too busy to think about putting anything up."

"You should not neglect to do so. Is life not about refinement as much as utility?"

"You'd know more about that than I do, but you're probably right."

"I may have lived a very long time, but that doesn't mean I know more about life than you or anyone else. No matter what I've done or where I've been, I've remained but a journeyman."

"Whatever you say. But anyone who's journeyed as long and as far as you must have picked up some knowledge along the way."

"Knowledge is not knowing." The old man sighed. "If only it were."

"That's semantic bullshit," Guthrie retorted with some irritation. He pointed to his front door. "After you go through that, it will still be there. But half the time I went out of your door, it vanished."

"It doesn't vanish," Tereba said. "If it did, how would I come and go in my own home?"

Guthrie rolled his eyes.

"Okay. So when it closes in one place, it opens in another. Pretty neat trick for someone with no knowledge."

"And there you have it. A trick. Did you ever consider that the door is always there, just hidden from view by a trick of light and angles?"

"A trick of light that fools the touch? I've been back out there and felt all along that wall, and when the door is not there, it's only a cement block wall."

"I had no idea it worked so well." There was amusement in the old man's eyes.

Guthrie's mouth twisted into a wry smile, and he shook his head.

"Must be lonely," he said.

"It is," Tereba acknowledged, giving his own sad smile. "But knowing you has brightened my life."

It sounded sincere, and maybe it was, but Guthrie could never be sure what ulterior motive might lurk within the unfathomable wells of the old man's dark eyes.

"How's your work?"

"It's good," Guthrie said. "Thanks to you, I don't have to take jobs I don't want, like photographing illicit affairs or chasing down bail jumpers."

He didn't bother reminding Tereba that he'd had no choice in helping the old man send Aswad Mar back to the hell that had spawned it. Tereba had given him no alternative, and if there was anything Guthrie hated, it was being given no alternatives, especially when his life and sanity were at stake. But the old man had been generous afterward, and the financial rewards had been the least of what Guthrie had received in compensation for the grueling ordeal.

"What about missing persons?"

"Depends," Guthrie said warily. "Is someone missing?"

"Someone is always missing. I suppose that is the nature of life."

"Are you trying to put me to work again?"

"You sound as if you don't like the idea."

"The last time, you killed me," Guthrie reminded him.

"Ah, yes," The old man shrugged. "It had to be done. And afterward I restored your life, did I not?"

"Only after I got rid of Aswad Mar for you." Guthrie peered at the old man and said pointedly, "Didn't you tell me it was the great guilt of your life?"

Tereba nodded thoughtfully.

"It was, and I am grateful for your help. I know it cost you dearly."

Shit, Guthrie thought. He should have known better than to try to back the old man into a corner. Somehow, Guthrie was the one who always came out on the defensive.

"Okay," he said. "I admit I paid lead for gold." He stared down at his hands for a moment, not really seeing them, then looked back at Tereba. "What do you have in mind?"

"I am not certain. I merely have a sense of powerful forces at work that I believe could lead to a situation of great gravity, but their exact nature is hidden from me. And who better to send into a grave situation to find out what lies buried there than one who has known death? Such as you, my friend."

"Can you be a little more specific?" Guthrie asked, not trying to hide his sarcasm. He didn't believe the friendship routine for one second.

"I have become aware that a report on a missing person—a specific missing person—has been filed with the police. And ignored. This person is at the nexus of the forces I just mentioned. But this person has disappeared from my range of perception. I simply wish for you to locate him and apprise me of the situation."

"Who is it?"

"Be patient," Tereba replied. "I'm sure you will reveal everything in good time."

He rose and went to the front door. Guthrie followed and opened the door.

"That's it?" Guthrie asked. "Where do I start if I don't know anything about this missing person?"

"I've given you all you need, Mr. Guthrie," Tereba said, stepping out onto the front porch. "Take care."

That'll be difficult, Guthrie thought, if I'm working for you.

"I will," he said. "You, too, Master Tereba."

The old man stepped spryly off the porch, walked to Wu's burgundy sedan, and got inside. He waved as Wu backed the sedan out of the driveway, and a moment later the car was out of sight.

Guthrie went back inside, wondering what kind of bad karma it was that had brought him into contact with Tereba. Or was it dharma? After all, the old man had helped him come to terms with his own perfidy and guilt, not to mention helping make it possible for Guthrie to set up his own investigative business.

Whatever it was, it didn't appear that Tereba was going away any time soon, even if it had taken him some time to show up again.

Sighing, Guthrie stared around the living room, puzzling over what, exactly, the old man expected. Whatever it was, Li Wu seemed to think it might occupy some time, but Tereba hadn't given Guthrie more than obscure hints.

But as Guthrie neared the sofa, where he intended to sit and relax and try to put Tereba out of his mind, he noticed the book the old man had been reading sitting on the coffee table. A slip of paper jutted from the pages like a bookmark. When he pulled it out, he saw it was a business card for a place called the Zephyr Gallery.

"Crap," he muttered, recalling Tereba's comment about the lack of art on his walls. A frown on his face, he changed into street clothes, locked up the house, and went to his car to go shopping for art.

2

WHILE HE DROVE, GUTHRIE THOUGHT about time and aging because Tereba was a real puzzle there. Apparently, he'd somehow managed to eliminate the aging process. Guthrie suspected he was many centuries old at least, but he could be even older. The references he frequently made to figures and events from the distant past always rang of direct familiarity. Of course, it all might be a come-on, but Guthrie didn't think so. Wu was nearly as enigmatic as Tereba, but over the past three years, Guthrie had gotten to know the tai chi master pretty well, and Wu didn't strike him as the kind of man who'd follow either a charlatan or a criminal. Wu gave the old man the sort of veneration and fealty due someone who possessed not just age and experience, but powerful and influential authority, and that told Guthrie more about Tereba than the old man would ever divulge himself.

The Zephyr Gallery was located in a brown brick house a few blocks from the north edge of Rice Village, on a street where other similar houses also had been turned into small businesses: a restaurant, a hair salon, a dentist. Guthrie had never noticed the gallery before, though it was possible he'd passed it—or the house, at least —on the infrequent occasions that he drove through this part of town. But he wasn't usually scouting for art.

Not that he didn't like it; his life just hadn't included art in its boundaries. When he'd married Alice and had been rising through the police ranks, trying to make detective, he'd been too preoccupied and poor. And after he was shot and Alice left him, he was poorer yet in money and spirit. If he was better off now—psychologically and emotionally as well as financially—than he'd been before, it was only because mysterious old Tereba had helped rescue him from his first clients. And, most of all, from the deadly mire of his personal guilt and self-destruction.

Since then, business had been good, as if a cloud of benevolence hung over him. Good enough that he could turn down the sleazier types of cases, like shadowing unfaithful spouses and seeking bail jumpers. The former brought back too many bad personal memories, and the latter reminded him too much of his self-destructive years as a cop. He wasn't rich, but he had a nice buffer in the bank, was working steadily, and was better than breaking even—enough that he could afford to fix his formerly ramshackle bungalow, buy a new car, and open a small office in Office City, a circa 1960s office park just inside 610 Loop, about two miles from his neighborhood. He still couldn't afford a secretary, but at least he was making an attempt to separate his work from his life.

His life, such as it was. He had money in the bank, and after years of ruinous self-contempt, he could now look in the mirror and see a human being staring back. But he couldn't say he had much of a life beyond those rudiments. Certainly no one to share it with, to ease the loneliness. Sometimes, he wished Alice was here to see how much he'd changed, though it wasn't likely he'd ever see her again. As Tereba implied, it was foolish to ignore facts and let fantasy control your life. Alice was gone, and too much negativity had passed between them for him to ever break through the barriers even if he did run across her. But that didn't mean he couldn't start something new—and better—if he could find the right person.

Maybe Tereba was right. Guthrie's walls were sound and freshly painted, but they were barren. He could use a little art to brighten up the place. It might help reintroduce him to a greater joy in living and open him to new possibilities.

The gallery's little front yard had been converted into an asphalt parking lot grafted onto the concrete driveway that ran beside the right side of the house. Behind the house, the driveway widened in front of a large garage apartment that occupied most of the property behind the main structure. The parking lot and front of the house were tastefully bordered with low shrubs and flowers in neat raised beds constructed from landscaping timbers. All five spaces were empty. Guthrie pulled his Xterra into one of them and went inside.

The house, like many in the area—and indeed in Guthrie's own neighborhood of Park Place—had been built sometime in the 1930s or 1940s. Inside, a wall had been removed to combine the original living room and dining room into a fair-sized exhibition space. There was a small desk just inside the door. No one was sitting at it, but a sign-in book, its top page about half filled with signatures, sat on top, and next to it, a decorative jar held a couple of business cards. Guthrie ignored the book but dropped one of his cards in the jar, wondering why he was here.

Walking through the main gallery and into the back of the house, he saw that two of the bedrooms had been converted into smaller exhibition spaces. The door to the third bedroom was ajar, and from what he could see, it was an office.

He seemed to be alone, so he returned to the main gallery and started looking at the paintings on the walls. They were all abstract cityscapes executed in an expressionistic style. The signature was the same on all of them, but to Guthrie it was an illegible scrawl. A card affixed to the wall next to one of the paintings said the artist was somebody named Jeff Harcombe. Guthrie didn't recognize the name, but he basically liked what he saw. He worked his way around the room, then he went into one of the bedrooms. The art here was completely different—collage work by another artist—Paul Stevens—and he liked this stuff better. It consisted mostly of strange landscapes fashioned from photos and drawings clipped from magazines and newspapers. After a few minutes, he came out, intending to go into the second bedroom, but in the hallway, he nearly collided with a woman carrying a large framed photograph.

"Shit!" the woman cried, drawing back tensely.

"Sorry," Guthrie said. "I didn't mean to startle you."

"I didn't realize anyone was here," she said, catching her breath. "Friday afternoons are usually kind of slow."

The woman was nice to look at, in her early thirties, about five-six, and maybe 130 pounds. Her medium-length light brown hair was pulled back in a careless ponytail, and a few wisps of it had escaped to float around her temples. She wore blue jeans, sneakers, and a tan, short-sleeved button blouse with the tails tied around her waist, and it looked like she'd been working. She also seemed nervous with a tension that went beyond being startled.

"Just let me put this down," she said.

She took the photograph into the second bedroom, and Guthrie could see that other photos—all black-and-whites—hung on the walls except for a couple of blank spaces. The photos showed odd but interesting angles of portions of hard-edged contemporary buildings, and each one sported a close-up of a tasteful nude whose sensuous curves belied her stark setting. The woman leaned the photo she'd been carrying against the wall below one of the empty spaces then turned to Guthrie.

"I was out in storage," she explained. "I sold three of the photos yesterday, and I was bringing in replacements. Do you like them?"

"I was on my way in when I ran into you," Guthrie explained. "But I caught a glimpse." He nodded. "They're nice, but I like the collages best."

"Yes," she agreed. "Paul's work is first-rate. I'm thinking of doing a whole show around him."

"Should sell," he said.

"Think so?" She peered at him. "Are you an artist?"

"Do I look like an artist?"

She smiled. "More like an artist than an art buyer, but if I'm mistaken, don't let that stop you from picking something out."

"I was thinking of buying something for my living room," Guthrie said. "But I'm just browsing right now. I don't want to keep you from your work."

"Okay," she said. "Call out if you need help."

Guthrie thanked her and returned to the room with the collages and looked them over once more. There were a couple he liked a lot, and the prices seemed reasonable. He didn't think that buying art was what he was really here for, but since he wasn't sure just what he *was* here for, he might as well do something about his empty walls. He went back to the room where he'd left the woman and saw she'd hung another photograph in the second empty space and was eyeing it to see if it was straight.

"Excuse me," he said. "I see something out here I like. Can I buy it right now?"

"Of course." She followed him into the other bedroom. "One of Paul's collages? Good thing you came today. These are going down this afternoon, and I'm hanging something else in here tomorrow morning. Which one did you want?"

"This one," Guthrie pointed.

"You have a good eye. It has excellent composition."

Guthrie wondered if she was trying to flatter him, but she seemed sincere—and a little too preoccupied to be consciously calculating. He decided to take her comment at face value, though he really didn't know what constituted good composition in a piece of art. He just liked the piece's overall impression, and it was complex enough that he thought he could look at it a lot and not get tired of it.

"Let me go wrap this up," she said as she lifted the collage from its hangers, which consisted of long wires hooked to heavy crown molding. Good way not to have to keep putting holes in the wall, Guthrie thought.

"Why don't you wait in here?" She led him into the hall and pushed open the door to the office with her foot. The center of the room was occupied by a wooden desk that looked like it had been bought at IKEA. She cleared a purse and a half-filled plastic grocery sack off a visitor's chair and pulled it up to the desk for him to sit in. "Make yourself comfortable. I'll be right back."

The office was organized and clean but not especially tidy. Several filing cabinets sat against one wall, and another was lined with bookshelves that matched the desk. Books and magazines on art and several dozen loose-leaf binders sat on the shelves. Paintings—large and small—occupied every available section of wall, and small sculptures decorated the shelves.

The windows opened onto the back of the house, giving a good view of the garage apartment. The two roll-up doors beneath the apartment were shut, but the people door beside the left one was ajar. A newish Ford Escape sat in front of one of the roll-up doors.

The woman returned a few minutes later, carrying the collage neatly wrapped in heavy brown paper. As she propped it against the door, she saw him looking out the windows.

"My storage facility," she explained with a smile. "The bottom, that is. The top is home sweet home."

She sat at her desk, took some forms from a drawer, and began filling them out.

"Zephyr is an interesting name for a gallery," Guthrie said. "Poetic."

"I've always like the word," she replied, glancing up from her paperwork. "The problem is it starts with Z. I should have named it AAAZephyr so it would be first in the Yellow Pages."

Guthrie chuckled then watched in silence until she passed two of the forms to him.

"These are both bills of sale," she said. "One for you, and one for me. Sign here on both."

Guthrie did and handed one back along with his debit card. She processed the card, returned it, and a moment later gave him the receipt to sign.

"Thank you, Mr. Guthrie," she said after the transaction was complete. "I hope you enjoy the collage. Would you like to be put on our mailing list?"

"I put a card in the jar," he said as he stood.

"Don't worry," she replied, a twinkle in her eyes. "We don't sell our clients' names to spammers."

He chuckled as he picked up the wrapped collage and headed for the front door.

"Please tell your friends about the gallery," she said as she let him out.

"I will," he said. *If I had any friends to tell*, he thought.

He went out, and she shut the door behind him. As he slid the collage into the back seat of his SUV, he wondered once again why Tereba had sent him here. Shrugging that he'd undoubtedly find out soon enough, he started the car and returned home, where he dropped off the collage. He then drove to Dot's Coffee Shop across the freeway from his office to grab a bite to eat before going to his office to see if anything was shaking.

In his office building, he collected his mail from the bank of boxes in an alcove just off the main hall, and a few moments later, he was inside his office, shuffling through the envelopes. Two bills had somehow managed to weasel their way into the junk mail. He tossed them into a tray and the junk into the trash can, then he turned to his phone and saw that the message light was lit.

"Hello," said a tense woman's voice. "My name is Diane Weston. You just came to my gallery—the Zephyr—and bought a collage. I was wondering if you could call me. I think I need some help. Please. It's important."

3

GUTHRIE DIDN'T CALL. INSTEAD, HE locked up the office and went back to his Xterra. Twenty minutes later, he parked in the Zephyr Gallery's small front lot.

Inside, he noticed that the jar that held the business cards was empty.

"Hello," he called out.

"Yes?" came a woman's voice from the back, followed by footsteps. The woman he'd bought the collage from emerged.

"You left a message on my voice mail," Guthrie said.

"I didn't know you're a detective," she said, brushing stray wisps of hair back from her temples. "I thought you'd call."

"You said it was important, and I knew you were here."

"It is. Thank you for coming back. Let's go into the office."

Guthrie sat in the same chair he'd recently occupied, and she went around the desk to her own chair.

"Oh, yes," she said. "I'm Diane Weston." She stuck out her hand.

"Pleased to meet you," Guthrie said, giving her hand a brief shake.

"Not as pleased as I am to meet you. Again." The tension Guthrie noted earlier was back. "I don't know any detectives. It's lucky you came by and left your card."

Yeah, Guthrie thought. Lucky. If you only knew. "Your message didn't say what your problem is."

"It's one of my artists," she said quickly. "Howard Graham. He's missing."

Surprise, surprise.

"Have you gone to the police?"

"Yes," she said. "I filed a missing person report, and they said they'd investigate, but I don't think they really did. They said there's nothing they can do. There was no evidence of foul play, and people move all the time and lose contact with people they know. And since I'm not family, I don't have any legal rights. I think they decided it was just a case of a guy dumping a girl who just didn't get it." The tension in her voice was tinged with bitterness.

Guthrie might have been inclined to agree, except for one fact: Tereba had sent him here to look for a missing person.

"You don't think he's just moved or gone off somewhere?"

"No. I'm Howard's agent. Besides, I've known him for years, and there's no reason for him not to get in touch with me or to return my calls."

"Forgive me for asking, but *did* he dump you? Are you lovers?"

"Is that relevant?" Her shoulders stiffened, and her jaw set.

"I don't know. Are you?"

"No," she said, shaking her head a little too quickly. Then she caught Guthrie's stare, shrugged her shoulders slightly, and gave a nervous little laugh. "All right. We were, for a time. Nearly four years. But it wasn't much of a relationship, really. You could say that Howard is married to his work." The bitterness surfaced again, this time at the corners of her mouth.

"So, it ended?"

"A few months ago. I don't know what happened, exactly. He just made it clear that I was no longer part of his personal life. He still wanted me to represent him, though. That's why it's really strange I haven't heard from him."

"How long since you last talked to him?"

She pursed her lips. "Two months. A little less."

"That seems like a pretty long time for an artist to be out of touch with his agent."

"Also long enough to stand up a very important client. Howard is a great portrait artist. He's very good at capturing both the image and the essence. That's how he makes his money. He'd already cancelled one appointment with this client a couple of weeks before he disappeared, and he just didn't show up at the rescheduled time."

"People can get distracted," Guthrie ventured.

"Responsible people don't let distractions undermine their livelihoods," she said brusquely, as if she were peeved but worried, too. "The last time I actually saw him, we argued about it, but he just brushed it off, even though the client was angry and could damage his reputation. All he cared about was that...."

She stopped suddenly and glanced up at Guthrie then down at her desk, but not before Guthrie caught a furtive look in her eyes.

"Cared about what, Ms. Weston?"

"Nothing," she said, absently fiddling with some papers on her desk. "It's not important."

"Let me ask you something about art," he said.

"Yes?" She looked up, curious. And maybe a little relieved that he'd changed the subject.

He pointed to a painting on the wall to his right—an excellent lifelike landscape with a shallow creek flowing in front of a rocky abutment that was studded with scrub trees and brush.

"In the water, the artist...."

"Howard," she interrupted. "That's one of Howard's paintings. He made his money doing portraits, but he preferred painting landscapes."

"Okay. See where Howard put those little white highlights on the water?"

"Yes."

"What would happen if he'd left those out?"

"Well, he wouldn't have," she said. "That's what gives the water motion, what gives life to the painting."

"So this apparently minor detail is really what pulls everything in the painting together?"

She gave a frown, but it wasn't an angry one. More like one of pain. "I get your point," she said reluctantly. "But I really don't see what it could possibly have to do with anything."

"Tell me, anyway," Guthrie insisted, not believing her because she didn't seem to believe it herself.

"Howard was working on a landscape." She paused. "For a couple of weeks just before he disappeared." She snorted. "Working is too mild a word. I'd call him obsessed. He was so excited. He said he was developing a technique that was a quantum leap above anything else he'd ever done. He showed it to me a couple of times—

once early on when it was just blocked in and again when it was about three-quarters done. The second time, I thought, my God. It was incredible. The subject was an almost barren landscape, and superficially, it looked a lot like his other West Texas landscapes, though it didn't have any particularly interesting or defining features. In the foreground were a few oddly shaped, scrubby trees interspersed with some other weird plants and a large boulder. A rocky hill in the background was the central focus, and more of the scrubby trees were growing sparsely on the slopes.

"That sounds normal enough when I say it, and aside from the strange plants, which looked a little like something out of a sci-fi book cover, there wasn't anything strange about the painting. Or shouldn't have been. But it was strange. At first, I thought that was because of the technique. That was just incredible in its depth and detail. Everything just popped out like it was vibrantly alive. There aren't many painters who can do something like that, and he hadn't even finished it. But the more I looked at it the weirder it seemed. Not the subject." She paused, took a breath, and gave Guthrie a look that mixed embarrassment with resignation. "I know this is going to sound nuts, but the painting just put out a creepy vibe. Maybe it was something about the composition, but I didn't see it long enough to analyze it." She shook her head and shrugged.

"I said that the plants were unusual, and at first I thought that his hyper-realistic depiction of them was what bothered me. He said the scene wasn't important. It was just something that came to him. A challenge to test his new-found technique. When he was done experimenting, he planned to apply the technique to a larger painting that someone had commissioned. After that, he'd use it on his normal subject matter. I should have been suspicious. As his agent, I should have known who commissioned the larger painting, but I didn't. I imagine now that I can see a hint of guilt on his face in the image in my memory, but at the time, I was too awed with what he was accomplishing to have any doubts. I knew that if he applied what he was doing to any normal sort of subject matter, he would move right into the upper pantheon. Beyond it. He'd make history.

"I went to the studio a few days later to check on him. Right after the first time he missed the appointment with the client. I went to tell him I'd arranged another sitting, but I was equally curious about the new painting. When I asked him about it, though, his behavior grew very strange. Almost threatening. He'd lost weight, and he hadn't bathed in days. He'd always been driven, but now all his energy was directed into that painting, and it was consuming him. He seemed disturbed that I asked about it, like I was controlling and prying at the same time. He wouldn't even let me see it. He said it wasn't turning out as he expected, and he didn't want to sell it."

"Was that odd?"

"Howard could just about sell his signature on a blank canvas, and from what I'd seen, he could sell this new piece, weird as it was, for a small fortune to the right collector. He said he was close to something and couldn't quit, and he told me to leave so he could get back to work."

"Close to what? Finishing the painting?"

"I don't think so. I think he'd finished it and was getting ready to start the larger one. He seemed to mean something else, like a breakthrough of some sort. The new painting was going to be quite large: eight feet by eight. I know that only because he was building the panel when I was there. He'd never tried anything that size before, and when I said something about how large it was and asked if he was using his new technique on it, he got really upset, like he was angry and frightened at the same time. I reminded him of the portrait sitter's second appointment, he told me he wasn't sure he had time to meet the sitter.

"I probably should have just left without arguing, but to tell the truth, I was hurt. Things had grown strained between us for months, and I was feeling rocky emotionally. I couldn't let things go like that. I begged him to tell me what was wrong, but I couldn't get through to him. He wouldn't let me. He told me our relationship was over and not to come back without calling. Then he just shut me out, literally as well as figuratively. That was late in March.

"He missed the client's second appointment, and the client cancelled the commission. I called Howard about it several times. Our relationship may have been over, but I was still his agent, and my reputation was on the line, too. Besides, I had a couple of checks for him. But I couldn't get hold of him. I even went to his studio. He wasn't there, but his files looked like they'd been ransacked. And the big panel he'd been building was gone, along with some art supplies."

"And you didn't hear from him again?"

"I did. About a month later. He called the gallery phone and left a message."

"Doesn't he have your cell number?"

"Yes. But it was late when he called. Well after midnight."

"What did he say?"

"I still have the message. Do you want to hear it?"

Guthrie nodded, and she fiddled with the desk phone for a couple of seconds, then a man's voice came from the speaker.

"Diane," the voice said. "It's late, and I didn't want to wake you. Please forgive my behavior. I'm not in my right mind, and I've let my work come between us. It's all that bitch Adriana's fault, but it's my fault, too, for falling so blindly into her trap. I was too greedy. But I want you to know I'm finished with her. I only have to do one more thing, and it'll all be over, I promise. Please believe me. I know I treated you shabbily, but I want to make it up to you. Please meet me at Pasha tomorrow at six. Please."

The message ended.

"What's Pasha?" Guthrie asked.

"A little Indian restaurant near here we used to go to. He didn't show up. That hurt more than the last argument we'd had. I could get angry over that, but this just left me feeling abandoned."

"How does he sound to you?" Guthrie asked.

"Agitated and exhausted," she said. "And maybe frightened. But he also sounds determined."

"He said he had something to do," Guthrie said. "Any idea what?"

She shook her head.

"I was hurt, and the next day, I called him to tell him off, but he didn't answer. I called every day for a week without reaching him, and finally, I went over there. His car was there, so I was sure he was, but he didn't answer the door, so I went inside."

"How did you get in?"

"I have a key," she explained. "The break-up was so sudden, he didn't ask for it, and giving it back was the last thing on my mind at the time. I went in, but he wasn't there. There was a pile of mail beneath the mail slot, and, like I said, his car was there, but he wasn't. I didn't know what to do, so I just came back here."

"Was that when you went to the police?"

"Not yet. I was worried, but figured he was just out with someone. I tried calling him some more, but he still didn't answer. I went over again about a week later, but nothing had changed except there was more mail. That's when I called the police."

"But that didn't get you anywhere."

"No," she said, shrugging. "I've called them a few times since, always with no results. Like I said, they seem to think I'm just a clueless jilted lover."

"Is it possible that he went off to work on some other paintings? Sometimes creative people want to get away from everything they know. Be alone."

"For this long?" she asked helplessly. "Where? He has the studio. His car was there." Her shoulders slumped as if to acknowledge that Guthrie cared as little as the police had.

"Don't worry," he assured her. "I'll look into this if you want me to."

"Would you? I don't know where else to turn."

"I'll need to see Howard's studio."

"I can take you. Just give me a minute to close up here."

"Before you do," Guthrie said, "maybe we should talk about financial matters. I hate to bring it up...."

He lowballed his lowest fee, mostly to make sure she'd hire him. He would have taken the case for free since Tereba had sent him, but he didn't want to arouse her suspicions. In the end, Tereba would foot the bill. If there was an end where a bill could be footed.

"That's fine," she said, though Guthrie thought she probably was calculating how long she could pay if her missing person didn't turn up quickly. "So, you'll look for Howard?"

Thinking of how he'd been led here by Tereba, Guthrie replied, "I don't think I can resist, Ms. Weston."

4

AS GUTHRIE DROVE TOWARD HOWARD Graham's address, he pondered the fact that Tereba had introduced him to this case. That made him nervous because it meant that he wasn't just looking for a missing artist—he was looking for trouble that was sure to be strange and probably dangerous. But he didn't let the thought deter him. It wasn't that he felt he owed the old man anything. They were even as far as Guthrie was concerned. The old man had saved him, and he'd saved Tereba in return. Nor was it that he was fatally drawn to danger. But his last encounter with Tereba had shown him that anything Tereba directed his way would be as profoundly important as it might be dangerous, and those were lures he couldn't resist. If Tereba once again was having Guthrie do his bidding, Guthrie would do it without question.

But why Graham?

"How long have you known Howard?" he asked, glancing at Diane, who sat as stiffly in the passenger seat as if he were ferrying her to a funeral.

"We became friends while I was in college," she said. "The University of Houston. He was a young assistant professor teaching a course in studio arts when I entered as a fine arts major." She chuckled. "It wasn't long before I realized I didn't have the kind of talent it takes to be a professional artist. Actually, Howard was the one who clued me in, though he never said it directly. But he dropped enough gentle hints that I finally got the picture. When I did and told him I was thinking of changing my major, he said it would be a terrible waste if I left the art world and suggested I take a master's in art history. His career was starting to blossom about the time I finished my degree, and when I told him I was going to open a gallery, he said he'd be interested in having me represent his work. And things just kind of took off from there. He was my first major artist, and he's stuck with me ever since, even though he could easily go to any gallery he wants."

"He's gotten pretty famous?"

"Howard is a realistic painter of the first water," she said. "His real love is landscapes, but he's one hell of a portrait painter. Like I said, that's his principal support."

"What's his background? Any family?"

"Is that important?"

"Maybe he's gone to stay with relatives."

"He's from Michigan originally. No family, though. At least, not any more. He was an only child, and his parents were killed in a car wreck about eight years ago. He may have some other relatives somewhere, but he never mentioned them or went to see them as far as I know. Turn here."

She directed him west on Washington Avenue and, soon after, onto a side street. The area once had been a business and warehouse district mixed with small old neighborhoods grown decrepit during the last half of the twentieth century. But now, urban renewal had sent its invading clutch well into its core. Guthrie drove past bulky town homes crowded onto lots that once held bungalows, and many of the old stores and businesses were being demolished for loft apartments that reminded Guthrie of ant mounds. He would have chuckled at the phoniness of the pseudo-Victorian architecture mingled with ultra-modern but cheap-looking structures, but the sight was too common in the districts surrounding downtown to elicit more than a wisp of dry regret at neighborhood character disintegrating beneath the trampling mind-set of Houston's developers. In Houston, historical perspective was a historical marker set in the sidewalk in front of a new building and a vague and vanishing memory that things once had been different.

When they finally reached Graham's address, though, he couldn't help but give a nod of approval. The century-old two-story brick building sat on a corner lot, with its long axis along the main street. Another old, two-story brick building sat to its left, and a narrow asphalt parking lot enclosed by a chain link fence lay behind it. A row of new townhouses occupied the remainder of the block on the far side of the lot. The building had a neat, if not new, coat of light gray-green paint with burgundy trim. Only the front of the lower story had windows, which were tall, wide, faced with frosted glass, and guarded by burglar bars. Regular, unbarred, double-sash windows circled the second floor.

"Nice place," Guthrie commented as he parked on the side street near the door, which was inset at an angle in building's front right corner.

"I believe it was originally a hardware store," Diane said. "It had been abandoned for fifteen years or so before Howard bought it. His studio is on the ground floor, and he has an apartment upstairs."

They got out of the car and went into the entry alcove. There was a bell, and Guthrie pushed the button.

"I have a key," Diane reminded him.

"Maybe he's come back and wouldn't appreciate us barging in."

Diane nodded but dug her key ring out of her purse anyway.

After a minute of silence from the other side of the door, she stuck one of the keys into the lock, opened the door, and quickly punched a code into the alarm panel just inside the door. Florescent fixtures dangling from the open-beamed ceiling flared into life when she flipped the switch by the alarm panel, but the lights weren't really needed because the room was flooded by diffuse daylight coming in the tall, frosted front windows.

"Hello!" Guthrie called. "Howard?"

The silence inside the building felt empty. The interior was an artist's loft in the true sense of the word. The front two-thirds of the ground floor, which was about thirty-five by fifty feet, was one large open room. Two rows of metal support poles were spaced about every twelve feet along the long axis, and a wall built along the second row of poles ran the full length of the building. The wall was pierced by three doors, all open. A long single flight of iron stairs ascended along the end wall to their right. All the walls were painted a light industrial gray, and the stairs were black. Linoleum squares of a gray a little darker than the walls covered the floor.

The open space was furnished with three heavy easels, all lined up about ten feet from the front windows, and two adjacent work tables were crowded with paints, bottles, brushes held upright in glass jars, and other painting tools. The first two easels faced the windows, about ten feet away, but the farthest was turned to give the painter a good view of a nearby easy chair set up in front of a muted canvas backdrop near the front left corner of the room. The chair was angled so the sitter would be bathed in natural light coming in the windows. A large wooden drafting table flanked by a pair of metal storage cabinets sat against the middle of the built-in wall, and a work table covered in papers stood against the built-in wall near the stairs. Under the stairs sat two stacked flat files and a large lateral filing cabinet. A rich, tangy odor of oil paints and solvents permeated the air.

All the drawers in the flat files and lateral filing cabinet were open, and the floor in front of them was littered with papers that had been pulled from them, but otherwise, there didn't seem to be any mess that couldn't be considered normal clutter.

"You said Howard had built a large panel," Guthrie said.

"Yes. Two sheets of plywood on a two-by-four frame."

"Where is it?"

"I don't know. I saw him building it, but it wasn't here the first time I came after he disappeared."

"The door was locked, and all this was like this?" Guthrie waved toward the scattered papers in front of the flat files and filing cabinet.

When she nodded, he went over, squatted, and picked through some of the papers.

"Those are his archives," Diane said. "All the sketches and notes he works up when he's planning a painting."

"So the sketches for the landscape that he wouldn't let you see should be here?"

"Probably," she answered, sinking beside Guthrie and hastily shuffling through the papers. "I didn't really see the bigger painting, just the panel, and I'm not seeing anything like the smaller one here. But it could take days to sort through all this mess."

Guthrie helped her scoop up the papers and dump them back into the drawers.

"Did you look for the new landscape the times you were here?" Guthrie asked when they were done.

"No, I wasn't thinking of it. I was worried about Howard."

"Where would he keep it?"

She pointed to the right hand door in the back wall.

"That's his storage room. Do you think we should look for it?"

Guthrie wasn't sure the painting had anything to do with the case, but looking for it would occupy Diane, who was visibly depressed at the empty studio.

"Might be a good idea," he said. "And I'm curious to see it." He followed her inside the storage room.

The space, about twelve by twenty, was built out with racks constructed of two-by-fours and plywood. Paintings filled the racks, grouped by size. Diane found the rack holding medium-size canvases.

"It was two by three feet," she said. "It should be in here."

Guthrie watched over her shoulder as she flipped through the paintings. There were portraits, a few cityscapes, and a number of landscapes that looked like they'd been painted in Central and West Texas. From the little he saw, he could understand what Diane meant when she said Graham was a realist of the first water.

"Nothing?" Guthrie asked when she'd finished and come up empty-handed.

"No." Disappointment tinged her voice.

They left the storage room, and Guthrie stared across the studio. Light flooding through the frosted windows illuminated the room with a bright but soft illumination. Of the three easels, only two held paintings. The one nearest the door was a half-finished landscape of a hilly countryside coated with bluebonnets, and the far one bore a partially completed portrait of a distinguished older man in a dark suit. He looked like a generic CEO.

Guthrie walked over, threading his way between the easel and work table, to take a closer look. The portrait was large: nearly four feet tall and three wide. Although the painting was only half-finished, Guthrie could see that it was—or would be—an expert piece of work. Even so, there was something unsettling about it. Guthrie couldn't tell if it was the expression on the face or in the eyes or the tilt of the head. None of these seemed out of place or suggestive when he examined each in detail, but the effect of the whole put him off. Diane had said that Graham could capture the essence as well as the image. Maybe this CEO was a real shit.

"That's John Eggers," Diane said. "He's the sitter Howard stood up."

"Looks like someone who doesn't like to be kept waiting," Guthrie said, scratching absently at the talisman tattooed beneath his navel during his first case for the old man.

Tereba called it a kuei—or more properly, the Talisman of the Armor of Heaven—and it consisted of a quartered square depending a pair of wavy lines and surrounded by eight little stick-figure men. The talisman was twitching, which it hadn't done since that first case, and Guthrie took it as a sure sign that something was off kilter.

"He's on the board of a major international bank headquartered here in Houston. He's not the kind of person you keep waiting, whether he minds it or not. Come over here. I want to show you something."

She led him between the easels and the windows to the easel nearest the door.

"You probably wouldn't notice," Diane said, "but I know this place well. Look there."

She pointed to the floor, and Guthrie could see that the linoleum was spattered with paint.

"It looks like something used to be there," he said.

"Another work table with paints and supplies. It's gone. It was gone the first time I came here after he disappeared."

"Maybe he took it to paint the landscape elsewhere, as I suggested."

She shook her head.

"The table, too?" She shook her head. "It's too big and heavy. Besides, he has a field set-up in one of the cabinets in the work room." She gestured toward the middle door in the back wall.

"Where's the third door lead?"

"A washroom. His washer and dryer are in there, too."

Guthrie went over to the door and glanced inside. Cabinets, counters, and shelving had been built into the back wall. Beneath the cabinets sat a clothes washer and dryer. A toilet and sink were along a second wall.

"Let's go look at the work room."

The middle door opened into a room almost as large as the storage room. Directly across from the door was a large steel door painted black and set with a small, wire-mesh window. It looked like it might have been the loading dock when the building had been a hardware store. It had crossbar brackets as well as a substantial knob lock. The door was shut and the knob latch was locked, but the crossbar itself was lying on the floor.

"Was this like this before?" he asked, bending and picking up the crossbar, which was a two-by-four about six feet long.

"I'm not sure," she said. "I didn't come back here."

Guthrie propped the crossbar in the corner and looked around the room. Lining the back wall were cabinets, countertops, and two deep stainless steel sinks that were, nonetheless, stained with paint. One of the cabinet doors was open, and painting supplies lay haphazardly on the counter and floor below it.

He turned again to the back door and peered through the window. Outside was a narrow parking lot paved with old asphalt and surrounded by an eight-foot chain-link fence trimmed with razor wire. A metal carport was to the left of the door, and the back right corner of a late-model dark blue Explorer parked beneath the corrugated tin roof was just visible.

"Is that Howard's car?" he asked.

Diane peered through the window and nodded.

"Yes."

"Let's go out and look."

Guthrie unlocked the door, twisted the knob lock, and pulled the door open. He went outside, Diane following, and stood there for a moment, surveying the parking lot. The electric gate was completely shut. He turned and walked over to the Explorer. It was covered with a layer of dust— even the windshield.

"He hasn't driven this in a while," Guthrie commented as he swiped a finger through the grime.

"Does that mean something?"

"I don't know," Guthrie said. "Let's go back inside."

They returned to the work room, and after Guthrie locked and barred the door, they went into main room. Guthrie pointed toward the ceiling.

"The apartment is upstairs?"

She nodded and followed Guthrie up the metal treads.

The second story was nicely laid out in a spacious apartment. The top of the stairs opened into a large living room whose back left corner was a dining area. Diane gave him the tour. The wall behind the dining area concealed a kitchen. A few dishes encrusted with dried food lay in the sink, and the food in the refrigerator appeared to be months old, judging from the plastic bag of muddy looking slime that had once been a head of lettuce and the way the remaining milk in the half-gallon jug had completely separated and congealed.

A door at the back of the living room opened into a hall that led to three bedrooms. The two smaller bedrooms had a shared bathroom between them. One of the bedrooms held bedroom furniture, but it had a dusty, unused feel. The second bedroom obviously served as an office, and it had a desk, bookshelves, several filing cabinets, and an easy chair flanked by a side table with a lamp. All the drawers had been pulled out, and papers and office supplies covered the floor.

The master bedroom lay at the end of the hall and had its own large bathroom. The bed was unmade, the closet door stood open, and the drawers in the dresser were pulled open. Several items of clothing lay strewn in front of the closet and dresser. Guthrie couldn't tell if any clothes were missing, but there was no sign of a suitcase in any of the closets.

Guthrie went into the master bath. Toiletries were missing from the bathroom, but there were a few feminine items lying around.

"Are those yours?" he asked, pointing.

"Yes. It all ended so abruptly I didn't have a chance to clear them out."

Nor had Howard, Guthrie mused, which meant that he didn't have a serious girlfriend who might have come into his life after Diane.

"Did you see all this mess when you were here before?" he asked.

"I didn't come up here. Too many memories."

Guthrie glanced around the bedroom. Despite the clutter on the floor—or maybe because of it—the building seemed even more empty than before.

5

WHAT DO YOU THINK?" DIANE asked as they drove away from Graham's studio. The tension lines around her eyes were tighter than ever.

"I think things look fishy," Guthrie answered. "But let me play the devil's advocate. There still could be a reasonable explanation for Howard's disappearance. Maybe he decided to take a vacation. You said he'd been working obsessively. He probably needed some time off."

"But what about him not being at the restaurant when he said he would?" she asked. "What about the missing art supplies? The large panel? His place is a mess, and his car's still there."

"Let's say he just suddenly wanted to get away from it all. Well, you're part of it all. You told me you argued about his priorities. He's kept away from you because he just didn't want to talk to you. He was in a hurry, so he left the studio a mess, took a cab to the airport, and flew off somewhere. After he's unwound, he'll call you and tell you he's in the Bahamas or something. As for the big panel, who knows? Maybe he made it for someone else. Or maybe it wasn't for a painting."

"He was gessoing it when I saw it," she said angrily."

"Like I said, Miss Weston, I'm just playing the devil's advocate. I didn't say I thought this was the case, but these are possibilities we can't ignore. It looks like Howard packed some clothes and toiletries, and he also took some art supplies with him. You have to realize that he may be off somewhere working or relaxing and having a good time."

"I still think he'd have called me by now."

"I do, too."

She shot him a look of suspicion mixed with a slight underpinning of hope.

"Then you believe something happened to him?"

"I'll do my best to find out. Just remember, it all may turn out innocently, and even if it doesn't, I might not be able to find him."

"I know that. But I have to do something. I owe the success of my gallery to him. And besides, Howard isn't just my client, he's my friend."

And still something more despite everything, Guthrie thought.

"Howard mentioned someone named Adriana."

"Adriana Lycoris," Diane said, nose wrinkling.

"You don't like her much?"

"That bitch." Diane lowered her eyes and shook her head. "I don't know what Howard sees in her."

"Tell me about her."

"Howard met her last fall," she said. "At the opening of one of his shows at my gallery. She bought one of his landscapes, and when she paid for it, she gave me her business card and said she wanted Howard to paint her portrait."

"She must have some money, then."

"I guess so, but I don't see how. As far as I know, she's little more than a gypsy fortune teller, although I think she has a high-class clientele. I guess even the rich get worried about the future. But I really don't know much about her."

"You know enough not to like her." Guthrie wondered if Diane was jealous. Maybe this Lycoris woman was the reason Howard had broken off his relationship with Diane. "Did he do the portrait?" he asked.

"He must have. I never saw it, but she paid for it."

Guthrie couldn't keep skirting the issue.

"So, what is it about her you don't like?"

After a thoughtful pause, Diane said, "She has a face made to frown, but she smiles all the time."

Guthrie had to laugh, but Diane flashed him a look that held as much impatience as hurt, so he sobered.

"Sorry," he said. "But there has to be more than that. Do you think she has something to do with Howard's disappearance?"

"I wouldn't put it past her."

"That sounds like anger talking. Would she have a motive?"

"I guess she'd have to have some sort of motive," Diane said, and she shrugged. "She monopolized Howard's time, and I barely saw him after he met her. They went to art openings together and socialized. He seemed impressed with her, but I always thought she was kind of creepy and not very nice."

"Were they romantically involved?" Guthrie asked, listening carefully to the tenor of her reply.

"I don't know. She's attractive, even though she's into middle age. He never said, and I never asked. But I don't think so."

"Why?"

"I'm not sure I can say why. It just never seemed to me that he thought of her that way, and she just doesn't seem the kind to want a relationship."

"Independent?"

"You could say that. More like aloof. A relationship has to have some give and take, and Adriana isn't the type to give." There was a note of sadness in her voice that said she knew about that the hard way.

By now, they'd reached the Zephyr Gallery, and Guthrie pulled into the small parking lot in front.

"What now?" Diane asked.

"I think I'll have a chat with Adriana Lycoris. Do you have a phone number for her?"

Diane seemed surprised.

"You just said you didn't think she had anything to do with it."

"No, I just asked if she had a motive. But you told me Howard didn't start behaving strangely—painting obsessively, standing up his clients, and not talking to you—until after he met her."

"Well, I never thought of it like that, but I guess it wasn't long after that. Come inside, and I'll get her number."

They got out of the car, and she unlocked the gallery's front door and led him to the office, where she seemed to take comfort from the mundane, familiar surroundings. Guthrie sat while she turned on her computer, opened her address book, and jotted a phone number on the top sheet of a note pad. She ripped off the sheet and handed it to him.

"Thanks. One last thing for now. Do you have a photo of Howard?"

She opened a file drawer, rummaged for a moment, then pulled out a small, three-fold color brochure and handed it to him. It advertised an opening of a show by Graham at the Zephyr.

"That was from last year," she said. "Happier times. Howard's photo is inside."

Guthrie opened the brochure and found the photo. It was a professionally done portrait that showed a long, angular face topped with short, dark hair. Guthrie wouldn't have called Graham conventionally handsome, but he was striking looking without having any features in particular that stood out. A faint smile touched his somewhat narrow mouth, but his eyes were somber and, Guthrie thought, a little tired looking.

Guthrie refolded the brochure, slipped it into the inside pocket of his jacket, and got up.

"I'll call you later."

"But what can I do?" she asked.

Guthrie knew the look in her eyes, knew the feeling, the need to do something, to keep occupied so the demons of fear and doubt couldn't latch on and make life hell. But he couldn't help. There was nothing she could do.

"Keep busy," he advised as he turned to go, but her hand on his arm stopped him.

"Be careful. She's a snake."

"I will," he told her, thinking, yeah, a careful detective. Must be like a painter who never handles paint or canvas.

Back at his office, Guthrie logged on to the law enforcement criminal databanks using the bootleg password he'd set up after the shooting that nearly crippled him but before he'd officially left the Houston Police Department. Every time he used it, he waited with trepidation for a message denying him access. Eventually, HPD would do an audit or upgrade the system and close down his back, but once again, the system opened its secrets to him.

The first thing he checked out was the missing persons report that Diane had filed. The notes attached to the report showed that she'd called about the artist three times, and the notes also indicated that the detectives assigned to the case believed Diane was little more than a jilted lover. The case had been officially closed soon after her third query. It seemed that Howard Graham had called the police two days later to say that he was not missing but was on an extended camping trip in the Texas Hill Country. The police believed the call because two game wardens with Texas Parks and Wildlife—a Gonzalez and Johnson—had verified his identity.

Guthrie thought the entry curious for several reasons. First, how did Graham know that Diane had filed a missing persons report? Second, if he'd bothered calling the police to say he wasn't missing, why hadn't he called Diane, which would have been just as easy? And finally, Howard didn't seem to be the camping sort, and Guthrie hadn't seen any signs of camping equipment in his studio. And as Diane had pointed out, Graham's car was parked behind the building.

Puzzled, he turned to Adriana Lycoris, but the background check on her took only a few minutes because there was surprisingly little to find. She didn't have a criminal record or even a driver's license, at least in that name. Nor could he find a birth record, so he couldn't even discover her age. Apparently she lived almost entirely off the grid.

He picked up the phone and punched in the number Diane had given him. A woman's voice answered, "The Eternal Flame. May I help you?"

"Uh, yes. Can you tell me where you're located?"

"Certainly. Nine-oh-six Pequot. We're open from nine to four every day except Sundays."

"Thanks," he said, and he set the phone back in its cradle.

The Eternal Flame? That could mean just about anything from a retailer of gas fireplace logs to a dating service. He looked it up online and found a lot of references to the John F. Kennedy Memorial, a song by the Bangles, some gaming group, and about a million other hits that could take tedious weeks to sift through. He switched tactics and did a search on the Harris County Appraisal District for the address on Pequot, which was located in the Montrose Area, and discovered that it was owned by a closely held corporation called EF Imports & Exports. That in turn led him to the EF Imports & Exports website, where he learned that the company did a web-based mail order business selling natural beauty products and herbal remedies. Apparently the mail order business took place at a second property, which was some sort of commercial building off the northwest corner of the I-610 Loop. The website did not mention any names, but a quick search of the county records for businesses revealed that Adriana Lycoris was EF Imports sole shareholder.

He checked out the addresses for both the house and the commercial property on Google Earth and saw in street view that the former was a two-story Victorian. The commercial property was a simple, boxy, tilt-wall cement warehouse structure shaped like two thick-bodied L-shapes back-to-back, with the base of the Ls at the rear of the lot, parallel to a railroad line. Wide driveways went about half way down each side of the building and ended at the top of the base of the L in a loading dock with a large roll-up door.

It was too late to drive to the Eternal Flame, whatever it might be, before it closed, so Guthrie went home and contented himself with eating dinner. After that, he hung the collage he'd bought from Diane Weston. There was plenty of blank wall, and he finally chose a space directly across the room from the sofa. Maybe the collage would eventually have companions.

He put away the tools, found the book he'd been working through, and settled onto the sofa to read. But his mind kept wandering, and at last, he put the book down. What was it? he wondered, staring at the collage.

But he already knew. It was a single artwork on his otherwise barren walls. It was the absolute silence in the house, a silence so stark that the sound of his own breathing sounded loudly in his ears and he could feel the thump of his heartbeat.

Memories of Alice tried to flood into his mind, but he pushed them down. No use in dredging up all that, he thought. It's over and done with a finality that forbade hope. But the sounds of her kept impinging on his consciousness, especially the happy, wordless tunes she used to hum to herself as she moved around the house before everything turned sour, then rotten. Even worse, the rottenness had been his own, driving her into the arms of another man, driving his revenge, and finally, driving her utterly from his life.

Why was he thinking about this now? He didn't need distractions, especially the distraction of thinking about how royally he'd screwed up his life. Maybe spending even a little time around an attractive woman like Diane Weston had reminded him of just how much he'd lost and how unlikely it was that he'd ever find anything like love again. Tereba had helped save Guthrie from his own perfidy before his dissolution was complete, but the old man could not erase Guthrie's dark past nor light his future. Only Guthrie could do that. And for a time, the work of solving the problems of others and putting some order into his own life had been sufficient in gaining some space between who he'd been and who he now was. But seeing the complexities of his own life mirrored in the collage set against the bare wall around it, Guthrie realized that the work wasn't enough, nor was the order. There had to be some larger purpose. Some reason.

What had Tereba asked him at the time? Was Guthrie ready not simply to face the challenges and difficulties of life, but to embrace the joys as well?

It wasn't just the energetic collage on the empty wall or the silence in a house haunted by the gentle refrains of lost love and companionship that lent a painful acuity to this question. Even more haunting was Diane Weston's very real anxiety over Howard Graham—a man who had, in essence, done as Guthrie had done to Alice by spurning her love for his own self-involvement.

Maybe Guthrie couldn't change his own past, undo ArtDurward's death, and bring Alice back, and maybe he was doomed to the loneliness of a perpetually silent house and empty walls. But, as he rose and went to get ready for bed, he vowed to himself that even if he couldn't help himself find happiness, he would do everything he could to give Diane a chance to rekindle something with Graham.

But first, he had to find him.

6

THE NEXT MORNING, GUTHRIE DROVE to the Eternal Flame. It turned out to be a shop that sold candles, herbal remedies, and books. It fit in with the inventory of EF Imports & Exports. EF had to stand for Eternal Flame. The shop occupied the first floor of the two-story Victorian house Guthrie had seen in Google Earth. The house's outer walls were pale gray shiplap siding, and the ginger-bread trim was painted yellow and red. From the curtains over the windows, the second floor appeared to be an apartment.

Now that he saw it in person, Guthrie could tell the house wasn't one of those faux Victorians that had sprung up recently, mostly in the form of townhouses, but the real thing, built some-time around the turn of the nineteenth to twentieth century. This part of the Montrose Area had a number of such houses that reflect-ed Texas oil money. But with urban flight during the 1960s, they'd become run-down palaces occupied by hippies. The years since had been kind. Thanks to revitalization of the area, houses like this now were even more desirable—and expensive— than they'd been in their heyday. If Adriana Lycoris was a gypsy fortune teller as Diane had said, her shop certainly was several steps up from the usual run-down bungalow slapped with garish but faded paint and boasting a crude sign with a stylized palm outlined on it.

The driveway went down the left side of the house and ended in a garage apartment over a triple garage. A green Chevy Suburban was parked in front of the left garage door, and Guthrie jotted down the license plate number. A brick sidewalk, guarded by a security company sign, led to the front steps. He mounted them to a wide porch surrounded by a wooden rail painted white and covered by a sloping gabled roof. Even before he opened the door, he could smell the shop's wares as well as see them through the front windows. The odor, a mixture of fruits, flowers, and herbs, was incredibly complex and quite nice.

And much stronger—cloyingly so—inside the cool, dim interior. The place reminded Guthrie of a cross between Tereba's highly functional apothecary shop, with its shelves and bins of herbs, roots, and other, often indefinable matter, and a candle shop you might find in a mall. Nothing was especially kitschy, but whatever real functionality that lay in the bottles and packets on the racks covering one wall was eclipsed by a glass counter filled with herbal cosmetics and tiny bottles holding essential oils for aromatherapy.

No one was behind the counter, so Guthrie turned to the wall that held shelves of books. The titles were a smattering of esoterica, from witchcraft and Wicca to feng shui and esoteric philosophy. He didn't see anything on UFOs, ghosts, or Bigfoot.

He was just reaching for a volume on sacred art when a rustling sounded behind him.

"May I help you?"

The voice belonged to an extremely attractive young woman standing behind the counter. She appeared to be in her mid twenties and had thick, dark, wavy hair that fell past her shoulders from a center part. Guthrie could barely see her because, in the dim light, the variegated fabric of her long, loose dress nearly blended in with her surroundings. She stood so still that she could have been there when Guthrie walked in, and he might have missed her.

"I'd like to speak to Adriana Lycoris," Guthrie said. "Is she available?" As he stepped closer, he noticed that she was visibly pregnant, though her baby bump barely inflated her loose dress.

"And you are?"

"Clay Guthrie. I'm a private investigator looking into the possible disappearance of somebody Ms. Lycoris knows."

"Howard?" the young woman asked. Guthrie couldn't tell if that was trepidation in the young woman's voice or contempt.

"Why would it be Howard?" Guthrie started to ask, but he never got the chance.

"I'll speak to Mr. Guthrie."

A light-brown paisley-print curtain covering the door in the wall behind the counter parted with a rustle, and a beautiful, busty, dark-haired woman of around fifty emerged. Her hair was cut in a bob, and she wore a dark brown, gown-like dress. The two women looked remarkably alike, except for their ages. Mother and daughter? Twins born twenty years apart?

"Go finish the parching," the older woman said, and the younger woman disappeared behind the curtain.

"I'm Adriana Lycoris," the older woman said to Guthrie. "Are you here about Howard?"

"I am," Guthrie said. "How did you guess?"

"Simple deduction," she said, smiling. "I've been trying to reach Howard for some time, and he hasn't returned my calls. We're quite good friends, so it's very unusual. And now you show up, looking for a missing person. It could only be Howard."

She smiled again, and Guthrie couldn't help but reflect that Diane was right. Even if Lycoris smiled a lot, she had a face made for frowning. Which was just what she should be doing right now.

"Apparently, he's been missing for a couple of months. I wondered if you'd heard from him in that time."

"No. As I said, I called him numerous times, but he wasn't home."

"You don't seem concerned."

"I'm not, really. Howard is an artist, and artists can sometimes be temperamental. He's probably off painting somewhere. He told me he was tired to death of painting those portraits Miss Weston kept pushing him to do." She peered at Guthrie. "I'm sure she told you about me. Is she the one who hired you?"

"Sorry, I can't divulge...."

"Of course you can't. How silly of me to ask. But it has to be her. Howard had very few friends, and Miss Weston was more than that to him once. And she was, rightly or wrongly, his representative. She needed him much more than he needed her."

"You don't think she was the person for the job?"

"He was stifled by her. She simply wasn't big enough. Howard should have been with a major New York gallery, not some hole-in-the-wall place in Houston."

"I had the idea that Howard liked being low-key."

"I'm sure Miss Weston told you that, but you wouldn't have heard it from Howard. He might have been content being with her for the time being, but his career was about to take a huge leap forward, and I don't think he'd have stayed with the Zephyr for much longer."

"Did Miss Weston know that?"

"She must have noticed that he was becoming restless. He made no secret of it to me."

"Being good friends, you must have visited his studio."

"Yes. Quite often. And he came here a lot."

"Then you saw that unusual landscape he was working on."

"Unusual landscape?" She was still smiling, but something hardened in her eyes. "Unusual in what way?"

"Painted in a hyper-realistic style. Very advanced technique."

Lycoris laughed.

"All Howard's techniques were very advanced. He was an excellent realist. Did Miss Weston tell you she saw an unusual landscape?" Her tone indicated that Diane most probably was a liar, but her unconscious use of the past tense when referring to Graham indicated that she definitely was.

"What about a really large painting? About the size of a garage door."

"That is quite large. Howard never painted anything larger than four by six. Most people don't have wall space for anything larger." Now her tone implied that maybe Guthrie was the liar, and if he wasn't, he was a fool. She smiled again then waved dismissively. "Who knows? Howard was always working on something."

"So, you didn't see him working on the landscape or anything larger than he normally worked on?"

"No. As I said."

No, he thought. As you failed to say.

"You met Howard at the Zephyr?" Guthrie asked.

"At one of his shows there. I bought one of his landscapes and was impressed enough that I commissioned him to do a portrait. Would you like to see them?"

56

"If it's not too much trouble," Guthrie said, wondering. Lycoris said Howard disliked Diane pressuring him to do portraits, yet Lycoris had done the same thing.

"No trouble at all. Come on around the counter and through here."

She opened the curtain and ushered him into the back. One room that he could see seemed to be for storage, the kitchen served as a work area, and a second room was an office.

"Melanie," Lycoris called. "Watch the front until I've finished with Mr. Guthrie."

The young woman came out of the kitchen, wiping her hands on a small towel, and went through the curtain, into the shop. Meanwhile, Lycoris led Guthrie into the office. The portrait occupied a prominent position on the wall opposite Lycoris's desk, but the landscape sat on top of a credenza, leaning carelessly against the wall. The landscape looked like a West Texas locale, with stubby, rugged mountains ranging behind a stream lined with cottonwoods and mesquite. It was a nice piece of work, but it certainly didn't fit in with the decorative ambience of the rest of the Eternal Flame.

The portrait was as well executed as the landscape and showed Lycoris in a soft light that both brought out her beauty and softened the dour expression that threatened to overtake her features. If Diane—and Lycoris—had pressured Graham into doing portraiture, the results certainly didn't show a lack of enthusiasm.

"They're both very good," Guthrie said, wondering why Lycoris would hide them in her office instead of using them to decorate her home, which was presumably upstairs.

"Yes," Lycoris replied. "It was while I was sitting for the portrait that Howard and I began our friendship, and we associated quite a bit after that."

"Miss Weston said as much."

"I'm sure she did. I believe she was somewhat jealous of me."

"Was there a reason for that?"

"Howard meant a lot to her. She may still have had a crush on him, though I'm not certain of that. I didn't pry into Howard's past. But I'm closer to Howard's age, and we had a lot more in common than he did with Miss Weston. As our friendship blossomed, theirs waned."

"The yin and yang of things," Guthrie commented, and Lycoris gave him a curious look.

"Your command overrules your style as much as your style overrules your command," Lycoris said. "It appears that you are a true man, Mr. Guthrie."

"I hope that's a good thing," Guthrie said, not exactly sure what she meant.

"Good is a relative term."

"Yes."

"Was there anything else?"

"I suppose not, if you haven't heard from Howard. But if you do, you'll pass on the message that Miss Weston needs to speak with him about some business matters?"

"I'll tell him as soon as I see him."

She said it as if she really didn't expect that eventuality. She gestured toward the curtain, ushered Guthrie through it, and walked him to the door.

"Come back anytime," she said insincerely.

"Thanks," Guthrie said, and he stepped off the porch. By the time he had, she'd closed the door.

Guthrie drove to the Zephyr Gallery, pulled into the little parking lot, and went inside. Diane was in the room that had held the collages. The collages were gone, and she was in the process of hanging a colorful framed quilt on one of the walls. She was dressed in jeans and a dark brown T-shirt, and a few strands of hair had escaped the elastic band that held the rest in a careless ponytail. She was fetching, and Guthrie felt a momentary twinge of jealousy at the missing artist.

"You're just in time," she said as he came in. "Would you mind helping me hang this?"

"Show me what you want me to do," he said, pushing down the desire that had surfaced unexpectedly.

The quilt was mounted in a wooden frame built like a shallow box with a front of Plexiglas. Diane already had hangers dangling from the crown molding, and Guthrie helped her lift the frame then held it while she hooked the hangers to the back.

"How would you do that without someone to help?" Guthrie asked, stepping back and looking at the quilt. Its odds and ends of material were stitched together into quadrants that held representations of four domestic scenes: a kitchen table bearing a feast, a living room, a boy's bedroom, and a backyard with a tire swing hanging from a tree limb. It was like a microcosm of a happy home held together by the quilt's invitingly warm color scheme.

She pointed to a pair of stools in the middle of the room.

"I was going to prop it on those, but it's a lot easier with another person."

"It's a really nice quilt," Guthrie said

"Yeah. All of these," she waved at the other quilts in the room, two already hung and two more leaning against the walls, "are by Mae Albertson. She's a black woman living in the Third Ward. Lived there all her life. Now urban renewal is taking over her neighborhood and pushing her out."

"I can see why it's in an art gallery instead of Gallery Furniture."

She chuckled but quickly sobered. "There's something wrong with it," she said.

"Doesn't look like it. What?"

"Here." She pointed through the glass to the left edge of a patch of fabric that was used to depict the bed in the bedroom. The fabric wasn't completely sewn. It's edge was loose and frayed, as if the bedspread wasn't completely tucked in.

"It's not finished," Guthrie said. "Did she forget to sew that part?"

"Believe me, she knows about it. But she let it stay that way, even though it would have been relatively easy to fix it."

"Something must have affected her."

"It did. She was working on this quilt when she learned her son had been killed in Afghanistan. She put it aside, and when she came back to it, she couldn't bring herself to finish that one part. She left it undone as a memorial to her son—the patch in the quilt of her life that couldn't be completed."

"I'm surprised she's selling it."

"She doesn't want to keep it because it reminds her too much of that day," Diane said. "Said others, even if they know, won't be distressed in the same way and can probably tolerate having it around.

But not her." She paused, and her eyes pinched with distress as she turned to face Guthrie. "Do you suppose I'll feel like that if I never see Howard again? Like something is permanently undone?"

"Yes," Guthrie said. "That's how you'll feel."

"You sound like you know from experience."

"Most people know something like that to one degree or another." He shrugged. "It's all in how you deal with it afterwards."

"You seem to manage."

"That's a good way to put it. You just work through it."

"Like a twelve-step program? Missing Persons Anonymous?"

"You find something to do, and you do it." He waved at the quilt they'd just hung, then at the others in the room. "This thing happened to her, and she went on."

"Ignore it? Is that what you're saying?"

"You can't ignore it. But sometimes problems like this can't be solved on a rational level, and chewing at it with your mind only makes things worse. You have to give the rational part of the mind something to worry at while you work through your feelings. Also, completing mundane practical tasks helps make life seem less crazy and more organized."

"So you detect."

"Yeah. You can immerse yourself in the art world and your gallery."

"What about Adriana? Did you meet her?"

"I did," Guthrie said. "She's quite an interesting woman."

"Not you, too," Diane said with forced exasperation that had a touch of sincerity.

"I didn't mean it like that."

"The dispassionate detective?"

"You may think she put some kind of hex on Howard, but she didn't on me."

Not that I'm not vulnerable, he thought, remembering Barbara Sidel and her sexy witchery.

She blinked then flushed and looked down.

"I'm sorry," she said. "I'm just tense."

"That's understandable."

"So, what did the gypsy bitch have to say?"

"She says she didn't know Howard had disappeared, but she didn't seem too concerned. She implied you're being overly protective."

"Somebody has to be worried."

"And nobody better than you," Guthrie agreed. "Actually, I think she was trying to get under my skin to see how much I know about you and Howard."

"Did she tell you that I'm jealous of her?"

"In almost those exact words."

Diane snorted. "If I was going to be jealous of anyone or anything, it'd be Howard's work. But that would be stupid." She looked Guthrie straight in the eyes. "I might be a little afraid of her, but I'm not jealous. Until you said that about her hexing him, I hadn't thought about it. But I have now, and now I think she did something to him that made him turn away from me. I don't think it was sex, but there was something strange going on between them."

"What?"

"I don't know. I just wish he'd never met her." She shrugged helplessly and stared up at Guthrie. "But I don't care about that. I don't even care about what happened between him and me, anymore. I just want him to be safe."

"I asked Adriana about the landscape and big panel," Guthrie said. "She says she doesn't know anything about them."

"That has to be a lie," Diane spat. "They spent a lot of time together, and the painting was the only thing he was working on. Compulsively. For two weeks. She has to know about it." She sat tiredly on one of the stools.

"If she does," Guthrie said, "I'd like to know why she denied it." And why she seemed surprised—and maybe angry—when I mentioned it, he thought.

"Do you think she's involved?"

She'd asked the question before, and he'd said he doubted it. But Lycoris's denial of something as simple, obvious, and innocent as knowing about a painting Graham had been obsessively working on or that he'd built an oversized panel afterward did not lend credence to anything else she might have said.

"I don't know," he answered. "I'd like you to write down all the people and places Howard normally visits. His friends, professional acquaintances, grocery store, barber, and so forth."

While she wrote out the list on a piece of studio stationery, Guthrie looked at the art on her office walls and wondered what it would be like to create such things. Maybe, he thought, it's all just a way for the artist to delve into the mysteries of life. Like a detective, just using a different medium.

7

OVER THE WEEKEND, GUTHRIE FOLLOWED up on the leads Diane had written down, but to no avail. The list was relatively small for so well-known an artist. Diane had said Graham was married to his work, and apparently his marriage tended to exclude friends. He wasn't a loner, exactly, but he wasn't much of a socializer, either. Most of the few people Guthrie talked to didn't even realize he had been incommunicado for two months. Only his dry cleaner had noticed.

Guthrie also did some research on Graham and Diane, but there was nothing in either one's background that hinted at anything clandestine or underhanded. Graham's website, set up through the Zephyr's website, displayed a wide variety of his works. Guthrie had seen some of the actual pieces in the racks in the studio, though only fleetingly. The screen images didn't do justice to Graham's minute technique, but the work was impressive, anyway. Guthrie particularly liked the West Texas landscapes, which managed to evoke a sense of fortitude and endurance despite the semiarid desolation.

He also ran the license plate number he'd gotten off the green Suburban. It was registered to EF Imports & Exports as part of a company fleet. The other vehicles were a brand new Lexus sedan and a GM cargo van a couple of years old. It was a small fleet but a pretty nice one for a gypsy fortune teller. Lycoris's retail shop didn't seem to do a lot of business, but the import and export business must be doing well.

By Thursday evening, Guthrie was still puzzling over how to pry into Graham's disappearance, but he was no further along than he had been after interviewing Adriana Lycoris.

When all else fails, he thought, go back to the beginning.

He picked up the phone and punched in Diane's number. She answered on the second ring, expectation in her voice.

"Nothing, yet," he told her, hating to have to disappoint her but knowing it was inevitable this early in the investigation. "I'm calling because I'd like to go back to Howard's studio tomorrow."

"Why? We know he's not there."

"It's the last place anyone knew he was. We may have overlooked something the first time we were there."

"I'm closing the gallery tomorrow, but I'll be working inside. Pick me up at ten, and we'll go to the studio together."

The next morning, Guthrie grabbed an early breakfast at Dot's then spent an hour in his office before driving to the Zephyr. The front door was locked, and he knocked. Diane, dressed in jeans and a long-sleeved blouse with the sleeves rolled halfway up her forearms, answered a few moments later.

"Still hanging the stuff for the next show?" Guthrie asked.

"I started to, but I couldn't concentrate. I've just been waiting for you."

"Let's go, then."

They were mostly silent on the drive to the studio. Guthrie parked in roughly the same spot he had on their earlier visit, and he followed Diane to the entry alcove and waited while she found her key and unlocked the door.

"Oh, no!" Diane gasped as soon as they were inside and she deactivated the alarm. She raised the back of her hand to her mouth and turned away.

"Are you all right?"

She nodded quickly but unconvincingly.

"Punch in the alarm code," he prompted.

She nodded and turned to the alarm panel, then back to Guthrie.

"It's already off." Her voice was subdued with tension.

If the studio had been a mess before, now it looked officially ransacked. All the drawers in the file cabinets and flat files again stood open, and the drawings and papers lay piled on the floor around them. The metal cabinets against the built-in wall were agape, their contents cast on the floor. And through the open door to the storage room, they could see that almost every painting had been pulled from the racks, and the canvases lay strewn around like a scattered deck of large, colorful playing cards.

Diane looked at Guthrie, stunned panic in her eyes.

"Somebody was here since we were."

"Howard!" Guthrie called, loosening his gun in its holster. There was no answer.

"Who could have done this?" Diane asked.

Why? was what Guthrie wondered. He stared around the studio. The only things intact were the easels with their unfinished paintings. The portrait of John Eggers, stared at them from across the room. If only he could talk, Guthrie thought. He's seen everything that's gone on here.

"I'm going to look upstairs," Guthrie said, turning and heading for the iron stairs.

The rooms that had been relatively neat and orderly on their first visit were now completely torn apart. Everything was pulled from shelves and closets, and drawers from the wooden desk in the office lay around like a handful of large children's blocks amid the litter of their former contents. The mattress had been overturned, and it and the box springs had been slit open.

"I have to go back down," Diane said. "I can't leave all those painting just lying there." She looked ashen.

Guthrie followed her to the first floor, and while she went into the storage room to pick up the jumbled paintings, he checked the other two back rooms. In both, every cabinet and closet had been emptied of its contents. The work room had been a mess before, now it was a wreck. He had to nudge cans, bottles, and jugs aside with his feet to get to the back door. It was bolted, but the crossbar was on the floor. Through its small window, Guthrie could see that Graham's Explorer still sat out back beneath its coating of grime, but its back driver's side door was wide open.

The back door is bolted, Guthrie thought as he went outside to close the car door. And the front door had been locked with its dead bolt, but the alarm was off. Whoever searched the studio had a key and the alarm code.

He went back into the building, locked and barred the back door, then went back to the storage room. By now, Diane had returned the undamaged paintings to the racks, and those that had suffered harm were leaned up against the walls and racks.

"That's two years' work down the drain," she said despondently, surveying the damaged paintings.

"What about the sketches and papers all around the filing cabinets?"

"I can't do that," she said, voice defeated. "Not now. I just can't."

"We can't just leave them on the floor," Guthrie said. He went through the door to the lateral and flat files. "Howard can organize them later."

He hoped is voice sounded as if the artist's return was inevitable. He bent and began picking up the papers, jogging them into some semblance of order, and putting them into the drawers.

Diane went across the room to the chair set up for sittings and slumped in it while Guthrie finished cleaning up the sketches. When he was done, he walked over to her.

"I still don't understand it," she said, looking up at him. "If they were trying to steal Howard's art, why isn't anything taken? Why did they just throw everything around?"

"They were looking for something in particular," Guthrie said. "That last landscape he painted."

"How would they—whoever 'they' are—know about it? And why would they want just that?"

Because I told them, Guthrie thought. He remembered that Lycoris had seemed both surprised and subtly upset when he'd mentioned the unusual landscape to her, but at the time, that fact had barely registered against her denial of knowing anything at all about it.

Lycoris and the painting—maybe two paintings: one small, one much larger. It all kept coming back to Lycoris and the paintings. It could be that she now possessed Graham's two masterworks and had done him in to ensure that she had the best—and most valuable—that he'd ever produce, but Guthrie didn't think so. The rewards wouldn't be significant enough for someone like Lycoris. Besides,

Tereba wouldn't have brought Guthrie in to investigate something so prosaic.

Guthrie remembered seeing an answering machine attached to the landline phone on Howard's desk.

"Let's go up to the office," he suggested.

They were there in a minute, Diane picking up her purse from where she'd dropped it beside the entry. Guthrie glanced at the desktop computer.

"Do you know Howard's email password?" he asked.

"Not by heart," she said. "But I have it written down in my purse somewhere." She rummaged in her purse for a moment before coming up with a small leather-bound address book. While she switched on the computer and activated Howard's email, Guthrie activated the answering machine. There were a couple of hang-up calls and several messages from Diane ranging in tone from urgency to distress. There were none from Lycoris, which gave lie to her statement that she'd tried calling him numerous times without success. True, she might have called Howard's cell phone, but if she was really worried, she'd have tried the landline, too. Diane had. It could be the two hang-up calls were from her, but that would have been strange, too. If she were such a good friend and so concerned, wouldn't she have left some sort of message, as Diane had?

"Let me take you home," Guthrie told Diane. "There are a few things I want to follow up on."

They rode back to the Zephyr Gallery in silence, and Guthrie let Diane out with the promise to call her later. Then he drove to the Eternal Flame. He parked along the curb a couple of houses down from the shop, and as he went toward the brick walkway that led to its front door, he noted that the green Suburban wasn't in the driveway.

The shop's interior was exactly the same as it had been on his last visit. Melanie Lycoris stood behind the counter in another variegated dress that nicely camouflaged her against the racks of wares behind her.

"Hi, I'm Clay Guthrie. I was in the other day."

"I remember. You were looking for Howard." Her voice was flat, her eyes suspicious, and her shoulders tense.

"I wonder if he's contacted you since I was last here."

"No."

"Is Ms. Lycoris in? I have a few follow-up questions."

"She's not here right now. I don't expect her back today."

Melanie's demeanor said she didn't want Guthrie here, either.

"When you see her, would you please tell her I came by. I'll try to come by again."

"She won't be here. She's taking the week off."

"I see. Well, thanks for your time."

Guthrie left, went back to his car, and sat there for a few minutes, staring at the front of the shop. Then he pulled out his phone and typed the address of Lycoris's commercial property into the map app. The map appeared with his route marked out. He twisted the key in the ignition and drove off.

Twenty minutes later, he exited the North Loop at Ella Boulevard. The street he was looking for—Judiway—was about a mile north, just across railroad tracks raised above the rest of the terrain on an earthen berm. After going up and over the berm, he turned left and cruised down Judiway, passing a couple of narrow blocks of tiny shabby houses, a city service center whose parking lot was filled with blue garbage trucks, and a cluster of small industrial buildings housing an auto repair place, a metal fabricator, a commercial painting company, and a door factory. Most of the buildings were built primarily of sheet metal, though two had brick fronts, and one appeared to have originally been a frame house. Next was what looked like a simple church that must have been built by a modest congregation. Even the sign out front, erected on a pedestal of brick the same color as the buildings, gave that impression, although there was no wording on the sign's weathered white face. The other side of the street was lined with wooden and tall chain-link fences that marked the back side of a neighborhood.

Lycoris's property was between the church and a lot holding a group of three more light industrial metal buildings. The front of the Lycoris's building was about sixty feet across, and he could see down the wide driveways on either side of the building to the loading docks with their large roll-up doors. It was easily the most substantial building on the block aside from the similarly constructed service center.

Guthrie remembered from observing the property earlier with Google Earth that the building nearly filled the lot, with only narrow gaps between its exterior walls and the surrounding fence line. The gaps appeared to be weed choked in the Google Earth images, and Guthrie could see that they still were beyond the loading docks on either side of the structure. But the driveways to the loading docks were clear, and he could see a personnel door in the wall adjacent to each of the loading docks' roll-up door.

The building was faced with sheets of tinted glass, and there were two front doors, as if it had been built to house two businesses. The modest sign over the left-hand entrance read, EF Imports and Exports, Inc. There was no sign over the right-hand entrance, and the windows on that side were covered with sheets of brown wrapping paper taped to the inside of the glass. A thirty-foot-deep parking lot separated the building from Judiway, and there were three cars in it: a black Lexus SUV, a white GM cargo van, and the green Suburban Guthrie had seen parked behind the Eternal Flame.

The fleet is in home port, he thought.

Guthrie cruised on by, going past another modest commercial building clad in sheet metal, the twin rows of a small and dilapidated apartment complex, and two more commercial buildings, one housing some sort of martial arts school, before coming to the end of the block. To his left, across the intersection, was a ratty convenience store, and to the right was a city park with tennis courts, a swimming pool, and a lots of airy space underneath tall oaks and pines. A neighborhood lay beyond the park, and more industrial businesses occupied the left side of the street past the convenience store.

After turning around in the convenience store lot, Guthrie drove back down Judiway toward Lycoris's building. Like all the lots on this side of the street except those for the church and apartment complex, hers was fronted with a chain-link fence topped with strands of barbed wire. But Guthrie noticed that the electric gate across the driveway on the left side of the lot was open, and taking a breath, he steered into the parking lot, got out of his car, and went through the door beneath the EF Imports sign.

He found himself in a room that spanned the left half of the building. It was about ten feet deep and furnished with two plain, cheap wooden chairs with padded vinyl seats. An equally cheap end table sat between them, a neat pile of old magazines in its center. A tall counter reached completely across the room, except for a narrow gap at the far end. On the other side of the counter stood two tall stools, but they were sitting at an angle that said they were props, not furniture—a diagnosis verified by the dust on both seats. Besides, there was nothing on or, from what he could tell, behind the counter, either. The room felt slack from disuse.

A wide, open door was in the right-hand side of the featureless wall behind the counter. Guthrie peered through the door, but all he saw was a short hall blocked by a door at the far end. The odor in the room was similar to what Guthrie had smelled in Lycoris's shop but considerably muted and mixed with the scents of cardboard and dust.

In the background, he could hear music playing—a sort of rhythmic chant accompanied by a modulated droning that sounded like it was created by a combination of stringed instruments, horns, and a humming that was at once brassy and ringing and set his teeth on edge. There were a lot of deep bass tones, too, that vibrated the soles of his feet. Here in the front office, it was muffled, but it must have been pretty loud in the back.

No one was in the room, but the button for a buzzer was set in the counter, and Guthrie pushed it. After a few moments, a husky middle-aged man with graying dark hair and heavy features came through the doorway.

"Yes," he said. "What can I do for you?"

"Hi," Guthrie said amiably. "I'm looking for a warehouse rental space in the area, and I noticed that the space next door looks vacant. Do you know if it's for rent?"

The man seemed surprised by the question.

"No. It's not."

"It's just that I saw the paper taped over the windows, and there's no sign, so I thought it was vacant."

"It's being used," the man said.

"I see," Guthrie said, looking around. "Too bad. This is a nice space. Perfect for what I have in mind. I saw that your company is called the EF Imports & Exports. What's that?"

"Beauty and health products," the man said.

"Yeah, lots of ugliness out there that needs to be fixed. Say, you wouldn't mind if I had a look around, would you? Like I said, this is perfect for what I need. Might help me find what I'm looking for."

"I'm afraid not. We're very busy right now. We have a major shipment going out soon. In fact, I need to get back...." He indicated the door behind him with a twitch of his head.

"Yeah, sure. Okay. Thanks for your time."

Guthrie went out the door. He got into his car and stared back at the building in time to see the man go up to the entrance, lock the door, and stare out at Guthrie.

Not very hospitable, Guthrie thought as he started the car and pulled out of the parking lot onto Judiway. He drove to the end of the block, turned right, and crossed the railroad tracks. As he went over the berm, he looked down the rails, seeing nothing but a dead-straight run that receded into the distance. It looked like both sides of the right-of-way were fenced in, but at the next street, he made another right, just to make sure. This street was a major thorough-fare, and after a thin strip of businesses on the right, most of the long block was taken up by a high school.

A parking lot occupied the far end of the school property. It was open, and Guthrie pulled in and found he could drive all the way to the back, right up to the chain link fence demarcating the railroad right-of-way. Directly across from him were the back fences of the businesses on Judiway. Most were old chain link, but the ones behind EF Imports and the church were wooden, both decayed and sagging.

Not much else to see or do here, Guthrie thought, so he headed for his office.

8

FOR THE NEXT THREE DAYS, Guthrie followed Adriana Lycoris. Even though her shop remained open, except for Sunday, she didn't spend much time there, apparently leaving its daily operation to her daughter. Her mornings started at seven, when the heavy-featured man Guthrie had talked to at the warehouse emerged from the garage apartment behind the Eternal Flame and went to the shop's back door and knocked. Lycoris would come out, and the two of them would get into the Suburban and drive to the warehouse. The heavy-featured man seemed to be Lycoris's personal assistant or bodyguard because she never went anywhere without him, and he always drove. Guthrie recalled that she didn't have a driver's license.

At the warehouse, the two of them went inside and remained until nine or ten at night, when they emerged and drove back to the shop. The Lexus and white van were always in the warehouse parking lot except when one or the other of two rough-looking men Guthrie hadn't seen before came out of the warehouse, got into the Lexus, and left for varying amounts of time—usually to get take-out food.

Something was going on in there. Guthrie was sure of it. Every one of the people going in and out carried an air of expectancy, and all of them—even Melanie Lycoris—were there on Sunday. Guthrie didn't believe it was, as the heavy-featured man had told him, because of a big shipment going out. In the three days that Guthrie watched, he didn't once see any deliveries, either coming or going, which was peculiar for any wholesale or mail-order business.

When he got home Sunday night, stiff and weary from spending days sitting in his car and going nowhere, he contemplated taking the next day off. But he knew he couldn't. He had no other leads besides Lycoris. Guthrie set his alarm for five to give himself plenty of time to wake up and shower so he could get to the Eternal Flame by seven. He was dead asleep in minutes.

The next morning, Lycoris's pattern remained the same. Guthrie followed the Suburban to the warehouse and settled in to wait and watch. Today, though, the routine was interrupted just after eight when his cell phone chimed.

"Clay, it's Diane." Her voice sounded distressed.

"What's wrong?"

"Someone came by yesterday, looking for that landscape Howard painted. At least I think it was the same one. I told him I didn't have it. Then last night, someone broke into the gallery."

"I'm on my way."

Morning rush hour had picked up, but Guthrie made it to the Zephyr in about twenty-five minutes, cursing the traffic the whole way. He mounted the steps and was surprised to see that the front door was intact. It was locked, but he didn't have a chance to knock before Diane opened it. She quickly let him in before shooting the dead bolt. She was so agitated that Guthrie suggested they go to her office, where she could sit down.

"Yes," she murmured, leading the way.

"What happened?" he asked when they were seated.

"Maybe I'm panicking over nothing," she said.

"Tell me anyway."

"A man came by late yesterday afternoon. Just before closing. Two men, really, but only one of them talked. The other one was a big guy. He looked like a goon, and I didn't like the way he stared at me."

"Did he threaten you in any way?"

"Not exactly. Neither one did. The one who did the talking was Gavin O'Neil. He said he knew I had a special painting that Howard had done, and he wanted to buy it. He was very businesslike, but he made it clear that he wouldn't take no for an answer."

"You know this O'Neil?"

"Unfortunately. He calls himself an art dealer, but art shark is more like it. He doesn't give a shit about art. He's just in it for the money."

"Buys cheap, sells dear?"

"That, too, but sometimes worse. This is rumor, so I don't know if it's really true, but apparently he's resorted to blackmail a couple of times to pry paintings from owners reluctant to sell. Most reputable galleries won't work with him. He deals mostly with individual clients. I've never had to deal with him since most of the people I represent aren't famous enough to bring in the really big bucks, but Howard was moving up into the level where O'Neil would be attracted."

"What did you tell him?"

"I said I didn't have what he was describing, but I think he knew I knew what he was talking about." She smiled ruefully. "I'm not a very good liar, even when I'm not lying. He could tell I knew something about the painting."

"But he didn't threaten you?" he asked, and she sobered.

"I think he might have done something to me if a couple I know hadn't come by the gallery to visit. He and his goon left. Thank God. They scared me to death."

"How would he have known about the painting? Would Howard have approached him?"

"No!" she spat. "O'Neil is slime! Howard wouldn't give him the time of day."

"But he was looking for a special painting. It has to be the small landscape. Tell me about the break-in."

"I'm not sure when it actually happened. When I closed last night, I went out for dinner with the friends I mentioned, and afterwards, we went over to their place. I was shaken by O'Neil and didn't want to be alone, so I spent the night with them. When I got home this morning, I saw that someone had broken into the storage garage beneath my apartment."

"Don't you have a burglar alarm?"

"Yes, but I guess it didn't go off. I never got a call."

"Did the burglar take anything?"

"I don't know. I was too frightened to go in. I locked myself in here and called you."

"Let's have a look."

They went outside, and he asked her where the phone service box was.

"Around the corner there." She pointed.

Guthrie stepped around the corner and saw a gray plastic box attached to the wall. The door stood open, and wires were pulled out.

"That's why your alarm didn't go off," he said. "Whoever broke in knew how to disconnect the security system." He stuffed the wires back into the box and closed the door. "Let's go to the garage."

They walked across the pavement to the two-car garage beneath her apartment. Both garage doors were down, but the entry door stood wide open. The frame around the lock showed the marks of a pry bar.

The space inside was big enough to hold two cars, with extra room to one side, but it was very clean, and obviously no car had resided there for some time. Racks for paintings lined three walls and the fourth wall had shelves holding sculptures. A large work table supported by four flat files dominated the open space in the middle. The air was cool and fresh.

All the paintings were out of the racks, leaned up against the racks and flat files or scattered around the floor.

"Anything missing?"

"I can't tell, but he must have been looking for a painting because that's all he looked at."

"I'd say it was that landscape. Someone is looking for it. They searched Howard's studio and now your storage facility. I'd like to know what's so important about it. I could see all this happening over a masterpiece from the Louvre, but not a contemporary and completely unknown landscape, no matter how well executed. Especially when you're the only one who's seen it." He scratched his cheek. "I need to find out more about O'Neil. Did he leave any contact info?"

"Yes. It's inside."

They went back to her office, where she handed him a business card. O'Neil's name wasn't on the card, which simply read, International Fine Arts and Antiques, followed by a phone number. There was no address.

"Do you think I'm in danger?"

"It's a possibility but not likely if O'Neil doesn't think you have the painting. But just in case, is there someplace else you can stay for a few days?"

"The friends I stayed with last night. They'll put me up, but I can't simply close the gallery. I have that show coming up, and there's a lot to do."

"You'll probably be okay during the day. Call me if there's a problem, but call the police first if it's an emergency. One last thing. May I have the key and alarm code to Howard's studio? I might want to look it over again."

She dug her keys out of her purse, removed one, and handed it to Guthrie. Then she jotted the code on the top sheet of a yellow stickie pad, tore off the little square, and passed it over.

"You'll call?" she asked anxiously.

"I will."

Guthrie left the Zephyr Gallery and drove straight to his office, where he checked into Gavin O'Neil.

Diane was right in thinking the art dealer was on the far side of shady, but she probably didn't realize just how far over the line he actually was. Although the authorities only rarely had been able to conclusively pin anything on him, his involvement in a large number of illicit art dealings, including selling forgeries and international trafficking in stolen fine art and looted artifacts, was certain if unproved. In one case, he was a suspect in the murder of an art collector and, in another, implicated in the kidnapping of a child ransomed with a portrait by Renoir. He'd operated his business under several different names during the last decade, the most recent being International Fine Arts and Antiques, the same name on the business card Diane had given Guthrie.

O'Neil's criminal record wasn't open to the general public, but that didn't mean he wasn't almost universally reviled. While Guthrie was in the process of discovering that International Fine Arts and Antiques didn't have a website, he Googled several webpages and news stories that mentioned O'Neil in unflattering terms. None of them called him a murderer outright, but extortion was more than hinted at since he'd been convicted on racketeering charges related to a Picabia he'd tried to force a wealthy couple to sell at a bargain rate in exchange for his silence on the finer points of their son's pursuit and abuse of prostitutes.

Guthrie found the address for International Fine Arts and Antiques in the public records for businesses. It was located in a cluster of office buildings off I-10 West, outside the Beltway. He also learned through property records that O'Neil owned a townhouse in the Memorial area.

He contemplated driving to O'Neil's to pay him a visit but decided against it. By now, it was mid afternoon, rush hour traffic would be building, and O'Neil's office was all the way across the city and would be closing soon for the day. Instead, Guthrie went home.

He changed into his workout clothes, went out to the garage, and practiced his tai chi form. Afterward, feeling simultaneously relaxed and energized, he went back into the house through the early dusk.

He was hungry and thought about preparing a meal, but the way the studio had been left in disarray after Graham's disappearance and later ransacked kept annoying his mind. And now the Zephyr had been broken into. Guthrie had visited most, if not all, of Graham's friends and acquaintances, and despite his prompting, none of them mentioned seeing him painting a landscape of unusual vividness. But then, most of them hadn't seen Graham in a while, either. Even so, it all came back to the painting. Or paintings. Two of them. One small and finished, one large and, presumably, being painted by Graham. The smaller one that Diane had glimpsed was of excellent craftsmanship, though Guthrie didn't think its quality alone was the reason behind what was going on.

But it was involved, whatever was happening, and the more Guthrie thought about it, the more he knew he needed to see it. He also knew that it was still out there to be seen since people kept looking for it. Unless Graham had an off-site storage facility that Diane didn't know about, which seemed unlikely, that left only one place to look: the studio. That was the last place Graham had been, and it was the place where he lived and worked.

So instead of eating, he got into his Xterra, and drove toward Graham's studio.

9

DARKNESS HAD FALLEN BY THE time Guthrie parked in front of Graham's building, went up to the door, and let himself in. He snapped on the lights and looked around. The place was exactly the same as when he last entered. There didn't seem to be any further damage, and all the paintings that Diane had returned to the racks were still in place.

He wandered around for a few minutes, taking in the odor of paint lingering in the air and picking through the tubes and brushes on the workbenches next to the easels. The portrait of the banker sat unfinished, collecting a veneer of dust. Or was it the patina of an antique? Whatever it was, the talisman tattooed beneath Guthrie's navel started itching.

He went upstairs and looked through the apartment, finding only what he'd already seen. Nothing seemed to be missing that had been here the last time he'd visited the studio. In the bedroom office, Guthrie squatted and sifted through the papers scattered around. He found utility bills, papers on the purchase of the building, and financial records, both personal and of his sales, but nothing that pertained to any unusual paintings or Graham's disappearance.

Guthrie went downstairs to the filing cabinets and flat files and flipped through the sketches and notes that he'd cleaned up on his previous visit. This time, he looked them over more carefully than he had the last time he'd handled them. There was a copious number of sketches and more-finished drawings and a lot of photos of Graham's work, but not a single image representing anything out of the ordinary.

But why was he looking for something out of the ordinary? Diane had described the scene in the painting as just another landscape, aside from its unusual depiction of plants. She'd simply said that the painting made her feel creepy. Guthrie could have thumbed through any number of sketches for the work and not realized it. But Gavin O'Neil had told her he was looking for a painting that was special. What the hell did that mean, aside from its hyper realistic execution?

Guthrie went and perched on the stool that sat in front of the easel holding the banker's portrait, wishing the portrait could speak of what it had witnessed. Staring around the studio, he tried to imagine he was Graham. Somewhere in the studio was a painting that Graham had compulsively created using a highly advanced technique that even his agent and former lover didn't know about. Soon to arrive was someone who would take or lure him away, along with a large panel and art supplies. Guthrie thought it was the former because the work room and files had been left a mess, and Graham didn't strike Guthrie as the sloppy sort. And then, after Guthrie mentioned to Lycoris the possibility that a smaller painting existed, someone—or more than one person—had ransacked the studio, presumably looking for it. It had to be the smaller landscape since Howard hadn't yet painted the larger panel—or was currently painting it. Guthrie didn't know much about painting, but he didn't think Graham could have completed something that size this quickly.

But if Graham had so compulsively created the smaller painting and used such an advanced technique, it would seem he should be proud of it. So why hide it? And what had become of the larger panel? And Graham?

The list of unknowns was growing steadily, but one thing Guthrie was sure of: Graham had been frightened and desperate, and his fear and desperation revolved around the landscape.

Why?

Guthrie looked up, and saw the banker staring back at him. Although the portrait was merely inanimate paint worked into a semblance of life, Graham's work showed his excellence. Even this close, the eyes and most of the face had a vibrancy that went deeper than mere representation. It boggled Guthrie that a person could create such a thing.

"Too bad you can't talk," he said to the portrait. The painted eyes stared back with impassive power just waiting to be released.

On the table next to it lay a sketchbook half-buried in tubes of paint. The top sheet, which was dog-eared and detached from the rest of the pad, showed a detailed rendering of the portrait on the easel, and askew on top of it lay a pair of photographs of the subject. The photos—8x10 color glossies—were expert work themselves. Guthrie picked them up and glanced back and forth between them and the paintings. Even though the photos were exact replicas of the real-life man, they didn't begin to approach the vitality conveyed by the leavings of Graham's brush.

Even so, there was an odd quality about the portrait that wasn't evident in the photos. Something unsettling. Something that made Guthrie's protective tattoo itch. Was this how Diane had felt viewing the missing painting?

He set the photos back on the sketch pad and stared at the portrait. Graham had obviously begun with the eyes. Guthrie knew that most of facial recognition centered on the eyes and nose, so that made sense. The face was nearly finished, with only portions of the sides of the head and hair incomplete. The background was merely shaded in, and it was light enough in color that it appeared to cast an aura around the head, which seemed odd to Guthrie, because the aura effect dampened the facial features, much like trying to see the face of a backlit person. It was a defect that Graham undoubtedly intended to solve once he got back to work on it.

But the client had canceled, so that wouldn't happen.

Guthrie stared around the studio again, surveying the damage. Had whoever taken the place apart found what they were looking for? The extent of the disorder suggested they hadn't. If you find what you're looking for, you stop looking. Maybe the painting wasn't here. Maybe Graham had destroyed it. But Guthrie thought not. The missing landscape was still hidden somewhere.

But not here. Guthrie had searched, and others had, too.

Cursing silently at one more dead end, Guthrie got up from the stool and headed for the door, wondering if there was someplace he hadn't checked. Hadn't thought to check. Some place that didn't seem like it needed checking? At the door, he scanned the room again, taking in the flat files and filing cabinet beneath the stairs, the drafting table and flanking cabinets, and the work stations with their easels: one empty, one holding an unfinished landscape and the other the banker's portrait.

Shrugging, he opened the door, turned off the light, and stopped.

The banker was glowing in the dark. Or rather, the aura of unfinished canvas around the head was glowing.

Guthrie shut the door and hurried over to the portrait, the protective talisman below his navel crawling. He carefully tilted the portrait off the easel and turned it around. Nestled inside of its stretcher frame was a second canvas, its face to the back of the portrait. It looked to be about two by three feet, and light leaked around its edges like light around an ill-fitting door.

Despite the fact that his protective talisman was itching like crazy, there was no way that Guthrie wasn't going to pull the painting out of its hiding place and look at it. He flipped the portrait and carefully set it onto the easel, face down. Then he grasped the sides of the nestled canvas's stretchers and pulled it free. As he did, the light emanating from the face of the painting splashed over the easel and floor. He carried the painting to the empty easel, being careful not to touch its surface, and set it on the easel's tray. Oddly, instead of giving off an odor of oil paints, the canvas exuded a brassy smell that began to permeate the room.

The painting showed a rocky hill whose lower reaches were a mile or so away on the right side. It looked a thousand feet high, maybe more. A rough-textured, arid flatland dotted with huge boulders stretched into the far distance between the base of the hill and a rocky abutment on the left side of the painting. The closest boulder, maybe eight feet tall, was only about thirty feet from the picture plane and about one-third of the way in from the left. Despite the obviously arid conditions, the landscape wasn't barren, though plant life grew only sparsely. In general outlines, the painting was like the one Diane had described, but there the similarities ended.

In this painting, the landscape and its features were warped, twisted, and sagging, as if everything was made of wax and a momentary but great heat had washed over it. Even the plants were deformed, though unlike the terrain, they weren't melted looking but seemed diseased, misconceived, and cancerous. No two were even remotely similar. Some of the plants were spindly and spiky, some with putrid-looking, lobular leaves that varied in color from blue-black to ragged mixtures of green, red, and gray. Others were like grotesque crosses between vegetable and animal. Most reminded Guthrie of rotting, moldy vegetables kept too long in a refrigerator bin, though these things obviously were alive and growing despite their odious appearances.

Even more repulsive was the one true animal in the scene—a large, dark, leather-winged creature that squatted on the large boulder near the picture plane. It was so realistically rendered that Guthrie had to shake his head to dispel the image that the creature was staring right at him.

The thing appeared to be fairly large, and its body bore a vague resemblance to a pterodactyl with sickly skin mottled pink, gray, and chartreuse. Guthrie could see the wrinkles where the splotchy, leathery skin twisted with the head turn. And the way the thing's eyes seemed to stare right into his own reminded him of an article he'd read about the hypnotic gaze that predators such as snakes turn on their victims to paralyze them.

The thing looked real enough to reach out and touch, only you wouldn't want to. Its head looked like a huge fist had crushed it into asymmetrical deformity, and below the bulging yellow reptilian eyes, the dozens of ragged, needlelike black teeth in the creature's obscene hole of a mouth looked like they could take your arm right off. The teeth were rimmed with blubbery and wrinkled pale pink lips, and long, thick strands of gray drool hung, almost quivering, from the lower lip.

The creature's leathery wings draped lazily on either side of the boulder it stood on, and its feet were armed with four long, crooked toes ending in sharply hooked black talons. Guthrie could even see places where the claws had scratched gouges in the surface of the rock—a subtle hint at the kind of reflexive power that resided in the heavy, tendon-driven legs.

The painting was one of the most hideous things Guthrie had ever seen, but not because the disgusting landscape and deformed creature it depicted reeked of some drug-induced nightmare made real and rendered all the more bizarre through Graham's photorealistic painting technique. All that was bad enough, but the horrific quality of the painting didn't come from the imagery alone. The canvas itself seemed to exude a dissonant, sick apprehension.

And how was it giving off light?

Diane had said that the landscape she'd seen had creeped her out, but if she'd seen this one, she'd have been terrified. And what about the larger painting? If it was anything like this, Guthrie thought, no wonder Diane was concerned for Howard's sanity as well as safety. Only someone seriously psychotic could produce a work like this.

Suddenly, the pterodactyl creature launched itself straight at Guthrie in a predatory surge of flapping wings.

Gasping, Guthrie fell back against the table flanking the West Texas landscape, knocking it over and sending brushes and tubes of paint flying across the floor. His hand groped instinctively for the 9mm nestled behind his right hip, but his hand had barely brushed its butt when the pterodactyl's disgusting, hideously frightening head jammed through the frame of the painting, mouth hissing with reeking breath and snapping with the black, needlelike teeth. A sinuous, gray-green tongue stretched back into a gaping and gulping puss-strung gullet, and gobs of stinking gray mucous spewed onto the floor.

By now, Guthrie had his gun out, and he drew a bead on the thing as it reared back and struck again. With intense will power, Guthrie held his fire. He was now ten feet away from the painting, and the thing was obviously too big to get more than its head through the frame.

The thing struck at him several more times in quick succession, like a huge, featherless raptor, each time with the same results. Guthrie feared that the painting's frame wouldn't be able to withstand the force, but he noticed that the painting didn't budge at all, no matter how powerfully the creature tried to surge through it. He breathed a sigh of relief but didn't holster his gun. Just because the frame had resisted so far didn't mean it would stand up to relentless battering. Or a stronger thrust.

The creature wheeled and began clawing through the painting with its powerful back legs, the black talons slashing empty air.

"Shit!" Guthrie yelled as the creature suddenly backed up and gathered itself for a more powerful strike. He leapt forward, grabbed the painting, and threw it face down onto the floor.

"Eat that, motherfucker!"

The canvas lay there, inert, but the light leaking around its edges flickered wildly for several more moments, accompanied by the sound of something hard striking the tiles. Then the flickering and impacts stopped.

If the thing had been able to see him, Guthrie thought, now it must be looking at the linoleum. Not much appetizing about that, even for a creature like the one that had moved on the other side of that painting.

That window?

Now he knew why light issued from it and why Howard Graham had been afraid. He was the one who'd done this. This was his art, as impossible as it was horrible. Guthrie wasn't sure what he thought or believed about it, but his former experience with Tereba had taught him that things weren't always what they seemed and that reality had a dimensions to it that most people didn't recognize and couldn't accept if they had. He'd never heard that a painting like this was possible, but now that he'd seen it, there was no argument in his mind.

There was only the question of what to do about it.

Guthrie picked up the stool he'd knocked over along with the table, propped himself on it, and watched the light around the rim of the canvas remain steadily bright for another ten minutes. Then he went to the light switch, turned off the lights, and in the dim street light filtering in through the studio's frosted windows, returned to the painting. He grasped the top edge of the stretcher frame, and gingerly lifted it, bending to peer, almost like peeking around the edge of a reverse hatchway in a floor. Ragged gouges furrowed the linoleum like miniature canyons in the light spilling from the painting.

The winged creature was still there, standing on the ground about half-way between the painting and the boulder where Guthrie had first seen it, but it was no longer staring in the direction of the painting. Instead, its head was twisted to the left on its blotched, leathery neck, as if was watching something to the side, hidden from sight off the right edge of the painting.

Thank goodness for small favors, Guthrie thought. Without the thing's mesmerizing eyes on him, he felt a little less intimidated. He returned the painting to the easel then stepped back into the gloom of the studio. With the studio lights out, he just had to keep out of the direct sunlight coming through into his side of the painting to remain unseen. Guthrie shifted to the left side of the painting and looked in the same direction the pterodactyl thing was staring.

His position close to the left side of the frame gave him a wider range of the view through the window of the painting, and he could see that more boulders lay strewn about on that side. As he watched, a snout edged around one of the boulders, and a moment later the new creature's body was in full view. It was some sort of alligator thing with a thick body armored on top with ridges of spikes that looked as sharp as the rows of snaggled teeth protruding from a mouth made for ripping and tearing.

The pterodactyl thing began to shy away from the newcomer, who spotted the movement and, without a second of hesitation, charged, mouth gaping. Voicing a muffled moan, the pterodactyl thing launched itself into the air just as the alligator slammed across the space where it had been standing, mouth snapping at the flyer's ascending legs.

Guthrie faded back into the shadows, hoping the new creature wouldn't see him. Despite its bulk, it was blindingly fast, and its head nearly came up to the height of the picture frame. He watched it mill around for a few minutes, sniffing at the rock where the pterodactyl had perched before it noticed what probably looked like, from its side of the painting, a black rectangle floating in the air. It came over and reared up on its legs, but before it could paw though the painting, Guthrie grabbed the canvas and lay it face down on the floor.

There was no way he was going to get a good look at the painting as long as freaky monsters kept attacking from the other side. Guthrie rummaged around in the cabinets until he found an artist portfolio about the right size to hold the painting. By the time he got back to the painting, both monsters had vanished. He quickly slipped the canvas into the portfolio, wishing it was a metal box instead, and zipped it shut. Then he left the studio, locking the door behind him.

10

AFTER GUTHRIE PULLED INTO HIS long shell driveway and stopped in front of the wooden fence that separated the front yard from the back, he got out, opened the Xterra's hatch door, and pulled out the portfolio holding the painting. He didn't really want the damn thing in the house. On the ride home, the little tattooed men of the talisman beneath his navel had felt like they were crawling beneath the skin, and he doubted he'd be able to sleep anywhere near the painting. But he couldn't leave it in the car all night.

He locked the car and started down the sidewalk toward the front door, but he didn't get farther than halfway before a sudden tiredness suffused his limbs and dragged him to a halt.

Low blood sugar, he thought. I must be hungrier than I realized.

But two heavy footsteps later, he found he just couldn't go on, and the real reason dawned on him.

The Old Master's Talisman.

When Guthrie had helped Tereba exorcise Aswad Mar, the old man had painted a protective diagram on Guthrie's door. A watchdog, he'd called it, that would protect the property from evil influences. Guthrie had met a similar entity during that case, and that one had called forth and amplified Guthrie's psychological deterioration. He'd always wondered how his own watchdog might affect intruders, but the one time he'd witnessed its work, he'd been too occupied facing down Corbin Ingram to ask Ingram how it felt. Now he knew: total lethargy.

He looked down at the portfolio, its handle gripped loosely in his enervated hand.

Evil influences.

Retracing his steps down the narrow sidewalk, he skirted his car and went through the side gate, feet still dragging sluggishly. He slogged toward his detached two-car garage, feeling lighter as each step took him farther from the house. The garage probably would be a better place to keep the painting, anyway. It had a new cement-slab floor, was dry inside, and since he used it as his laundry room and gym and never parked his car in it, the floor was clean.

Guthrie unlocked the personnel door, took the portfolio inside, and opened it. He pulled out the painting and gave it a glance. No monsters, just an ugly, melted landscape and disgusting flora ruffled by a slight breeze and dripping nastiness onto the arid soil. There was a sudden movement from the boulder where the pterodactyl thing had been crouching when he'd first seen it. Guthrie started then stared. No monsters, but something had moved. Then he saw what it was and felt like he might be losing his mind. Off center in the boulder, close to where the pterodactyl had gripped the rock with its vicious talons, was an eye, and it was looking right at him.

For a crazy second, Guthrie thought the boulder might actually get up and rush him. If it did, he didn't think his gun was going to do a hell of a lot of good.

The eye blinked—the same movement that had first attracted his attention—but the boulder remained in place.

Guthrie lay the canvas face down on the floor then left the garage, locking the door behind him. If it wasn't safe here, he thought, fuck it. He went to the house, feeling as normal as a person who possessed a possessed painting could feel, but at least as he went through the door into the kitchen, the creeping sensation beneath his navel subsided.

He spent the next hour fixing his dinner and watching the news on TV. After he cleaned up, he returned to the garage and lifted the painting from the floor. No creatures were in sight, but the eye, which had been looking off to its right, turned to stare at him. Guthrie unfolded a couple of webbed lawn chairs, propped the canvas on one, and sat in the other, staring at the painting.

With the creatures absent, he could take in the rest of the painting in a way he hadn't done before, though the eye staring back from the boulder was disconcerting. The creatures might have left, but that didn't make the painting any more palatable. Maybe it was the painting's proximity to his watchdog, but it seemed more loathsome than before, and the tattooed talisman on his stomach was more uncomfortable than ever. The same brassy odor wafted through the opening, now infused with fetor from the deformed and blighted plants.

If the thing had started out as a painting, it was a masterpiece of technique, the brush strokes so minute and well blended that they were completely invisible. The hideous plants were rendered in sharp, detail, each moldy flake, thorny protrusion, and glistening rivulet of slimy decay as real as the bark and leaves of the pecan tree arching over the driveway in front of Guthrie's garage. Even the blasted and fused terrain was photo-realistically etched. Guthrie marveled at so steady a hand and so fine an eye, and he wondered again about what could have driven Graham to use such a refined and magical technique to create a monstrosity like this. Couldn't he as easily have painted a paradise?

But then, had it always depicted the kind of foulness it now did? This had to be the same one Diane had seen, and while she'd said it gave her a creepy feeling, she'd described it as a conventional scene, not a melted landscape blighted with corruption and crawling with monsters. Maybe it wasn't the same painting, but Guthrie thought it had to be, though the reason for its transformation was beyond him.

He had the same reluctance to touch the painting that he would have had handling a dog with mange, but he had to. He expected his hand to go right through, and it did. He quickly pulled it back. No telling what lurked behind his window view.

Keeping close to the edge of the window, he moved around, getting as wide a look into that other world as he could. When he squatted, he could see almost nothing but sky. A speck up there appeared to be a bird wheeling in the air. A sun that looked more orange than the one he was used to in normal reality was a few degrees left of being directly overhead. He remembered that the angle of the shadows in the other world had distinctly slanted toward the left when he'd first seen the painting. So, it had been morning out there a few hours ago, and now it was just past midday. In that world beyond the surface, the day was progressing just as it did here on Earth, but it wasn't in sync with Houston time. He'd seen something similar out of the windows in Tereba's home, but at least the view from the old man's house was a normal landscape.

Dropping his eyes, he saw something he hadn't noticed before. About halfway across the ragged plain to the hill, a wide swath had been cut through the landscape. It was as if a gigantic road grader had plowed the ground, leveling everything in its path.

Guthrie couldn't stay this close to the painting any longer. It was too repugnant, and his tattooed talisman was writhing beneath his skin. He stepped back, wiping his palms against his pants, and stared at it. After many minutes of watching, his patience was rewarded when he saw the bird that had been soaring in the sky far above swoop low over the terrain in the near distance. Only it wasn't a bird. It was the warped pterodactyl again. The thing banked to the right, out of sight, and Guthrie got up and moved closer to the left side of the painting so he could track the creature's movements. As he did, he noticed that the garage light behind him dimly cast his moving shadow across the ground on the other side of the painting's interface.

Horrified, he realized that the pterodactyl had seen the movement, too, when it abruptly banked again and headed right toward him. As soon as its shadow flitted across the boulder, the eye in the rock closed so tightly that Guthrie couldn't tell where it had been. Within seconds, the pterodactyl landed on the boulder. The diseased plants dotting the alien landscape were repulsive enough, but the thing's predatory stare was far worse.

Before it could spring at him again, he leapt toward the painting and lay it face down on the floor. Maybe the thing would leave if all it saw was a rectangle of cement instead of a square meal. For a moment, he thought he could see the light around the edges of the canvas flickering from the creature's efforts to get through, but then he realized it was he who was shaking. Wishing again that he had a safe or metal box to store the painting in, he moved it to the back right corner, out of sight behind a floor-stand punching bag. Then he locked the garage and went back into his house. He was more tired than he'd been in a long while.

At his desk, he punched Tereba's number into the phone. He wanted to show the painting to the old man and see if he could explain how a painting could open onto an alien world where disgusting plants grew and hellish creatures moved. After three rings, Tereba answered.

"Hello, Mr. Guthrie. I believe you must have found something."

"You need to come over here, Master Tereba. I don't think I'm qualified to handle this job."

"You are the only one I can rely on in this situation," the old man answered. "Why do you need me to come to your house?"

"I have this painting," Guthrie said. "Only it's not a painting. More like a window. It looks like hell out there, or some part of it. My watchdog wouldn't let me bring it in the house."

He described the scene, the monsters, the plants, the eye in the boulder, and the swath plowed across the landscape.

"The pterodactyl thing saw me and tried to get me, but it was too big to get through."

"I see." There was a pause, then Tereba said, "I'm afraid that I cannot come to see your unusual painting."

"I really need you to," Guthrie insisted.

"It would not be safe. There is something far worse than monsters in that place, and my presence close to the painting might attract it. Your monster couldn't get through, but this thing would."

"Well, what can I do with it?"

"Keep it covered. Predators ignore the inedible."

"What about this other thing? The one you're afraid of?"

"I did not say I was afraid."

"You didn't have to."

"Yes," Tereba admitted. "I am afraid, and not just for myself, but for all of us. This painting isn't a window. It's a leak between two layers of reality. And in this case, not a beneficial one. Like a pail of water leaking onto a fire."

"Or a plague carrier arriving in a city?" Guthrie asked, thinking of the diseased plants.

"A most apt metaphor," Tereba replied. "All that thing out there needs to infect our world is a means of ingress. After that, there's no power on this earth that can stop it."

"There's another one," Guthrie said. "Painting, that is. Or will be. But a lot bigger. The artist is the missing person you sent me to find."

For a moment there was silence, and Guthrie could almost see the old man on the other end of the line pondering that news.

"You must find him," Tereba said at last. "And you must find the other painting and destroy it."

"How?"

"You are the detective, Mr. Guthrie. Both this painting and the artist are out of my range of perception, so I cannot help you. I can only rely on your courage and judgment."

"But...."

"I must go now, Mr. Guthrie. My friends and I have to prepare for what will occur if you fail. Good luck."

The line went dead, and Guthrie hung up the phone. He sat there for a few minutes, digesting what Tereba had said.

"Shit," he exhaled at last, and leaned back in his chair, staring at the ceiling and wondering what the hell he'd done to deserve this. Whatever "this" was.

At last, he went into the living room and tried watching a program on History Channel, but the two-dimensionality of the TV screen only reminded him of the window out in his garage masquerading as a painting of hell. He turned off the TV, got ready for bed, and fell into a troubled sleep.

11

IT WAS BETWEEN MORNING RUSH hour and noon, but the traffic on I-10 was dense, even going outbound. The interstate from downtown to the western reaches of Houston had been under almost constant construction and widening for thirty years, but Guthrie didn't suppose anyone would be happy—or that the traffic would flow smoothly—until the damn thing was forty lanes across. Maybe not even then.

The building where Gavin O'Neil had his office lay beyond the Beltway. After parking in the visitor's lot, Guthrie rode the elevator to the eighth floor and found a door with unobtrusive lettering on the plastic plaque that read, "International Fine Arts and Antiques." Behind the door was a reception office as unobtrusive as the sign. Guthrie would have expected it to have a sampling of original art on the walls, but the only things there were several reproductions of colorful antique art festival posters framed in burnished metal.

"May I help you, sir?" the receptionist asked. She was a beautiful, svelte blond in her early thirties and dressed more chicly than her plain surroundings warranted.

"I'd like to have a word with Mr. O'Neil," Guthrie said.

"Do you have an appointment, sir?"

Of course not, or you'd already know about it, he thought. "No, but I think Mr. O'Neil will see me."

She looked him up and down, assessed the off-the-rack quality of his attire, and said, "I'm afraid he's very busy, sir. If you would like to leave your name and number...."

"He's not as busy as you will be tomorrow," Guthrie interrupted.

"I beg your pardon?" Hardness glinted in her frosty blue eyes.

"When Mr. O'Neil learns that I was here and you didn't even make an attempt to let him know about me, he'll be handing you your walking papers. Tomorrow, while I'm talking to him, you'll be looking for a new job."

"I don't think that's terribly likely."

"Don't worry." Guthrie smiled at her. "Worse things have happened."

He took a slip of note paper from the tasteful dispenser on her desk and quickly wrote down Howard Graham's name and the number of a burner cell phone he carried in addition to his own. He tried to hand the slip to the receptionist, but she just looked at it like it was diseased.

Maybe some of the hellish painting's ambience has rubbed off on me, he thought as he dropped the paper onto her desk.

"Bob Jones is the name, and this is my cell. I suggest you give it to O'Neil in the next few minutes—or as soon as he's finished with his latest scam."

She stared at Guthrie, eyes snarling, but he just smiled at her and left. A few moments later, the elevator deposited him on the ground floor, but before he had a chance to leave the building, the prepaid phone rang.

"Yes?" he said after he flipped it open.

"Mr. Jones?"

"Yes."

"This is Mr. O'Neil's office calling. Mr. O'Neil will see you now."

"I'll be right up." Guthrie closed the phone and went back to the elevator. While he rode up, he pulled out his real cell phone and punched in his office number. When his voice mail answered, he said, "This is Clay Guthrie. I'm entering the office of Gavin O'Neil, a crooked art dealer." He recited the address, date, and time, then put the phone, still on, into his inner jacket pocket. If something happened to him, at least there'd be a record.

The office looked the same as when he'd last seen it, but the atmosphere was distinctly more frigid. As soon as he entered, the receptionist, glaring at him, picked up the phone, punched a button, and said, "He's here."

She put the receiver down, got up, and opened the door into the rest of the office suite.

"Follow me."

Guthrie did, watching her hips twitch stiffly as she led him to an office and ushered him inside.

"Close the door, Stella," said the man behind the desk. "And tell Waite to go to the library."

"Yes, sir." She closed the door.

"Sit down, Jones," O'Neil said, the name slipping off his tongue as if he believed it were genuine or didn't care if it wasn't. He waved to one of the two chairs in front of his desk. "I understand you want to talk about Howard Graham. What is your interest?" O'Neil was a medium-sized, fleshy-faced man in his early fifties, with thinning and graying dark hair. He wore a very nice gray suit, but it looked out of place on him, as if he ought to be wearing used-car-salesman plaid.

"Did you know that he's missing?"

"Missing?" O'Neil shook his head. "I don't keep up with all the artistic gossip. There's far too much of it, and most is extremely trivial. Do you mean missing in that something might have happened to him?"

"That's a possibility."

"Are you looking for him?"

"That's right."

"Who hired you, if I may ask?"

"You may ask, but I won't answer."

"Ah, yes. Client confidentiality, and all that." O'Neil paused and stared at Guthrie for a moment. "But why have you come to me?"

"I understand that you recently inquired about a Graham landscape. A very special landscape."

"I might have inquired," O'Neil shrugged, waved, and gave a small, self-deprecating smile. "But surely that's no indication I know anything about Graham's whereabouts. Why would I have anything to do with his disappearance?"

"Good question," Guthrie said, and was rewarded with a hardening of O'Neil's eyes. "I spent a couple of hours last night going over your criminal record, O'Neil. It's pretty impressive for an art dealer. I don't doubt you'd stoop as low as you need to get what you want, and I think you want that landscape."

"I hope you're not implying...."

"The landscape you inquired about was known to only two people before a few days ago. One of them was the gallery owner you tried to intimidate Sunday, and the other was Graham himself. Now I know about it, but apparently so do you. How is that, Mr. O'Neil?"

"We're done talking." O'Neil rose from his chair and pointed to the door. "I want you to leave."

"Not yet," Guthrie said, remaining seated. "You haven't heard my offer yet."

"I don't want to hear your offer."

O'Neil punched a button on his phone, and Stella's voice answered, "Yes, sir?"

"Send in Waite," O'Neil said tersely. Then to Guthrie he said, "I strongly suggest you leave before Mr. Waite arrives."

"And I strongly suggest you call off Mr. Waite until you've heard me out."

"I've heard all I want."

"But not all I'm going to tell you."

"I think so," O'Neil said as the door opened and a man with short, sandy-colored hair entered. He was a big man, but he moved well. "Mr. Waite, escort this man out of the office and make sure he gets on the elevator."

"Yes, Mr. O'Neil."

Moving quickly forward, Waite grabbed Guthrie by the jacket collar and dragged him out of the chair. He spun Guthrie around to aim him at the door, but Guthrie kept spinning, and suddenly, he was behind Waite. Before Waite could react, Guthrie chopped a foot down on the back of his right knee. Waite's leg collapsed, and he crashed to his knees. To his credit, he managed to keep from going all the way down, and he lashed out, his right hand balled in a meaty fist. Guthrie caught the hand with his own right hand, flipped it over, bore down with his left above Waite's inverted right elbow, and used the leverage to force the big man's face toward the floor. Then he saw Waite's left hand groping toward his jacket and knew he was going for a gun. Guthrie twisted a little harder and shifted the angle of pressure on Waite's elbow. A small popping sound came from the elbow, and the man grunted in pain. His tai chi training under Li Wu was coming in handy.

"You can take the gun out now," Guthrie said. "Slowly, or I'll ruin your arm."

Waite carefully dragged out a heavy semiautomatic.

"Toss it to your left."

Waite complied, and Guthrie shoved him down then let him go and stepped quickly to the gun and picked it up. It was a .45 Beretta Storm.

"Nice gun," Guthrie commented, pulling the slide back far enough to see a chambered round.

By now, Waite was rising, rubbing his arm, his face flushed with anger and the corners of his eyes pinched with pain.

"I'll get you for that," he snarled.

"Not today," Guthrie said. "Go stand in that corner." He gestured casually with the pistol. While Waite complied, Guthrie looked at O'Neil. "I hope you don't have one of these that you're thinking of pulling out."

The art dealer was looking back with cool calculation, apparently undisturbed by the sudden violence but obviously irritated that it hadn't gone his way.

"I still have nothing to say," he said, sitting down again.

"Keep your hands on top of the desk," Guthrie ordered, and O'Neil obediently put his hands in place. "I want to know where Graham is, and you're going to tell me."

"Or what? You'll shoot me?"

"Well, it would have to be you, since you probably wouldn't give a shit if I shot Waite."

O'Neil laughed. "Perhaps not, but Mr. Waite would care a great deal if you shot me since I pay him quite handsomely."

"To intimidate and kill owners of art who might be reluctant to sell?"

"Mr. Waite can be quite useful at the bargaining table."

"How about it, Waite? You also kidnap artists?"

"Fuck you."

"I just want to find Graham," Guthrie said, ignoring the jibe. "Well, O'Neil? Want to tell me where he is?"

"If I knew, which I don't, I wouldn't tell you."

"Not even for payment?"

"I doubt you have the resources."

"Aren't you in the least bit curious about what I have to offer?"

"Okay. In the least bit. Give me the quick version."

"The Howard Graham landscape you tried to buy from Diane Weston. She never had it. But I do, now."

Guthrie saw O'Neil's eyes narrow and shoulders stiffen.

"Is that right?" A calculating look crossed O'Neil' face. "I suppose you're here because you want to sell it. What do you want for it?"

"Howard Graham."

"You propose a trade? The painting for Graham?"

"That'll do."

"I can't promise anything," O'Neil said after a pause, "but I have a certain client who might be interested. I'd have to contact him and relay your proposal."

"You do that, and get back to me as soon as possible." He turned to Waite. "Okay, big boy. Drop your pants and lie down on the floor."

"Like hell," Waite said, turning around, his heavy face flushed.

"Don't get all huffy. I'm not trying to take you up on your offer of sex. I just want a chance to get out of here without you running after me."

"Do it, Waite," O'Neil ordered.

Waite hesitated then undid his buckle, unzipped, and let his trousers fall around his ankles.

"Down." Guthrie gestured with the pistol, and Waite lay down. "Now you," Guthrie said to O'Neil.

Without a word, the art dealer came around the desk, dropped his slacks, and got down on the carpet.

"Call soon," Guthrie reminded him. "Remember that paintings are fragile. They burn and tear easily."

"So do artists," O'Neil replied.

Guthrie opened the door to the outer office and hurried through, barely glancing at Stella, who obviously didn't know what had transpired in her boss's office and just shot him a nasty look.

Out in the hall, Guthrie waited impatiently for the elevator, hoping that O'Neil wouldn't have his goon follow him. A trashcan sat next to the elevator doors, and he dropped Waite's gun into it after wiping it off with his handkerchief.

The elevator came without incident, and as he rode down, Guthrie pulled the phone from his jacket pocket and ended his call to himself. Inside of two minutes, he was back on the freeway, heading toward Graham's studio. There, he let himself in and went straight to the storage room. After a few minutes of searching, he found a West Texas landscape the same size as the painting—the window—in his garage. He put it into a portfolio, left the studio, and drove home.

12

EARLY THE NEXT MORNING, GUTHRIE went to his office, where he distractedly flipped through the mail that had accumulated in the mailbox during the last few days. Among the advertisements, credit card offers, and come-ons was a check from one of his most recent clients—a woman he'd helped in tracing the whereabouts of her father, who'd disappeared when she was a child, soon after her parents had divorced. Turned out he was working for an insurance company in Philadelphia, and he was overjoyed his child had sought him out. He had a different version of the events of the separation. After the divorce, his ex-wife had remarried and moved without telling him her new address or new name, and he'd never seen his child again.

They sure had some problems to work out, Guthrie thought as he set the check aside. He wished them luck. His bank was just across the freeway, and he'd make the deposit when he went out later. He killed a few minutes by cleaning his M&P. When he was done, he snapped the magazine into the pistol's butt and slid the gun into the holster riding his right kidney. He fished another full magazine from a locked desk drawer and dropped it into his pocket, smiling. Twenty-four rounds should be sufficient for an art deal. He got up to pour himself a fresh cup of coffee.

By noon, he was getting antsy. He tried calling the Zephyr again, but the gallery's voice mail picked up on the fourth ring. He left a short message and hung up then called Diane's cell and home phones and got voice mail at both, as well. He was a little puzzled but not too worried. He'd told her to lay low. Maybe she was still at her friend's or some place she had to turn off her cell phone.

Making a mental note to try back in an hour or so, Guthrie left his office, drove under the freeway overpass to his bank, and deposited the check that had been in the mail. Then he pulled onto Woodridge, turned right onto the feeder, and stopped at Dot's, where he ate a BLT with fries and drank another cup of coffee. Afterward, he drove home.

When he arrived, he went immediately to the garage and gingerly lifted the painting off the floor. There weren't any monsters visible, so he propped it on the washing machine.

The shadows out there were longer and angling to the left, as if the sun might just have risen. The pterodactyl thing had vanished, but for all Guthrie knew, it or the other creature he'd seen, was lurking behind the painting.

And that brought another interesting point: What did the back of the painting look like, there on that other world?

Guthrie looked for the eye he'd seen earlier in the boulder, but couldn't spot it. Maybe it was asleep, he thought. What kind of dreams do boulders dream?

He thought about destroying the painting, but he was reluctant to do that until the case had been resolved. He might still need it as a bargaining chip. Then, he'd be glad enough to be rid of the damn thing so it wouldn't give his tattooed talisman the heebie-jeebies.

He lay the painting face down on the floor and went into the house, where he occupied himself with domestic chores. Forty-five minutes later, his prepaid cell phone rang. The caller ID read "Unknown Caller," but Guthrie recognized Stella's voice.

"Mr. Jones?" she asked coldly.

"Yeah," Guthrie replied. Why waste time being conversational with someone who hates your guts?

Apparently, she felt the same way, because she simply put him through without another word.

"Jones?" It was O'Neil's voice.

"You talk to your client?"

"He's interested."

"If he's interested, he must have Graham."

"I have no idea what you're talking about. I want no part in this transaction. The actual nature of the merchandise and payment exchanged will be between the two of you. I will put you in touch, then I'll be out of it."

"All right. What's the plan?"

"Since I am sure you and he are reluctant to share names and phone numbers, perhaps a discreet meeting would be in order."

"Make it a public place."

"Of course. Some place where the payment can be held safely until the actual exchange."

"Suggestions?"

"There's a Starbucks on Kirby, a few blocks south of Sunset. It has a small patio right next to the street. Be there at three sharp with the painting. Sit on the patio by the rail. He'll meet you there, and you can make the exchange."

"Sounds simple."

"Then that's all you need from me." O'Neil cut the connection. Guthrie checked his watch and saw that he didn't have a lot of time before the exchange. He tried Diane's numbers again but, as before, only got voice mail. He slipped his phone back into his pocket. Just before three, he neared the Starbucks, but even at this time of day, its small lot was full, so he had to park on the side street just to the north. Before he got out of his car, he chambered a round in the M&P, just in case.

As he walked toward the small building's entrance, carrying the portfolio with the painting he'd taken from the studio the day before, he reflected that he was less than a mile from the Zephyr. Inside, he ordered a coffee. Two of the five tables on the patio were unoccupied, and he sat at one, facing Kirby, and propped the portfolio against the wooden rail that separated the patio from the sidewalk that bordered the street. The coffee was too hot for him to do more than sip at it, but coffee wasn't what he was here for.

Surreptitiously, he surveyed the people at the other tables. Two men and a woman, all in their early twenties, sat at one. A laptop was open on the table in front of one of the men, and all three were engaged in an animated conversation. Obviously students from Rice University, which was just a couple of miles southeast.

A man and woman at another table were engrossed in a conversation that seemed intimate, and their hands kept touching across the tabletop. Guthrie felt a twinge of jealousy that highlighted his own isolation. People everywhere had someone. He knew he'd blown his marriage in the worst way possible, but he was different now. Maybe it wasn't too late. But he had no idea about how to approach a relationship, even if the opportunity arose, which, in his case, didn't seem likely.

A lone, middle-aged man sat at the third table, and he seemed pensive. Was he the one Guthrie was here to meet? As the minutes passed, Guthrie began to doubt it. For one thing, the man's business casual clothing didn't seem to be in context for a high-level art collector, even of bizarre art. And for another, aside from a casual glance when Guthrie first sat down, the man showed no interest in him. Instead, he stared reflectively across the street as he sipped his coffee, and after a few minutes, he pulled a small brown leather notebook from his hip pocket and began writing in it.

Guthrie turned so he could watch the parking lot. Cars were coming and going—most through the drive-thru—and half a dozen people drifted in and out of the doors, but none gave Guthrie a second look. Three o'clock came and went, and so did the other people on the patio.

He was alone when, at two minutes after three, an unmarked white cargo van pulled up and stopped on the street next to the patio. Its license plates were obscured by mud, but it looked like the same one he'd seen parked in front of EF Imports & Exports.

As traffic backed up impatiently behind the van, the cargo door slid open, and a burly black man emerged. He had close-cropped salt-and-pepper hair, wore an expensive but ill-fitting suit, and carried himself like he meant business. A slender white man with a scruffy beard masking a narrow chin sat behind the steering wheel, staring straight ahead. Another white man, this one with muscles bulging beneath a loud Hawaiian shirt two sizes too small, was half visible on the bench seat at the back of the van.

Ignoring the blaring horns from the cars trapped behind the van, the black man stepped across the sidewalk to the side of the rail and held out his hand.

"The painting," he ordered gruffly.

"Where's Graham?"

"You wanna see Graham?" The black man turned to the open cargo door, and as he did, Guthrie could see he had a Colt 1911 in a holster at his waist. "Show him Graham."

The muscular man in the back of the van reached to his right and hauled a struggling figure to the opening.

It wasn't Graham. It was Diane.

The muscular man's right hand gripped her hair, pulling her head back, and his left pushed the muzzle of a chrome .357 into the soft flesh beneath her jaw. Her mouth was duct-taped, and more tape wound her wrists and ankles. Her eyes held more fear than Guthrie cared to see, but her struggling said the fear wasn't all she felt.

At the sight of her, Guthrie started to his feet and surged against the railing. The burly man stepped back, hand on the butt of his gun.

"The painting or she dies," he told Guthrie. "And you, too. Now!"

As if to emphasize the order, the muscle man jerked Diane's head and hissed loudly into her ear, "Keep still, you!"

She stopped struggling, and the burly black man held out the hand that wasn't fastened to the butt of his gun.

"Now."

Guthrie handed over the portfolio, and the burly man unzipped it enough to see that there was a painting inside. He re-zipped the portfolio, put it into the van, and got in after.

"Hey!" Guthrie yelled. "Give me the girl!"

The black man just looked at him like he was crazy and slid the door shut with a bang. In a second, the van was accelerating into the angry traffic.

Guthrie raced down the patio, around the corner of the building, and across the small lot to the side street where he'd parked his car. Kirby was crowded almost any time of the day. He just might have a chance to catch up with the van before it vanished.

The Xterra was parked pointing the wrong way, and Guthrie pulled a quick U-turn, but the traffic worked against him instead of the van. By the time he'd muscled his way onto the busy thoroughfare, the van was gone. For good, he realized. Just a mile north was the Southwest Freeway, and in a couple of miles either way were freeway exchanges that could allow the van to escape in almost any direction.

Gut sinking, Guthrie pounded the wheel.

13

GUTHRIE FELT AS EMPTIED OUT as he had after Master Tereba had stopped his life force during his last case for the old man. The idea that whoever was behind this not only had Howard Graham but Diane Weston, too, made him want to lash out and eradicate them. But whoever they were, they weren't here, and he didn't even know who they were. Except for one, and that was himself. It was his fault more than theirs. He'd exposed Diane by dangling the painting as bait, expecting a fish to rise, not a shark.

But he was going to find out who they were, goddammit, and after that, they'd be sorry they ever thought about laying a finger on her or Graham.

And he had a good idea where to start.

O'Neil.

Guthrie steered his car toward the building where O'Neil's offices were, arriving in just under half an hour.

The elevator ride up to O'Neil's floor seemed nerve-rackingly long, but when he emerged, he still had no better plan than to barge in, gun drawn. Nobody was in the hallway, so Guthrie drew his pistol and, keeping it down by his leg, approached O'Neil's door.

It was locked, so he pushed the button beside the door frame. He could hear a buzzer go off inside, but there was no answer, and he pushed the button again. Still nothing. The door was too sturdy to break down, and though Guthrie probably could have picked the lock, he didn't have the tools with him.

Fuck you, O'Neil, Guthrie thought. You can run, but you can't hide. Didn't the bastard have a townhouse in Memorial?

Re-holstering the S&W, Guthrie returned to his car, where he looked up O'Neil's address on his phone. It wasn't far as the crow flies, and he arrived in less than half an hour. As he drove down O'Neil's block, he saw a moving van parked in front of O'Neil's townhouse. He pulled to the curb in front of the van while several Hispanic men in jumpsuits carted boxes and furniture out of O'Neil's door.

Guthrie walked boldly past them and into the townhouse, which already looked vacant. O'Neil wasn't there, but he found Waite in the kitchen, sitting on a stool, drinking a beer, and reading the *Chronicle's* sports section. The man's jaw dropped as Guthrie entered, and he started to stand, anger in his eyes, but he stopped when he saw the S&W appear in Guthrie's hand.

"Put your hands on the wall over there," Guthrie commanded.

"What you gonna do?" Waite's voice sneered. "Shoot me with all those moving guys for witnesses?"

"Yes. In two seconds if you don't put your hands on the wall and spread you legs."

Apparently, Waite believed him because he set the beer and newspaper on the counter and did as Guthrie instructed. Guthrie patted him down, keeping the S&W's barrel pressed to the man's neck. He found the .45 Beretta in a shoulder holster and a butterfly knife in Waite's front right pocket. Backing up, he holstered his S&W and pulled on the Beretta's slide, chambering a round. After that, he slipped the butterfly knife's blade into a drawer and snapped it off, then tossed the flopping, pointless hilt onto the counter.

"Okay, turn around slowly and sit on the floor." Waite did as he was ordered.

"Wadya want?" he asked when he was on the floor.

"Where's O'Neil?"

"Gone. On his way to Paris."

"Planned flight or spur of the moment?"

"He was pretty upset about your visit to the office. After you left, he made a couple of phone calls, then he had me drive him here. He packed up a couple of suitcases, got a couple more calls, and told me to be here today to supervise the movers. I drove him to the airport just after lunch."

"Where's he moving?"

"Nowhere. It's all going into storage. I don't think he plans on coming back."

"Left you holding the bag?"

"I'm flying out day after tomorrow. Looks like I'll be spending the rest of my life on the Continent."

"Not if you don't tell me what's happened to Diane Weston."

"I don't know any...."

"She's the owner of the Zephyr Art Gallery. O'Neil paid her a visit the other day, and being his good little lapdog, you went with him."

"Okay, yeah. I know who you mean. But I don't know anything about her."

Guthrie leveled the Beretta's barrel at Waite's face, his own taut.

"That's the only time I saw her," Waite said quickly. "I mean it. I didn't do anything to her. I just drove him and stood around while he talked to her. Ask her yourself."

"What did O'Neil want?" Guthrie demanded, keeping the pistol pointed at Waite.

Waite looked down briefly, then back up. He shrugged. "It ain't nothing to me. About some artist. Howard Graham. The guy you were talking to him about. O'Neil was trying to buy some painting he did, and he thought this Weston woman had it."

Guthrie jammed the Beretta's barrel toward Waite's face, and the big man flinched. "I know you had something to do with Howard Graham's disappearance. And Diane Weston's, too. Tell me."

"I don't know nothing more than I've told you...."

"Don't fucking lie to me," Guthrie snarled. "If you're not going to be completely honest, I have no further use for you."

His finger tightened on the trigger, and apparently Waite saw the truth that Guthrie had killed before and wouldn't hesitate to do the same to him because he jerked up his hands.

"Wait! Wait! Yeah, I admit I helped O'Neil and those guys bust into Graham's place, but I didn't do anything but help O'Neil swipe a few of his paintings. I didn't know anybody had snatched him or this Weston chick. I swear. You gotta believe me."

"Convince me," Guthrie said, keeping the Beretta aimed. "Who were they? These guys you're talking about."

"I don't know who they are. I never saw them before. I think they work for some client of O'Neil's. O'Neil and me met them there, and they were already inside Graham's place. I was just there to protect O'Neil if they tried any funny stuff and to help him lift some of Graham's paintings."

"Why was O'Neil there?"

"The client wanted O'Neil to help identify a painting Graham did for some broad, but I don't think it was the Weston chick. This was before she entered the picture, but I think it was the same painting we went over to her gallery to get later."

"How much later?"

"A long time. Maybe a month."

"It was you who broke into the gallery?"

"Yeah, that was me, but I couldn't find the painting."

"And you don't know who took Graham?"

"Not me. I never heard of him before we broke into his place, and I was there just the one time."

"What did O'Neil tell you this painting looked like?"

"He just said it was some landscape that might look kinda weird. He said I'd know it if I saw it, but hell, most of the paintings I see look weird to me. Anyway, I didn't find it."

"What kind of car were these other guys driving?"

"A white van."

"Any markings?"

"It was just a plain white van. Like a delivery van. The kind without windows. No name or anything on it."

"Who's the client?"

"I don't know that, either. O'Neil never told me that kind of thing. You had me pegged before when you said I'm just his muscle. Maybe Stella knows, but I sure don't."

"Is Stella in the office today?"

"I doubt it. He told her to shut everything down."

"Is she going Continental, too?"

"She's got the same flight out as me."

Damn, Guthrie thought. That eliminated her as someone to question. As soon as he let Waite go, he'd call to warn her Guthrie was looking for her. She'd be gone before Guthrie could learn her address. And O'Neil was out of reach, too.

Guthrie stared at Waite, wondering what else could be gained from him.

"What about the men who broke into Graham's studio? They didn't tell you their names? What did they look like?"

"No names," Waite said. "O'Neil didn't bother to introduce us. Hell, they just looked like guys. Only two came into the studio. One was a big black dude but, you know, going to fat. Graying hair. The other was younger. White. Looked like he lifted weights. A couple of real cold fishes. Outta my league. There was a third guy— a scruffy, skinny white guy with a beard. He was the driver, and he stayed with the van. He didn't seem like the other two. Dangerous, I mean. I didn't ask them anything, and they weren't conversational."

"Keep going."

"The other guys were already there when me and O'Neil showed up. They were getting some of Graham's stuff—clothes and art supplies and such—and O'Neil went into a room with all these racks of paintings and pulled them all out. He was looking for this one painting, but he didn't find it. Then he picked out a few of the others and told me to load them in the car. While I was doing that, O'Neil went through all these files, looking for some sketches, but I guess he didn't find what he was looking for 'cause he didn't take any of them. At the same time, the other two guys tore the place apart, looking for the painting, too. But it wasn't there. After that, the other guys tossed Graham's stuff in the van, but we drove off before they did. That was it. I don't know anything else. I swear."

Apparently, Waite sensed that the interview was coming to an end.

"What you gonna do?" he asked, looking nervous. "I told you everything I know."

"I'm going to let you go," Guthrie said. "But if I find out you've lied to me, I'll hunt you down and kill you. I don't give a shit if you are on the Continent or anywhere else. I know how to find people, and I'll find you no matter where you try to hide."

"I told you everything," Waite promised. "I don't know nothing else."

"Don't try to come out after me. And if I ever see you again, you'd better shoot first. Enjoy your Continental life instead."

Guthrie backed from the room, and as soon as he was out of Waite's sight, he stuck the Beretta into his jacket pocket to hide it from the movers, who were busily oblivious to what had taken place in the kitchen. Outside, he wiped down the gun and tossed it into some bushes beside the front door. In a few minutes, he was out of the neighborhood.

Only then did he notice how white his knuckles were on the wheel. He deliberately relaxed them, but he couldn't get the tension out of his shoulders.

He'd told Waite that he knew how to track people down, and maybe he'd sounded convincing, but was it really true? Howard Graham and Diane Weston were gone without a trace, and he wasn't any closer to finding them than he'd been at the beginning. Could he learn where they were and rescue them before something irrevocable happened?

14

GUTHRIE WHEELED INTO THE ZEPHYR Gallery's little parking lot half an hour later and, not bothering with the front door, hurried around the side to the garage apartment. Diane's car sat in front of the doors, and the personnel door beside them was open, keys dangling from the lock. Inside the storage room, paintings were lying on the floor and tilted against the walls and central work table, several of them torn and their stretchers broken. This had been a more thorough and destructive search than Waite had accomplished when he'd broken in.

Guthrie locked the door and pocketed the keys then took the stairs two at a time to the apartment. As he hit the landing, he saw that the front door had been kicked in, the frame around the lock splintered.

The neat, two-bedroom apartment had its kitchen separated from the living room by a bar fronted with a pair of stools. The décor was feminine and simple without being minimalist. And there was art on the walls. Among the abstracts, conceptual art, and still lifes were two Grahams—one a landscape that looked like it was a late afternoon scene of the Texas Hill Country and the other a portrait of Diane. He'd captured her perfectly.

And so had someone else.

There were a few signs of struggle but not many. They must have surprised and overwhelmed her. The black guy and the muscle builder wouldn't have had much trouble. Guthrie looked around, and though her attackers had left no obvious clues, they hadn't taken her purse. Inside it, Guthrie found her cell phone, which yielded nothing of interest on her call list or in the address book. He kept it, anyway.

After shutting the broken apartment door as best he could, he went downstairs and made sure the gallery was locked. Then he went to his car, wondering what the hell to do next. He seemed to have hit a wall. O'Neil had been his only lead, and the corrupt art dealer had effectively removed himself from play.

Guthrie drove back to his office and sat brooding as he hadn't done since he'd sought the Katib sculpture for Tereba. Where the hell could Diane and Howard be? Who had them? And why?

More importantly, how could he find them?

He refused to consider the possibility that they might not be alive. If the people who'd snatched them wanted them dead, Diane's body would have been in her apartment or found in some roadside ditch. No, whoever had Graham had her as well, and that meant purpose, not whim.

But where could he start looking? With O'Neil out of the country, that was a dead end. It was all dead ends.

Or was it? There was one other person who knew Graham and who knew about the paintings, although she'd denied it. Lied about it. Adriana Lycoris.

She'd told him to come back anytime, even if she hadn't meant it. The time was now.

Guthrie stuck a couple of extra magazines for the S&W into a belt pouch and clipped it on. Normally, he might try to be a little more circumspect, but in this case, he wasn't above out-and-out intimidation. Diane had trusted him, and not only had he let her down, he'd put her in jeopardy. He was going to get her back safely if it was the last thing he did. And Graham, too.

By now, the day was long past evening rush hour, so the worst of the traffic had died, but he still felt tension rising in his chest. With businesses closed for the day, he was afraid he'd arrive at Lycoris's shop too late to confront her. Of course, he could always come back tomorrow, but that would waste precious hours, and that might be all the time Diane and Graham had. Guthrie knew that whoever took them wanted them for some reason, but eventually their usefulness would play out, and then they'd be a danger to be disposed of. He couldn't afford to wait until tomorrow.

But when he arrived at the Eternal Flame, it seemed he would have to wait. It was closed and dark. Then he remembered that she probably lived on the house's second-floor. Around back, there was no green Suburban in the driveway, and the garage apartment, too, was dark. He saw a double flight of wooden stairs that led up to the second floor from a small back yard surrounded by shrubbery. As he climbed them, he loosened his pistol in its holster. On the little landing at the top of the stairs, he paused, carefully peering into the window just to its left. The last of the afternoon sun sent a shaft of light through the window, and he could see that the room inside was a kitchen, but beyond the door at the back, the apartment looked unlit.

He knocked loudly, waited half a minute, then knocked again. Either no one was home or they were hiding, and Lycoris hadn't struck Guthrie as the type to hide.

He'd brought his burglary tools, and he thought about breaking in, but the blue and gray shield-shaped sign he'd seen sticking out of the flower bed near the bottom of the stairs told him that the apartment was protected by a home security system. He could bypass the alarm easily enough, but he wasn't interested in spending hours tossing an apartment that probably would yield few clues. What he wanted was a live person he could intimidate into talking.

He returned to his car. Lycoris was now his only lead. Even though she might not know anything about Diane's disappearance, Guthrie suspected she did know something about Graham's. But Guthrie wasn't about to wait around for her to show up. If she wasn't here, she probably was at her warehouse. If she was, he was going to have a little chat with her, and she would tell him what he wanted to know. If she wasn't, he had his burglar tools. Might as well put them to good use. He'd wanted to get a look inside, anyway. He started the Xterra and headed toward Lycoris's warehouse.

The growing darkness was the perfect cover for a break-in, but he saw that unimpeded entry wasn't going to be the order of the evening. At least not this evening. The green Suburban and the Lexus were parked in front, and the electric security gate was closed. The white van was absent.

Guthrie drove past the building. The windows fronting the EF Imports side of the building were only dimly lit, but he could see brighter light leaking around the edges of the paper taped over the windows of the seemingly vacant warehouse next door.

He turned around in the driveway of the dilapidated apartment complex down the block, then came back by the warehouse. Just beyond the cluster of light industrial buildings, he turned into the short street next to the city service center. The street dead-ended at the chain-link fence bordering the railroad tracks. Another chain-link fence with a motorized gate to the right enclosed a half-acre parking lot that lay between the rear of the cluster of light industrial buildings and the railroad tracks. The lot belonged to the city service center, and the cement expanse was about a third filled with black home garbage bins and green recycling bins waiting distribution. The city employees were long gone, and the parking lot was empty of cars and locked up, but the whole area was well lit by lights from the service center and lot.

He pulled up next to a large recycling dumpster that sat next to the parking lot gate and got out. The razor wire looping the top of the tall, chain-link fence around the front of Lycoris's building elim-inated a frontal approach, so Guthrie scaled the fence bordering the railroad tracks and dropped to the weeds in the ditch that paralleled the berm supporting the rail line.

He scrambled up onto the tracks, and a couple of hundred feet of walking took him to the fence separating the warehouse from the tracks. There, he went down into the ditch and up the other side to the fence. The smooth side of the fence was toward the tracks, but as he'd noted earlier, the wood was gray and rotted. He stuck his fingers into a crack between two boards and pulled. The wood bent and creaked and finally split with a sharp crack. He grabbed the lower half and twisted its nails out of the bottom stringer then tossed the piece of wood into the weeds and peered through the narrow opening.

The warehouse's back wall was only about eight feet away across a weed-choked alleyway, dimly lit in the wash of lights from the high school across the tracks behind him. Nothing moved in the gap except for the tops of the weeds swaying in the light breeze. The wall was a blank, concrete cipher without features or character. If there were any security cameras watching the alley, Guthrie couldn't see them, but he did spot something curious. Smoke was drifting off the roof over the back left corner of the building. He couldn't see a chimney or a stack, but there had to be one up there. The smoke had an aromatic odor, and Guthrie wondered what was being burned. Old scented packaging? If so, why didn't they just throw it away instead of taking the trouble to burn it? Inside a commercial structure?

Guthrie pried out two more boards, slipped into the alleyway, and worked his way through the weeds to the corner of building to his right, behind the EF Imports & Exports' side of the warehouse. If the light coming around the paper covering the front windows was any indication, the building's occupants were on that side of the structure, so Guthrie intended to see if he could get in the EF's side door. More weeds choked the gap between the building and the fence, and he threaded his way through them to the corner of the loading dock.

No one was there, and both the loading dock roll-up door and the personnel door set in the adjacent wall about eight feet away were closed. And locked. Guthrie took out his lock picks and teased open the lock in the knob, hoping he was right in thinking that the lights being on in the rooms on the far side of the building meant that everybody was over there. He slipped the picks back into his pocket, drew his gun, and eased open the door.

15

PULLING THE DOOR TO BEHIND him but not completely closing it, Guthrie found himself in a large space with ceilings about twenty feet high. Rows of eight-foot florescent tubes hung from the metal rafters. The cavernous main room stretched to his right, between the exterior wall and a parallel concrete wall twenty feet in front of him. The second wall appeared to run the entire length of the building, but he couldn't see all of it because the space to his right, which was toward the front of the building, was almost completely occupied by tall rows of industrial shelving holding an assortment of boxes and crates. The air was filled to overflowing with flowery, fruity, and herbal scents.

To his left, the space expanded an extra fifteen feet because of the extra width created by the wing holding the loading dock. Much of the center of this space was open, and as he stepped around the corner to his left and into it, he could see the roll-up door immediately to his left. Shipping and receiving tables lined the wall adjacent to the roll-up door, a hand-operated pneumatic pallet jack sitting in front of them. A wide opening in the middle of the far wall showed another room beyond.

Guthrie paused and listened. The place seemed quiet as a tomb. He hurried over to the wide opening and took a quick peek around the corner. This room was about twenty by forty, another concrete wall along its long axis. That had to be the main divider between the two halves of the building. To his right was more shelving at the end of which a metal door was set in an unpainted wallboard partition.

To his left were two cubicle rooms flanked by a kitchenette with a cheap dining set. As was typical with buildings such as this, the cubicles had been constructed of two-by-fours and wallboard and stood only about eight feet tall, leaving a considerable gap between their ceilings and the iron-raftered roof.

The room was unoccupied, so Guthrie quickly threaded his way through the kitchenette furniture to the two cubicle rooms. Both were bathrooms marked for men and women.

He returned to the main room and looked down the length of the long wall. About forty feet away was another door that had been hidden before by the shelving. He trotted toward it, his sneakers barely making a scuffling sound.

The room beyond was a sort of office, with a desk, filing cabinets, a computer and printer, a copier, and a work table. An open door to his right looked into the unlit front reception area where Guthrie had talked to the saturnine man on his first visit here. On the left was another built-in room with a door that was shut. He glanced into the reception room and saw that it was empty, then he stepped to the closed door of the room to his left. Inside was another office, obviously the business's main nerve center.

Just past the office door was the entrance to a hallway, one side of which was the main dividing wall. Another metal door was set in the wall at the end of the hall, and about ten feet down the concrete wall was an opening. Guthrie crept down the hall to the opening and was surprised to see that it hadn't been original to the construction of the building but had been cut out after the building had been constructed to allow access between the two halves of the building. And fairly recently, judging by the rawness of the concrete's edges and a lingering odor of cement dust.

All he could see through the cut-out entry was a wallboard wall, but when he peeked around the corner, he saw another hall like the one he was in, a closed metal door about five feet to his left. To the right was the second warehouse's front room with its paper-covered windows. Unlike the half of the building where he'd entered, the front room on this side wasn't divided into a reception area and small office but was an open space. The lights were on, and the room down there looked empty, but faint sounds filtered around the corner.

Guthrie went to the metal door at the end of the hall he was in and eased it open. He wasn't sure what he'd find, but all he saw was the smaller area of shelving he'd already seen and, across the space, the kitchenette and rest rooms.

Guthrie shut the door, returned to the cut-out opening, and eased into the hall beyond. This time, he went to the right, into the entry room of the right side of the building. It was completely empty except for dust swirling in the air beneath the florescent tubes.

As with the other side of the building, an office had been built into the back of the room, but when Guthrie opened the door, he found it, too, was empty. Also as with the other side of the building, a doorway pierced the far concrete wall. It was open, and the sounds, now louder, came through the opening. Guthrie glided over and peeked around the edge of the frame.

The space beyond was a mirror image of the first room he'd seen —the one filled with rows of shelving. But this room was nearly vacant. Most of the way down the far wall, he could see the personnel door like the one he'd entered on the other side of the building. But unlike the other side, here a floor-to-ceiling wallboard wall completely blocked off the loading dock and shipping area. A door was set in the middle of this wall, but it was closed.

About halfway down the wall directly opposite Guthrie was a TV on a stand. A tattered sofa sat in front of the TV, flanked by end tables and several folding chairs. Two men, one eating from a bag of microwave popcorn, were sitting on the sofa, watching the TV, their backs not twelve feet from Guthrie. They were the same two Guthrie had observed coming and going during his stake-out of the warehouse. A pump shotgun was propped against the nearest arm of the sofa, and the snout of an AR-15 protruded above the arm on the far end.

Despite the sounds from the TV, Guthrie could hear two voices—a man's and a woman's—coming from behind the tall wallboard wall, but he couldn't distinguish what they were saying.

There was no way Guthrie could get closer to the wall without being seen, so he went back to the hall and cracked the metal door.

Beyond was the mirror image of the space occupied by the kitchenette, rest rooms, and shelving on the other side of the building. Here, though, the area that was occupied by shelving on the other side contained a pair of built-in rooms constructed just like the rest rooms and offices. They were separated from the building's central dividing wall by a narrow hallway barely wider than the doorway Guthrie now peered through. About ten feet beyond the end of the second room was the doorway of the left-most of the two rest rooms for the warehouse on this side.

The voices were louder, now, as they drifted down the narrow hall. The doorways to the two rooms both opened onto the hall, though both were shut. Four quick strides carried Guthrie to the first one. It had a metal door with a bolt on the outside. He twisted the knob and nudged it open with his foot, hoping no one was in it.

Nobody was, and Guthrie paused there, holding his breath and listening for a change in the tenor of the voices that would tell him that his quick, furtive movements had been heard. But the voices went on, so he relaxed and glanced around the room.

It was dark, but light wedging through the open door showed it was about ten by twelve feet and furnished as a crude bedroom. Two of the walls were concrete, and the other two walls and ceiling were not faced with wallboard but with unpainted plywood.

The room might have served as a bedroom, but it also was an effective holding cell. The linens on the single mattress bed were rumpled, and a lump of dirty clothes lay wadded in an open suitcase that sat in one corner. The air smelled of sour, stale sweat. Guthrie ignored the cheap dresser. No time to search that now. But he did pick through the pile of dirty clothes and lift up a pair of khaki trousers and a T-shirt, both stained with splotches and smears of paint.

He dropped the clothes back to the floor and returned to the door. The voices had diminished in volume, as if their owners had stepped farther away.

Guthrie took the opportunity to hurry to the second door—this one a regular wood-panel door without a lock. Inside was another bedroom that was similar to the first, except that this one was faced with painted wallboard instead of bare plywood. And it had a small closet that held men's clothing on hangers. It also was a lot neater.

The bed was made, and dirty clothing was in a large, open-topped cardboard box on the closet floor.

Guthrie eased out the door and over to the corner at the end of the hall. The voices were louder, as if the speakers were just ten or fifteen feet away.

"Many since have perverted the teachings, diluted them until they are as water compared to the wine of everlasting power and joy," the woman's was saying, and Guthrie recognized the voice as Adriana Lycoris's.

"The perversions and those who speak them will not prevail," the man replied. Guthrie thought he might be the saturnine man.

"They will wither before the true wine of haoma," Lycoris said in a tone of agreement. "It will cleanse us with its radiant fire, burning away the dross of frailty, imperfection, and age. Only we, the chosen, are the true steel that can be tempered in those flames. Only we will experience the renewal and metamorphosis that will transform us with the power to exploit the world's manifold weakness and imperfection and allow us to bring forth a new age."

She paused then let her smooth, powerful voice slip into a tone of dramatic confidentiality edged with affection and satisfaction.

"Brother Gregory," she said. "You are among the chosen, and I am so grateful for your assistance in this difficult undertaking."

"As you have often said, Danae, unity of spirit is of ultimate importance in these final days of which the Prophetess spoke."

"But you have held fast, Brother Gregory. Only you believed that our goal was not simply worthy but attainable. I know there must have been times when you did not believe that Chinvat Bridge could truly exist. Or perhaps you believe that it, like our sacred flame, is only a metaphor."

"Danae...."

"Say nothing, but listen. I assure you that Chinvat Bridge is real, and this very night I will prove it to you beyond a shadow of doubt. Tonight you will see it, and, at the other side, Hara Berezaiti."

"Can it be true, Danae?"

"Yes. But first, let us reflect upon the eternal flame."

Guthrie heard the sound of retreating footsteps, and he risked a quick glance around the corner. He saw Adriana Lycoris, Melanie, and the saturnine man walking through a door, into the space beyond and out of his range of vision behind the edge of the doorway built into the floor-to-ceiling wall that masked the shipping area and loading dock.

Guthrie, safely out of view of the Lycorises and Brother Gregory, slipped across to the left of the door they'd entered. He almost didn't make it, not because he was seen, but because what he saw almost made him stop. Centered on the concrete wall opposite the door was a square object about the size of a garage door, draped with black cloth. A worktable to the front right of the square was littered with tubes of paint, bottles, and a jar of brushes. A stool was carelessly shoved to one side. And to the left of the square object, Howard Graham slumped in a metal folding chair.

He didn't appear to be in very good shape. His shoulders sagged, a short, untrimmed beard nearly hid his hollow cheeks, and his hair was an unkempt mess. His hands lay listlessly in his lap. He was looking at the floor near his feet and didn't notice Guthrie pass across the doorway.

Guthrie risked a peek around the door frame. If he was spotted, it would only speed up the inevitable. He was going to brace Lycoris and Brother Gregory anyway; he just wanted to do it in a way that nullified the threat of the men watching TV in the next room.

As he'd suspected, the room had the same dimensions as the shipping area on the other side of the building. In the corner to his far right was the inside of the roll-up door for the loading dock. All the walls were painted a neutral light brown.

Adriana, Melanie, and Gregory were less than twenty feet away from Guthrie, in three-quarters profile facing away from him. Gregory was wearing a long, dark robe, and both Lycorises were really decked out in radiant white gowns girdled with wide white belts of some sort, though from where he was, Guthrie couldn't tell what they were made of.

The three had mounted a low stage or dais made of brick, about twelve feet deep, fifteen feet wide, and two feet high, centered along room's back wall. In front of them, at center stage, was a flat-topped altar about six feet square and two high, also constructed of brick. A low fire flickered in a brazier set in the middle of the altar, and above it, a metal hood attached to a long metal pipe siphoned the smoke through the ceiling. In the corner at the left side of the dais sat a heavy, ornately carved wooden box about the size of a steamer trunk filled with what looked like sticks.

Guthrie's tattoo was itching like crazy.

Lycoris stood there in front of the altar for a moment, arms outstretched and palms up, as if embracing the spirit of the smoke before her.

"You know our flame, Brother Gregory, for you have kept it burning here continually, year after year, since we performed the ritual cleansing of the temple and consecrated the first brand, which I lit with my own hands. And it burns still, helping light our way through this land of sin and immorality, this time of trial and travail. How can a simple flame do this? Because our sacred fire has meaning. Because it is alive and mirrors the fire that burns within us all."

Lycoris stared for a moment at the fire, then she looked at Brother Gregory again and gestured imperiously to the dais in front of the altar.

"Get down on your knees before the flame," she commanded.

"Danae?" he asked, even as he knelt.

"Have no fear. Your loyalty is about to be both challenged and rewarded. Henceforth, you shall no longer be a mobad. I now designate you dastur of this Fire Temple."

"Danae," the man gasped. "You honor me."

"Because you have honored our Fire Temple. Rise now, Dastur." As he got to his feet, Lycoris said, "Please turn off all false illumination."

Brother Gregory—or was it now Dastur Gregory?—turned toward the doorway from which Guthrie was peering. Guthrie whipped back, not sure if he'd been quick enough.

Gregory's footsteps clicked across the cement, and Guthrie waited to be discovered, pistol heavy in his hand. But the footsteps weren't hurried, and when they reached the door, Gregory paused in the threshold only long enough to flipped off the light switch. Then his footsteps retreated, and after a moment, Guthrie slid along the wall and peered around the door frame.

The room was not in complete darkness thanks to the flickering light emanating from the fire. He watched the shadow of Gregory's shape return to the Lycorises.

"The fire is low, Danae," Gregory said after he mounted the dais. He waved toward the wooden box. "Shall I fetch more sandalwood or cedar?"

"Change is immanent, Dastur. More than immanent, for it comes tonight. And for the true illumination to be born, we must let our sacred fire die."

"Die?" Gregory might have been promoted to dastur, whatever that was, but his voice sounded weak. "But what will we do?"

"We must take courage from the eternal flame, even as it dies, and embrace inevitability because the time is here to behold at last the true eternal flame of the spirit. The flame that does not consume in order to shed its light. The flame that is cast from within."

She paused, taking in her audience of two.

"I have told both of you often of Chinvat Bridge, which will allow us to cross the demon-spawned seas of chaos to the land where the chief of the elder gods, Angra Mainyu, rules. Once there, Angra Mainyu will guide us up the slopes of sacred Hara Berezaiti and lead us to the place where haoma grows in such abundance that we may harvest it to our heart's content. And when we have partaken of haoma's divine flesh, it will ignite the holy fire within us, imparting wisdom. Only then, with that wisdom lighting all with numinous truth, will Angra Mainyu bestow his power upon us. Is that not what we have been working for all these years?"

"I cannot tell you, Danae, how I anticipate that moment." Gregory's voice was almost a moan.

"Then rejoice, for that moment is at hand, and you will see with your own eyes what we have worked to create."

Lycoris stared at the altar, where the flame was barely visible now. Then she knelt and reached out as if caressing and soaking in the fire's last flicker.

"I'm afraid, Danae," Gregory's pleading voice came from the growing darkness.

"Are you afraid, Daughter?" Adriana turned to Melanie.

"No, Danae," Melanie said, voice firm. "It is as the prophecies foretold."

"You see, Dastur?" Adriana said sternly to Gregory. "We must have courage to seek the true light." She looked back at the dying fire.

"Silence, now! Have respect for the death of our old friend, for it is the death of our own childhood with all its ignorance and imperfections."

The fire sputtered and went out, leaving only glowing embers.

The pitch blackness inside the room was cut with a fearful moan from Gregory.

"I feel your pain," Lycoris said soothingly. "Yet I rejoice, for I know that the flame we have nurtured for these many years was but a symbol of the true light that haoma will impart within each of us after we allow it to enter our lives. Come with me."

She stepped off the dais, and only then did Guthrie realize that the room did not lay in absolute blackness. Across the room, light cast a dim halo onto the wall from beneath the edges of the cloth draping the large square shape.

"I give you a new light, Dastur, and this one is no mere symbol. It is as real as this room, as real as you and I. It is the true light of Hara Berezaiti and the holy haoma bringing order to the disorder around us and light to illuminate deception. See! Even now, its true light is manifest, just as Angra Mainyu's power is absolute, just as haoma's gifts are divine."

Lycoris stepped around Howard, who didn't appear to react, grabbed the edge of the cloth, and pulled. The curtain slid off the panel with a swishing hiss, and the room was flooded with light that could have been shining through an opening the size of a garage door.

"Behold!" Lycoris said. "Chinvat Bridge!"

Gregory gasped, and Guthrie nearly did, too. The one in his garage was nothing compared to this. And nothing like it, either, except for the incredible level of lifelike detail. The scene was dominated by a rocky mountain sparsely covered by odd looking trees with lobular leaves and brush no less strange. The mountain didn't look especially tall and appeared to be easily scalable. It was close—the painting's point of view seemed to be located at the base of a low foothill that connected to the main bulk of the mountain by a narrow ridge. The mountain wasn't snow capped, but the world out there looked too warm and dry to support snow, even at higher elevations.

Unlike the one in Guthrie's garage, this painting did not depict warped and twisted land forms, and no monstrous animals or blighted and diseased plants were visible, for which Guthrie was grateful. But the tint of the sky looked the same, and he had a sense that this was the same world upon which the painting in his garage opened, though he had no idea why this view showed something relatively normal and the other a landscape that reeked of insanity. But he did remember that Diane had said the scene in the smaller painting was prosaic enough when she'd seen it.

Guthrie could see that the painting was far from being finished. Portions were more detailed than others, and several small areas remained simply blocked in. But it was obviously finished enough to let light through, though unevenly, as sunlight through a dirty windowpane.

As with the smaller painting, the world's sun wasn't visible, but it seemed to be late afternoon out there, and the illumination pouring through backlighted Lycoris and Gregory and cast a strong wash over the rest of the room. A casual observer might have thought that some clever stage lighting was responsible for making it seem as if the illumination was coming through the painting rather than from hidden lights, but Guthrie knew this painting provided its own luminescence.

"Can you feel it, Dastur?" Lycoris asked without turning. "Can you feel its power?"

"I feel it," he murmured.

Even Guthrie could feel it, but the feeling wasn't pleasant. And his talisman was crawling.

"Forgive me for ever doubting," Gregory said.

"Our goal is in sight, Dastur," she said, "but we do not yet have it in our grasp." She turned to stare at Howard, who was still slumped in his chair, staring at the floor. "Do we, Howard?"

Graham didn't look at her, but Guthrie saw his shoulders tense.

"If you think this has been unpleasant for you," she said, "don't think it hasn't been equally unpleasant for me. But it's necessary. It is imperative that you finish that painting."

"Imperative for whom?" he asked. "Me? Or you?" His voice sounded raw and defeated.

"Does that matter? Right now, what's good for me is good for you. It would behoove you to comply, and continue with the work. You promised the painting for the power to paint it. I gave you the power, and now you owe me the painting." She turned from him and stepped up to the painting, lifting her hands to let her palms hover inches over the surface. "I know you're getting close. I can feel it."

"You feel that thing out there," he said. "Not some mystical plant. I don't think it cares much about us or what we think."

"Maybe it doesn't care about you," she said. "But it knows me. It has called to me and my mothers since before the dawn of history. It spent centuries giving us the power to set it free, and it gave me the knowledge to make you the instrument of that freedom."

"I'm done," Howard said. "There's nothing you can do to convince me to finish it."

"Observe," Lycoris said in a scathing tone, turning to Gregory and gesturing at Graham. "This is the weakness that stands between us and Angra Mainyu, bringer of all that we desire, granter of all our wishes, redeemer of the beliefs we have so long nurtured and striven to make real. He who will lead us to bounteous fields of haoma. Our Fire Temple, our very bodies and lives will be transformed forever in the radiance of haoma's wisdom and Angra Mainyu's power, but not until our instrument can be persuaded to honor his commitment."

At that moment, a loud, insistent pounding sounded from the side door next to the loading dock. As the pounding came again, Gregory reached beneath his robes and pulled out a pistol.

"No need for that, Dastur," Lycoris said, laying a hand on his forearm. "Persuasion, and our glory, are at hand."

16

"TURN ON THE LIGHTS, DASTUR," Adriana ordered.

As Gregory came over to the doorway, Guthrie ducked back. Gregory toggled the light switch for the big room with the fire pit and painting—the Fire Temple. Then he went to Adriana and Melanie, who had walked over to the door set in the tall wall. Through that door lay the large front room where the two armed guards were watching TV. It also had the side door adjacent to the loading dock.

Lycoris nodded to Gregory, who opened the door, and she went through it just as one of the armed guards opened the side door, which wasn't visible from his angle, but when two newcomers did come into view, they squelched any plan he might have had to bully Graham away from his captors. One of them was the burly black man who'd taken Diane and the decoy painting.

The other was a complete stranger, but he was obviously the one in charge. Adriana stepped up to him, while Gregory stood off to the side, hands—and gun—hidden beneath his robes. The newcomer was a little over average height with short, dark brown hair and appeared to be about fifty. Although he was obviously fit, and he was good looking enough, there was something raw about his appearance and mannerisms, as if he had a feral energy that couldn't stay still. Or contained.

Maybe he wasn't in charge, Guthrie amended, when Adriana started in on him.

"You're late," she snapped.

"I didn't know I was on a schedule," the man shot back. "I had business to attend to."

"No business of yours is as important as what's going on here."

"What's going on here is only possible because of my business."

"I will always have my own means."

"Then I guess you no longer need the money I regularly deposit into your bank account or the services of my accountant to help you launder the proceeds from your smuggling operation, or the men I pay to protect you. Don't forget, Adriana, that you need me more than I need you, especially now."

"Danae...," Gregory protested, but Lycoris silenced him with a wave of her hand.

"It is the price we pay, Dastur." She turned back to the newcomer. "Do you have it?"

"No. The man who calls himself Jones gave us a painting, just not the one you want."

Adriana stiffened, and when she spoke, her voice was filled with barely controlled rage.

"You let him go."

"No choice at the time," the man replied with a shrug that implied he wasn't concerned about her anger.

"Do you think he's that detective?"

"Who knows? But if he really has the painting, he'll be back. In the meantime, aren't you going to let me see what our talented artist has been working on?"

"Very well," Lycoris said. "You may enter the Fire Temple, but not them." She waved at the black man and other, unseen people in the room, which included the two armed guards and maybe more.

"Stewart goes where I tell him," the newcomer said, and he gestured to the black man to follow as he walked past Lycoris, into the Fire Temple. He went over to the painting, Lycoris close behind him, and stared at it for a few moments.

"This is it?" He turned to look at Adriana, who stood next to him, then he reached out and touched the surface. "The light thing is a pretty neat trick, but it still feels solid to me."

"Patience, Karl," she said without returning his look. "Soon, all our efforts will be rewarded."

"Where are the monsters you promised would be out there?" the man asked, then he looked at Graham, who still sat, looking dejectedly at the floor. "Where are the monsters, Howard? Why didn't you paint any monsters?"

"I don't need to paint them," Graham said, looking up at the man. Karl. "They'll be along presently. The thing that made them will be along, too. That's why I'm not going to finish it."

Karl laughed.

"Oh, you're going to finish it," he said confidently. "But not here." He turned to Lycoris. "It's obvious that you've lost control of the situation, Adriana. It's time I took over. He can finish the painting at the ranch."

"No!" Lycoris almost shouted. "My power alone was strong enough to open Chinvat Bridge, but I have to oversee his work on the painting."

"If it's that important to you, come on out. Bring your daughter, mother, and priest if that makes you happy. There's plenty of room. But that's where we're going, whether you like it or not. This place isn't secure enough, anyway. Not if the creatures out there are anything like you describe. I've built a special room for it. When Howard's done, we can go out exploring together for your precious haoma."

"I won't paint it there, either," Graham said.

"You will," Karl said, and he waved toward the black man, who left the room and went out the side door. He was back a moment later with the muscle man in the Hawaiian shirt and Diane. She was still trussed and gagged with duct tape. The muscle man hauled her over to Graham, who surged out of his chair, only to be knocked down by the black man.

"Diane...," was all Graham could say.

"You *will* finish that painting," Karl said. Graham looked up at him, defeat making his body slack. "Don't bother saying anything. I have to stay in Houston for a few more days to attend to some business. You'd better be working on the painting when I get to the ranch, or she will pay the price. Do you know how long I can make her suffer? How many ways I can make her suffer? And I'll make you watch every second. And then I'll do worse to you, if that's possible."

He nodded to the muscle man, who shoved Diane down to the floor next to Graham. The artist instantly folded her in his arms.

"Andrews," Karl called out, and the man with the AR-15 appeared in the doorway.

"Go out and have Porter bring the truck. Then you and Bailey help him load up this." He jerked a thumb toward the painting. "And be careful. If you fuck it up, I'll fuck you up."

Andrews disappeared through the outside door, and Karl turned to the muscle man. "Help them load up the painting and all the art supplies. Make sure they do it right" Then he looked at Stewart. "Take Howard back there and get his clothes."

Oh, shit, Guthrie thought as the black man hauled Graham to his feet. "Back there" was right where he now hid.

17

As Stewart pried Graham's arms from around Diane and pulled him off the floor, Guthrie stepped back from the doorway, keeping in the shadows. If he was lucky, he'd be able to make it to the hallway beside the two bedrooms before Stewart brought his captive into the room where Guthrie was.

He was almost lucky, but Stewart must have seen furtive movements in the shadows, because he shoved Graham aside and went for his gun.

"Hey!" he shouted. "We got an intruder!" He started toward the door.

Guthrie had already drawn his own weapon, but he couldn't risk a shot toward the black man for fear of hitting Diane or Graham, so he shot into the air over his head. The rounds ricocheted off the concrete wall and punched through the roll-up door. As Stewart ducked, Guthrie raced for the hall. Seconds later, he burst through the door at the end. Two bounds took him to the cut-out hole in the dividing wall, he swung to the right, and slammed through the door into the EF Imports side of the building. He heard feet pounding after him as he raced around shelving and into the shipping and receiving area. The door he'd entered was about thirty feet away, and he hoped he could make it out and into the night before his pursuer could get a clear shot at him.

Guthrie had just made it across the space when Stewart came around the corner behind him and fired. Flakes of cement stung Guthrie's neck as he tore around the corner of the shipping and receiving area and jerked open the door, thanking foresight for not completely closing it when he'd entered the building. Then he was through it and into the night, heading for the back of the building. But he was a long way from being safe. The skinny van driver appeared around the front corner of the building and fired with his own assault rifle, the shots scoring the cement wall behind Guthrie as he ducked around the back corner.

Guthrie lost no time in thrashing his way through the weeds to the hole in the fence. Without slowing, he dove toward the opening. He was a little off center, and his shoulder slammed into the board on the left side of the opening. The rotted old wood snapped, and he fell through, his shoulder feeling like it was dislocated. In an instant, he toppled down the short slope into the weed choked ditch that paralleled the rail line.

The ditch saved him as two shot gun blasts shredded the old wood above him, showering him with splinters.

He scrambled ten feet down the ditch, weeds and underbrush tearing at his face and arms, then burst out onto the gravel-covered right-of-way beside the tracks. Throwing a glance toward the hole in the fence, he saw a head poke through, and he fired at it. He couldn't see where his bullet struck, but the head jerked back.

He ran like hell down the tracks, hoping to get as far as he could before the men behind him came through the fence after him. He didn't have far to go. The parking lot partially filled with black household garbage bins appeared to his left behind its chain-link fence, and his car was parked just on the other side of it, next to the recycling dumpster. If he could get far enough ahead of his pursuers, he might have enough time to scale it before they got close enough to shoot him.

A bullet sparked off the gravel next to him and whined off down the tracks. Another followed. He could hear footsteps crunching behind him, but he didn't waste energy looking back.

Forget the fence, he thought. There was no way he could get over it without being hit. Zigzagging as much as he could without tripping on the ties or slipping on the bulky gravel, he ran on, trying to remember what lay ahead. To his right was the unbroken fence line that ran behind the school, and to his left was the equally unbroken fence behind the city service center and the lot for the garbage trucks. The only difference was that the ditch and margin between the tracks and the school fence were well manicured, while those behind the city service center and lot were overgrown. More shots rang out behind him, and he heard one round rip the air dangerously close to his head.

Just ahead to his left, beyond the garbage truck lot, loomed a dark patch of tall trees—a tiny neighborhood, he remembered, whose single street dead-ended at the railroad tracks. Just beyond was Ella. Cars were driving on it, over the hump the tracks rode on. Guthrie didn't think that the men behind him would chance shooting at him close to the neighborhood or tracks. So far, all the gunfire had taken place in the relative anonymity of the tracks sandwiched between the light industrial area on Judiway and the school, and while they'd have been heard by people in the neighborhoods across Judiway and by anyone in a business still open on the street the school was on, it was unlikely they could have said exactly where the shots had come from. But the closer Guthrie and his pursuers got to the main thoroughfare, the more chance there was that someone in the little tiny neighborhood just ahead or a passerby would hear the shots distinctly, and maybe even spot muzzle flares.

Taking his last opportunity, Guthrie ground to a halt and whirled. Three shadowy figures were coming down the tracks, maybe a hundred and fifty feet behind him. Without really aiming, Guthrie emptied his magazine in their direction and saw two of them dive into the ditch behind the service center and the third topple down the short slope on the school side of the tracks.

Guthrie made it past the end of the row of houses on the near side of the short, dead-end street, and was gratified to see that, while there was a wooden fence between the first house and the tracks, only a barricade painted in chipped, grimy, and faded red and white stripes blocked the end of the street. He scrambled into the ditch, and paused to eject the spent magazine from the S&W and replace it with a full one. He was about to crane his head to see if the men were still following, when he saw something else that made him crouch lower in the brush and weeds.

A police car driving slowly up Ella had emerged into view from behind the small used car lot that faced the thoroughfare, its back to the school's playing field. The cruiser's rooftop lights weren't flashing, but the spotlight beside the driver's side view mirror was on. The car rolled slowly up the mound of the right-of-way then paused as the driver aimed the spot down the tracks then swung it over the brush where Guthrie crouched.

Guthrie didn't dare move for fear that the weeds would shake, indicating his presence. He just hoped that the cop or cops in the cruiser didn't get out to inspect his hiding place. Apparently, they were content to stay in the car, and after a couple of minutes, the car descended the mound and drove on.

The instant the patrol car was out of sight, Guthrie came out of the ditch, vaulted the barricade, and ran two houses down the street toward Judiway before he stopped to hide behind the bole of a large oak. The police car had turned down Judiway, and it hesitated at the end of the dead-end street, but then it moved on, and so did Guthrie. Doing his best to dodge behind trees and telephone poles in case his pursuers were still behind him, he made his way to Judiway and stopped at the corner. By now, the police cruiser was nearly in front of Lycoris's warehouse, but it didn't slow. At the end of the long block, it went straight ahead, between the park and the industrial area beyond.

He nervously waited while the cop car vanished in the distance, looking back toward the railroad tracks to see if his pursuers were still following. When he was reasonably sure the cop car was gone, Guthrie gave one more glance backwards and saw no one, so he emerged from the end of the street and hurried down the garbage truck lot fence line.

That first stretch, which was open, exposed, and well lit, looked to be the most dangerous, but he made it without a problem. He angled across the front parking lot of the city service center toward the place he'd parked his car, but before he reached the corner of the building and came in sight of the recycling dumpster and his Xterra, he halted.

He wasn't sure if he'd hit any of his pursuers when he'd emptied his gun at them back on the tracks, and he'd seen no sign of them since. After the police car had passed and he'd disappeared into the tiny neighborhood, they'd probably given up and headed back up the tracks toward the warehouse. But that would have taken them behind the city service center, and his car would be clearly visible just beyond the fence line.

Would they have decided he'd already fled the neighborhood, or would they suspect that the SUV was his and wait nearby so they could ambush him when he returned? They'd have gone by several minutes before Guthrie came up—plenty of time to climb the fence and take positions.

He wanted to take a look, but the front of the service center was brightly lit and his head poking around the corner would make an obvious silhouette. And target. To give himself a less conspicuous profile, he lay down on the crisp grass, praying that there wasn't a fire ant mound nearby, and inched his head forward, around the corner at the base of the wall.

Directly across from him was the small door manufacturing company and then the beginning of the chain-link fence that separated the parking lot holding the household dumpsters from the dead-end road where his car was. Even from his low angle, he could see the recycling dumpster with the front right corner of his car sticking around it only a hundred and fifty feet or so away. He didn't see anybody, but that didn't mean anything. The light was dimmer down there, and all three of the men chasing him could hide behind the dumpster, and he'd be none the wiser until they stepped out, guns blazing.

He knew he couldn't just lie here, peering, for very long. His pursuers might have gone back to the warehouse to get a car to cruise around looking for him, or the police car might come back. Or someone might drive down the street, hauling stuff to the recycling dumpster. To any one of them, he'd look suspicious lying in the grass by the corner of the service center. He had to act, but he didn't want to walk down the street to his car, totally exposed and with absolutely no cover between the service center and the chain-link fences lining the door company property and the dumpster parking lot.

But maybe there was some cover. The stainless steel rectangle of a telephone service box mounted on a concrete base jutted from the grassy margin between the road and the junction of the fences for the door company and the dumpster parking lot. It wasn't much, but it was large enough to hide behind, and the circuit boards and wiring inside would be dense enough to stop any but the most powerful rounds. Even better, it was offset slightly in relation to the recycling dumpster. If he could make it to the box, he might be able to see if anybody was hiding behind the dumpster.

If he made it to the box at all. It was closer than the dumpster but still a hundred feet away across open ground.

He ran for it, his feet swishing through the grass of the narrow side yard then pounding on the pavement. As soon as he hit the road, a man wheeled from behind the dumpster. There was just the one, but it was Andrews, the man with the AR-15.

As Guthrie rushed across the road, the man hastily jerked the muzzle down, but Guthrie fired at him as he ran, and Andrews flinched. His first burst gouged asphalt from the street behind Guthrie's feet. The AR was fully automatic, and the man's second burst shredded the face of the telephone service box a split second after Guthrie dove behind it. Folks around here were going to have a phone trouble for a couple of days, Guthrie thought inanely.

He had to move fast before the other men—or the police—were drawn by the gunfire. Guthrie didn't know how big a magazine his opponent's rifle had—probably thirty rounds since it was full-auto — but he had to convince the man wielding it to empty his load.

"Those cops'll be back any moment!" he yelled. "Do you know what they'll do to you if they catch you with that thing?"

He could hear cautious footsteps approach. Sticking the muzzle of his pistol around the edge of the telephone service box, Guthrie fired twice. Shooting so quickly from a blind position, he didn't expect to hit Andrews, so he wasn't disappointed when the man didn't go down. But he was satisfied to hear the assault rifle stutter into life again as he jerked back behind the box. But instead of stopping, he came around the other side, hoping like hell the man had emptied his magazine.

Andrews saw him, and both of them aimed their guns. The AR barked twice then went silent as the bullets hissed by Guthrie. Guthrie's own two shots, more carefully aimed, took the man in the chest, and he collapsed in a heap.

Rushing toward his car, Guthrie dragged his keys out of his pocket and punched the button on the fob. The Xterra's lights flashed and Guthrie snatched at the door handle and scrambled inside. He started the car, threw the gearshift into drive, and peeled out, twisting the wheel to avoid running over the inert body lying at the edge of the road.

He kept the headlights off as he whipped around the corner to his right, toward Ella, which would take him to the freeway. Just as he wheeled onto the thoroughfare, his rearview mirror showed flashing lights turn onto Judiway at the far end of the block. He hoped that the distance and darkness had masked his car, and as soon as he'd gone thirty feet, he turned on his headlights and drove rapidly, but not too fast, toward the freeway.

As he sat at the intersection waiting for the light to change so he could go under the freeway and turn left onto the east-bound feeder, two more police cars zoomed down the west-bound feeder and spun around the corner onto Ella, heading toward the scene of the shootout. Then the light changed, and a few moments later, Guthrie was on the Loop, heading for home.

He managed to make it a mile or so down the freeway before his hands started shaking.

18

GUTHRIE DIDN'T KNOW WHERE KARL and his henchmen had taken Diane and Graham, but he did know where Lycoris lived, and he drove straight there. But any hopes he might have had of confronting her were dashed when he arrived at the Eternal Flame and drove down the street, going a speed that he wouldn't arouse suspicion. He got only a brief look at what was going on in the driveway behind the house, but that was enough.

The Suburban was parked in front of the garage apartment, lit by porch lights from the apartment and the back of the Eternal Flame. Lycoris and her daughter were out there with three men: Gregory; the man who'd driven the van, Porter; and the guard with the shotgun, Bailey. All three men were armed, and Bailey's shotgun was visible as he watched the others load suitcases into the Suburban. There was just too much firepower for Guthrie to face down. After the gunfight on the railroad tracks, he was low on ammo, anyway.

He turned around and parked at the end of the street, got out, and hurried down the sidewalk. As he neared the Eternal Flame's driveway, he ducked behind a tree where he could see that they were nearly finished. Lycoris said something to Bailey, who nodded and went up the back stairs to the upstairs apartment. The rest of them got into the Suburban.

Guthrie ran back to his Xterra, but he was still fifty feet away when the Suburban backed out onto the street and came his way. He flattened himself against the backside of a large oak. As the Suburban went by, through the windshield he caught a glimpse of

Porter in the driver's seat and Gregory on the seat next to him. Presumably Lycoris and her daughter were in the back seat, but it was too dark to see through the tinted windows. As the vehicle reached the end of the street, turned right, and disappeared, Guthrie dashed for his car.

He jumped behind the wheel, started the engine, and turned around and followed, but by the time he got to the corner, the Suburban was out of sight.

Which way? He didn't know where they were going, but it sure wasn't back to the warehouse. The man named Karl had mentioned a ranch. They had to be headed there. That meant they'd most likely be taking an interstate out of town, but ranches lay in almost every direction around Houston.

Guthrie hurried through the neighborhood and made several turns onto side streets, but the Suburban had vanished. And in this part of town, there were several ways it could have gone to find interstate access, each in a different direction. Guthrie knew it was hopeless to try to follow.

But if Lycoris was gone, the man they'd left behind—Bailey— was probably settling in by now. Guthrie intended to disturb his comfort.

In five minutes, Guthrie swung onto the street where the Eternal Flame was located and drove slowly by the closed shop. Only the ambient glow of night-lights lit the lower floor, but the lights in the upper story were on. The guy probably was up there.

Guthrie parked in the next block. Before he left the car, he opened the box beneath the armrest between the seats, pulled out a stun gun, and slipped it into his pocket. Then he got out and walked back toward the shop, doing his best to keep his approach hidden by trees, shrubbery, and fences just in case the man at Lycoris's was actually doing his job and watching the street. Guthrie really only had to worry when he passed beneath the pools of light cast by the street lamps and the occasional well-lit front porch. At last he was at the corner of the Eternal Flame's lot, and he peered around a bush at the front of the building. Seeing no one, he crept toward the right corner of the wide front porch. Reaching it, he climbed up and over the rail then crouched beside the window and peeked inside. Bailey wasn't in the shop, or if he was, he was hiding.

Guthrie took the chance that the man was upstairs, not watching out of the shop windows, and crossed to the other end of the porch.

There, he went over the rail and hurried up the driveway, keeping close to the house. He stopped at the corner and gave a quick glance around it. Most of the lights that had lit the backyard a short while ago were now off, but the light for the small porch at the top of the stairs was still on. It cast its glow into the yard below, but Guthrie saw no one. Bailey might be concealed in the shrubbery surrounding the back yard, but Guthrie still thought he most likely was inside the apartment.

The next minute or so was the most dangerous. If Bailey was hiding outside, he'd have the drop on Guthrie, but there was nothing to do but go ahead. Guthrie chambered a round in the S&W and held the gun down by his leg. Then he boldly emerged from the corner, went straight to the stairs, and hurried up them.

He reached the top, breathing a sigh of relief before giving a quick glance through the window into the kitchen. The lights were on, but it was empty. A door in the far wall opened onto a short hallway, and dim light shone from the room at the end of the hall, augmented by a faint flickering glow.

Bailey wasn't watching out the windows. He was watching TV.

Guthrie pulled his lock picking tools from his pocket, and very quietly eased the tumblers open. They made only a faint clicking, and Guthrie waited a few moments to see if the man had heard, but there was no indication he had.

Afraid that it might make more sound than the lock had, Guthrie didn't try to open the door yet. Instead, he went back down the stairs and around front. The ambient light in the shop showed that the room was as empty as before. It took him but a moment to pry a brick paver from the front walk. Hefting its cool, damp weight in his hand, he went up the steps, where he heaved the brick through the glass of the front door.

In an instant, he was off the porch and racing down the driveway, half expecting to hear the blare of an alarm. But aside from the barking of a few neighborhood dogs, silence lay over everything. Air conditioning, he mused briefly, is the burglar's best friend in a neighborhood where people live behind insulated walls and closed windows. But while he was relieved that the neighbors weren't responding, Guthrie hoped like hell the noise had been loud enough to alert the man upstairs.

The back door yielded to his touch as he pushed it open as quietly as possible and stepped into the kitchen. Was the man still upstairs, or had he gone down to the shop to investigate? Guthrie could only hope it was the latter. Gun drawn, he crept quickly but carefully down the hall toward the glow of the TV.

The room—the living room, it appeared—was empty, but a glass, beaded with condensation and half full of ice and a dark liquid like cola sitting on a coaster showed it hadn't been that way for long. Through an archway, Guthrie could see a foyer, and the door in the opposite wall was open. He hurried toward it as quietly as possible and glanced through. A stairwell descended to a landing then turned out of sight. Guthrie could hear Bailey moving down there.

Guthrie eased down to the landing and listened some more. He heard footsteps crunch over broken glass, followed by a subdued curse. Then the footsteps got louder as Bailey returned to the bottom of the stairs. Flattening himself against the stairwell wall, Guthrie pulled the stun gun from his pocket and waited as Bailey hurried up toward the landing. Would he expect Guthrie?

As the man climbed the stairs, Guthrie heard a faint electronic beeping noise, and a moment later, the man rounded the corner. His shotgun was held absently in his right hand, and his left thumb was poised above the keypad of a cell phone.

Guthrie didn't let Bailey do more than give a surprised expression before he jabbed the stun gun against his neck and pressed the stud. Bailey jerked convulsively and collapsed onto the landing, dropping the shotgun and cell phone.

Before Bailey had a chance to recover, Guthrie had his arms behind his back and cuffed with thick twist-ties. A quick pat-down revealed a hammerless snub-nose .38 in an ankle holster, and Guthrie confiscated it, along with the shotgun and cell phone, the latter of which he pocketed.

"Don't do anything stupid," Guthrie said when the man could understand him. He'd holstered his own gun and aimed the shotgun at him.

"I think I already have," Bailey responded glumly, his words slurred. Then his eyes lit with recognition. "You're that guy from earlier. You killed Andrews."

"That's right, so you know I won't hesitate to use this." Guthrie gestured with the shotgun. "Do what I say, and you won't get hurt."

"Okay."

"Let's go upstairs."

Guthrie backed up the stairs, keeping the shotgun on Bailey as the man cautiously got to his feet and followed. In the apartment, Guthrie pulled open a door that looked like it was a closet and found he was right. He motioned the man inside

"Sit on the floor."

Bailey complied, his head brushing clothing hanging from the bar.

"I'm very upset," Guthrie said calmly, aiming the shotgun between the man's eyes. "And I don't have a lot of time or patience. You can answer my questions right now, or you can die right now."

"Okay," Bailey said, fear dulling his gaze.

"Where's Karl taking the artist and the woman?"

"I don't know. Honest. I work for the Danae, not Mr. Banning. They're going to his ranch, but I never been there."

"Where is it?"

"I don't know. I swear. Pretty far, I think. They hunt there."

Bailey was obviously fearful of Guthrie and was being cooperative, but that didn't mean he wasn't holding back. Guthrie wondered what the man knew that he wouldn't divulge unless asked a direct question about it.

"Why did they leave you here?"

"They don't need me at the ranch. Mr. Banning's got plenty of guys there. Like I said, I work for the Danae. She left me here to take care of the old Danae."

"Stay in there," Guthrie ordered. "Don't come out or I'll cut you down with your own shotgun. Understand?"

"Yeah."

Guthrie shut the closet door then jammed a chair against the knob. It wasn't foolproof, but if Bailey tried to get out, he'd make a lot of noise. Guthrie thought the man would do as ordered. He wiped down the .38 and the shotgun and shoved them beneath the sofa cushions, but he kept the phone.

The apartment was neat and clean and devoid of anything that wasn't domestic. There wasn't even a desk to hold household bills. All that, he realized, must be downstairs. But there was something unexpected. In a third bedroom, an old woman lay on the bed, hooked up to a nebulizer and an IV drip.

She must be the old Danae, as Bailey had put it.

She was gaunt of face, but the still-strong bone structure beneath the parchment skin showed a remarkable resemblance to Adriana and Melanie. A halo of white hair circled her head. Her body might have been feeble, but the malevolence of her burning gaze was enough to make Guthrie want to shrivel. He moved away from the doorway and took one step toward her, and she sat bolt upright in the bed and hissed at him.

That harsh, prolonged sibilant voiced a lot of warning, but her feeble body wouldn't let the warning become an actual threat.

"Sit back before you have a stroke," Guthrie said.

She glared at him and leaned back against her pillows, but her nerves were wire taut. Guthrie would have bet she'd bite the crap out of him if he got too close.

"You must be Adriana's mother."

"How did you get in here?"

"Your guard wasn't efficient enough."

"What do you want?"

"Your daughter helped kidnap two people. I want them back."

The malevolence of the gaze didn't waver in the woman's cold, stony features. She said nothing.

"I won't ask politely again." Guthrie took a step toward the bed.

"I don't know where they are," she snapped. "And I wouldn't tell you if I did know. I want them where they are even more badly than you want them back."

Guthrie closed the distance and grabbed the old woman's arm. It felt frail in his grip, and he twisted, wondering just how far he was willing to brutalize an old woman to get the answers he needed.

"I'm not into elder abuse," Guthrie said, "but I'll hurt you if you don't tell me where Karl's ranch is."

"I don't know," she whimpered, trying to pull away from him. He twisted harder, and she tried to bite him, but he shoved her head back onto the pillow. "You'll get nothing from me."

"Who's Karl Banning?"

Her lips drew into a sardonic line.

"A nobody. A tool. Just like you."

"Tell me," he demanded, twisting her arm harder. But she just glared up at him through a grimace of pain.

"Go on and kill me," she said. "You can't stop what's happening, and I won't help you try. Now, get out."

Guthrie dropped her arm. It was that or torture her, and he wasn't up to torturing an old woman, no matter how nastily she behaved. Without another word, he turned and left the room. Moments later, he paused beside the closet where he'd locked Bailey.

"I'm still here," he called out. "Don't do anything foolish or I'll kill the old woman."

The man inside gave no reply, but Guthrie, figuring he'd gotten the message, headed down the stairs.

He spent half an hour going through Lycoris's office. Most of the files pertained to the herb and candle business, and the desk held only a minor clutter of papers. Invoices were arranged in a set of stacking trays. Next to the trays was a letter holder shaped like a heavy wire spring set sideways in a wooden base. A dozen or so envelopes were stuck in the spring, and Guthrie shuffled through them finding mostly new bills and invoices. But there was one envelope that was different.

On the surface, it looked innocent enough: almost square instead of the usual elongated shape and hand addressed in neat, blocky lettering. Inside was an invitation whose front read, "Safaris to Hell." Guthrie opened it, and a slip of paper fell out, onto the desk. He picked it up and saw it was a check for $20,000 made out to EF Imports & Exports. It might have been payment for a shipment of some sort, but the note inside the invitation, written in the same blocky hand, read, "This should keep you going until he finishes the painting. Thought you might like to see the invitation before I send them out. Don't worry. It'll be an exclusive mailing." It was signed "Karl" in a cursive not far removed from the blocky lettering of the rest of the message.

Inside, the invitation's printed message continued: "Hunter's Challenge personally invites you on the safari of a lifetime. You won't want to miss this exclusive opportunity to bring back trophies impossible to attain anywhere on earth."

The postmark on the envelope showed it had been mailed in Houston a week earlier.

Guthrie tossed the check onto the desk but pocketed the invitation. He didn't bother going back upstairs but left the Eternal Flame through the front door instead, being careful not to cut himself on the broken glass. Outside, he hurried to his car.

19

DESPITE ALL THE ACTIVITY OF the day—or maybe because of it—Guthrie slept poorly and not long enough. He resented the downtime, but he knew it was necessary, and even restless sleep was better than mentally chewing over a problem he couldn't solve in the middle of the night anyway. He woke groggy, though after eating a bowl of cereal and drinking a cup of coffee, he felt a little more human. But that didn't make the seemingly impossible task of finding Diane and Graham any easier. He got a second cup of coffee, sat at his computer, and did an Internet search for Hunter's Challenge.

Ten minutes of browsing the Hunter's Challenge website showed him that the company offered hunting trips for every budget, from weekend trips to deer leases in Texas to real safaris in Africa and other places. There was no mention of Hell.

The name Karl Banning wasn't mentioned, either, but there were no names at all on the site, so that didn't necessarily mean anything. The company's office was on the North Loop, and Guthrie jotted down the address. It was still a little early, but he called Hunter's Challenge on Bailey's cell. A pleasantly masculine recorded voice told him to leave a name and number. Guthrie hung up then shuffled through Bailey's cell menus, but found nothing helpful. The short contact list consisted of the numbers for the Eternal Flame, EF Imports, and one other number with an area code in Ohio. Guthrie called the number only to hear the querulous voice of an old woman answer.

"Jimmy?" she said. "I thought you'd call yesterday."

Guthrie hung up. Apparently Bailey was a man devoted to his work and his mother.

He spent the next hour taking a shower and drinking a third cup of coffee. By the time he was finished, the clock read a little after nine. Hunter's Challenge should be open for business by now. He went out to the Xterra, got in, and drove toward the Loop. He didn't have a plan, really, but he had an address for Hunter's Challenge, his S&W, and an invitation to Hell. Those would have to be enough.

Inside the foyer of the eight-story building where Hunter's Challenge had its offices, Guthrie stopped and scanned the directory hanging on the wall across from a bank of three elevators. The company occupied offices on the top floor, and Guthrie got into the first available elevator and punched the button for eight. No one was with him, so he unholstered the S&W and pulled back the slide to chamber a round. Then he slipped the gun back into its holster and waited until the elevator doors slid back.

The entrance for Hunter's Challenge was a pair of glass doors to the left of the elevators. Guthrie went through the doors and found himself the focus of a dozen pairs of glass eyes staring down from mounted trophy heads on the wall. Actually, one wasn't just a head but half the body of a huge water buffalo, its skin a rich dark brown that was almost black. It jutted from the wall as if it had just charged through it, and the fearsome horns curling from its bony brow made the possibility seem plausible.

Guthrie forced his eyes from the thing to the receptionist behind the desk. She smiled with very white teeth. She was a good-looking brunette with tawny skin that showed a mix of color in her genes. Her eyes were anything but glass.

"Hello, sir."

"Pretty impressive fellow," Guthrie said, pointing to the buffalo.

"Our African Cape buffalo? Yes, sir."

"Doesn't he get a little intimidating?"

She gave a short laugh.

"He's really quite tame." Her tone said she'd used that line before. "May I help you?"

"I'm thinking of doing a little hunting," Guthrie said. "Your company seemed like it might be able to help me out."

"Certainly, sir. I'm sure we can. Would you care to sit down and look at some of our brochures while I contact one of our associates?"

"How many associates do you have?"

"Three on staff, but one of them is Brazil at the moment."

"Nice."

"Yes, sir. May I have your name?"

"Bob Jones."

She gestured to a trio of armchairs spread behind a coffee table made of close-grained, dark wood. Guthrie obediently sat while she disappeared down a hallway that intersected the back side of the reception area. He picked up one of the brochures from the coffee table and began leafing through it. It showed in living color all the exotic animals of Africa that he could render quite dead. The blurbs and captions made it all seem like such adventurous, heroic fun.

He glanced at the fearsome but inert water buffalo and other heads on the wall and wondered if they had found the experience all that enjoyable.

The receptionist came back with a dark-haired, tanned, fit looking man in his late thirties and dressed in a dark suit. She returned to her desk while the man stepped forward. Guthrie stood and came around the coffee table as the man extended his hand. Guthrie shook it.

"Mr. Jones, I'm Kevin Bartlett. I understand you're in the mood for a little hunting."

"That's right."

"Come on back to my office, and I'll show you what we have to offer." Bartlett turned and went down the hall, and Guthrie followed. "We have a wide range of options," Bartlett said over his shoulder. "I'm sure we can find exactly what you're looking for."

"I hope so," Guthrie replied.

They passed a door that opened to a room on the right, where another man in a dark suit sat working at a computer. Two more doors were down the hall on the right. One was closed, and from the slice of tile floor that Guthrie could see through the other, it probably led to the office kitchenette. Bartlett ushered him through an open door to the left.

"Have a seat." Bartlett waved to a comfortable looking chair in front of his desk, and Guthrie sat while Bartlett took his own seat. As with every other room in this place, the walls bristled with trophy heads.

"Have you done much hunting?" Bartlett asked, surveying his client.

"Some," Guthrie replied, surveying him back. "Mostly here in Texas."

"There's a lot of great hunting here," Bartlett smiled. "I got that fella there," he pointed to a many antlered deer, "and him," this time a javelina with gleaming yellowed tusks, "in Texas. We offer all sorts of trips, including canned hunts if you don't have the time or inclination to beat around in the bush. You pick the one you want then pick him off." Bartlett chuckled at his own joke.

"Yeah, right," Guthrie said, then shook his head. "No, I like the pursuit as much as bringing down the prey, especially if the game is dangerous."

"A man after my own heart," Bartlett nodded, his eyes narrowing. "So, what did you have in mind?"

"Something out of the ordinary."

"We offer a number of trips to Africa, Asia, and South America. And we can arrange to beat the bush for just about any game you want. Within reason, of course." Bartlett spread his hands apologetically.

"Nothing illegal, I suppose." Guthrie tried to inject a touch of disappointment into his voice.

"Legality often differs from country to country. If you want something bad enough, we have enough pull in some locales to make it happen."

"What about a snow leopard?"

"I can think of fewer exotic prey," Bartlett said. "But that would be highly illegal. Even displaying a trophy would be problematic."

"I'm sure these are all just for public consumption, Mr. Bartlett," Guthrie said, waving around at the heads on the wall. "You must have your own problematic personal collection at home."

Bartlett stiffened.

"If you're implying that I engage in illegal...."

"Relax," Guthrie soothed. "I can be pretty problematic myself. Like I said, I like the danger. Anyway, I'm not interested in a snow leopard. Not exotic enough."

"It doesn't get much more exotic than that," Bartlett said. He didn't look soothed, but he relaxed a little, though he was still wary. "What did you have in mind, then?"

"What about this?"

Guthrie pulled the invitation out of his pocket and showed it to Bartlett. He didn't dare open it and reveal Banning's personal message to Lycoris, but he thought the front of it probably would be enough.

It was.

"Where did you get that?" Bartlett snapped, sitting bolt upright in his chair.

"Safaris to Hell," Guthrie said, ignoring Bartlett's question. "Sounds like just the thing for me. How do I sign on?"

"I asked where you got that."

"And I ignored you," Guthrie pointed out. "What does it matter, as long as I have it?"

"It matters a great deal. Those were sent to only a select few clients...." Bartlett shut up then, realizing his anger was causing him to reveal things he shouldn't.

"What clients?"

"That's confidential. I'm going to have to ask you to leave."

Bartlett stood, and started coming around the desk, but Guthrie simply drew his S&W and aimed it at the man's chest.

"Sit down."

Bartlett stopped, hands bunching. He didn't seem particularly afraid.

"If you shoot, you won't get out of here alive," he snarled.

"Neither will you." Guthrie got up and quietly shut the door without taking his eyes off Bartlett.

"I don't know who you are," Bartlett said, "but you're barking up the wrong tree."

"Obviously not. Sit down." Guthrie gestured with his chin toward the desk chair, and Bartlett sat. "Keep your hands on the desk. If you put them out of sight for one second, I'll kill you."

Bartlett sat.

"What do you want?"

"Information about this." Guthrie waved the invitation then stuck it back into his pocket.

"You're not going to get it from me," Bartlett said.

"Then I'll kill you."

Bartlett must have seen the truth in Guthrie's eyes.

"I can't tell you," he said in an ameliorating tone, "because I don't know anything."

"The invitation came from Hunter's Challenge. What do you do when the clients call? Tell them it was all a mistake?"

"No. I just take the names and numbers and pass them on to my boss."

"That would be Karl Banning?"

"How...?" Bartlett began, then his mouth snapped shut.

"Not 'how,' Bartlett. 'Where.' Where can I reach Karl Banning?"

"I don't know.... Wait! I'm just an employee. He doesn't tell me where he is."

"But you know how to reach him."

"He could be anywhere. Anywhere in the world."

"But he's not. I saw him yesterday."

"If you saw him, then you already know where he is."

"That's right. But what I really want to know is where he might be. So, you're going to give me all his contact information."

"Okay, okay. I'll write it down."

"I have a better idea." Guthrie pointed to the computer sitting on a side desk. "Get on that and print out your address book."

"But that's got all my clients on it."

"If they have nothing to do with this, they'll be ignored. I'm not interested in some yahoo out to shoot another hogzilla in a pen."

Bartlett hesitated, and Guthrie rose and stepped forward, stance radiating menace.

"Kind of like a canned hunt, isn't it?" he ground out. "How do you like being the one in the pen?"

Bartlett's jaw knotted, and his lips quivered and pulled back in a half snarl, but he didn't move.

"Five seconds, Bartlett."

Bartlett rolled his chair over to the computer and began punching keys. "Do you want them on a disc? That would be quicker."

"Discs damage too easily. Put a bullet hole in one, and it's trash. Shoot a paper list, and it's still a list."

Bartlett made a few more key strokes, and a moment later, the printer spit out what seemed like thirty sheets of paper. "Print out your bookmarks while you're at it."

"What do you need those for?"

"Maybe pick up some good links to porn sites," Guthrie said, and he smiled inside as he saw Bartlett's face turn red.

More paper spit out of the printer, and Guthrie waved Bartlett back into a corner.

Take off your belt and strap it around your ankles," Guthrie ordered. Bartlett complied. "Now lie on the floor with your hands behind your back."

"Don't kill me," Bartlett said. "I gave you want you want."

"Maybe," Guthrie said.

When Bartlett was prone, Guthrie knelt and zipped a pair of plastic restraint ties on his wrists. He pulled Bartlett's handkerchief out of his back pocket, rolled Bartlett onto his back, and stuffed the handkerchief into his mouth.

"If anybody comes out of this building after me, I'll kill them, and then I'll come back and kill you," Guthrie promised. "You hear me?"

Bartlett nodded, his eyes glaring with anger and humiliation. Guthrie turned and went to the door. He opened it, using his own handkerchief on the doorknob. Holstering the S&W, he left the office. The man down the hall was still hunched over his computer, and the receptionist gave him a friendly smile. But as Guthrie pushed through the glass doors and paused to wipe the handle clean, her smile faded.

Guthrie strode to the elevator and waited impatiently for the car, keeping an eye on the receptionist through the glass doors. She stared at him for a few moments then punched numbers into the phone on her desk. When she didn't get an answer, she rose and disappeared down the hall toward the offices.

Thankfully, the elevator came, and Guthrie went. No one followed him outside, and inside of three minutes, he was on the freeway, heading back to his office.

20

KARL BANNING. IT WAS JUST a name, but it belonged to a man not to be taken lightly.

Guthrie looked over the intel he'd gathered. Some of it—the sanitized version—had come from Banning's company profile, some of it from old newspaper and oil industry publication databases, and some from law enforcement databases.

Banning had been born in southern Louisiana and worked his way through LSU on oil rigs in the Gulf of Mexico. About twenty years ago, he managed to make a quantum leap by buying a small oil drilling company in Houston and renaming it Hunter Petroleum. The name was a little too much like Hunter's Challenge to be coincidence. Since then, he'd chewed his way up the food chain, turning Hunter Petroleum into one of the most successful independent oil exploration companies in the country.

Banning was on top, and Guthrie couldn't find any sign that his underpinnings were shaky. All his business dealings seemed on the up-and-up, he paid his taxes, he wasn't involved in any bribery of public officials that was overtly apparent, and he even funded a professorship in subsurface geoscience at a Houston university. Apparently he was single, and it seemed that his only passion, aside from Hunter Petroleum, was big game hunting.

Guthrie had to wonder where he managed to do that, these days. Half of Africa was in the grips of too much violence, and the other half tended to strictly control hunting. The same was true most places that had any game that could be called "big." But he supposed a man with Banning's money could go anywhere and hunt anything he liked.

Such as artists who painted gateways to Hell.

Certainly, Banning was the sort of man Gavin O'Neil might have as a client. But at the moment, O'Neil couldn't tell him that—only Banning could.

The sole phone number Guthrie could find for Banning was the one for Hunter Petroleum's main office. But he did have Banning's home address as well as the address for the company. Banning had told Howard that he would be in Houston for a few days, but the question was: How was Guthrie going to penetrate the Hunter bureaucracy—small as it might be—to get to Banning himself?

Barge right in, of course.

Guthrie checked the time. It was past two. Time enough for Banning to have returned to his office from lunch, assuming he left his office for lunch.

Hunter Petroleum's company offices were located in a black glass office building just inside the West Loop, within sight of the Galleria. Expensive real estate just a ten-minute drive from Hunter's Challenge. Guthrie parked in the visitors' lot and rode the elevator to the eleventh floor. Banning's company occupied the entire floor, and the foyer in front of the elevator doors served as the reception area.

"Welcome to Hunter Petroleum," said the perky-looking blond receptionist as he stepped up to her desk. Her voice was just as perky and blond.

"I'd like to speak with Mr. Banning."

"Do you have an appointment?"

"No, but it's important."

"What is your name, sir?"

"Bob Jones."

"Just a moment." She pressed a button on her phone with an immaculately engineered fingernail. "A Mr. Bob Jones is here to see Mr. Banning.... No, he doesn't.... He says it's important.... Yes, ma'am."

She hung up and smiled at Guthrie.

"Mr. Banning's personal assistant will be out in a moment. Would you care for anything? Coffee, water?"

"I'm fine." Guthrie didn't think he'd have time to drink a cup of coffee, and he was wired enough, anyway. He sat on one of the chairs against the wall.

After about two minutes, an attractive brunette in her forties came in, spotted Guthrie, and walked over to him."

"Mr. Jones? I'm Susan Widrig, Mr. Banning's personal assistant. You wished to see Mr. Banning?" Her voice was a lot less perky than the receptionist's.

"That's right. Is he available?"

"I'm afraid he's quite busy at the moment. May I take a message?"

"Tell him that Gavin O'Neil told me to get in touch. I may have something pertaining to Howard Graham that he'll be interested in."

The names didn't seem to register with her.

"Very well. Is there a contact number?"

"I'm afraid Mr. Banning will have to make a decision on this very quickly. I'll be here for the next five minutes, and then I'll be gone. If he's interested, we can talk now. If he's not," Guthrie shrugged, "that's all right by me."

"I'll tell him," Widrig said, looking equally irritated and puzzled, probably because even if she was Banning's personal assistant, she didn't know of O'Neil or Graham or what any of this was about.

She left the room, and Guthrie sat down again, this time under the curious stare of the receptionist. Guthrie smiled at her, she smiled back, and that was about all they had time for before Widrig returned.

"Mr. Banning will see you now," she said a trifle woodenly.

Guthrie rose and allowed himself to be ushered into Hunter's inner sanctum. Banning's office was at the end of a short hall. As they neared, Guthrie could see an impressively sized lion's head mounted on the wall that was visible through the doorway. Widrig took Guthrie inside, announced him, then left the room, closing the door behind her.

"Bob Jones, eh?" said the man behind the desk. He gave a thin smile. "I'm Karl Banning. Have a seat."

Banning gestured to a chair in front of the desk, and Guthrie stepped up, sat, and got a close look at the man he'd seen in Lycoris's warehouse the night before. Banning was an indeterminate fifty, with a husky, powerful-looking body that was thickening in the middle. His short hair, once dark but now shot with gray, was combed back from his high, squarish forehead. He sat solidly and straight in his chair, staring at Guthrie from hard dark eyes.

"Bob Jones," Banning said again, rolling the sound around on his tongue like he was tasting it. His eyes looked amused. "Seems like I heard of another Bob Jones just this morning."

"I know several," Guthrie said. "We have a convention every year."

"Well, Bob, I understand you have something I might want."

"No might about it, Karl," Guthrie said, noting that Banning didn't appreciate the familiar use of his first name. Reaching into his jacket pocket, he pulled out a folded piece of paper, unfolded it, and slid it across the desk to Banning. It was a printed copy of a photo of the painting in Guthrie's garage.

Banning stared at it for a moment then set it on his desk.

"Weird shit, eh?" Guthrie said. "Things move around in it. I understand you might be interested in buying it."

"Gavin O'Neil told me you two had a chat. Do you mind telling me how you came by this?" He gestured toward the paper on the desk.

"That's simple. I did Graham a favor once, and he repaid it by giving it to me."

"Must have been one hell of a favor."

"Must have been," Guthrie said, picking up the paper, refolding it, and putting it back in his pocket.

"Why are you coming to me directly? Why didn't you contact O'Neil?" Banning asked.

"He's in Europe," Guthrie said. "Incommunicado. Or didn't you hear?"

"I didn't," Banning said, sounding as if he didn't like it.

"Besides, why work through a middleman when you can go straight to the source?"

"But why would I buy this painting?" The implication was that he had everything he already needed.

"What art lover wouldn't like a painting that is really a window? And what hunter wouldn't like access to a world filled with monsters ripe for shooting? I'll tell you, Karl, some of the beasties I've seen out there would positively make your mouth water. Besides, it strikes me that a man like you would prefer to own everything associated with something like this."

Banning laughed, and though his eyes remained hard, a calculating look crept into them.

"I'll give you one hundred grand cash," he said. "No questions."

"You've already asked several questions. And you already refused my first offer to trade it for Graham. Now that both he and Diane Weston are out of the picture, I'm only interested in money. Make it three hundred."

Banning again laughed without humor. "Watch it, boy, or you might get kicked in the taco."

"Is that right?" Guthrie got up, turned, and took a few steps toward the door, loosening his jacket button.

"Jones!"

Guthrie turned, letting his jacket fall open, revealing the S&W at his belt. The sight of it didn't seem to bother Banning, but Guthrie could tell he noted it.

"Where are you going?"

"This painting means nothing to me," Guthrie said. "I think I'll go home and maybe kick it in the taco."

"You'd be throwing away a lot of money."

"I don't know about that. I'm familiar with another buyer who's definitely interested in this painting, too. I could give him a call and find out what he'd give for it." Guthrie glanced around the office and then pursed his lips thoughtfully. "I think he has more resources than you do, and if he learns that you have the Chinvat Bridge painting, he might be apt to do something serious about it."

It was a bluff, but it worked. A flicker of astonishment twisted through Banning's eyes, though his face remained stony.

"All right," he said. "Three hundred. But that buys your silence, as well." The words came smoothly enough, but the tone that carried them tightened.

"Of course. That's what you're really paying for, isn't it?"

"It's a deal, then. But you'll have to wait. I won't be able to get that much cash until tomorrow."

"Tomorrow, then," Guthrie said. "It's been a pleasure."

"That remains to be seen."

"Cheer up, Karl. Tomorrow you'll have it all. Call me on Bailey's cell when you have the cash."

Guthrie had the satisfaction of seeing surprise in Banning's eyes as he left the office. A few minutes later, he was on the Loop, heading toward his office.

21

GUTHRIE WASN'T SHY ABOUT MAKING unexpected visits, but he didn't think he'd be able to surprise Tereba. If Tereba was home, that is, and Guthrie could find his door.

The shopping center on Bellaire looked no different than it had during his first case for the old man and the few times he'd visited it since then. A grocery store occupied the right third of the center, and a series of ten or so shops trailed off to the left. At this time of night, nothing was open except for the 24-hour washateria on the end opposite the grocery, but no one was in its brightly lit interior. He steered the Xterra around the washateria and entered the wide service way at the back. Enclosed at the rear by a tall, grayed wooden fence and strewn with half a dozen dumpsters, the service way ended at the back left wall of the grocery store where the loading docks for delivery trucks were located.

The service way was just as harsh and grimy beneath the streetlights atop their creosoted poles as it had been every other time Guthrie had seen it. But Craig Stanton wasn't there, waiting for him and, thank goodness, would never be anywhere else again, except maybe Hell.

Turning his attention to the back wall of the center near the grocery, Guthrie wondered if he'd be able to see Tereba's door. Most of the times he'd been here, the wall was simply a blank expanse. But every once in a while, it was occupied by the door. This time, he was gratified to see the door set in the cement block wall, its Old Master's Talisman carved in bas relief beneath the thick red lacquer surface. Would the door be visible to anybody else who might chance down the service alley, or would they simply see Guthrie vanish into a blank wall?

Guthrie shrugged off the thought. Probably nobody else would be allowed back here right now. He was just glad that the old man deigned to talk to him. Maybe Guthrie would even be able to fathom what he said. Or rather, what he meant.

Guthrie parked by the door, got out, went up to it, then hesitated. He wasn't afraid to go in, exactly. Peacefulness and interesting smells pervaded the old man's apothecary shop and home, but the door was no simple entrance. Guthrie felt a sense of dislocation every time he crossed Tereba's threshold, and he knew that Tereba's home did not actually exist there behind the cement block wall at the back of a nondescript shopping center in southwest Houston. It was somewhere else—or perhaps nowhere—and it disturbed Guthrie's sense of the order of things to know that he could so quickly and profoundly lose his bearings by doing such a simple thing as entering a door.

He operated the latch, stepped across the sill, and let the door shut behind him, braced for the touch of vertigo that came and passed as quickly as a breath.

"Hello, Mr. Guthrie."

Tereba perched on a tall stool behind the polished wooden counter, engaged in some activity on the workbench beneath the countertop.

"Hi Master Tereba. Thanks for seeing me."

As he neared the counter, he saw that Tereba was grinding up dried plant matter with a small porcelain mortar and pestle.

"Your thanks are misplaced," the old man said, his eyes twinkling. "I didn't even know you were coming."

"Your door did, then."

Tereba chuckled.

"It is, indeed, a very wise door."

"Let me ask you something. What would happen if they tore down the shopping center? What would happen to your door?"

"It is only a door," Tereba shrugged. "And a door only requires a wall. Does it matter where the wall is located?"

"It does in my reality."

166

"Yet you have used my door several times. Perhaps it does not matter as much as you think."

"It's also not there more often than it is."

"As I said," Tereba shrugged again, giving a tiny smile, "it is a very wise door."

"Ever hear of something called a Fire Temple?"

"Fires are sacred to many religions. A sacred fire is the heart of the religion called Zoroastrianism. The fire is kept burning in what they call a Fire Temple. They believe that the world will end in an all-devouring fire."

"Do they worship an evil god?"

"Evil?" Tereba looked troubled. "No. They worship a single, transcendental god named Ahura Mazda, whom they believe to be the one uncreated creator. Mazda brings truth and order, and Zoroastrians, so named for their prophet, Zoroaster, believe that active participation in life through good thoughts, good words, and good deeds is necessary to keep chaos, falsehood, and disorder at bay. It is a very old religion, though still practiced. Religious studies experts consider it to be the root of many Eastern and Western religious traditions, Christianity and Islam included."

"But those have an opposing concept of chaos and falsehood, so I guess Zoroastrians might have their version of Satanists."

"Anything may be perverted for wealth or power. What are you getting at, Mr. Guthrie?"

"Ever hear of someone or something called Angry Manu?"

"Angra Mainyu," Tereba corrected. "It is, you might say, Zoroastrianism's equivalent of the devil. Mainyu means something like mind or mentality, and Angra means destructive or malign."

"How about Chinvat Bridge?"

"The Bridge of Judgment. The bridge that separates the world of the living from the world of the dead." Something frightening flashed in the eternal depths of Tereba's pitch black eyes, and Guthrie felt a palpable force emanate from the old man's lean form, almost like a steady wind that blew not on Guthrie's body but on something inside him. "Where did you hear of these matters?"

"From a woman named Adriana Lycoris. Ever hear of her?" Guthrie wanted to retreat from the flush of the old man's power, but he knew that the power wasn't directed at him, so he forced himself to stand steady.

"Some sort of fortune teller with a number of wealthy clients. She is not without power, but only of the middle realm. She is, I believe, a pharmakis."

"Like a druggist?"

"Not pharmacist," Tereba corrected. "Pharmakis." He spelled it. "The words are etymologically linked. Pharmakis was the ancient Greek word for witch, particularly one versed in herbs, plants, and potions. In fact, it is the oldest word for witch in Western literature."

"Never heard of it before."

"You might also be interested in another variant from the same root: pharmakos."

"What's that?"

"A person already condemned to death who was sacrificed as an act of purification or atonement for a city or community."

Guthrie winced, remembering all too clearly how Tereba had halted his life force so he would be immune to Aswad Mar. And with Tereba again sending him into the jaws of death—or worse—the word struck a little too close to home for comfort.

"If Adriana Lycoris is a witch with knowledge of herbs, she might be interested in a plant called homa?"

"Haoma. The divine plant. Mythic, now, but perhaps once a genuine herb. Reportedly, it imparts divine wisdom in those who consume it."

"A sacred drug?"

The old man nodded.

"It's loosely identified with the equally mythic soma. No one knows what it was, although there are several possibilities, none of which fully satisfy the historic descriptions. Present-day Zoroastrians use a plant that contains ephedrine, but that drug is a stimulant, like caffeine, rather than a true entheogenic." He saw the blank look cross Guthrie's face. "A psychotropic substance that produces a spiritual effect. LSD, psilocybin, and peyote are commonly known examples in Western culture."

"And it grows on a mountain called Hara Berezaiti?"

"That's the name of a legendary mountain around which, the Zoroastrians believe, the stars and planets revolve," Tereba clarified. "I never heard it specifically associated with haoma, which reputedly grew in an arid environment." He eyed Guthrie. "But what does any of this have to do with the matter at hand? I sent you to help a young woman find her missing friend."

"Why?"

"For the last few months, I've felt a nexus of dangerous power gathering around Mr. Graham, and then the power vanished from my range of sensations, and so did he. I want to know what that power is and where Mr. Graham went."

"I can't tell you that yet, but I can tell you that Adriana Lycoris is some kind of high priestess with a Fire Temple off the northwest corner of the Loop. I think she somehow gave Howard Graham the power to paint gateways or windows into another world. There are two of them. The small one in my garage I already told you about and a much larger one that Graham hasn't finished. She calls the larger one Chinvat Bridge."

Tereba didn't seem surprised, but he did look thoughtful.

"I did not know this. That is why a detective like you is indispensable. Tell me more."

"She was holding Graham captive in her temple building, where he was painting Chinvat Bridge, but apparently, he's balked and won't finish it. Some guy who's associated with her named Karl Banning has taken Graham and Diane Weston to an unknown location where he's going to force Graham to complete the painting by threatening to harm Diane if he doesn't."

"And what is Lycoris's purpose?"

"She says Angra Mainyu will lead her to haoma, which she believes will give her and her high priest ultimate insight. Then, Angra Mainyu will give them the power to solve all their problems."

"All religions are right when they say we're all united at some esoteric level, but they lie when they say they alone know the true name and nature of God." Tereba's black eyes stared into Guthrie. "And what about this Karl Banning?"

"I don't know what their exact association is, but he's a businessman and big game hunter, and I think he's there to protect Lycoris from the monstrous creatures that are running around in that other world. He put out an invitation offering Safaris in Hell to a few select clients, if you can believe it."

"This is all most disturbing." Tereba rose from the stool and paced the worn parquet floor.

"Do you know what's going on?"

"Know?" The old man shook his head. "No. But I have suspicions." He stopped pacing and faced Guthrie across the counter. "I believe that Lycoris has found a way to penetrate to another realm—to break through the veil, if you will, that separates this world and reality from others. It is no easy task, and there are manifold reasons not to do so, not the least of which is that the inhabitants of one reality often are incompatible with the inhabitants—or even basic nature—of others."

"Are you afraid Lycoris might do if she crosses Chinvat Bridge?"

"I'm more worried about what she might bring back or inadvertently let through. The landscape you described when you first told me about the smaller painting does not sound natural—or even amenable to life. Something must have affected it to make it that way."

"Angra Mainyu?"

"A convenient name for anything that destroys. But the real thing?" Tereba shrugged. "I think that Angra Mainyu, if it exists, is a demon of the soul, not of the flesh. Perhaps it's out there, but it's not the monsters you mentioned. Creatures of that ilk would consume the body rather than the spirit."

"Howard said that something else is out there. Something that made the monsters. He was afraid of it, and maybe he has a right to be." Guthrie quickly described the warped, twisted, and diseased world he'd seen through the window of the small painting, but how Diane had merely seen an odd landscape. "The Chinvat Bridge painting looks more like what Diane described. What changed the smaller one?"

"What, indeed? Perhaps this Angra Mainyu."

"But why would she try to attract something like that?"

"People see things, they hear things speak inside themselves, beckoning with promise. They think it's some deity because it holds and wields power. But they do not always recognize the truth that lies behind that which beckons. Not everything that calls with promise is beneficent."

"Lycoris seems to believe otherwise."

"As I said, her power is merely of the middle realm. She obviously has a weak grasp of the true nature of reality if she has so carelessly endangered us all. We must finish her project in a way not to her liking."

"By 'we,' you mean me."

"Who better?"

"I was afraid of that."

"The painting is the key."

"I'm more concerned about Diane and Graham," Guthrie said.

"I'm sure that you will do your best on their behalf. But I cannot emphasize enough that if you fail to destroy the painting, the fates of Miss Weston and Mr. Graham will be but a drop in a bucket already filled with the rest of us." Tereba peered at Guthrie. "You must find this painting as soon as possible and destroy it."

"What about Lycoris?" Guthrie asked. "Won't she just get another artist to paint another gateway?"

"Not if I deal with her first."

22

GUTHRIE DROVE TO HIS OFFICE. He had no intention of keeping any sort of appointment with Banning or anyone he might send, even if he did call to set up a meet. The first time hadn't gone well, and there would be no second. The photo of the painting had gotten Guthrie the information he needed: a read on Banning's personality. He had no intention of handing over the painting to Banning or anyone else. The only real question was, where was Banning's ranch?

It didn't take Guthrie long to find what he wanted on Bartlett's address list. In addition to owning a home in the Memorial area, Banning had an apartment in a high-rise in Dallas and, more interesting, a ranch northwest of Uvalde.

Guthrie found the place on Google Earth and printed out several images. After that, he left his office to go home to pack an overnight bag. He also stowed his S&W, several extra magazines, and a Bersa .380 he could strap to his ankle. Then he dropped by a map store on Bissonnet Street and bought a topographic map for the county where the ranch lay.

He left for Uvalde early the next morning. It was about an hour and a half west of San Antonio on U.S. 90, which, in turn, was about three and a half hours from Houston. He arrived just after noon and checked into a motel. After a quick meal at a nearby restaurant, he went back to his room and surveyed the topo map and aerial photos of the area of Banning's ranch.

Uvalde lay at the lower edge of the Edwards Plateau, a vast limestone region that was unsuitable for farming but was ideal for cattle, sheep, and goat ranching. The area also supported abundant game and wildlife, drawing hunters from around the state.

Banning's ranch was on the plateau, where the terrain was hilly and rugged but not wrapped in the tortured contours that might be found in the Trans-Pecos region farther west. It was reached by a county road that skirted its eastern perimeter, and the aerial photos showed a long graded dirt road beginning at the county road and winding among the hills for nearly four miles before halting at a fenced-in enclosure that was about the size of two football fields laid side-to-side.

The resolution of the photos wasn't high enough for Guthrie to make out finer details, but nearly a quarter of the way back from the fence defining the western border of the enclosure sat a group of three buildings that surrounded the irregular blue oval of a swimming pool. The main building wrapped around three sides of the pool, and the other two, each a quarter the size of the first, enclosed the rear. Near each of the corners at the enclosure's eastern end stood a large outbuilding or barn, and both barns were flanked by what looked like corrals. Animals of some sort clustered in one of the corrals at the northeast corner.

He studied the maps and photos for some time, trying to memorize what he could, and at last he folded them, carried them out to his car, and steered out of the parking lot.

It took forty-five minutes to reach the junction where the county road met the state highway, and another twenty to find the perimeter of Banning's ranch. It wasn't hard to spot—a ten-foot chain-link fence topped with coils of barbed wire delineated the property. A closer look told him that a strand of electric wire was strung along the fence top, through the coils of barbed wire. Just inside the fence ran a dirt service road on the other side of which was another fence similar to the first, though without the electric wire. It was pretty tight security for property that seemed to be little more than a semi-dense cover of short, gnarled trees, scrub brush, and cactus fleshed in by sparse, waist-high grass.

Guthrie drove along the county road until he passed an electric gate that blocked the ranch's entrance road. A similar gate was in the second fence. He slowed but didn't stop, noting that the gates were monitored by a pair of cameras. He drove for another ten minutes before he reached the corner of the ranch, where the fence angled west and ran out of sight into the brushy woods. There, he pulled off onto the grassy shoulder to consult his map and aerial photos.

The county road passed several more large ranches and went through a couple of small towns before meeting up with a minor U.S. route coming down from a town called Junction. The section of county road he'd just driven was the only public road that bordered the ranch, but his topo map showed an interesting feature just ahead, and he pulled back onto the road and drove to it.

It was a stream bed that passed under a short bridge. Like most stream beds in the area, it was dry now, but water rushing through it following past rains had eroded the rocky soil to a depth of about twelve feet. It was the sort of feature that was easy to ignore, but Guthrie stopped, got out of his Xterra, and stared up its course. According to the map, it ran this direction from Banning's ranch. That meant it had to go under the fence. He locked the car and set off upstream.

It was maybe a mile from the bridge to the fence, and sure enough, the stream bed, now only about three feet deep, went under the chain-link. But if Guthrie had thought he might be able to crawl under, he saw now that he couldn't. At least, not easily. Although the fence went straight across the dry culvert, an additional semicircle of chain-link, supported by metal rods and anchored by metal stakes, had been wired across the gap.

The semicircle of fencing was half-clogged with grass, leaves, and other water-washed debris, including the torn and dirty wrapper of an energy bar and a dingy plastic water bottle whose label had faded nearly to white. He brushed away the debris and saw that just inside was a two-foot corrugated plastic pipe to channel water flow beneath the road between the fences.

Guthrie figured he could get through, but it would take some real work to undo the heavy wire twists that held the extra fencing in place if all he used was his bare hands. He'd need wire cutters or pliers, and he had neither.

Hell, if he had a shovel, he could just dig under the fence anywhere along its length. At least that was his initial thought, but as he pulled more of the water-washed debris from the fencing to get a better look at the anchoring stakes, he noticed that the fence was set in a concrete ribbon. The ribbon went into the ground about eighteen inches from what he could see where the ribbon met then dipped beneath the gully, Digging deep enough to be able to crawl under that would be a major task in such rocky soil. Going through the fence would be much simpler.

The security made Guthrie itch to see what was inside. But that would have to wait at least a few hours. He'd return to town eat and find a hardware store where he could buy wire cutters and a flashlight. He'd come back tonight and see what lay beyond the fence.

He clambered out of the ditch and started back toward his car, stopping when he judged it was only a couple of hundred feet away to relieve himself on the parched soil. He zipped up and went another thirty paces toward the road then froze.

He could just see his car, and parked behind it was a midnight blue pickup whose side was painted with the logo of Texas Parks and Wildlife. Beneath the logo, red letters spelled out Game Warden. Two men were outside the pickup, one jotting down Guthrie's license plate number, the other scanning the brush with a pair of binoculars. He hadn't yet spotted Guthrie.

Shit, Guthrie thought, ducking behind a clump of scrub brush. He hadn't thought that game wardens would be patrolling the roads, but it made sense in country where hunting was common and local ranchers wouldn't want poachers coming onto their property.

The real problem was Guthrie's guns. He had a license to carry them, but the game wardens might interpret the fact that he was carrying them out here as an attempt to do a little illegal hunting and hassle him about them.

What the hell, he thought. I'm coming back tonight. Better to be slightly inconvenienced than be hauled off to spend several hours being asked questions he didn't want to answer.

He unstrapped both guns, made a nest for them in the grass surrounding the brush he'd hidden behind, and covered them with more grass. Hoping the cache looked natural enough, he stood and walked toward his car and the game wardens, making an effort to blunder along.

The officer with the binoculars spotted him quickly enough, and a few moments later, Guthrie emerged onto the road.

"Hi," Guthrie said, smiling.

"Is this your vehicle, sir?" asked the warden who'd taken down the license plate. He was Hispanic, and the nameplate clipped to the shirt pocket opposite his badge read, "Gonzalez."

"Yes. Is there a problem?"

"What are you doing out here?" asked the other, this one white.

"Just driving around, looking at the countryside," Guthrie said.

"Why are you stopped here?" the second warden asked a bit impatiently. "What were you doing out there?" he gestured in the direction Guthrie had come from.

"I had to take a leak," Guthrie replied, noting that this warden was named Johnson. The two game wardens who'd supposedly verified that Howard Graham had not vanished but was merely on a camping trip were named Gonzalez and Johnson.

"Are you aware that this is private property?" the first officer asked.

"Well, no," Guthrie said hesitantly. "I saw a fence back that way," he gestured toward Banning's ranch, "but it ended. I thought it would be okay."

"Show us where you took this leak," the second warden said.

The request didn't seem kosher to Guthrie, and he began to feel trepidation at having left his guns behind. But he tried not to show his concern.

"Sure," he said. "If I can find it. This way."

He led the wardens through the brush and trees to the spot where he'd pissed. The arid soil and air had nearly dried the stain, but it was obvious what had happened. As the wardens looked, Guthrie glanced at the cache holding his guns. It appeared natural enough to him, but these guys were used to being outdoors and might notice. But they didn't.

"Okay," said the first one. "Let's go."

They went back to the road.

"You can go," the second warden said. "But next time, don't stop on the road. Find a service station."

"I'll do that, officer. Thanks."

Guthrie got into his car and pulled off. The pickup followed him all the way to the next town. Rather than further incite the wardens' curiosity, Guthrie followed another state highway to the east and finally worked his way back down to Uvalde, arriving there in late afternoon.

He stopped at an Ace Hardware store on the U.S. 90 and bought the items he'd need, then he went to the motel to eat and rest. It was nearly dusk as he pulled into a space near his room, got out, and opened the back door to retrieve his purchases. When he straightened, he found himself staring into the barrel of a Colt .45 1911.

23

THERE WERE TWO OF THEM: Stewart, the burly black man with salt-and-pepper hair, and his younger muscular companion. Stewart was dressed in what looked like the same suit he'd been wearing at their first encounter, but the muscle boy had traded the Hawaiian shirt for a lime green tank top. Sweat glistened on his bunched shoulders.

"Drop the bag," the black man ordered.

Guthrie let the plastic sack holding his purchases clatter to the pavement.

"I remember you," the younger one said. The .357 he'd held on Diane back in Houston was in his hand, pointed at Guthrie. His armpits were shaved.

"Check him out." Stewart gestured with his Colt. "Banning says he's carrying."

"Maybe we shoulda killed him then," the younger man commented dispassionately as he frisked Guthrie.

"Maybe," Stewart said, "but the boss wants him now." To Guthrie he said, "You going to come peacefully, or do we have to get rough?"

"He's clean," the muscular man said, straightening.

"You've got the guns," Guthrie shrugged. "I'll come without a fuss."

The muscular man picked up the bag Guthrie had dropped, peered inside, then held it out, opened, in Guthrie's direction.

"Empty your pockets," he said.

Guthrie cleared his pockets, putting everything into the bag. When he was done, the muscular man tied the bag shut with its handles.

"Over there," Stewart ordered, pointing with his chin to a Chevy Trailblazer parked in the next isle. The light had fallen enough that the vehicle's color was hard to tell, but Guthrie thought it was a dark gray. The muscular man opened one of the back doors, and Guthrie got in while Stewart slid behind the wheel.

"Buckle up," Stewart said. "We don't want any accidents."

Guthrie did as he was ordered, and the muscular man shut the door and got into the front passenger seat. The burly man locked the doors.

"Child-proof locks in the back," he said dryly as he started the engine. "So don't act childish."

Guthrie wasn't about to because the muscular man had turned around in his seat and was keeping him covered. Staring into the open maw of a .357 was a powerful inducement for compliance.

"We going to the ranch?" Guthrie asked as the Chevy pulled out of the parking lot.

"Ask us no questions, we'll tell you no lies," Stewart said. The muscular man just stared indifferently at Guthrie over the barrel of his revolver.

The rest of the ride was in silence except for the hiss of the tires on the road. By now, it was dark enough outside that, once they left Uvalde, not much could be seen except yard lights, but Guthrie knew from the direction they'd taken out of town that Banning's ranch was their destination. He settled back and closed his eyes, and if he didn't catnap, he rested. It had been a long day, and it probably was going to get a lot longer.

At last, the SUV slowed. Guthrie opened his eyes as it turned into the dirt road to Banning's ranch. Stewart reached up and touched a button on one of two gray control boxes attached to the sun visor. The first gate rolled aside. Once they were through, he stopped, pushed the button again to close the gate, then pushed the button on the other box. The second gate opened, and Stewart accelerated through. Without slowing, he punched the second button again.

Guthrie didn't bother to turn to watch the gate shut. Instead, he stared through the windows, but there was precious little to see, just the headlighted glare of roadside brush as the Chevy rolled steadily down the dirt road.

The road was in good condition, though washboarded in a few spots, and occasionally it wound around low hills. Guthrie could see them darkly silhouetted against a sky barely brighter. His memory of the terrain from the maps and aerial photos helped him visualize approximately where he was. But it's one thing to look at a map and another to experience the terrain. The fact that it took them nearly fifteen minutes of slow but steady driving to reach the house gave Guthrie a sudden realization of just how big Banning's ranch really was.

At last they approached the ranch's inner compound. Stewart punched the button on the first control box, and the gate rolled aside. There was an open parking area in front of the house that was well lit by floodlights on creosoted poles. Half a dozen other vehicles sat around the dirt and gravel lot, including a white van, presumably the same one he'd last seen Diane in. Little else could be glimpsed beyond the glare of the lights except the facades of the main house and the large outbuildings that Guthrie had taken for barns. Both were industrial buildings fabricated from sheet metal painted a dull reddish brown.

Stewart didn't pull into the parking area in front of the house but continued down the dirt road to the right, toward the barn in that direction, which sat a couple of hundred feet away. When he stopped the Blazer in front of the barn, the muscular man got out and, after Stewart popped the locks, opened Guthrie's door, keeping him covered.

"Out," he said.

Guthrie complied as Stewart came around the Chevy, drawing his own gun.

"In there." Stewart pointed to a door that the muscular man was opening in the front of the barn.

As Guthrie entered, a strong animal odor assailed his nostrils, though the odor's source was not immediately apparent. Guthrie had been right in assuming it was a barn, though the room he found himself in, which occupied a small square of the building's front right corner, was a simple office containing a desk with a computer and a couple of filing cabinets.

"Sit over there," Stewart said as the muscular man moved a molded plastic lawn chair against a blank space of wall well away from the door.

Guthrie did as he was told, and Stewart picked up the telephone handset from the unit on the desk and punched three numbers.

"It's Stewart," he said into the phone a moment later. "We have him. Yeah, in the cages. Talbot's got him covered. Right."

He replaced the receiver and looked at the muscular man.

"He'll be over in a couple of minutes."

The first minute or so passed in silence, but that was abruptly shattered by a loud roaring from beyond the wall at Guthrie's back. Startled, Guthrie sat up.

"What the hell was that?"

Talbot laughed. It was the first semblance of emotion Guthrie had seen in him.

"Your cell mate," he said.

Before Guthrie could ask for clarification, the door opened, and Karl Banning entered, followed by two other men. The first was a beefy white man with a shaved cranium. The second was Porter, the skinny, scruffily bearded man who'd driven the van during Diane's abduction. Porter directed a hostile look at Guthrie as he trailed the others into the room.

"Well, if it isn't the ubiquitous Mr. Jones," Banning said, perusing Guthrie, his upper lip twisting sarcastically. "Or would that be Clay Guthrie?"

"What's in a name?" Guthrie shrugged.

"Leverage, for one," Banning said. "A man without a name has nothing to protect."

"Well, I don't have much of a name," Guthrie said.

"But you do have something to protect." Banning smiled again. "Miss Weston."

"Where is she?" Guthrie couldn't bring himself to ask if Banning had done anything to her.

"She's in the main house. Quite well, considering. And, in case you're wondering, Howard Graham is there, too. I might even let you see them if you're smart and tell me what you know."

"Diane Weston hired me to find Howard Graham. I tracked you by intimidating Gavin O'Neil and burglarizing Adriana Lycoris's house, where I found your invitation for Safaris in Hell. I'm sure you already know about my conversation with Bartlett. That's about the size of it."

"Not quite. What about the paintings?"

"I don't know how, but they are more than paintings. More like doors."

"That doesn't seem to surprise you."

"You don't seem surprised, either."

Banning laughed.

"You're really quite remarkable. Most people would simply balk at the idea, yet you look through the door to contemplate the world beyond. As for me," he chuckled again, this time a little more soberly, "Adriana and I go back a long way, and very little she can do surprises me. Our...relationship, you might call it...is one of mutual effort, trust, and antagonism. We do favors for each other."

"You sound like an old married couple."

Banning's mouth expressed wry mirth, but his eyes didn't.

"That's exactly the case. Maybe I'll tell you about it if there's time." His eyes narrowed. "But right now, I want to know about the other painting. If there is another painting, and it wasn't simply some ruse."

"It's at my house."

"I'm a little disappointed you didn't bring it with you. I'd like to get a glimpse of what I'll be dealing with."

"Sorry," Guthrie said. "But since you already have the big one— or will soon—I thought I'd hang on to the smaller one."

"No matter," Banning said. "I'll send someone to retrieve it from your home."

Good luck getting in, Guthrie thought.

"Is it true that there are monsters out there?" Banning asked.

"You haven't seen any through the new painting?"

"Not yet. Light is coming through, but so far, the scene is still static."

"Still looks normal?"

"Normal? In what way?"

"The ground looks like ground, the animals look like animals, and the plants like plants."

"I suppose so. The plants are different than anything I've ever seen, and believe me, I've been almost everywhere." Banning's eyes narrowed again. "Why? Is there something that shouldn't look normal?"

"Monsters," Guthrie said.

"So there are monsters?"

"I've seen a couple," Guthrie said. "Freakish abominations. Aren't you worried they'll come through into this side?"

"The monsters are the whole point as far as I'm concerned. Adriana needs me to protect her while she's out there looking for that precious plant of hers, and I want what she needs protecting from. Besides, I have plenty of safeguards in place. None of those beasties over there will get out—at least, not until we bring them out as trophies."

"And what about Angra Mainyu? Aren't you worried about that?"

"I might cater to Adriana's fantasies," Banning said with a chuckle, "but that doesn't mean I believe in them."

"Howard says something's out there that's worse than the monsters."

"Yeah, the thing that made them, he says." Banning's jaw tightened, and hardness glinted in his eyes. "I hope so. I'd like nothing better than to mount its head right next to those of its offspring."

"The biggest game of all?"

"Not quite, but very close."

"I hope to hell you're right."

"I always am." Banning looked at the man with the shaved head. "Hayes, you and Porter take him to the cages then meet me back in the main house." To Guthrie, he said, "I'll allow you to visit with Miss Weston and Mr. Graham later. Right now, though, I have some important business to attend to, so you'll permit my men to show you to your temporary quarters. If you'd called first, I might have had time to make better arrangements."

Banning went out the front door, followed by Stewart and Talbot. Porter, who was carrying an AR-15, aimed its snout at Guthrie, and Hayes drew a pistol then opened the door to the main area of the metal building.

"After you," he said.

Guthrie rose, and as Porter shoved him through the door, the animal odor Guthrie had been smelling all along hit him like a sandbag. And now he saw why. The cavernous room was lined with cages made of heavy chain-link fencing, some large, some small. Although many were empty, most held animals.

"Is this some kind of private zoo?" he asked.

"Shut up," Porter snarled, jabbing Guthrie painfully in the small of the back with the barrel of his gun.

As Hayes and Porter moved Guthrie along, he realized that if it was a zoo, it was one that specialized in predators. There were large cats of nearly every species, bears, wolves, hyenas, and huge constrictors. He didn't know a lot about snakes, but these seemed too big to be boas, so they probable were pythons. None of the animals seemed too happy to be caged, and they all went wild as the three men passed, setting up roars, shrieks, and howls.

About half way down the building's right side, Hayes moved ahead and pointed to an empty cage sandwiched between a male lion and a tiger.

"Inside," he ordered.

"You're keeping me in there?"

"Can't think of a better place," Hayes commented dryly, his voice almost lost in the furor being raised by the two big cats.

Guthrie went into the cage, and Porter locked it behind him. The two men departed, leaving Guthrie alone with his new neighbors.

24

THE LION FINALLY QUIT ROARING and settled into watchful silence, but the tiger kept snarling, pacing, and occasionally lunging at the chain-link barrier separating it from Guthrie. The fencing seemed frighteningly flimsy compared to the beast's tremendous weight and power.

Guthrie sat at the center point of his own cage's rear wall, which was the outer wall of the metal building, and tried to stay calm. His back leaned against a mechanically operated lift-up door that wouldn't, despite his best efforts, raise. Each of the cages along the outer walls had one, and he remembered from the aerial photos that the building's sides were embraced by enclosures—yards or corrals where the caged beasts could exercise.

Guthrie wondered how long it would be before his own door was raised. The only other question was, would he have company in the yard?

At last, tired of sitting, Guthrie got up and went to the front of his cage. The tiger voiced a sound between a snarl and a howl and flung itself at the chain-link, while the lion surged to its feet and also bounded forward. Guthrie tried to ignore them as he ran his fingers over the fittings binding the chain-link's heavy gauge wire to the support poles. They were fastened with nuts and bolts, and there was no way he could get them loose without tools. The door had a horizontal slot about two feet wide and one tall. Too narrow to squeeze through.

For the tenth time, he surveyed his surroundings. The room was fifty or so feet wide and a hundred in length, both long walls lined with ten-by-ten-foot cages, more than half of which contained animals. The larger beasts were one to a cage, but others, such as the wolves and snakes, were doubled up. Wildlife ranches weren't uncommon in the Texas Hill Country, though most featured herbivores, and a few were home to species from the African veldt. But Banning's collection of predators was truly impressive and probably in violation of dozens of wildlife preservation acts and importation laws. And none of the animals seemed too happy about it, either— especially the wolves, who were surrounded by predators far larger and more dangerous than themselves. Only the snakes seemed calm, but who knew what went on inside the mind of a constrictor that might take on an alligator if it was let loose in the Everglades?

Boxes and crates were stacked on pallets in the barn's center area. Some of the boxes looked like they held veterinary supplies and food, but most were unmarked. Clustered toward the back stood half a dozen camouflaged Kawasaki ATVs, and nearby sat a dozen or more red metal five-gallon gas cans. A large roll-up door was in the wall at the far end of the room, at the left side, and next to it was a smaller personnel door. Beside that, a long hose attached to a spigot was neatly coiled on a bracket fastened to the wall. The back right corner of the barn was occupied by a room about fifteen feet square. From the look of the door and the faint but steady hum that came from that direction, Guthrie thought it probably was a walk-in freezer or cooler.

Every once in a while, one of the lift-up doors would activate, and the caged predator inside would leave, presumably to let it exercise in the outside enclosure. As soon as it came back in, the door would close and another open. This went on along both sides of the room. Guthrie never saw anyone, and he couldn't tell if the process was automated or if someone was watching and operating the mechanisms. He decided it had to be the latter since it didn't seem to be on a regular schedule and none of the doors to the empty cages opened. He scanned his surroundings again but didn't spot any surveillance cameras on the walls or up among the metal rafters.

It was a long night. Guthrie was thankful that the cage's cement floor had a drain hole in the middle where he could relieve himself. He even managed to doze a little, though the concrete floor was hard on his butt and the metal door cold against his back. The building had no windows, but apparently some of the roof panels were translucent, because eventually they began to lighten, telling Guthrie that morning wasn't far off.

Not long after, a man Guthrie didn't recognize entered the barn. Ignoring Guthrie, he went to the walk-in freezer, opened the door, and disappeared inside. He wasn't gone long, emerging with a two-wheeled, bin-like plastic cart with a shovel handle sticking out of it. He steered the cart to each of the big cat cages in turn, and used the shovel to toss what looked like huge gobs of ground beef through the door slots and into the cages. The wolves received smaller portions.

Breakfast, Guthrie realized.

"Nothing for me?" Guthrie asked as the man passed by his cage.

"You want this slop?" the man asked, focusing a blank stare on Guthrie.

"Two eggs over medium, sausage, whole wheat toast. Grits, if you have 'em."

The man turned away and pushed the cart to the tiger's cage, then on to one holding a cheetah. When he was done with them, he went back to the freezer and came out with two five-gallon buckets of fish, which he fed to the polar and grizzly bears. He didn't give anything to the constrictors. After that, he cleaned up and left.

Another hour passed, and the animals were let out and back in through their mechanical doors. Guthrie began to think that the system was automated in some way. Maybe a sensor told the system when an animal had returned and shut the door then opened the next in turn. Guthrie's own door never opened, which worried him. In addition to getting hungry and thirsty, he had to take a dump. He'd been dubiously eyeing the drain hole for half an hour when Hayes and Porter came into the building and over to Guthrie's cage. Hayes held a .45, and Porter cradled his AR-15.

"Boss wants to see you in the main house," Hayes said, unlocking the cage door and stepping back to let Guthrie out.

They took him through the office at the front of the building and out into the sunshine. It was a beautiful day, but what Guthrie really appreciated was the fresh, crisp air after the odor of wild animals permeating the atmosphere in the barn. The gray Blazer sat waiting outside, and Hayes drove them to the house while Porter sat behind Guthrie, the snout of his AR-15 jammed into the seat back.

The drive was short, so they weren't outside long enough for Guthrie to do more than get his bearings with regard to his memory of the aerial photos of the ranch and note the presence of his Xterra parked next to the white van on the dirt and gravel front lot.

The main house was an impressive two-story, blocky modernist structure made of limestone and cement, with a wide and deep covered veranda laid with granite pavers. Beneath it's shadowed length gleamed broad windows that were, incongruously, barred. Inside the house, the air was cool beneath high, timber-raftered ceilings. Hayes and Porter took him down an entry hall, and a quick glance to the left showed wide entries to the living room and dining room. To the right was a den and, just past that, the open door to a hall wash room. Straight ahead was a glass wall with a sliding glass door.

As they led him through the sliding door, his memory of the house's general layout visible in the aerial photos was confirmed. The house was U-shaped, its center courtyard occupied by a swimming pool surrounded by a pebble-paved patio, the fringes planted with bushes and tropical plants set in mulched beds. Two bungalows— both single-story—sat behind the main house's wings, completing the courtyard's back perimeter. All three buildings were separated from one another by paved walkways bordered with low shrubs. Like the main house, both of the smaller houses were built of concrete and limestone, but with smaller windows.

Hayes pointed for Guthrie to go around the left side of the pool, toward the bungalow in that direction. All of the courtyard's interior walls were glassed-in except the wall to his left, which held long windows showing, first, the interior of the dining room, then the inside of the kitchen. A hallway ran the length of the wing on the far side of the pool, and the wall beyond was pierced by only two doors. The first was the hallway bathroom he'd just seen, and the second was located about fifteen feet farther down the wall. A wall long enough to conceal two or three rooms, so probably a suite lay through there.

When they reached the bungalow on the left, Hayes opened the door and ushered him inside.

"Your stuff's in the bedroom," he gestured. "The john's that way. Go get cleaned up. We'll wait here."

Sure enough, his overnight bag from the motel was in one of the two bedrooms. Guthrie pulled out a change of clothes and his shaving kit and went to the bathroom, used the facilities, took a quick shower, and put on fresh clothes. While he did, he noticed that all the windows that didn't look onto the courtyard were barred. When he was done, he found Hayes and Porter sitting in the living room. It didn't seem like he'd interrupted a conversation.

"I just want you to know that Andrews was my buddy," Porter grated as he stood. "You remember Andrews, don't you? He's in the police morgue back in Houston."

"His taste in friends was as lousy as his choice of employers."

Porter stepped forward, a snarl twisting his lips, and raised his AR, but Hayes stepped in front of him and pushed the gun down.

"Cool it," he said. "Mr. Banning isn't finished with him."

"Yeah." Porter lowered the gun but didn't relaxing any. "Me, either."

After that, they led him back into the main house through the sliding door, then left, past the half-bath, and down the hall to the second door. Inside was an office that took up a little less than half the space behind the wall. Unsurprisingly, the office walls bristled with trophy heads—many of them animals Guthrie knew were illegal to hunt. Three stuffed bald eagles hung from the beams like a squadron of huge, feathered model airplanes. A metal door with a keypad lock was set in the wall near the back left corner.

"Sit down, Guthrie," Banning said jovially from behind the desk. "I trust you had an uncomfortable night." A tiger skin, complete with head and paws, was stretched diagonally across the wall behind him, reminding Guthrie of his recent roommates.

"You could have let me stay in the motel and picked me up this morning," Guthrie said as he took the chair in front of Banning's desk. He saw that his maps and aerial photos were spread across its surface.

Banning laughed.

"But you were on your way over here already, I believe." He waved over the maps and photos. "No sense in delaying things."

Guthrie made no response, and Banning didn't seem to expect one.

"Anyway, I wanted to give you a taste of how unpleasant your stay can be if you don't choose to behave."

"You mean I have a choice?"

"Hunters always have choices, Guthrie. Unlike prey."

"I'm not much of a hunter," Guthrie said.

"You hunt men," Banning said. "The most dangerous of game."

"Not in the way you hunted those." Guthrie nodded toward the heads on the wall.

"Perhaps not, but I know you've killed men. It may not have been in sport, but the danger is there all the same."

"Maybe, but I don't see a deer or a bunch of doves fighting back."

"That's exactly why I haven't hunted that kind of game in a long time. Now, I only pursue prey that can do me real damage in return. There's an energy that predators have that prey can't comprehend. It's like an aura, but it's more than that. A predator strikes, and it may miss, but it strikes again and again until it overpowers its prey. The prey can't understand it because they don't have that kind of drive. They just fall before it."

"No canned hunts for you? Hunter's Challenge offers them."

"They're a way to turn a profit from weak snots who think that real killing is like a video game." Banning shrugged. "I'll take their money, but the man who scorns canned hunts is the one who interests me. It's one way to weed out incompetent hunting partners."

"Somehow, I don't think we're going to be hunting partners," Guthrie said, and Banning laughed again.

"Don't be too sure of that. The future is always optional. But in the meantime, I want to offer you more comfortable quarters than you had last night. Did you find the guesthouse to your taste?"

"The bars on the windows are a little disconcerting."

"Oh, those. They're not to keep people in. They're to keep the animals out. You probably noticed them on this house, too. Anyway, I'm sure that a man of your talents would find the door a much easier way to leave. And that's why I want your word that you won't try to escape."

"What are the consequences if I don't give it?"

"You can spend your time here in the same cage where you spent last night for as long as I need you to remain my guest."

"And if I give it and try to escape?"

"Well, there are several consequences for that. The first is that my men and I would hunt you down and kill you. And I assure you, I know every inch of this ranch intimately. You wouldn't get far."

"I might."

"Yes, but in that case, I would have to resort to other measures."

"Such as?"

Banning pushed a button on his phone and said, "Bring them in."

Stewart entered with Howard Graham, and behind them came Talbot escorting Diane Weston.

"Clay!" Diane tried to step forward, but Talbot restrained her. "How did you find us?"

"I'm a detective, remember?" He meant it to sound light, but he couldn't keep self-deprecation out of his voice.

"Now he's got you, too."

"That's right, Miss Weston," Banning said. "And while we're all together, let me make the ground rules clear."

Guthrie looked at Banning.

"First ground rule: I have you all. I would have preferred to have none of you, but it seems Howard couldn't stand to just paint the painting for Adriana and be done with it."

"You have no idea how dangerous it is out there," Graham said. His voice was deep but raspy with tension and exhaustion. Dark circles dragged beneath his eyes.

"Of course I do. If Adriana gave you a gift, it would have to be dangerous. She gave me gifts, and I relish them, but you're a coward. She gave you a gift, yet you refuse to pay the price of using it. But it seems that having Diane close has given you new strength." Banning spread his hands as he surveyed his prisoners. "So, now we have ground rule number two: As long as Howard continues with his work, no one will be hurt. As for ground rule number three, we've already begun discussing that. If you play ball, Guthrie, you can sleep comfortably while you're here. If you don't, it's back to the cage."

"And if I try to escape, you'll hurt Miss Weston."

"A lever can work in two directions. But I have other ways to enforce compliance. You remember the occupants of the cells adjoining yours?"

"They kept me up half the night."

"Well, I'm going to let them out tonight. Without dinner. I don't know if you noticed, but the entire perimeter of the ranch is surrounded by two fences, and the compound is surrounded by its own fence. The cats won't be able to get away, but they'll be very hungry. They'll start looking around for something to eat, but they'll be lucky to find even a raccoon or possum. I've had all the deer and other game rounded up and put into a safe enclosure. The cats will wander around, getting hungrier and hungrier. And remember, Guthrie: They know your smell." He shrugged. "In any case, if you escape the cats, I have men patrolling the perimeter between the fences. And if they don't get you, well...." He glanced meaningfully at Diane.

"He's not going to hurt me," Diane said. "Not if he needs me to make Howard paint."

Guthrie knew differently. Banning could hurt her badly and still have plenty left over to force Graham to do his bidding.

"No one has to be hurt at all," Banning said suavely. "I only need you here long enough for Howard to finish painting the gateway." He looked at Guthrie. "That's all I want. After that, I no longer need him, which means I'll no longer need Miss Weston as leverage. They will be free to leave, and you won't have to protect either of them. I'm sure you noticed that your car is here. When Howard is done, I'll give you the keys, and you may drive them back to Houston."

Banning rose and came around the desk.

"I have business to attend to right now, so you'll have to excuse me. But I'll see you later." His eyes bored into Guthrie. "Don't try to leave. Let matters remain on course, and when the painting is finished, everybody will be happy and free to go about his or her business." He turned to Diane. "Your friend must be hungry. Why don't you and Howard show him the kitchen? It'll give him a chance to meet Howard. After all, he's been looking quite hard for him."

"It's this way," Diane told Guthrie.

The three of them left the office, followed by Hayes and Porter, and the heavy door thumped shut behind them as they went down the long hall.

25

THE KITCHEN WAS SPACIOUS, WELL lit, and modern, with a break-fast table set off to one side. Hayes remained by the door they'd come through, while Porter jerked his chin toward the table.

"You two sit there," he ordered Guthrie and Graham. "She can fix your food."

"I guess he never heard of women's equality," Guthrie said to Diane.

"Shut up," Porter snapped.

"Or what?" Guthrie stared at him.

"You'll see what," Porter said, taking a threatening step forward. Guthrie laughed.

"I doubt your boss would like that. Why don't you just go stand in the corner like a good little boy?"

Porter growled and started to raise the barrel of the AR-15, but Hayes quickly stepped in and pushed it down.

"He's just trying to needle you. Go watch the back door."

Porter, face red and shoulders tense, moved toward a closed door at the rear of the kitchen that Guthrie surmised led to the carport.

"Don't cause more problems for yourself than you already have," Hayes advised.

"I only want to know one thing," Guthrie said. "If he actually tried to kill me, would you have shot him?"

Hayes just gave a thin smile and shook his head in amazement. Then he ambled over to the coffee maker, passing Diane, who was coming toward the table carrying a carafe of coffee and two mugs.

"Are bacon and eggs okay?" she asked.

"Just what I ordered," Guthrie said. "I haven't eaten since noon yesterday, so supersize mine."

While she went into the cooking area, Guthrie filled his and Howard's cups and looked the artist over. Howard was more gaunt than he had appeared in the photos, and his skin was pallid, as if he'd been ill. He gave Guthrie a wan but sincere smile.

"Diane told me about you," he said. "Thanks for all you did for her."

"You mean let her get kidnapped?"

Graham's smile turned rueful.

"At least you didn't cause her to get kidnapped."

Actually, it probably *was* me that did that, Guthrie thought glumly.

"Did you know that would happen when you first got into this mess?" he asked.

"The desire to accomplish something greater than oneself is a powerful motivator," Graham said. "It can fool us into disregarding potential consequences. But if I'd known we'd all be here like this, I'd never have started."

"We all live with unintended consequences," Guthrie said. "What I want to know right now is how we got here."

"It's not a long story, but it's complicated."

"And it starts with Adriana Lycoris."

"Yes, with Adriana."

"Hey, you two," Porter said from across the room. "Quit whispering."

"Is she here?" Guthrie asked, ignoring Porter.

"Yes. And Melanie and Gregory. They're in town right now."

"So tell me what's going on."

"Adriana started coming to my shows, and she wanted me to paint her portrait."

"I told you to shut up," Porter snarled, leaning aggressively forward.

"I've seen it," Guthrie said. "Nice work."

"It's funny," Howard said. "In two months, she knew everything about me, but I knew nothing about her. I didn't even know she was married until Banning showed up to bring me here."

Actually married, Guthrie thought.

"Adriana has a lot of practice getting information out of people without divulging anything," Guthrie said. "She'd be the envy of all detectives if she chose to take up law enforcement. You were a sitting duck."

"I suppose so. And you'd think I'd know better. Portrait painting, in part, is reading the person who's sitting. Hell, I might as well have painted a black widow spider," Howard snorted. "But I didn't know that at the time."

"I told you to shut the fuck up!"

Porter stepped quickly toward the table, half raising his AR-15.

"Back off, Porter," Hayes said from where he leaned against the counter next to the coffee maker.

"Not until this fucker does what I say."

Guthrie looked up at Porter, a sarcastic gleam in his eyes, and snorted. "You got a problem with me?"

"I don't like fuckers who shoot at me and kill my friends. They're the kind of fuckers who get fucked back."

"Bet you like all that fucking back. And forth," Guthrie said. Rage washed over Porter's face, and he swung the AR's muzzle toward Guthrie, his finger snapping off the safety. But Guthrie was already out of his chair, his left arm sweeping up and across the AR's barrel then down and around, partially wrenching the weapon out of Porter's grasp. An instant later, Guthrie's right hand, cocked back, palm up, knifed into the left side of Porter's neck.

The man went down in a tumble over Guthrie's chair, and suddenly the AR was in Guthrie's hands, muzzle two inches from Porter's nose.

"Do you mind if my friends and I have a little space here? After all, Mr. Banning gave us permission to chat. Are you bucking Mr. Banning's orders?"

Porter, blinking back pain, stared into the little round hole.

"All right, Guthrie," Hayes said. He had his own gun out, and it was aimed. "You made your point."

Smiling down at Porter, Guthrie straightened and stepped back. He dropped the AR's magazine, ejected the live round, then tossed the weapon to Hayes and set the magazine and round on the counter.

Porter scrambled to his feet as if he wanted to charge Guthrie.

"Get those," Hayes snapped, gesturing at the magazine and round, "and get the fuck out of here. Just be glad I don't tell Mr. Banning what a fuck-up you are. Tell Spencer to come in here."

"I'll get you for that," Porter snarled at Guthrie.

"I said get out," Hayes said. He held out the AR.

Porter snatched the rifle and, shoulders bunched, turned and stalked out the back door, into the sunshine. When the door slammed behind him, Hayes turned to Guthrie and gestured toward his fallen chair.

"Porter's an idiot," he said, contempt in his voice.

"Good help is hard to find," Guthrie replied.

He picked up his chair and sat down. Only then did Hayes relax and holster his gun.

"Jesus," Diane breathed, her eyes bright. "You don't think they're going to kill us, do you?"

"That would be the simplest thing. Once Howard's done, Adriana and Banning won't need any of us."

"But there's nothing we can do to him," she said. "If we went to the police, they're not going to take our word over Banning's. And no one would believe it about the paintings. We'd just look like a bunch of crackpots."

"I can do plenty," Guthrie replied. "And it wouldn't matter if I promised I wouldn't. Banning's not going to believe me, and he isn't the type to leave loose ends. He'll string us along until the painting opens up, then he'll take whatever steps he's already planned."

A man wearing a straw boater hat and wraparound sunglasses came in the back door. He left his hat and sunglasses on the counter by the door then joined Hayes by the coffee maker. They had their own whispered conversation.

"I'm scared, Clay."

Guthrie smiled, despite himself. She didn't sound scared, and she wasn't trembling. She was just still. Still with the anticipation of change, of movement.

"We'll get out of this," he promised. "All of us. And Lycoris and Banning will pay."

"What are we going to do?"

"I don't know." He turned to Howard. "How close are you to finishing?"

"A few days at the most."

"Can you drag that out any?"

"A week, maybe. But it'll be hard. Adriana's been monitoring my progress. She'll be able to tell if I'm stalling."

"Listen," Guthrie whispered. "My Xterra is parked out front. If worse comes to worse, I'll create a disturbance and go off into the woods...."

"What about the big cats out there?"

"I'll have to chance it. Banning's men won't risk that I might escape, and they'll have to hunt me down even though the big cats will inhibit them as much as me. That'll draw most of them away. You two get to my truck. There's a hidden set of keys in a little box welded to the frame underneath the driver's door. Get in the truck and leave. Crash through gates if you have to, but go."

"We can't just leave you."

"You have to. Hopefully I can keep away from them until you've had a chance to find the police. But listen. If you see a couple of game wardens in a dark blue pickup, don't stop. And if they try to stop you, don't let them. I think they're on Banning's payroll."

"I don't like it," Howard said.

"I don't either, but it's all we've got. Until then, I need to know everything."

26

"I'M SURE DIANE HAS TOLD you...," Howard said.

"You don't know what she's told me," Guthrie said. "And she doesn't know what you know."

"All right. Well, during the sitting, which took place over several weeks, we talked—Adriana talked—and she was quite flattering about my work. I didn't pay much attention at first, but she began to point out some of the minor flaws she noticed in various paintings. Not in a cruel or vindictive way, but more like a good art instructor or critic might. She wasn't a painter, but she had a damn good eye, so I started paying attention to what she said.

"After I finished the portrait, we started going to various exhibits and the museums together, and she would show me this or that about different paintings or styles, and I saw that she understood the crux of what was being done, even if she couldn't do it herself. Then one day, while we were at a visiting show of Rembrandts at the MFA, she said she had a way she could enable me to paint in so realistic a style that my paintings would appear to be windows instead of two-dimensional representations. 'You're going to give me art lessons?' I asked her, feeling amused but also intrigued since she'd demonstrated a deep understanding of art. 'No,' she said. 'I'm going to teach you about essences.'

"I wasn't sure what that meant. Sure, as a painter you have to capture form as well as cover a surface, and a good portrait painter can invest the image with some of the subject's personality. I've found that comes with the way the subject behaves and holds his- or herself, the expression on the face, and especially the look in the eyes. But essence is something a painter can't really reach. Hell, I doubt most people can do more than blindly grope for it in themselves."

"I've found it difficult enough," Guthrie agreed wryly, and Graham went on with another wan smile that quickly faded.

"Adriana insisted that she could teach me to endow my paintings with the essence of the subject—any subject, be it person, place, or thing. I laughed it off at first, but she kept at me. You have to understand that all this took place over the course of several months. She spun it a little at a time, gradually wrapping me so totally in her web that even when I acceded, I didn't realize how inevitable her trap was. I was practically drooling to accomplish what she suggested was possible.

"That's when she told me there would be conditions. A price. I suppose there is a price for everything, and if it isn't the sweat of honest effort, it's something less pleasant. But what she demanded didn't seem so difficult at the time. I had to agree to paint a large landscape that would come to me in dreams. She said it had to be the first painting that I would do with my newfound powers and that I shouldn't paint anything else until I'd finished it. I'd give this painting to Adriana without charge, and after that, I'd be free to use my new ability in any way I chose, with no further obligation."

"That must have sounded pretty good," Guthrie said. "You get heightened abilities for the price of a single painting. What artist wouldn't jump at the chance?"

Graham glanced at Diane over by the stove, guilt in his eyes. He looked like he wanted to say something but couldn't bring himself to spit it out. Diane, her attention on the bacon popping and sputtering in the skillet, didn't notice, but Guthrie did.

"Something else, Howard?" he prodded, but Graham quickly shook his head and turned to stare at the table.

"I thought she was going to teach me some kind of technique," he said after a pause, "but she just laughed and said I already had the technique, it was just that my inner eye was asleep and she was going to awaken it. I already knew that painting is done with the mind, not the hands, so when she said I'd have to learn to see in a different way, it made sense.

"She wanted to perform some kind of procedure on me. I had to fast beforehand then drink an herbal potion she concocted. The experience was very strange, and I don't remember much about it. It was like she hypnotized or drugged me. Maybe both. There wasn't any kind of mumbo-jumbo or candles or incense, just me lying on her couch and listening to the drone of her voice. Then suddenly, I felt something...I don't know...twist inside my head. That's the only way I can describe it. Like that feeling you get when someone startles you, and you sort of jerk inside before your body moves, only this was without the fear or adrenaline you might associate with that.

"After it was over, I just got up and drove home. For several days, I felt very hung over, like I was still slightly drugged, and I couldn't even begin to think about painting anything. But every night I dreamed vividly of this odd sort of landscape. I was like a disembodied eye soaring around, surveying it, and I knew this was what Adriana wanted me to paint. Even when I was awake, I could see it vividly in my mind, like a place I'd lived or visited many times.

"When I came out of the state enough to paint, I experimented with a landscape on a small canvas just to see what would happen. I knew I was violating my agreement with Adriana by painting it, but I couldn't help myself. And I was amazed at the results. I swear, I could see that world in my mind more thoroughly and deeply than I'd ever seen anything before, and that insight somehow was translated to the work. I watched the paint go onto the surface from my brush, and for a time, the surface was tangibly apparent. But then, at some point when the painting was nearly picture-perfect, something happened that sent chills through me. I came down to work on it, and the entire painting was black.

"I couldn't believe what I was seeing. There was no explanation except that somebody had painted it over while I slept. After the initial shock wore off, I realized that the door was locked and the burglar alarm was on. Nobody could have sneaked in, vandalized the painting, and sneaked out without my knowing about it. And why would they do that, anyway? My next thought was that the paint had somehow turned bad, but that was ridiculous. I was using the same paints I always did. And anyway, even if one pigment turned—which it wouldn't—they all wouldn't at the same time.

"Despair started to creep up on me, but I was too fired up to heed it. Fuck it, I thought, and I began to prep another canvas. But by the time I was done, I noticed that the first painting was gradually reappearing, as if out of a murky background."

"Dawn," Guthrie said.

"Yes." Howard peered curiously at Guthrie. "You believe it? You don't think I'm mad?"

"I might if I hadn't seen the painting."

"You've seen it? Where?"

"I found your clever hiding place. The painting is currently face down on the cement floor of my garage."

Howard's shoulders sank.

"Then they'll have it, too, now that they know who you are."

"I don't think so," Guthrie said. "I have a very good watchdog."

"They'll just shoot it."

"Not this one."

Howard looked puzzled, but before he could ask what Guthrie meant, Guthrie told him to go on.

"It was dawn," Howard nodded. "As the light came up, I realized that. The painting had gotten to the stage where it was visually permeable, and it changed from being a static scene to something more like a window. And things moved around it. The plants blew in the wind, and there were animals."

"Monsters?"

"No, not yet. If there had been, I might have stopped. They were more like insects, birds, lizards of various sizes, and a few small, furry creatures. You can't imagine how I felt: shock, awe, elation. Power." He cast his eyes downward. "Fear. I told myself that it was impossible and it was just lack of food and sleep and my overheated imagination playing tricks with my mind. But the movement was unmistakable. I could doubt my sanity, but I knew I wasn't crazy. This was real. So I went on. I could still touch the surface, but I found I had to develop a special mental technique to make sure the paint went where I wanted it to go, especially during the final stages, when the painting barely seemed to have a surface. If something was close to the surface, I'd think about applying the paint close to me, and if it was far away, I'd stretch with my mind to take the brush deeper into the painting.

"And then, after I'd applied the last few brush strokes, it was a real window. An open one. I could smell what was out there on the other side, feel the breeze and the temperature of the air. And I could reach through it. That scared me, but not for the reason you might think: that I wasn't painting just another picture but some sort of reality. What scared me was the sense of power that welled up inside me. But I was too excited to think twice about the fear. Instead, I thought about working on something larger. Full-scale. I felt exhilarated and invincible and, most of all, ambitious. I thought, god, if I can apply this to conventional portraits and landscapes, I'd make Rembrandt and all the rest footnotes. But first, I had to pay the price and paint Adriana's painting. That didn't bother me. Not then. Like I said, the world out there looked pretty benign at the time, and if she wanted a gateway to it, that seemed reasonable. I wanted to go out there too, to experience what it was like to actually be on another world rather than just imagining and depicting it.

"I called Adriana and said I was ready to start her painting. I didn't tell her about the test painting, of course. She came by my studio, and we discussed what she wanted. She had as vivid a mental image of that other world as I did, and she had a specific scene in mind. She even had a rough sketch of the location and could describe how to find it in my mind. I don't know how she did it, but she did, and I could see the exact scene and perspective, not too far from the scene I'd already painted. Then she took me to some warehouse just outside the North Loop. She wanted me to paint the gateway there."

"Wouldn't your studio have been a better place to work?"

"Adriana's painting is too large. Eight by eight. The largest surface I've ever worked on outside of some modernist experiments when I was younger. It was easier and safer to paint it in situ rather than paint it and move it. So I built and prepped the panel in my studio then transported it and a work table and supplies to the warehouse and started the painting there.

"Usually, a canvas that large is reserved for abstracts, not something as detailed as I had to do. I might have felt intimidated, but instead, I was excited, delirious, driven by a power I'd never felt before. I'd made some preliminary sketches, but in the end, the landscape was so vivid in my mind that I didn't need them. I just painted, oblivious to what was happening. I was desperate to fulfill the compulsion, to see if it really would come to life like the smaller one. My reputation was suffering, and Diane tried to help, but I couldn't tell her what was going on, and I couldn't stop. We just quarreled, so I quit talking to her."

Graham sighed and glanced over at Diane again, who was cracking some eggs into a skillet and scrambling them. In his gaze, Guthrie saw a combination of longing, a sense of opportunities missed and lost, and a resolve not to miss others. But overlaying it all was a fear that already everything was irrevocably lost.

Guthrie had to repress a sneer—not at Graham and Diane and their reconnection, no matter how tenuous, but at his own situation. They had a house, and maybe it was about to burn down around them, but there was always hope that the fire department would arrive in time to save it. Guthrie's own house wasn't even worth burning. But, he reflected, maybe that is as it should be. After what he'd done, could any woman ever trust him? Could he ever trust himself or feel joy or loss at his own prospects? But that was his problem, not Diane and Howard's, and of minor importance right now. Right now, he had to concentrate on getting them out of here alive and intact.

"I forgot everything else—everyone else—and poured myself into the painting," Howard went on. "As the weeks progressed and it came to life like the smaller one, I had to adjust my schedule to what was going on once I reached that initial stage of visual permeability since I could only paint while it was full daylight in that other world. In those days, they still allowed me to go home, which I did every night—night on that other world, that is.

"But I went home less and less. The painting consumed me, even when I couldn't work on it. Bailey set up a room for me at the warehouse, and they brought in food. I was completely obsessed and worked for weeks in a dazed frenzy, refining and adding details. That world became more familiar and tangible to me than the real world here.

"But then, one day, I remember sort of coming to and finding myself wandering aimlessly around the warehouse, a brush in my hand. At first, I rationalized that I was just overworked, but something was disturbing me on a deeper level. I thought I just wanted the damn thing done so I could go on to something else, but that really wasn't it, either. I'd been so obsessed, that I hadn't given myself a chance to notice what was going on in that world out there.

"Some of the picture elements were different. I don't mean the obvious changes, like moving clouds, passing animals, or the progress of day to night. These all began happening when I had most of the painting nearly picture perfect. That's when it stopped being a static scene and acted like a closed window. I'd gotten used to those, but these new changes were different, even if they weren't obvious at first—just a twist of something here or a minor degradation there. Mostly of these were in the distant landscape, but some of the creatures wandering across the foreground began to look deformed in unpleasant ways. Something wasn't right. Something about the painting was dangerous in a way that defied the relative normalcy of the scene it depicted."

Diane came over with their plates of food, set them down, then handed out plastic utensils.

Guthrie looked at the flimsy utensils then up at Diane.

"It's all they let us use," she said with a shrug as she sat next to Howard.

"Don't want you hurting yourselves in Mr. Banning's absence," Hayes said dryly from across the room.

Guthrie nearly wolfed his meal, though Howard merely picked at his own food.

"I began to realize," Howard went on, "that it wasn't the scene or the painting that was off. It was something else. Something that was out in that world. Adriana thought she was the one who gave me the power to paint the gateway." He shook his head sadly. "It wasn't her. It was something else. She was just the messenger girl." He snorted a bitter laugh. "That bitch doesn't know what she's dealing with."

"Maybe she does," Guthrie said.

"No," Howard replied, looking up. His long fingers writhed together and his face twitched. "If she did, she wouldn't force me to keep on painting. Something is out there in that world. Something terrible."

"I've seen the monsters," Guthrie said.

"Not them," Howard said with a shudder. "The thing that made them."

"I heard you say that at the warehouse," Guthrie said. "Angra Mainyu?"

"What's Angra Mainyu?" Diane asked.

"Some sort of entity. Adriana thinks it's is going to guide her and Brother Gregory in their search for a psychotropic plant."

"Whatever it does," Howard said, "it won't be guiding anybody anywhere but hell." He paused, drank a sip of coffee, then went on. "As I said, in those days, they allowed me to go home, though I hadn't for weeks. But I had to get another look at that first painting. I hadn't seen it since I'd begun the large one. I don't know why. At the time, I thought I didn't want to let the sight of it sully my current work. Make the new painting somehow derivative. But truthfully, I was scared. Scared of having painted a portal to another world. Scared that I wouldn't be able to do it again with the large one. And now I was scared of what might happen if I did.

"So after I saw the changes that had been wrought in the large painting, I went home on some pretext and got out the smaller one." He shook his head, mouth a grim line as he looked at Guthrie. "Diane told me she described the painting to you—the painting in its earlier stages. The scene looked normal then. The plants and animals were odd—alien, even—but not monstrous. And the terrain wasn't warped and desolate. It was covered with long grass, and the hill in the background was lightly forested. You've seen it. Does it look like that?"

"I'd say it looks horrible, if that's what you mean," Guthrie answered. "That's why I laid it on the cement floor."

"That won't stop Angra Mainyu," Howard said. "I was there when it came. Until then, the scene looked normal, but by then, I could feel that it wasn't. Something was out there, looking for the painting from the other side. Knew it was there but just couldn't pin down where it was. It came within a hundred yards, but at an angle that would have made the painting look like just a vertical sliver to it. And there were the plants all around. Even though a lot of them morphed into ugly caricatures, I guess their vertical stems helped mask my vertical slit.

"But I could see Angra Mainyu almost completely. When I first saw it, I instinctively turned toward the movement. But once I had and could see what it was, I froze. I sensed that there was a connection between us, that it knew I was there, somewhere. I realized that if I moved, I'd attract its attention, and then it would be all over. Either I'd tear up the painting or let that thing through into our world.

"Thank goodness it didn't see me, and finally it left. Still looking, I guess. But I knew then that I could never finish Adriana's painting. That thing's just using her like she used me." He hung his head.

"You wouldn't be the first person to make errors of judgment when dealing with life," Guthrie said. "The important thing isn't that you lost, but that what was lost is now found."

"At what cost?"

"An old man once told me this story," Guthrie said. "There was a peasant farmer who worked his land with his only son. One day, a stray cow came onto their farm. The farmer tried to find the owner, but no one claimed the cow, so he decided to keep it. 'What great luck!' exclaimed the farmer's neighbor. 'We shall see,' the farmer replied. Not long afterward, the cow kicked the farmer's son while he was milking it, breaking his arm. 'What misfortune!' exclaimed the farmer's neighbor. 'We shall see,' the farmer replied. A week later, the emperor's army came through the region, conscripting all the able-bodied young men. Because the farmer's son's arm was broken, they passed him over. 'What great luck!' exclaimed the farmer's neighbor. 'We shall see,' the farmer replied. So, to you I say: We shall see."

"Maybe," Howard said, "but you haven't seen what I've seen. This thing out there, this Angra Mainyu, is a corruptor. It's like a huge amoeba infecting the skin of reality. It crawls around within the surface, and everything in its direct path melts into a smooth, uniformity. And it has a huge...I don't know—an aura, I suppose. You can't see it, but whatever passes through it transmogrifies and warps. The landscape just gets melted looking, but normal plants and animals morph into those disgusting growths and monsters. I could feel it even a hundred yards away, like an itchy madness plucking at my mind as well as at my flesh.

"I went back to the warehouse and told Adriana I was going to stop. Had to stop. That her world was too dangerous. But she wouldn't listen. She was as obsessed as I was. More. I'd been involved for only a few months, but she'd been involved her whole life.

"I managed to get away and go back to my studio. I was going to destroy the smaller painting. And I guess I thought I'd be safe there, but I was a fool to think Adriana would let me go. I called Diane to ask her to meet me, but before I could burn the smaller painting, Banning's men came for me. I managed to hide it before they got in. They took me and some clothes and supplies back to the warehouse. They made the room where I'd slept into a cell and locked me up when I wasn't painting or eating. I was guarded around the clock.

"When they brought me back, Adriana threatened me. Told me that if I didn't finish her painting, she'd have her men break my fingers, and I'd never finish another one. I had to go on. I couldn't let her destroy my career. But that's a weak excuse." He lowered his eyes. "I guess I was secretly glad at first that I was being forced to do what I knew I shouldn't do because I found I didn't really want to stop. By then, I'd become drunk with the power of being able to do what I was doing. I didn't care what kind of world it was out there. I just knew I'd retain the power after I finished Adriana's painting, and I fantasized about how I would wield it after I got out of her clutches. What worlds I would create!" He lifted his eyes again. "But I vowed I'd never go back to Adriana's world again. I would find a real paradise to paint.

"I went back to work, but I knew something now that I hadn't before. I realized she'd never let me go. I had the power now, and she couldn't let me run loose with it. I knew they'd have to kill me when I was done, but even that fact did little more than slow me down." He snorted. "My newfound power had driven me to paint something terrible and dangerous, and if this was to be my final painting, it would by my masterpiece. But the more I contemplated the scene that flowed from my brush, the more deeply I considered my own miserable life and the path that had brought me to this point. I'd been blinded by my own ego and the drive to succeed, and even if I hadn't meant to trample on Diane's feelings, I had done just that. And I saw, at the same time, that success isn't exclusive of attachments to other people, but partly because of them. So, feeling nothing but revulsion for myself, I finally understood how badly I'd treated Diane." He looked at her, sadness in his eyes, then back at Guthrie. "How I desperately I missed and needed her. That I loved her. And that changed everything. If I finished the painting and Adriana unleashed Angra Mainyu on us all, Diane would suffer."

"So you stopped again."

"I couldn't go on. Wouldn't."

"And then they captured Diane."

Howard nodded.

"Now," he said, "all I can do is dread the day when I try to put on one more brush stroke, and my hand goes right past the surface."

27

AFTER THE MEAL, HAYES ORDERED Howard back to work, then he and Spencer took Guthrie outside. Apparently, Diane, like Howard, was confined to the house because she stayed inside.

"You have free run of the guest house, yard, and pool, but don't try to go into the main house or any of the other buildings," Hayes told Guthrie. "And, like the boss says, if you're smart, you won't try to climb the fence and get away."

He nodded toward the predator barn. As if his gesture was a signal, one of the animal doors opened, and the lion emerged into the corral, which was surrounded by a tall chain-link fence. The lion paced around the enclosure for a moment before it realized the outer gate was open, and when it did, it quickly trotted through it and into the trees and scrub at the edge of the compound. A few moments later, the tiger followed.

"Norris didn't feed them this morning," Hayes said pointedly. "Bet they're hungry." He turned to Spencer. "You're on. I'll relieve you in a couple of hours."

Hayes went back into the house, leaving Guthrie standing in the middle of the dusty yard with Spencer, who had donned his straw hat and sunglasses.

"Go on," Spencer said. "Take a look around. Just don't leave me out in the sun too long. I'm prone to skin cancer."

Turning away, Guthrie stared around. Obviously they were letting him run around loose because they didn't want to do anything to jeopardize Howard's work, and damaging Guthrie would be counterproductive. Banning wanted his victims to cling to any remnant of hope, no matter how tattered, that they'd be released when Howard was done. But Guthrie knew it was rotten cloth. When Howard's hand painted that last brush stroke, he, Diane, and Guthrie were doomed. But what form would that doom take? With Banning, there would be many options.

Well, doom wasn't upon them, yet, and Guthrie didn't plan to stand around idle, waiting for it. If they were going to let him run around, he was going to make the most of it. He started by making a circuit of the compound's perimeter—or as much of it as he could reach. Spencer followed about forty feet behind. Far enough to be safe from a surprise attack, but close enough to use the assault rifle to rip Guthrie to shreds with very little effort or aim.

The ten-foot chain-link fence was topped with razor wire and ran all the way around the perimeter of the compound. Like the fence that marked the boundaries of the ranch, it had a concrete ribbon set into the ground beneath it. To make it hard to dig under, Guthrie presumed.

The main house was sited a little less than a third of the way back from the compound's front fence, straight back from the front gates, which were electrically operated and watched by surveillance cameras. The tan, gravely dirt driveway didn't run straight to the house, however, but branched to the left and right just inside the front gate. Both branches continued toward the back of the corners of the compound and the two barns, but they also connected at a wider parking area in front of the house, leaving a roughly oblong island of weeds and a few scraggly prickly pear cacti about fifty feet across. The parking area was currently occupied by several vehicles that Guthrie easily recognized from the previous couple of weeks, although the green Suburban wasn't there.

The house was built on the rim of a shallow ridge, and while the property sloped gently downward toward the rear of the compound, it dropped more sharply just past the area where the dirt road wound in toward the front gate from the scrub oak woods covering most of the tract. The view out there was pretty nice and probably was even better from the house's second-story windows. But the house's combination of stone and glass gave Guthrie an unsettled sense of simultaneous substantiality and transience.

The two dirt driveways running toward the back corners of the compound and the barns turned and met each other, making a loop. The barn to right was the one he'd spent the night in. All the pens nearly surrounding the other barn held various types of herbivorous game animals: deer, bison, javelinas, antelope, a moose, a big-horn sheep, and even a couple of giant feral hogs. Banning's private zoo must have cost a fortune to assemble. And no doubt, Hunter's Challenge was doing boom business because it offered no challenge at all.

The area enclosed by the loop drive was nearly two hundred feet across. It had a lot of scrub oak and underbrush, with weeds proliferating in between. A little more than halfway from the house to the herbivore barn was a small, low wooden shed. An electric line ran to it from the house, and a low, steady hum emanated from it. Must be a pump house for a well, Guthrie thought.

He completed his circuit of the property, noting the surveillance cameras at the fronts and backs of both barns and on several poles around the perimeter. When he arrived back at the house, he walked around the front left corner, down a dirt driveway that ended in a carport. Hayes had said he couldn't go into the house, but he'd gotten a pretty good glimpse of most of the lower floor, and he had a general idea of the layout. The front left corner of the house held the living room, and just behind that was the dining room, then the kitchen. There were wide windows on the outer walls of each room, allowing Guthrie to easily see inside. All were protected by bars.

He passed beneath the carport and saw the kitchen through the open back door and, to the left, the door to a utility room. The gap between the main house and the smaller house where he was quartered was spanned with a tall chain link fence set with a gate and topped with razor wire. The gate's latch was held in place by a U-shaped bolt instead of a padlock, presumable for easy human egress. Ignoring the gate, Guthrie continued on down the side of his quarters, around the corner, and along the back toward the second smaller house. The gap between his bungalow and it was fenced and gated, and all the outward-facing windows on both houses were barred.

A turn down the south wall of the second bungalow showed more barred windows and another fenced gap between the bungalow and the main house. Across the gap, Guthrie encountered a structural anomaly. In the same place that was occupied, on the other side of the house, by the carport, a windowless, medium-sized room protruded. The room was adjacent to the second room behind Banning's office.

The addition didn't really fit architecturally with the rest of the house, and it looked as if it had only recently been constructed. Although it was cased in dressed stone similar to that used on the main structure, the stone looked slightly lighter, as if it had come from a different quarry or simply hadn't weathered as long. The cement of the thick foundation was raw and unaged. Even the low shrubs that lined the foundation were freshly planted.

The west wall of the addition, which faced the front of the compound, held a steel roll-up garage door. Was it a garage? Guthrie couldn't tell, but that would be odd considering its location and the presence of the carport at the end of the opposite wing. Also odd was the fact that the room behind Banning's office had no outer windows at all. It, like the addition and upper floor, were terra incognita, at least for the moment.

Guthrie went back to the gap between the main house and the second bungalow and let himself through the gate, whose latch, like those of the other gates, was held in place with a U-shaped bolt. He didn't bother to re-latch the gate but tossed the bolt to Spencer, who'd trailed him the whole time.

His eyes sought the front windows of the two bungalows. No bars. With all the outward-facing windows of all three buildings barred and the gaps between the buildings fenced across, that meant that the big cats were allowed to prowl the compound at least some of the time.

Through the window of the second bungalow, Guthrie could see that the living room was half filled with gym equipment and half with a TV viewing area. He watched Porter come out of one of the bedrooms, buttoning a shirt. So the second bungalow was a bunkhouse.

The main house was large, but not large enough for all the men under Banning's command. Certainly not now, with all the guests who were present. Probably the top ranked—surely Adriana, her daughter, Brother Gregory, Stewart, and Talbot had rooms in the house, while the others stayed in the bunkhouse. Guthrie wondered if he'd displaced anyone, but he thought not. His own bungalow was too neat and bore no marks of permanent tenants. Under normal circumstances, Banning probably used it as guest quarters. His canned hunters had to stay somewhere.

Guthrie turned left, down the narrow patio between the pool to his right and the wall of windows to his left. He passed the door to Banning's office—again closed—and then the door to the half-bath. He could see more of the room from this angle, but it was small and generic.

Guthrie turned the inner corner toward the sliding glass doors he'd been taken through just a couple of hours before. The big room beyond was a den, furnished with comfortable furniture, bookshelves, and a large TV monitor. He passed the sliding glass doors, saw more of the living room and dining room than he had before, then turned right and went between the pool and the solid wall, behind which was the kitchen and utility room.

At the end of the long, narrow patio was his bungalow, but Guthrie turned left and went through the gate and back out into the larger space of the compound. The day was already hot and dusty, so he walked around to the front of the house, mounted the steps to the veranda, and sat in one of the wicker chairs. Spencer propped himself against the bole of a nearby tree, his eyes still on Guthrie, but Guthrie paid him no attention. Instead, he stared out into the distances and thought about his situation.

It wasn't easy to work through, and he was still sitting there a couple of hours later when Lycoris's Suburban pulled up to the gate. As the gate slid back on its rollers, Guthrie's guard stopped lounging against the tree trunk and became more alert. Guthrie wondered if Spencer thought he might make a break for it. But the gate was more than a hundred feet away, and he'd be riddled before he made it a quarter of the way. Then the Suburban pulled through and the gate began to roll shut, and Spencer relaxed. Only then did Guthrie realize he hadn't been worried about Guthrie escaping but about the big cats getting into the compound with Adriana and her companions.

Not that there'd be much difference.

As the Suburban pulled around the circle drive to stop in the parking area in front of the house, trailing a low waft of dust, Guthrie could see that Brother Gregory was at the wheel. Nobody sat in the seat next to him, and the SUV's tinted back windows prevented him from seeing inside, but Guthrie figured Adriana and her daughter, Melanie, were back there.

Sure enough, as soon as Gregory got out, he opened the door behind him, and Adriana emerged, carrying a purse and a small paper shopping bag with handles. At the same time, Melanie got out of the other side and came around the Suburban, toting a similar pair of items. The two of them walked toward the house while Brother Gregory went to the back of the Suburban, opened the doors, and bent inside. He was just coming out with several plastic grocery sacks dangling from his fingers when Adriana and Melanie mounted the steps.

Adriana had spotted Guthrie sitting there when she'd gotten out of the car—probably as soon as the Suburban had pulled up to the gate—and her face was a frigid mask as she reached the flagstone veranda.

"Hello, Adriana," Guthrie said amiably. "What's a city girl like you doing in an out-of-the-way place like this?"

"You won't be flippant much longer," she said, the mean bite to her words mirroring the contempt in her eyes.

"I promise it won't matter to you, one way or the other, before much longer," he said with false bravado, noticing that Melanie was giving him an equally spiteful glare.

"You frightened my mother," Adriana said. "She's an invalid."

"Yeah," Guthrie snorted. "Right."

Hatred glared through Lycoris's contempt, and for a moment, Guthrie thought she might try to hit him. But apparently she realized that if she tried, she'd be dead before Guthrie's guard or Brother Gregory could do a thing about it. Instead, she turned stiffly away and stalked through the front door, into the house, Melanie following.

Brother Gregory trudged up the steps with his burden of grocery sacks, and gave Guthrie a nasty look of his own. Then he, too, disappeared into the house leaving Guthrie with the heat, the dust, and the lowering sun glaring into the veranda. Guthrie was tired of sitting, anyway. He got up, contemplating his options.

"When's dinner?" he asked Spencer.

"You and the other two can eat in the kitchen after the boss and his guests finish their meal. Someone will take you there."

"Well, they can come and get me. I'm going to take a nap. My cell mates snored too loudly for me to get much sleep last night."

Spencer chuckled then followed Guthrie around the house to Guthrie's bungalow. He didn't come in but sat in a shaded chair by the pool, facing Guthrie's front door.

Inside, Guthrie spent some time scoping the place for microphones and cameras. He found one of each in every room he could get into, and he assumed that the other bedroom suite, which was locked, was similarly bugged. Ignoring the cameras, he lay down on the bed and fell into a shallow sleep.

He was awakened just before six when Hayes and Spencer came into his room.

"Time for dinner," Hayes said as Guthrie sat up.

They took him into the kitchen, where Diane was frying three hamburgers in a skillet.

"I'm not much of a cook," she said apologetically as Hayes gestured for Guthrie to sit at the table.

"I could help," Guthrie volunteered.

"You could stay right there," Hayes said as he perched on a nearby stool. Spencer parked himself by the back door. Guthrie ignored them both.

"Where's Howard?"

"He's painting," Diane said. "They'll bring him in a few minutes."

Porter ushered Howard into the room just as Diane was putting the burgers onto the buns. He looked even worse than earlier: emaciated, unkempt, enervated, and slack-jawed. Porter took him to the table, where Howard sat heavily. He glanced at Guthrie for a moment with burning eyes before he lowered his gaze to stare at his long fingers twitching in his lap.

Diane put the plates on the table, sat, and looked at Howard. Guthrie could feel her concern washing over the stricken artist, but Howard was too embroiled in his interior turmoil to notice. He picked at his food, but Guthrie, still hungry from several days of low rations, dug in. He might not get a chance to act, but if he did, he wasn't about to let physical weakness hamper him.

Guthrie was almost done when the door opened, and Banning came in, followed by Stewart.

"I hope you will excuse me," he said, "but I have to go to Houston." He looked at Guthrie. "It seems my men are having difficulty breaking into your house. Some things you have to do yourself, and your keys will make it simple. I'll be gone a couple of days." He turned to Howard. "Don't slack off while I'm away, Howard. That wouldn't be good for anybody."

Then he and Stewart were gone.

"He said he was having trouble getting into your house," Howard said.

"I told you I have a really good watchdog," Guthrie responded, hoping that Banning wouldn't think to look in his garage.

28

WHILE BANNING WAS GONE, THE compound was Guthrie's world. If he wanted to get out of the heat, he could go into the guesthouse. But they locked him in his room at night, so he stayed outdoors as much as possible during the day, hoping to get a sense of the routine.

Of Stewart and Talbot there was no sign, so probably they were with Banning in Houston. But Banning still had four men on the property. Apparently, Hayes was in charge when Banning and his two personal bodyguards were absent. Beneath him were Porter and Spencer, and beneath them was Norris, the caretaker, who fed and cared for the animals. Norris had a room in the predator barn, above the office, and the other three slept in the bunkhouse.

Diane told him that there were six bedrooms on the second floor, parsed out to her, Banning, Stewart, Talbot, Adriana, and Melanie. Howard slept on a cot in the room where he was working on the painting, which seemed to be the odd addition off the side of Banning's office. Adriana's priest, Brother Gregory, was staying in the second bedroom in Guthrie's bungalow, but he spent very little time there and usually was attending Adriana and Melanie in the main house.

Guthrie only rarely saw Adriana, Melanie, or even Brother Gregory, despite the fact that Gregory shared Guthrie's bungalow. Guthrie was already safely locked away at night before Gregory came in to sleep. Most of the time, Adriana and Melanie kept to the house, as if they felt an antipathy to the heat and dryness that lay over the landscape. But sometimes they went out on excursions, though Guthrie had no idea where. Occasionally they came back with shopping bags of one sort or another, but at others, they returned bearing only weariness. Guthrie began to suspect that Adriana was keeping away so that she wouldn't have to deal with him, Diane, or Howard any more than she had to.

As for the routine, if there was a routine, one of the men—usually Spencer—always tailed Guthrie. Hayes generally stayed in or around the main house, though he sometimes traded off with Porter, who spent most of each day riding patrol of the property. At least, that's what Guthrie figured he was doing. There was a lot of property out there to keep track of. Guthrie thought Porter might drive one of the half a dozen Kawasaki ATVs, but he invariably took the gray Blazer. Maybe that was because of the air conditioning, but more likely it was because of the big cats roaming the scrubby woods. The only places safe from them were the compound and the alley between the ranch's twin perimeter fences. Guthrie occasionally saw one or the other of them lurking just beyond the compound's margin.

They know where the food is, he thought.

Porter didn't seem to be too happy with having to drive around in the woods all day. He's probably too afraid to get out of his truck to take a piss, Guthrie thought. Maybe he didn't usually have to do the job by himself and had traded off with Andrews. Whatever the reason, Guthrie was thankful that Hayes kept him away, and he understood why the man was left in charge when the others were gone.

Twice a day—breakfast and dinner—Spencer took Guthrie into the main house's kitchen to eat with Diane and Howard, and sometimes Hayes joined them. Diane seemed to be holding up, but the effort of completing the painting was taking a toll on the artist. His already gaunt body looked almost fleshless, and his skin was sallow. Worst of all were his eyes, which had become hollow pits of exhaustion with a coal burning deep within each. He rarely spoke, and he usually just picked over his food, though Diane encouraged him to eat.

He's running on nervous energy, Guthrie thought, and he wondered if the artist would hold up long enough to complete the painting.

"He's so tired," Diane said to Guthrie on the third night. Graham had begged off half-way through the meal, saying he wasn't hungry, and had gone to lie down on his cot. "It's like the painting is sapping his soul. I hardly see him. He's trying to finish as fast as he can so we can leave." Even as her mouth spoke the last few words, her eyes said she didn't believe them.

Banning had told them he'd release them, but Guthrie had stopped believing that less than one second after Banning said it. And Guthrie was anything but tired. The confinement of the past few days was beginning to wear thin, and worse was not knowing what Banning had in mind for them. Guthrie still had no coherent plan of his own, and he felt his nervous tension kick up a notch. He had to do something before it got too late to act, but the way things stood, he wouldn't have the chance. Banning had the situation sewn up. There seemed to be nothing Guthrie could do but ride it out.

Howard didn't show up for dinner the next day. Diane was already in the kitchen, cooking spaghetti.

"He's close," Diane said when she brought over Guthrie's plastic fork and a bowl of salad. "Another day or two." She leaned over and put the salad in front of Guthrie and whispered in his ear, "Mind your napkin."

Then she straightened and went back to the stove to stir the pot of sauce and check the noodles.

Guthrie left the napkin on the table, but he laid his left hand on it as he jabbed a piece of lettuce with the plastic fork, being careful not to break the flimsy tines. Something long and slender was folded in the cloth. He calculated the angle, and thought that he might be able to mask the napkin with his body if he leaned forward, so he did, lifting another forkful of salad to his mouth. At the same time, he lifted the napkin off the table and put it into his lap, trying to make the movement natural. He squeezed his legs together, then unfolded the cloth, dumped the slender object into the valley between his thighs, and laid the napkin over it.

He hadn't seen what it was, but he knew. It was a knife. The only question was, would he be able to secrete it on his body somehow without Spencer noticing?

He finished his salad, and Diane came back to the table a few minutes later, carrying two plates of spaghetti.

They ate in silence for a few minutes.

"I wish I'd known what was going on," Diane said at last. "With Howard and Adriana. Maybe I could have stopped it."

"You couldn't have," Guthrie told her. "Even Howard didn't want to stop. Maybe couldn't stop. Not at first."

"I had no idea that people like Adriana and Banning and these others exist in the real world," she said. "Only in movies and books. But these people are even worse. They're horrible. How can they stand to be like that and look at themselves in the mirror?"

"If I've learned anything," Guthrie said, "it's that evil does exist in the world, and it likes to be evil. It likes to harass the helpless and destroy the innocent. And many people, for one reason or another, are its willing tools."

"They make me sick," Diane said. She looked helplessly into Guthrie's eyes. "They're going to win, aren't they?"

"I think that if they win, we all lose," Guthrie said. "I'm not going to let that happen."

"But what can you do? They have the guns and fences."

"We shall see," Guthrie said.

"Yes." She wiped her mouth with her napkin, staring pointedly at Guthrie. She rose and reached for his empty plate, whispering, "I think I'm going to have a little accident."

Then she straightened and carried the plates over to the sink. Guthrie sat unmoving except for his right hand, which crept beneath the napkin on his lap and gripped the knife by its handle. Suddenly, Diane cried out and tripped. The dishes in her hand tumbled to the terrazzo tile floor in front of the sink and shattered. Guthrie pulled out the knife, lifted the front of his T-shirt, and tucked the hilt of the knife between his belly and belt, blade pointing upward.

No sense in cutting off my own balls so soon, he thought. Plenty of time for that later.

He twisted as he hid the knife to look in the direction of the commotion. Spencer hadn't moved, but his eyes, which had been on Diane, swiftly turned back to Guthrie, who was now turned toward Diane, both hands in plain sight. Breathing a sigh of relief that his guard hadn't noticed his sleight of hand, Guthrie stood.

"Need help?" he asked, taking a step toward Diane.

"No," Spencer said. "She made the mess, she can clean it up. Time for us to go outside."

Guthrie went out the back door, into the dying sunlight, feeling the cool length of the knife blade pressed against the skin of his abdomen. He'd have to get the thing out pretty soon before he bent over and cut himself.

"I'm going to lie down," he told Spencer.

Inside the bungalow, he lay down on the bed without removing his shoes. Conscious of the video surveillance camera mounted high in the corner, he rolled over and pretended to sleep. When he'd just about convinced himself, he slipped his hand beneath his shirt, eased out the knife, then slid it over the edge of the bed and dropped it onto the floor.

Not long afterwards, he rose and swung his feet over the side of the bed, nudging the knife underneath the box springs. Then he went back outside and sat on the veranda of the main house to watch the sun go down. That night, in the darkness of his room when the video camera was ineffective, he found the knife and examined it. Diane had chosen well. It had a heavy, sharp, six-inch blade. He spent half an hour fumbling around in the dark, fashioning a crude sheath out of a sock and strips of T-shirt that he could tie to his leg under his jeans. Then he slept.

29

BANNING RETURNED IN MID AFTERNOON on the sixth day after he left. Guthrie was sitting on the veranda when he saw the black Mercedes emerge from the scrub forest beyond the fence. The compound's electric gate whined back, the Mercedes drove through, and the gate slid back into place while the car came down the dirt and gravel drive and rolled to a stop in front of the house. Talbot was driving, and as the dust settled, Stewart, who had been in the front next to him, got out and opened the back door for Banning.

Banning climbed the steps to the veranda, and as soon as he ducked out of the sun's glare, he spotted Guthrie sitting there in the shade. He stopped and turned toward him. Guthrie couldn't read the expression behind his sunglasses, but Banning's entire demeanor radiated frustration mixed with excitement. The frustration emerged first, as soon as he saw Guthrie.

"I don't know what the fuck trick you have going on at your house," he said, "but whatever it is, works."

"Couldn't get in?"

"I'll have to find out how you do that." Banning waved, taking in the men scattered around the yard. "Get rid of some overhead."

Guthrie shrugged.

"I couldn't tell you. It was a gift from somebody."

"That other party interested in the painting?"

"One and the same."

"I'll have to search him out sometime."

"I wouldn't advise it," Guthrie said. Seeing a look of skepticism cross Banning's face, he amplified. "You're leery of Adriana. Well, my employer would make her quake."

"You sure about that? Adriana has some interesting powers."

"You've implied that her matriarchal line is old."

"A thousand years."

"So's he."

"A thousand years? Really?"

"Really. Personally."

"You work for this guy?"

"I have."

"Like now?"

"That's right."

"He know where you are?"

"Not yet, but he will."

"Then I'll have time to get ready to meet him."

"You'll never have that kind of time."

"That remains to be seen," Banning said. "But I certainly don't have time to discuss it now. Why don't you join me for dinner?"

"Sure," Guthrie said. "I have no other pressing plans. Does the invitation extend to Miss Weston and Graham?"

"This is just between the two of us. Man to man. Hunter to hunter." Banning laughed, turned away, and went into the house.

That afternoon, Guthrie noticed that security, which had grown lax the past few days with the big cats on the prowl outside, tightened considerably. With Stewart and Talbot back, Banning had six men on the grounds, not counting himself and Brother Gregory, and at least three of them spent the day patrolling the fence line.

In late afternoon, however, they all returned to the compound and stood around, looking nervously toward the predator barn. Hayes, Porter, and Spencer had exchanged their usual weapons for high-powered hunting rifles. Curious, Guthrie watched from the sidelines as Norris emerged from the predator barn carrying a bucket. He went around the corner of the barn to the corrals where the big cats had exercised, opened the gates, and went inside each in turn. Guthrie noticed that the doors in the metal wall were open, and Norris poured some of the contents of the bucket on the ground in front of each.

Then he went out of the gate, stopping to pour more of what was in the bucket before going to the gate in the perimeter fence. He unlocked the padlock, swung the gate wide, poured again, then proceeded until he was about half way to the tree line. With a heave, he tossed out the rest of the contents of the bucket in a red arc that splashed thickly onto the rocky, tan-colored dirt.

Blood.

Norris hurried back through the gate, leaving it open, and disappeared into the predator barn while the other men stood around, watching the trees, their weapons ready.

It wasn't long before one of the big cats showed up. It was the lion. As it cautiously approached the splashed blood, Guthrie could see that its ribs were beginning to show. It took a tentative lick of the bloody mud, but was startled by a sudden shout from the animal barn. Norris stood in front of the entrance to the lion's cage holding a shovelful of ground meat.

"Hey!" Norris shouted again. "Come and get it, you big mother!" Norris dropped the hunk of food in the doorway and ducked inside.

Cautiously, the big cat went into the enclosure next to the building and stopped beside the doorway, where it sucked up the fistful of food. Then, hunger more imperative than freedom, it went inside, and the door closed behind it.

The tiger took longer to come in, but it finally did.

Guthrie turned away, only then noticing that Stewart had come up behind him.

"Dinner is at 6:30 sharp. I'll come get you."

"I'll be waiting."

He was, with the knife strapped to his calf. But if Guthrie thought he might be able to knife Stewart and get his gun, the thought vanished when Talbot showed up, too.

They took him into the main house and through it to the dining room. Banning was already there, seated at one end of a long table and attended by Hayes.

"Have a seat, Guthrie," he said, waving to the chair at the opposite end of the table.

"What's on the menu?" Guthrie asked as he sat. Hayes vanished into the kitchen, but Stewart and Talbot remained casually by the door, strategically positioned behind Guthrie.

"Remember the python that was in the animal house?"

Guthrie remembered.

"Tastes just like chicken, I suppose," he said, and Banning laughed. "I'm surprised you eat vegetables," Guthrie went on, gesturing at the several covered dishes on the table between them.

Banning laughed again.

"The human body isn't made to eat nothing but meat," Banning replied as Hayes came back in with a bottle of red wine and filled Banning's glass. "But when we eat meat, we absorb the spirit of the animal we consume. Ever wonder why Americans, by and large, are such cowardly and docile herd animals? It's from eating all that chicken and cow."

Hayes came around the table and poured three fingers into Guthrie's glass.

"I might as well wonder why so many of them wallow in the sties of their own lives," Guthrie said. "Pigs."

"Hey!" Banning raised his wine glass in a salute, nodded, and drank.

"Well, just chalk me up to being a herd animal," Guthrie said, ignoring the toast. "I'll have a steak."

"There are exceptions to the herd rule," Banning said, his eyes narrowing a little at Guthrie's rebuff. "I think a man like you probably could eat nothing but chicken and still be a predator." He turned to Hayes. "A steak for Mr. Guthrie."

"Medium well," Guthrie added.

Hayes went back into the kitchen, and Banning looked at Guthrie.

"Yeah, we had one guy—some oil executive—who came up here to kill a buffalo. A bison. With a fucking bow and arrow. He was white, but he wore a loincloth and feathers. Whole bit. Said he was getting in touch with his inner Indian." Banning laughed. "Had us butcher it up afterwards and left us with a hindquarter. Talbot ate it, right, Talbot?"

"It was good, boss."

"I didn't eat any, of course" Banning went on. "Even if bison are pretty fierce and independent of men, they're still herd animals. Besides,

I think I was working on some cheetah steaks at the time. But the point is, we get all sorts who want to hunt our preserve. Even you. But you should know that we don't allow poaching. It's bad for business."

He stared at Guthrie, and Guthrie just stared back.

"I don't believe I've told you why I eat only predator meat," Banning said at last.

"Sure you did," Guthrie said. "Just now. To absorb their predator spirit. Tell me, are you going to eat all those animals in the barn out there?"

"Of course. That's why I have them here. Nothing like fresh meat. I think you'll notice your steak will be exceptionally tasty. Beef straight from my own herds. Range-fed, too, which you should definitely be able to taste. No growth hormones, either. As for the predators in the barn, somebody will hunt them first, just as if they're in the wild. We'll let the hunters have the heads, but the flesh will end up on my table."

"Canned hunts?"

"If you want to put it like that," Banning said. "But nothing so crude as tying them down or shooting them in a pen. We release them onto the property, and I let some fat ass corporate dickwad from Houston or Dallas pay me big bucks to go out there like he's on some cut-rate safari. He goes home with the head of a lion or bear he's shot in the wild, and I pocket enough cash to more than pay for the animal. And, I have fresh meat for quite a while."

"Your men eat that stuff, too?"

"Stewart will eat bear and shark. And I think he tried barracuda once, didn't you, Stewart?"

"Once, Boss."

"Did you like it?"

"It was okay."

"'Okay,' he says." Banning turned his palms up as if to say, what can you do with them? "It's really very sweet." He shrugged. "The rest of the men are like you: domestic meat eaters."

"Actually," Guthrie said, "I've been considering vegetarianism."

Banning chuckled, took another drink of his wine, then glanced up at the men waiting watchfully by the door.

"Why don't you two go relax? I don't think Mr. Guthrie is going to be any trouble at the moment. Wait in the living room. I'll call if I need you."

Stewart nodded, and he and Talbot vanished around the corner.

"Let me tell you why I eat only predator meat. Why I became a predator. It has to do with my father." He held up a cautionary hand. "Before you quip that it always has to do with the parents, let me assure you that my father was an extraordinary man. He was born into a crawfish farming family in southern Louisiana, and even though he was practically illiterate, he took a haphazard business and organized it at just the right time. People all over were starting to eat those damn mudbugs, and he had major clients throughout Louisiana and East Texas. He was the family's golden boy."

"But not to you," Guthrie said as Banning paused to take another sip of wine.

"You're right about that. He was a cold, heartless bastard. Didn't give a shit about anyone but himself or anything but his business. He beat me regularly—not always for punishment and not out of rage or because he was drunk. I used to think it was some sort of practical exercise—his way of toughening me up—but I came to understand that it was the only way he understood of showing emotion."

"Some way of caring."

"It wasn't caring. It wasn't that deep. It was...attention. I thought it was normal because it was the same way he treated my mother."

"He beat you to acknowledge you?"

"He also gave me work—chores around the house when I was a kid and a place on one of his harvesting crews when I got old enough. By then, I knew enough about the world—or as much as any kid born and raised in a dinky town on Pigeon Bayou can at sixteen—to know that something about my father was different than other men. I had friends at school, and I'd been to Baton Rouge and New Orleans and even Houston. I knew the kind of attention he visited upon me and my mother wasn't normal. I thought I could take it, but I saw that my mother's health was failing and she wouldn't last much longer under his fist. So I began making plans to take her out of there. Go to New Orleans, maybe. Or Houston. Or farther."

Banning shrugged. "I was a kid. I didn't know that what I planned would be impossible in that time and place. And then it became unnecessary. I'd thought it was my father's iron hand that was killing my mother, but it was something even harder. Liver cancer. Which remained undiagnosed until it was too late because my father didn't trust doctors or care to pay out money he didn't have to. By the time I turned seventeen, right at the beginning of my senior year of high school, she died. I sat up half the night with her and held her hand as she went. I could actually feel her spirit exit from her. After it was all done, I went to tell my father, and when I found him, he was with Shelly du Pré, the biggest slut on Pigeon Bayou.

"If I'd had a gun, I'd have killed him on the spot. I actually went home to get one, but when I got back to Shelly's, he was gone. Out into the swamps on one of his boats to boss one of his crews like it was just one more work day. I went home, wanting to cry for my mother, but I couldn't. My hatred for my father was too strong. It wiped away everything else. At first, I was going to kill him when he got home, but by the time he had, I'd fallen asleep. And the next morning, the hate was still there, but it had transmuted into something more implacable than the simple desire to just gun him down.

"What happened was that I realized I was wrong to hate him for that one indiscretion. No, I hated him for all the indiscretions and lapses and deliberate cruelties. In fact, I realized that I'd always hated him for those and for his temerity in spawning a progeny of loathing and despair such as I'd become. I knew right then, at that moment, that only I could wrest myself from the pits of self-contempt into which I had thrown myself.

"I made plans, similar to the ones I'd made for my mother and myself, though now, she would accompany me only in spirit. I would finish high school then go to college and make something of myself— something greater than my father ever imagined. Then I'd come back and lord it over him before I beat him to death with my own hands.

"I have but two tragedies in my life. One is that my father was shot to death by Shelly du Pré's husband before I had the chance to kill him more painfully. The second is that, no matter what I've done, all that I've accomplished is tainted by the spirit of his blood, and I'm never going to feel either remorse or satisfaction at his death. Nor am I going to feel personal satisfaction in my own life. He wasn't evil, but maybe he was worse—he was the embodiment of a crude and cruel weight that occluded his spirit. And no matter how valiantly my mother's blood strives for the light inside of me, my father's pulls me toward the ground.

"It wasn't until he died that I understood what a dutiful son I'd been—how I'd tried with conscious deed as well as unconscious thought to do as he wanted and be what pleased him. But if he wanted anything, it was something I couldn't give, and only pain brought him pleasure. He needed a jolt to get through the stupefaction of his crude senses. When he died, though, I came to my own senses as if emerging from a shadow. I realized that it all comes down to this: Some are afraid of life, and some are not. And with that, I knew I no longer had to make a show of being something that I was not, and I could be myself. Unfortunately, that self all too often resembles my father.

"I can't help it. As someone else once said, I am what I am, and that's all that I am. Not much, unfortunately, penetrates my senses anymore, so I have to have relatively powerful stimuli for me to feel anything. I can admit this because, intellectually, I am not especially impaired. My IQ is respectable, and my powers of ratiocination are fine. But let's just say I'm not the sensitive sort.

"That's why I became a predator, and after a while, being from superstitious stock and believing in sympathetic magic, I began eating only predator flesh, never that of a strict herbivore. And after another long while, I came to realize that man is Earth's greatest predator. That's what I want to be. The greatest predator of them all."

30

"BRANDY, SIR?" HAYES ASKED AS he cleared the table of the meal, eaten largely in silence.

"Two," Banning said.

"One," Guthrie said.

"You don't care for brandy?" Banning asked.

"I don't care to drink. Call it an old habit."

"I see." Banning glanced at Guthrie's untouched wine then back at Spencer. "One, then. And bring Mr. Guthrie another glass of water." After Hayes left the room, Banning turned to Guthrie. "As one hunter to another, I'd like to discuss technique."

"I'm not sure I can help you much there. You've got all the trophies, and I've never been hunting in my life."

"You hunted and found me, despite the fact that I remained well in the background of this affair."

"That wasn't much," Guthrie said. "Like I told you before, I burgled Adriana's apartment and found the invitation you sent. After that, I just had to do a little bullying, and here I am."

"But why did you suspect Adriana of involvement? She had no obvious connection to Graham's disappearance."

"Maybe not, but she knew about the landscapes Howard was painting—or at least one of them—and she didn't want to admit it. And she was too glib in professing her ignorance. Plus, she didn't seem particularly concerned that he'd disappeared."

"It's the instinct," Banning nodded.

"I knew she knew something," Guthrie shrugged. "That's all."

Hayes returned with Banning's brandy and Guthrie's water then took the rest of the dishes into the kitchen.

"What is Adriana's involvement?" Guthrie asked as Banning swished the brandy around in the snifter.

"You don't know? I'm astonished."

"I know she somehow gave Graham the ability to create that painting."

"Yes," Banning said, and he took a reflective sip of his brandy. "As I said earlier, Adriana has certain powers."

"But what's your connection to her. You've known her a long time?"

"A long time, yes, but I can't say I really know her," Banning clarified. "I met her about a year after I got out of college. I'd done well in school but was at loose ends and didn't know what I wanted to do with my life, so I was still working as a roughneck on the Gulf rigs. One night, on one of my off weeks, some friends and I were cruising the French Quarter in New Orleans. We were pretty drunk, and at one point, we stumbled down a side street to take a piss. There was this fortune teller's shop a couple of blocks down, and the sign was lit, so my friends convinced me to go in. I was drunk enough to do it, but not without some trepidation. I'd grown up in southern Louisiana, and people there don't take vodou or witchcraft lightly, even the cheap sort practiced by gypsy fortune tellers.

"There was a good-looking older woman inside, and she started out with a Tarot deck, but she'd barely laid out the cards when she scooped them up and gave me a powerful look. And I mean powerful. I was young and drunk, but something in her stare gave me pause. She put the cards away and called out toward the back. A moment later, a young woman in her early twenties appeared. Beautiful as all get out. She looked a lot like the older woman, and I supposed she was her daughter. The fortune teller told the young woman to get her bones, and the girl left, but she was back in a minute with a small black cloth bag that she handed to the fortune teller. The woman shook the bag a few times, and it rattled, then she dumped the contents onto the table.

"It was, as she'd said, a bag of bones. I don't know what kind. They didn't look like chicken bones. They were all small and dried and almost black from use. As soon as they scattered onto the table,

236

the woman bent over them for a few moments, then she looked up at me. She beckoned to the girl, who came close enough for the woman to whisper something into her ear. The girl looked at me with this blank sort of stare, then she left the room.

"'What do you see?' I asked, though I confess I felt pretty spooked.

"'In a moment,' the fortune teller said. She said she wanted to consult the tea leaves. Sure enough, the young woman came back in a few minutes with a cup of tea that the fortune teller insisted I drink. It didn't taste all that good, and I've never been a tea drinker, but something about the older woman made me comply. When I was done, she took the cup from me and stared into it for a few moments.

"'Well, what is it?' I demanded. By now, I was getting pretty antsy. 'Love,' she told me. 'You are about to meet the love of your life.' 'I don't love anybody,' I told her. 'And I'll never get married.' She just laughed, and after that, things got strange. The younger woman came back in wearing a peculiar gown, and around her neck was a garland of some kind of pungent herbs. The fortune teller said something in a language I didn't recognize, the young woman bent forward and kissed my forehead, and that was it. Then the fortune teller ushered me out into the night, where my rowdy friends waited impatiently for me."

Banning took another sip of brandy, then sat for a moment, staring into the caramel-colored liquid, a faint smile on his face.

"She was right," he said at last. "I did meet the love of my life, and it was that very night. My friends and I wandered around for another hour or so as the liquor and time gradually took their toll, and they dropped off one by one, leaving me alone. And then I wasn't alone. I don't know where she came from. Hell, I don't even remember where I was. Some bar. At first, I didn't recognize her. She was out of context. But she was young and gorgeous, and she bought me a drink. Then she offered herself to me.

"By the time she'd steered me through a maze of streets to a walkway leading up to a house, I'd sobered enough to realize who she was. 'You're that fortune teller's daughter,' I said. She just smiled and told me to come into the house."

"Adriana."

"Yes. And I went in with her. I don't think I could have helped myself. I was smitten, you see." Banning nodded. "Yep. Full-blown in love. And the fortune teller—Adriana's mother—was right. It was the only time, and it only lasted a couple of hours."

"She probably spiked your drink," Guthrie said. "Or the tea. Love potion number nine."

"You're a cynical man, Guthrie," Banning said, his lips twisting into a rueful frown. "Maybe she did. That's all right. All I can say is, if that was true love, once was enough. It was incredible. Adriana was passionate and insatiable, and I was completely enthralled. We must have fucked five or six times that night, but I was sober enough the first time to realize she was a virgin. Somewhere in there, I was thinking I never wanted it to end. But it did. As soon as morning hit the streets, she turned cold as a dead fish. She told me to get dressed and get out. I tried to protest, but she just shoved me out the door. I didn't understand. Maybe I still don't. But it was over.

"Well, not really over. The emotion and passion had evaporated, but some things lingered. When I got home and cleaned out my pockets, I found a business card that had the name of the owner of a small oil exploration company in Houston. Handwritten on the back of the card were the words, 'Your future lies in his hands, and a married man should have a future and provide for his family.'

"I knew it was from the fortune teller, though at the time, I didn't get the bit about being married or having a family. But I knew, somehow, somewhere deep in my soul, that the words were true, about both the future and marriage. Within a week, I quit my job, packed up my stuff, and drove to Houston. The man whose name was on the card was waiting for me. He gave me a job, showed me the ropes, and promoted me steadily. By the time I was thirty-five, I was running the company for him. When he died five years later, he didn't have any heirs, and he left it to me. I changed the name to Hunter Oil and Exploration, and here I am."

"It sounds like it was payment," Guthrie said. "But for what? Having sex with Adriana?"

"It looks that way, doesn't it? But payment is too cut-and-dried a way to look at it. It turned out that my benefactor was married to the fortune teller, and Adriana was his offspring. And he made it clear to me that I was just as married to Adriana as he was to the fortune teller. He told me that we were just the latest in long line of men who'd mated with the Lycoris women over the centuries, and the pattern was always the same: single men driven by a passion that wasn't wholly their own mating with a Lycoris to produce a daughter who would, in turn, mate with another driven man to produce another daughter."

"So," Guthrie said. "That makes Melanie your daughter."

"Undoubtedly, but so what?" Banning shrugged. "I never knew about her until she was a teenager, and she says as little as possible to me."

"So, it's all about wealth and power?"

"Why not?" Banning acknowledged. "The Lycori—which is how my benefactor referred to them—help their men become wealthy, and in turn, we have to support them. We're like a mutual aid society. His and my contribution was money, but theirs would be more abstract. And sure enough, all those years, I kept getting things in the mail—call them charms. Some were like lockets, only instead of having a picture inside, they'd contain a powder or a seed or something like that. Hell, half the time, I couldn't tell what it was. And sometimes there'd be a slip of paper with some writing on it. More like a pictogram than writing sometimes. Probably some sort of hex symbols to help oil the machinery, so to speak."

"So you're just an old married couple who hate each other's guts but can't separate because of legal and financial entanglements," Guthrie said, thinking, I'll have to warn Howard and Diane not to get like that.

Banning chuckled, then peered at Guthrie. "You don't seem surprised by any of this. Or skeptical."

"Let's just say I've seen the efficacy of such things before. You've met my watchdog." Guthrie sure wasn't going to tell Banning about the protective talisman tattooed into the flesh below his navel. Banning would probably skin it off and hang it on his wall.

"Watchdog? Ah, yes. The protection on your house." He took a sip of his brandy then said, "Anyway, not long after my benefactor died, I had a surprise visit from my old paramour. She was older, obviously, but still a strikingly good-looking woman. She was accompanied by her mother and a teenage girl who looked like her. They all looked like triplets born two decades apart. Adriana didn't formally introduce me to the girl, but I realized she must be my daughter. Adriana told me she was going to move to Houston. She didn't want to rekindle the relationship, if you can call a one-night stand of frantic fucking a relationship. At least not the sexual part. And frankly, I didn't want that, either. Love isn't part of my life, and I get all the sex I want from women who don't demand love in return.

"I suppose I should have smelled something back then, but I had other fish to fry, and I didn't really pay attention. She did want more money. Not exorbitant amounts, at least. Just enough to buy her shop and the warehouse, which was easy enough to do. And that's where matters rested for ten years. I saw her only rarely, and Melanie never acted like she gave a shit if I was her father or not, so their presence didn't bother me much. Then, about two years ago, Adriana said she wanted several things from me. The first was to find an artist for her. She didn't have a particular artist in mind, but she did have some parameters. He—and it had to be a man, and an unmarried, childless, heterosexual man, at that—had to be an excellent landscape painter approaching the top of his form who lived locally. I was to find such a painter and tell her who he was. That was it.

"It was a strange request, but Adriana is a strange woman. And, I know nothing about art. I much prefer my trophies. They speak to me in ways that paintings can't. But how could I refuse? I was wealthy and independent thanks to our liaison, whatever its purpose was to her. Besides, as you implied earlier today, Adriana is the only person who makes me the least bit...let's not say afraid. Cautious. She does seem to have some sort of otherworldly power. So I found Gavin O'Neil, who was knowledgeable enough, and unscrupulous enough, to help me in my search. He turned up Howard Graham."

"She didn't tell you that she wanted him to paint a painting that would open a gateway into another world?"

"I'm not surprised you know that since you've seen the smaller painting. Actually, she did, which surprised me since Adriana is never one to give me or anyone else any kind of power over her. But she had to. She's after something—a drug plant that she thinks will confer....I'm not sure what. Wisdom, she thinks. Or power. But she can't go out there unprotected because the other world has dangerous creatures. I have to admit that, at that point, protecting Adriana from anything wasn't high on my list of priorities. But the mention of hunting opportunities unheard of before intrigued me since I've grown bored of even the most dangerous animals here on Earth. I also realized that I could use such a portal to dispose of my enemies permanently and without an untidy mess. And I assure you, I have many of those. And now that I've seen things moving around in Howard's painting, I can't wait to get out there and hunt them."

"How does Adriana know about that other world out there?" Guthrie asked. "Or how to give Howard the power to paint a gateway to it?"

Banning shrugged.

"Two of her secrets," he said, "but she did tell me the Lycori have been working on this for centuries. Apparently from some sort of collective vision."

"It might interest you to know that she has an ulterior motive."

"Adriana always has an ulterior motive." Banning sat back, nodding, lips pursed and eyes narrowed. "Okay, I'll bite. What is it?"

"You know all those monsters you're aching to hunt? There's something even worse out there. Adriana believes it will help her out, but I don't think she knows what she's dealing with. Graham says that this thing, whatever it is, is what created all those monsters you're so eager to hunt. Something that not only corrupts the plants and animals but that warps the landscape itself."

If Guthrie thought the idea would spook Banning, he was dead wrong, and he knew it in an instant as the man's eyes lit up almost feverishly.

"So you said before. This Angra Mainyu thing. Howard talks about it, too, but he's half-crazed and would say anything to stop painting."

"Half-crazed or not, I'd listen. Nobody knows that world better than him, except maybe Adriana. And I'd trust Howard over her any day."

Banning's eyes turned shrewd, then he smiled.

"I am listening, and I hope he's right. I've always searched for the ultimate predator. Until now, that was man, but maybe there's something even more challenging."

"It doesn't bother you that that thing might get out and create the same hell on Earth as it has in that world?"

"I doubt that Adriana is foolish enough to do anything to endanger herself, and I certainly won't. I can take enough men and weapons out there to kill anything that lives. But speaking of hell, would you like to have a look at the painting?"

"Lead on," Guthrie said, feeling a dark futility settle over him and knowing that some things can't be eliminated by bullets.

31

THEY ROSE, AND AS THEY left the dining room, Stewart and Talbot fell in behind them. The way led back toward Banning's office. Inside, Banning went to the metal door set in the left side of the back wall and punched a code into the keypad lock. A humming click sounded, and Banning swung the door open and ushered Guthrie inside.

The room was about the same size as Banning's office, but it was only sparsely occupied. A pair of leather easy chairs and ottomans separated by a side table were arranged along the left side, but that was the extent of the furnishings. Instead, a taxidermied grizzly bear stood behind the chairs, and the majority of the floor space and mahogany-paneled walls were laden with trophies of predators Banning had killed. Most were big cats, but there were bears, wolves, and even a wolverine. A condor, its massive wingspread nearly spanning the room, was suspended from the ceiling. Four eagles surrounded the condor, like a squadron of fighter planes accompanying a giant bomber. Glass-fronted cases built into the wall behind the bear and to the right of the door displayed nearly two dozen hunting rifles, a few carbines, and eight or ten shotguns, many with ornate engraving on their metal parts. Fifteen or so handguns of varying calibers and models rounded out the collection.

A second metal door that looked like it belonged on a vault stood open in the long wall to their right, swung into the room beyond. The odd addition to the south wing of the house. As Guthrie turned to face the opening, his protective talisman felt like the little manlike figures that surrounded the quartered square were dancing beneath his skin. Banning led him across the threshold.

The room they entered was about the size of a large one-car garage and was constructed entirely of concrete except for the door they'd just entered and the roll-up garage door filling the wall to their right. There was a light switch next to the door, but Banning didn't bother flipping it because the room was completely lit by light streaming in through what appeared to be another garage door at the opposite end. A door that looked out on another world.

The painting was tightly set into a large niche in the concrete wall, and the niche had a gate of heavy steel bars that presently stood open. A table covered with painting supplies stood near the painting, and Howard Graham was in front of the painting, a look of intense concentration on his face that did not fade when he turned to see who'd entered.

"Keep painting," Banning ordered, then, as Howard turned back to his work, Banning waved around the room. "I had this specially designed. The walls are a foot thick and reinforced with carbon steel rods. Same for the roof, and the floor is even thicker. And this," he ran fingers along the edge of the metal door, "is solid and seals hermetically when it's closed. Same with the roll-up door, which also is made of carbon steel." He indicated the real garage door in the wall to their right. "Cost me a fucking fortune. Not even a whisper of air can get in or out. You could store gold in here and feel secure."

Guthrie wasn't really listening. Instead, he was looking at the painting. Through it.

At first glance, the landscape appeared to be normal enough, though the plants that were visible looked a bit odd. But at least they weren't the pustular, corrupted abominations that masqueraded as plants in the small painting Guthrie had already seen. But then, Diane had described that landscape as being normal enough when she'd seen it, and Howard himself said he'd seen it change before his eyes into the horrific parody of landscape and life it now depicted. Howard also had said this landscape had changed, too, though only in relatively minor detail. It didn't look any different to Guthrie than when he'd briefly glimpsed it in Lycoris's warehouse. Except for the three monstrous creatures that now inhabited it.

244

Only a dozen or so feet away, squatted a hideous cross between a bulldog and a toad covered with mangy brown fur. It was about the size of a hyena, but squatter. Its gaping mouth bristled with yellow fangs. On a nearby rock sat another pterodactyl-like thing—not the same one Guthrie had seen through the smaller painting, but about the same size and just as malevolently warped. The third creature was like a huge, tumorous sea urchin. Its misshapen, red and yellow mottled, slime-covered blob of a body was five or six feet in diameter, and its three-foot spines jerked spasmodically as the flesh beneath them twitched and writhed. All three were staring—if the sea urchin had eyes—into the room, as if they could see in as easily as the humans inside could see out.

Even as Guthrie watched, the bulldog toad lunged toward the painting, snaggletoothed mouth agape, revealing a purple slab of tongue with serrated edges. Guthrie flinched involuntarily as it hit the other side of the painting and fell back. It made several more lunges, but Howard didn't seem startled. He merely stopped painting until the thing finally backed off.

"Don't worry," Banning laughed. "The painting isn't fully open. Not yet. But Howard tells me it will be tonight. I think he'll have to do the last few brush strokes with the gate closed. Carefully, so he doesn't lose an arm. Don't you think so, Howard?"

Graham stiffly ignored Banning, who didn't seem to care.

Despite his revulsion, Guthrie couldn't help but be fascinated by the landscape and the horrible creatures inhabiting it. He stepped closer to get a better look, but Banning stopped him with a hand on his arm.

"You may look, Guthrie, but Stewart will shoot you if you attempt to touch. I can't afford to have Graham's work spoiled. Not now."

"I hear you," Guthrie said, pulling away but still staring.

He not only could see the creatures moving, but saw dust being raised by a slight breeze. And he thought he caught a medley of odors that blended vegetable rot, hot brass, ozone, and fetor. Was it warm or cold out there? Although the terrain was not melted or fused, it looked like much the same environment as he'd seen in the smaller painting. Even the odors were familiar, though less redolent of fungus and rot.

"Think of it," Banning said. "Monsters just waiting to be hunted. My own private monster game preserve. Safaris from Hell opens for business the day after tomorrow. I can barely wait."

"Are you sure you can shoot those things?" Guthrie asked.

"If they can kill and eat each other," Banning assured him, "I can kill them."

Guthrie didn't bother to tell him that some things that lived can't be killed—at least not by conventional means. He didn't think the argument would make any real difference. Banning was the sort who just wouldn't understand, and he'd already rejected the idea that he might not be a match for every predator he encountered.

"I hope so," he told Banning, "because I'd hate to be out there if they couldn't be."

"You won't have to worry about that," Banning assured him. "I have other plans for you. Before Safaris from Hell start, you and I are going to have our own little safari. A warm up just to get my juices flowing for the main event."

"What's that supposed to mean?"

"Let me show you something. Back in the trophy room." Stewart and Talbot drew their weapons and pointed them at Guthrie.

"It's your show," Guthrie shrugged.

He followed Stewart back into the room right outside the vault. Talbot came right behind, with Banning trailing.

"Talbot, let's show Mr. Guthrie the real trophies."

Talbot opened a drawer in the side table sitting next to the leather easy chair, pulled out a remote control, and thumbed it. A humming sounded from the gun cases, and one section of them swung away, revealing a glassed-fronted display hidden in an alcove. Mounted inside were more of Banning's trophies—the most disturbing Guthrie had yet seen in this fortress dedicated to the predatory instinct.

They were the heads of men. Seven of them. They were mounted in two rows, with plenty of room for more.

"He was a mercenary," Banning said, pointing to each one in turn. "A Chinese kung fu expert, another big game hunter, a Maori warrior, another mercenary, a Japanese karate expert, and this last one was a decorated Army Ranger. He was the toughest to bring down."

"I don't suppose any of them got much of a chance to fight back," Guthrie said.

"You are a predator, are you not?" Banning asked as Guthrie surveyed the gristly scene. "A hunter of men? That makes you, like them, the ultimate prey, at least here on Earth. So tomorrow, Mr. Guthrie, I'll be hunting you. And be assured—I will catch you and kill you. And when I'm done, I'm going to eat you, just as I do all the predators I hunt. Just as I ate them. Your trophy will go right up there." He pointed to the empty space to the right of the Army Ranger.

If Guthrie could have, he'd have killed Banning on the spot. But he'd never have made it closer than a muscle flinch.

"Leslie Banks got there first," he said.

"This isn't a movie, Guthrie. And you won't be taking Miss Weston and Graham away on a boat while I die on a window sill. Instead, you'll be up there with them." He gestured with his chin toward the heads in the alcove. "And Miss Weston and Graham will be...how shall I put it? Art history."

"What are you going to do with them?"

"They're prey," Banning said with a dismissive wave. "I hunt only predators, not prey. But my lion and tiger have to eat to keep up their strength before they are hunted themselves, and they have to maintain their hunting edge. I'll let Miss Weston and Graham loose on the preserve, and my pets will take care of them and get a little exercise to boot."

"Let them go," Guthrie said. "They know nothing of any of this," he waved around the room.

"Ah, but you do, and they'll know I've done something to you if I let them go and they never see you again." Banning shook his head. "No, I'm afraid it was destined to come down to this. But you have to acknowledge that I gave you a final meal fit for a condemned man, did I not?"

"I take no solace in being fattened up for the kill," Guthrie said. "Are you going to give me a weapon to even things up?"

"I'm a sporting man, Guthrie, not a fool." Banning turned to Stewart. "I think it would be best if Mr. Guthrie spent the night in a cage. Otherwise, he might be tempted to do something foolish." He looked back at Guthrie. "Until tomorrow, then."

Prodding Guthrie with his gun, Stewart, followed by Talbot, took Guthrie to the predator barn and locked him in his old cage between the lion and tiger. Then they left, turning out the lights, leaving Guthrie in darkness heavy with the rank odor of the big cats.

32

"HAVE A COMFORTABLE NIGHT?" STEWART asked, then he nodded to Talbot, who tossed four energy bars and a plastic canteen in a nylon sleeve through the bars.

Guthrie managed to catch the canteen, and in a moment, he'd scooped up the energy bars. He put three into his pocket and tore open the fourth and took a bite.

"Mr. Banning doesn't want to take unfair advantage by hunting a starving, thirsty animal," Stewart said. "When the door opens, you'll have half an hour lead time before Mr. Banning comes after you."

"Alone?" Guthrie asked.

Stewart gave a chuckle.

"Of course not. Hayes will go with him. The rest of us will patrol the perimeter."

"Just another caged hunt," Guthrie said dryly.

"You don't expect him to let you walk, do you?"

A walkie-talkie clipped to Stewart's belt crackled, and a voice Guthrie recognized as Banning's asked, "Is he ready?"

Stewart unclipped the walkie-talkie and raised it to his mouth.

"Affirmative, sir."

Stewart re-clipped the walkie-talkie.

"Ready or not, it's time," he said to Guthrie. "When that door opens, you'd better skedaddle, because he'll shoot you in here as readily as he will out on the grounds."

The door in the outer wall opened, and Guthrie hurried through it and the gate beyond. In a few moments, the compound was hidden by the patchy scrub forest that covered the ranch. He tried to keep his pace at a steady trot, wondering if video surveillance cameras hidden in the trees were watching his progress. Banning might not consider that sporting, but Guthrie wouldn't put it past him. Banning was the sort who had to win, whatever the stakes or cost and whatever the method. He'd cheat then smile up at Guthrie's head on the wall, call it a fair hunt, and brag about it to his next victim.

Guthrie was determined to make it as unfair as possible. He figured Banning would expect him to try to use evasive tactics and maybe even circle back around and attempt to get into the ranch house. But Guthrie had other plans, and he also had a pretty good sense of where he was, which direction he had to go, and how far his destination was. And once he was out of sight of the compound, he didn't waste a moment in heading north, toward the dry stream bed he'd scouted the day of his capture. The place he'd been rousted by the two game wardens.

The place where his guns were hidden in a clump of weeds half a mile beyond the fence line. Thank goodness it hasn't rained, he thought.

He kept up the pace for twenty minutes then paused to take a sip of water. As he stood there, hoping to hell he was going in the right direction, a thought struck him, and he looked more closely at the canteen. It was an ordinary plastic canteen available at any number of camping supply stores: a white plastic bottle covered by a lightweight dark blue nylon sleeve to which the web shoulder strap was sewn. Out of curiosity, Guthrie pulled the bottle out of the sleeve and turned the sleeve upside down.

A small black square fell out onto the ground. As Guthrie picked it up, he immediately recognized it as a homing chip.

You fucker, he thought. So much for a sporting chance.

But the presence of the chip meant that Guthrie would have to alter his tactics. He couldn't just head straight for his guns, because Banning already knew exactly where he was and his bearings and probably would try to head him off on one of the dirt roads that crossed the ranch. And it would take Guthrie several minutes to get through the wire fencing at the bottom of the gully—precious minutes that would give Banning plenty of time to catch up.

Guthrie stuck the plastic bottle back into the sleeve, slipped the homing chip into his pocket, and set off again, this time due west. This would take him a little while, but it also would make it look like he did intend to circle back toward the ranch house.

After he'd trotted in that direction for another twenty minutes, he judged he'd gone far enough. He tossed the chip into a small mass of prickly pear cactus, turned to the north again, and ran.

He had to get to the gully before Banning homed in on the chip and began tracking him in earnest. And Guthrie was under no illusion that Banning wouldn't be able to track him. The man was an experienced hunter, and Guthrie, like any prey, would leave a trail.

He hadn't gone more than a mile before he heard the faint roar of small engines behind him. Banning and Hayes must be using those Kawasaki four-wheelers.

Guthrie ran faster, dodging branches and swerving around brush and cacti, often not fast enough. At last, scratched and jabbed, he forced himself to slow to a steady trot. If he kept up the pell-mell pace, he'd leave a path that even a blind man could follow. He listened, but the sound of his pursuers' engines had faded. They must be circling the area where he'd dropped the chip, trying to pick up his trail.

Half an hour later, he reached the fence line and stared at the barrier in front of him: two lines of ten-foot chain-link twenty feet apart, each bedded in a concrete ribbon and topped with razor wire, with the dirt service road running between them. He knew that the gully was somewhere east of his current position. Keeping back in the trees, he turned right and trotted parallel to the fence line.

It was just as well that he kept hidden. Not ten minutes later, the sound of engines came up from behind him, and he crouched behind a short scrub oak, nervously watching the road through gaps in the skimpy foliage.

Two four-wheelers approached from the west, going slowly. Banning was in the lead, Hayes flanking him a dozen feet back. Both men wore side arms, and AR-15s were jammed into boots slung on the four-wheelers. Banning was scanning the road, obviously looking for footprints, and Guthrie was glad he hadn't climbed the first fence and stepped out onto the dusty surface.

After a few moments, the four-wheelers passed, but Guthrie remained where he was for ten minutes longer before he set out again, and even then, he moved deeper into the woods. He wasn't worried that he'd miss the gully because he knew it stretched for some distance into the ranch, but he didn't want to blunder into one of his pursuers lying in wait.

He didn't see anyone, and fifteen minutes later, he found a gully. He wasn't sure if it was the right one, but he didn't remember any others along this section of the ranch, so he turned and followed it toward the fence line. There, he found the black plastic pipe that channeled water beneath the dirt road between the fences, and he knew he was at the right place.

The dirt road looked empty as far as he could see in either direction, though he knew that Banning or his men might be hiding anywhere, just as he'd done, and he'd be none the wiser until a bullet shattered the life from him. At least it wouldn't be a head shot. That would spoil the trophy.

Guthrie had no choice but to brave the openness and get past the barriers that separated him from the outside. In an instant, he scrambled down to the semi-circle of chain-link that had been wired across the mouth of the pipe. As with the other end of the pipe, fencing was wired across it. The wire ties the held it in place would have confounded an animal, but they were no different than those used for any chain-link fence, and he had the knife Diane had stolen for him. He pulled it from the makeshift sheath tied to his leg and went to work.

In two minutes, he'd undone enough of the ties to bend back a flap of the chain-link, squeeze through into the pipe, and shimmy through the narrow conduit. The ties holding the semi-circle of wire covering the pipe's egress were tougher to undo because he had a hard time reaching them from his cramped position in the pipe.

He had fewer than half of the ties undone when he heard the muted snarl of one of the four-wheelers coming up the dirt road. Working frantically, he got enough of the ties loose to worm through the opening, and he scrambled down the gully and just made it around the first bend before the four-wheeler stopped where the pipe was. He halted, not wanting to make any sound that might bring pursuit, and listened as the four-wheeler's engine idled. Then he heard the crunch of boots on the gravel in the road. The footsteps stopped.

Guthrie flattened himself against the gully wall. If the pursuer came through the fence and into the gully, Guthrie would have no choice but to try to take him with the knife before he could use his gun. But instead of the sound of someone wriggling through the fence, Guthrie heard a voice.

"Porter here. I'm at the creek at the northeast corner," he said. "It looks like he went through the fence. Do you want me to follow?"

"No. Stay where you are," replied another voice, recognizable as Banning's despite the crackling hiss of walkie-talkie static. "I'll be there in three minutes. Just make sure he doesn't double back. Johnson and Gonzalez are out on the road, and when I get there, we'll go through the fence after him and trap him between us."

"Copy," Porter said. "Out."

Guthrie crept far enough down the gully that Porter couldn't hear him. Then, keeping his head low, he hurried along the channel toward the road.

He reached the spot where he'd hidden his guns and scrambled out of the gully, hoping to hell they were still there and that he'd find them before Johnson and Gonzalez arrived. They were, and he'd just finished strapping the .380 to his ankle and clipping the S&W holster onto his belt when he faintly heard a pair of car doors slam from the direction of the road. After jacking a shell into the chamber of the S&W, he quickly scurried to the far side of a clump of brush and weeds, hoping he hadn't left too obvious a trail, but knowing he had. The dirt he'd displaced when he climbed out of the gully and walked to his guns would tell the tale even to an urban dweller. But he didn't want to be trapped in the gully when Johnson and Gonzalez arrived, and they'd probably figure he'd be down there, trying to keep out of sight.

The two showed up moments later. Johnson was edging stealthily down the lip of the gully on Guthrie's side, Gonzalez on the other. As with the men on the four-wheelers, both carried AR-15s and side arms. Armed only with his two pistols, Guthrie knew his survival depended on surprise.

As the men neared, Guthrie tracked Gonzalez, aiming at his chest. A few seconds later, the man's eyes focused on the gully wall beneath Johnson's feet, and Guthrie knew he'd seen the spot where Guthrie had come out. Because of the angle, Johnson wasn't yet aware, but Gonzalez started to lift his eyes and the barrel of his assault rifle to point the way.

Guthrie shot him, and as he tumbled back onto the dusty ground, Guthrie jerked his gun toward Johnson.

The man was fast as a snake, whirling and crouching as he whipped the barrel of his assault rifle in the direction of the shot, firing even as he turned. The AR-15 was fully automatic, but Guthrie, still hidden in the weeds, didn't make an obvious target, and his reactions were heightened by desperation. He fired again, twice. One of his bullets caught Johnson in the right shoulder, lifting and turning him, and the second tore through the left side of his head.

With a spasmodic lurch, Johnson dropped the assault rifle, pitched over the lip of the gully, and disappeared from sight.

Guthrie surged to his feet and dashed to the edge and looked down. Johnson lay unmoving in a crumpled heap. Across the gap, Gonzalez was moaning and twisting in pain.

Shouts came from the direction of the fence line.

Guthrie picked up Johnson's assault rifle and ran for the road. As he came out onto the blacktop, he saw the game wardens' dark blue pickup parked on the shoulder, almost in the same spot it had been parked just a few days ago. He hurried over to it and saw keys dangling from the ignition. In a second, he was inside. He started the truck and, as quickly as he could, turned it around on the narrow road then slammed down on the accelerator.

Shots rang out behind him, the back window shattered, and two rounds starred the windshield to his right. He threw a glance in the rearview mirror and saw Banning and Hayes behind him, assault rifles aimed. Porter wasn't with them. Guthrie ducked as more bullets pierced the truck, then he was around a long bend and headed toward the ranch's front gate.

He got there quickly, but Banning must have radioed ahead, because Spencer was waiting and both the gates were shut. Not that it mattered. Guthrie rammed through them.

Spencer was just lifting his gun when the impact flung the second gate toward him. At the same time, Guthrie poked the barrel of his assault rifle out of the window and fired a short burst. The AR was a fully-automatic model. He didn't expect to hit anything; he just wanted to give Spencer something extra to think about.

Spencer ducked instinctively, the gate barely missing him, and as Guthrie wheeled the pickup through the gap, he fired again to keep him there. And then he was past, and Spencer leapt up and shot at the retreating vehicle, but his aim was off, and in a moment, the pickup was out of sight.

Guthrie figured he didn't have much time. He had to get to the house, find Diane and Howard, and get them out before Banning and the others arrived.

He doubted he'd be able to do it, but he had no other choice than to try.

33

JUST AS THE COMPOUND CAME in sight, Guthrie stopped the pickup. He couldn't see anyone, but he suspected that Norris, at least, would be around, and maybe Stewart, Talbot, and Porter, too. Banning would have left somebody to watch over Diane and Howard in case Guthrie managed to circle back. And now they'd know he was coming.

He pulled the magazine out of the assault rifle and checked it. Only four rounds left. He wished he'd had time to get another magazine off the dead game warden, but as it was, he'd barely escaped before Banning showed up. But there were still nine rounds in the S&W, and the .380's magazine held eight. It would have to do.

He floored the accelerator, and headed for the compound's gate, quickly picking up speed. Seconds later, he ducked as the pickup, jolting, smashed through the gate, tearing it out of its track and twisting it aside. Guthrie slewed the pickup to a stop in front of the main house, dust boiling from beneath its wheels. Opening the door, he rolled out onto the ground just as Norris popped out of the front door, blasting away with an AR-15. The pickup's windshield shattered, but the cloud of dust obscured Guthrie's exit, and he came around the back end and pulled the assault rifle's trigger.

The four-round burst was surprisingly brief, but Norris staggered back against the door frame, chest shattered. He crashed to his knees and fell across the threshold.

Guthrie went up the steps to the porch in two quick bounds, casting aside the empty AR. Pausing only to pick up the dead man's assault rifle and strip a belt-pouch of extra magazines from his waist,

Guthrie shoved the body out of the way and shut and locked the door. Keeping the assault rifle pointed at the doorway on the far side of the foyer, he moved slowly into the house. If anybody was inside, he'd have heard the shots and would know Guthrie was there.

The house was silent as Guthrie edged into the living room. Then, through the front windows, he saw Porter run around the front right corner of the house. He had to be heading for the back kitchen door. Banning must have sent him back to the house when he and Hayes had gone through the fence after Guthrie. Guthrie hurried to the kitchen and got there just as the door was opening. He leveled the AR-15 and sent three rounds through the panel about chest high and was rewarded by a howl. He didn't know if he'd hit Porter or not, but he wouldn't be trying the door again anytime soon—at least, not until Banning and the others arrived. Guthrie turned and raced toward the stairs leading to the second floor, shouting Diane and Howard's names.

As he rounded the top of the stairs, he was rewarded by a pair of slugs that gouged chunks out of the corner. He dropped back and risked a quick peek. Brother Gregory stood in front of one of the doors, holding a pistol. He fired another shot, but Guthrie had already jerked back. Guthrie jammed the barrel of the AR around the corner and ripped off four shots. Brother Gregory was completely exposed in the hall, and Guthrie heard him grunt, and then there was the sound of something heavy hitting the floor. He took another peek and saw Gregory lying in a heap.

The man might have been playing possum, but his pistol was on the floor about four feet from him, and Guthrie didn't have time to waste. He dashed around the corner, keeping his gun on Gregory. When he got to him, he saw that the man was dead. He scooped up the priest's fallen pistol—a Sig Sauer 9mm—and yelled Diane's name. Her voice answered from behind the door. It was locked, but the Sig Sauer was a universal key. Warning her to stay back, he blew the lock out and kicked open the door. She came out, eyes wide with worry and stress but with no sign of panic.

"We have to hurry," Guthrie said. "Let's get Howard."

He turned to start for the stairs, but Diane stopped him.

"He finished the painting last night, and they moved him up here."

"I'm in here," came the artist's voice even as Diane pointed to the door across the hall.

"Get away from the door!" Guthrie shouted, and he shot out the lock. In two seconds, Howard was beside them.

"Let's get the hell out of here," Guthrie snapped. "My truck's outside."

Guthrie in the lead, they headed down the stairs and turned left into the foyer. But as soon as they had, Guthrie heard the snarl of four-wheelers and shouts come from beyond the front door.

"It's them," he said.

"What now?" Diane asked.

"There's a phone in the kitchen," he said. "Keep low. Call the police." But before she could go, he said, "Wait."

She stopped, and he drew the .380, pulled back on the slide, and handed it to her.

"Porter was out back. If you see him or anybody else but Howard and me, don't hesitate to use this. Here," he said to Howard, handing over Brother Gregory's Sig Sauer. "Take this one."

Howard turned it over in his hands like it was an alien object.

"I never shot a gun before," the artist said.

"Me either," Diane said. "But I'm going to now if I have to."

"Aim like you're pointing a finger," Guthrie told them. "Hold the butt steady with both hands like this, and keep pulling the trigger until whoever you're shooting at is down. Most of these guys are used to shooting, not being shot at. Remember, it's them or us."

"Okay," Diane said, and she disappeared toward the kitchen.

"Watch the front door," Guthrie told Howard. "Shoot anyone who comes in."

Guthrie turned and edged into the living room to peek through the front windows.

Out in the parking area, four of the Kawasakis were drawn up near the white van. He could see Hayes and Spencer crouched behind the clump of four-wheelers. A second later, Porter ran from behind a tree toward the white van, ducking low. Nothing happened for a few seconds, then Banning, Porter hovering behind him, peered around the front of the van. At that moment, Stewart and Talbot roared into the compound on their own Kawasakis.

Before they could close on the group, Banning waved for them to go around to the back of the house. Kawasaki's snarling, the two men disappeared. As soon as they had, Banning signaled for Hayes and Porter to advance, and the two men started running for the wide front porch.

"Fuck," Guthrie snarled. He swung into the foyer and gestured for Howard to follow, then he hurried toward the kitchen.

Diane was just dropping the phone with a look that said the line was dead when Guthrie saw a shadow darken the holes he'd shot in the door.

He sent another burst through the panel. This time, there was no accompanying howl. Stewart and Talbot were too cool-headed for that. But the shadow backed off.

"This way," Guthrie urged, leading them back toward the front of the house.

It was a dangerous maneuver. Two of the walls—the one at the base of the U-shaped building and the one flanking the long hall to Banning's office were nothing but glass. If Stewart and Talbot were in the pool area, they'd have a clear shot at the fugitives. But the door to Banning's office was only a few long strides from the corner. They might have a chance.

Almost as soon as they emerged around the corner into the hall behind the sliding glass doors, both Stewart and Talbot came around the corner from the kitchen end, saw the fugitives, and started firing. Plate glass shattered, but Guthrie and his friends had a slight head start, and they rounded the corner to the long hall ahead of the bullets, glass showered the floor behind them.

And then, the glass wall of the long hall suddenly became their friend. Because of the oblique angle, Stewart and Talbot's rounds, aimed dead center on the escapees, deflected, and before the two could correct their aims, Guthrie was shoving Diane and Howard into the office and diving in after them. Just as he slammed and locked the door, a rattle of automatic fire came from the front of the house, followed by the sounds of heavy footsteps. Banning, or one of his men, had shot out the front door lock, and they were all inside now, closing in.

A moment later, Banning's voice bellowed out.

"Give it up, Guthrie. You're cornered, and you know what happens to cornered prey."

"They get desperate," Guthrie yelled back. "They kill their hunters."

"Not a chance," Banning said. "You're a dead man, Guthrie."

"I've been there before."

"You're outnumbered and outgunned," Banning pressed. "All we have to do is wait you out. We have plenty of time, and eventually you'll get hungry and weak, and then we'll have you."

"We have to go out there," Guthrie told his companions.

"They'll kill us," Howard said.

"No, not there," Guthrie said. "There." He gestured toward the door that led to Banning's trophy room and the vault.

Diane's eyes widened as the meaning of his words registered. "We can't," she breathed. "Those monsters will kill us."

"We can't stay here," Guthrie pointed out. "Banning is a worse monster than anything out there. In case you haven't been informed, tomorrow he was going to let you and Howard loose and have his lion and tiger hunt you down and eat you."

"What about you?" Diane asked, her face blanching.

"He was going to hunt me himself. I was supposed to be his dinner tonight. Literally."

"Oh, God," she breathed.

Guthrie didn't know the security code to the trophy room, so he simply shot out the lock and kicked open the door. When they were inside, he told Howard and Diane to close the door and block it. They started dragging the easy chairs in front of the door and piling the ottomans and side table on top.

While they did, Guthrie went over to the gun cases and opened the glass doors. He grabbed a pair of pump 12-gauge shotguns and found boxes of double-ought buckshot and more .223 and 9mm ammo in a drawer beneath. There was nothing for the .380. A small range bag sat in a cupboard next to the gun case, and he stuffed it with as much ammo as he could comfortably carry.

By now, Howard and Diane had joined him, and he handed shotguns to them along with a box of shells. He quickly showed them how to load and cock the shotguns and pistols they carried.

Then gesturing for them to follow, he went into the bunker-like room where the painting hung, shutting the door behind.

There was no visible difference in the painting in its niche, but the atmosphere in the room was noticeably denser and warmer than in the trophy room, and the now-familiar brassy and pungent odor of that other world filled the air. The iron gate was fastened over the painting, held in place by two heavy bolts. Clearly, Banning didn't think any of the creatures out there were smart enough or dexterous enough to warrant padlocks. Beyond the bars, the pterodactyl thing wasn't visible. Maybe it had gotten bored waiting. But the two other creatures— the one that resembled a diseased bulldog crossed with an equally diseased toad and the huge spiny blob—were still out there. Both were about fifty feet off to the right side of the gateway, where the mutant bulldog was examining the blob as if looking for a way to get its blunt snout through the protective spikes. The spiny blob probably moved pretty slowly, but the bulldog toad would be a major threat.

Tentatively, Guthrie reached between the bars and through the painting. He quickly withdrew his arm, and there was a taut silence broken after a moment by Banning's voice yelling, "Fuck, they're in with the painting!"

That was followed by the sound of piled up furniture being shoved aside.

"Get back," Guthrie ordered, and when Diane and Howard had stepped back, he pulled out the bolts and swung the gate to the side.

"Come on," he urged. "Out."

"What about those things?" Diane asked, gesturing to the two creatures outside. The sound of the commotion had attracted their attention.

"Run for that," Guthrie said, pointing to a gully a hundred feet to the left of the gateway. "The blob thing doesn't look like it can move very fast, and I'll kill the other one if it comes after us."

He hoped.

The sound of the last of the furniture toppling came dimly through the trophy room door.

"Now!" he yelled. "Run!"

They ran, feet pounding across the hard, dry ground. As soon as they came through the door, the two creatures began to move toward them. The bulldog toad was faster than Guthrie expected, but the humans, driven by desperation, were nearly at the gully by the time it went past the gateway through which they'd come. By then, Banning and his men were in the vault and the thing spotted them, judged them closer, and swerved toward the gateway. Guthrie threw himself into the gully a moment after his companions and peered over the rim.

From outside, the gateway was a strange square hanging suspended in the air about six inches above the ground, showing the inside of the vault, where Banning and his men were backing off as the creature surged toward them. Shots sounded, and the creature jerked and lunged again. Then the air roared as every man in the room emptied his weapon into it.

Blood and flesh erupting from its body, the creature lurched back and fell onto its side, writhing spasmodically, half blocking the gateway.

Banning, ramming another magazine into his assault rifle, leapt over the body and through the gateway. It was obvious that the creature had kept him occupied enough that he hadn't seen which way Guthrie and his friends had gone. He stood there for a moment, casting around. Stewart, Talbot, and the others followed, and they approached the spiny blob, which was still creeping toward them, and gunned it to slimy, squirming shreds.

"Remember, this is Safaris from Hell, Guthrie!" Banning yelled into the bleak air. "You'll be the first thing we hunt. If you live long enough."

34

GUTHRIE AND HIS COMPANIONS WATCHED Banning and his men mill around the gateway for a few minutes, then Banning pointed at the dead toad thing and said something. The distance was too far to hear what he said, but his meaning was clear as Hayes, Porter, and Talbot grabbed the creature's body by various limbs and dragged it with effort into the room. Then Banning, still staring around the barren landscape, backed in after them. He leaned his assault rifle against an inner wall, shut the gate, and yelled something to his men. A moment later, Stewart came up and handed something to Banning. A pair of somethings. Padlocks. Banning fastened them to the gate.

"The bastard's locked us out," Howard snarled.

Banning picked up his weapon, but he didn't leave immediately. Instead, he stood there, scanning the landscape. It was an odd sight watching him stand inside that disembodied rectangle. At last, he grew bored and left the room.

Or, Guthrie thought, maybe he's hungry and wants to see how his fresh kill tastes. He only hoped that it was as toxic as it was deformed. Guthrie sure wouldn't want to eat it. He nodded toward the disembodied gateway.

"Let's go see if we can get in."

As he approached, his tattooed talisman began itching again, and only then did he realize that the sensation had ceased while he and his companions had hidden in the gully. Nor did this place—this world—no matter how repugnant its creatures and plants were, elicit the same disturbing feelings that he'd associated with it when viewing it through the paintings. Guthrie now just felt physically afraid, not unpleasantly repulsed.

But as he neared, the sense of creepy dislocation rose again, and he realized that it was the painting—the gateway—itself, not this world, that produced the impression. Now that the sensation was dissociated from the visual aspects of this world, he recognized it as akin to the feeling he got every time he encountered something that wasn't steeped in one reality or another, such as when he stepped across the threshold of Tereba's mysterious door. When he'd come into contact with Howard's two paintings, it had been easy to conflate that feeling of dislocation with this alien world's desolate and repellent aspects. But this world, no matter how much its plants and animals filled him with fear and loathing, was only a place. Just not a very friendly place, he mused as he filled his lungs. The air was hard to breathe, but that wasn't only because of the pervasive brassy odor mixing with the smells of vegetable decay and animal rot. It was as if it was heavy but without enough oxygen.

When he reached the disembodied square, he put tentative fingertips to it, and they went through, into the vault. He circled behind the gateway and noticed that he couldn't see it at all unless he viewed its front surface. From behind, it was invisible, and he had a clear view of the landscape in front of him.

Diane laughed. "Can you see me?" she asked, leaning to her right as if peering around something.

"Clearly."

"I can't see you at all. Just the room inside."

"Let's see something." Guthrie took a couple of steps forward and reached out. Diane's eyes widened, though she didn't recoil. "That's really weird," she said. "Your hand's coming right out of thin air. What's it feel like?"

"Nothing," he said. "Like nothing's there."

He withdrew his hand, and she tried to touch him, but her hand just went past the bars, into the vault.

Guthrie waved his hand back and forth but couldn't feel the bars. Taking a chance, he stepped completely through the gateway from behind, then turned to stare with his companions into the room that was so close yet so far away.

"Can you shoot off the lock?" Diane asked.

"I could, but they'd hear and come after us."

"Maybe you could hide behind it and shoot them when they come out," Howard suggested.

"I thought of that," Guthrie said. "But Banning will, too. And there are a lot more of them than me and more heavily armed. I wouldn't stand a chance, and then he'd have the two of you." He shook his head. "No, we're going to have to think of something else."

"It's all my fault," Graham said morosely, and he stood there, slump-shouldered.

"You're only guilty of wanting to be a better artist," Guthrie said. "If anybody is guilty, it's Adriana Lycoris."

"She gave me the power, it's true," Graham said. "But I was the one who used it to create this."

"I don't think you created this anymore than you create the people you paint portraits of," Diane said. "You just showed what was there, even if nobody else could see it. Adriana knew, though. She gave you the power—maybe even the compulsion—to see this world and open a way into it, and she did it for a reason. If it hadn't been you, it would have been someone else."

"But it was me. And now you're involved. And Clay."

"Don't worry, Howard," Diane soothed, taking him by the arm. "We'll think of something."

"I don't see what. We're trapped here with a bunch of monsters in front of us, madmen with guns at our backs, and no food and water. In two or three days, if we survive the monsters, we'll be begging Banning to kill us."

"Maybe not," Guthrie said. "Don't forget that you made another painting of this place. Don't you see what that means?"

Graham's eyes lit.

"There's another entrance," he said. "Back in Houston."

"You once said it isn't far from here," Guthrie said hopefully.

"I don't know for sure," Howard said, his brow wrinkling. "When I saw this in my dreams, it was like I was flying over the landscape, and I wasn't paying attention to direction or distance. Walking? I'm not sure. A couple of days, at least. Maybe more."

Guthrie breathed a sigh of relief. Two or three days. They might have a chance.

"What about the monsters?" Howard went on. "We'll never survive long enough."

"We have these," Guthrie indicated their weapons. "And we don't have a choice. We might not survive long enough to get to the other painting, but we sure won't if Banning gets hold of us."

"He was going to feed you and me to the lion and tiger," Diane said.

"What about you?" Howard asked Guthrie.

"He was going hunt and eat me." Guthrie chuckled without humor. "But none of that will happen if we can get to that painting. Do you think you can find it, Howard?"

"How?" Graham answered. "It could be anywhere. There's a whole world out there." He waved his long arms helplessly around.

"Nobody knows this place better than you," Guthrie said. "You told me you'd spent enough time here that it became more real to you than the world outside your studio. You can lead us to the painting."

"I don't know every part of it."

"You don't need to know every part of it," Diane said, putting her arms around Howard's tense, wasted body. "You only have to find the way."

"Yes," Howard said, straightening. "Maybe." He paused and pivoted, staring around at the landscape. But I can't see anything from here. I need to have a wider view."

"Let's climb up there." Guthrie pointed to the ridge to their left —a shoulder of the mountain that Lycoris called Hara Berezaiti. The slope of the ridge was heavily furrowed with gullies and small canyons and looked fairly easy to climb. "Maybe you'll see something you recognize."

"That'll take us all the rest of the day," Howard said.

"We can stay here and wait for Banning's hunting party or more monsters," Diane said. "I think Clay's right. If there's even the faintest chance of finding the other painting, that's our only hope."

Between where they stood and the ridge, the playa was networked with dozens of shallow gullies like the one they'd hidden in, all of which fanned out from the deeper gouges marring the flank of the ridge. Guthrie led them across the flats and between the gullies for as far as he could, then down into one of the deeper ones. That quickly hid them from the square opening back into their own world, but it wouldn't save them from Banning, because their feet left obvious trails across the crusty, dried earth. But Guthrie had suggested the ridge not only to scout the terrain but also to thwart Banning. It was only a matter of time before the hunter came after them, and he'd be using the Kawasaki four-wheelers. The slope would stop those cold, and Banning's party would either have to abandon their vehicles or drive no telling how many miles across unknown territory before the ridge's elevation dropped enough to let the machines cross.

Guthrie took the lead and Howard the rear. All of them kept their guns ready as they entered the gully. The one Guthrie chose ran for about a half a mile before it gradually deepened and narrowed then wound up the side of the ridge. Not long afterward, it became the lower reaches of a shallow, steep cut that climbed between a pair of the ridge's knobby knees and rose up its final elevation. For the most part, the cut wasn't particularly steep and the walking was made even easier by whole stretches where weathered rocks that had tumbled from the sides of the cut formed crude steps.

About half way up and well within the shadows of the valley, they paused to rest. There were no plants at all on the slopes of the ridge, and the terrain spread below them was nearly as barren. But they'd seen no monsters, either, and that was one thing in their favor, at least.

"I wish we could have some of this," Guthrie said, shaking the canteen. "But we don't have much, or food, either, so we're going to have to conserve what we have."

His companions nodded, eyes grim.

Guthrie turned to survey back the way they'd come. Something large and dark-colored was moving slowly and almost aimlessly across the ashen ground. One of the monstrous creatures? Guthrie could see three more, now, at various places on the flats. Two seemed to be converging on the area from which he and his friends had come, perhaps drawn by the sound of gunfire or the scent of blood. More important, he didn't see any human activity.

"Can you see the gateway?" Diane asked.

"Not from here," Howard said. "It's too far, or we're at the wrong angle."

"We better get moving," Guthrie said, and they began climbing the slope again.

The cut widened and grew shallower as they neared the top of the ridge. At last, panting, they scrambled over the rim of the ridge and could get a view of the landscape beyond. Except for Hara Berezaiti rising to their right, the forbidding terrain spread out before them was dominated by arid, rough flats separated by low but rugged ridges and several lowland areas. From their position, they couldn't tell if the lowlands were shallow valleys or hid steep-walled canyons. A solid band of dark, serrated mountains stretched across the horizon. The scenery was similar to what Guthrie had seen in West Texas. No wonder Lycoris had courted Howard, who was experienced in painting such landscapes.

A feature angling across the playa at the far side of the ridge caught Guthrie's eye, and he pointed.

"I don't know much about geology," he said, "but that doesn't look natural."

A wide swath cut across the terrain below. It seemed to have no beginning or end, and at first, Guthrie thought he was seeing a road. Then he realized it couldn't be a road. It was difficult to judge sizes from their height, but the swath had to be two hundred feet across. And though its surface appeared to be paved—or at least much smoother than the surrounding terrain—its color was no different from the earth around. It was as if a huge road grader had crawled across ground, leaving a broad trail of flattened earth and rock. Guthrie recalled spotting something similar through the window of the smaller painting.

"You ever see anything like that? I saw one in the first painting."

"One of Angra Mainyu's trails," Howard replied flatly. "It leaves them like a slug leaves a trail of slime."

"Look," Diane pointed. "There's another over there."

"Or the same one," Howard said.

The swath—or trail, if Howard was right—came out of the desert and approached the ridge before it ran down the length of the ridge toward its lower end then angled off into the desert again.

"Well, whatever made it isn't here," Guthrie said. He turned to Howard. "Can you tell which way we need to go?"

Howard pivoted, scanning the landscape.

"I don't know," he said despairingly. "I don't know where it is."

"Stop looking with your eyes," Guthrie suggested. "You saw this place in dreams and meditative states. Sit down, close your eyes, and do the same."

Howard complied, and his gaunt face went slack as his mind traveled over the landscape. At last he opened his eyes, stood, and pointed.

"That's it," he said excitedly. "See those hills that way, near the horizon? The other painting is just on this side."

"Are you sure?"

The hills looked like a good two-day walk from where they were, and Guthrie didn't want to go there if it wasn't the right place. On the other hand, what other choice did they have except to hang around Banning's room in the probably futile hope that they'd somehow manage to sneak back inside?

"Positive," Graham said.

Guthrie pulled out the canteen and handed it to Diane.

"Only a sip," he warned. "It's all we have."

While they drank, Guthrie glanced at the position of the glaring sun. When they'd first emerged into this world, it had been midway up and to their left. Now it was high and to their right. If they were on Earth, they'd be looking south.

From their vantage, he could see that the space between Hara Berezaiti and the distant chain of hills was filled with rugged flats that were intermittently wrinkled with gullies and low ridges. The mound of a lone low hill lay roughly a third of the way to the hills. It was mashed down the middle, and the elevations that rose on each side looked less than a thousand feet high, though it was difficult to judge from this distance.

"See that?" Guthrie pointed to the hill. "I want to try to reach that by sundown."

"Why that?" Diane asked.

"The monsters seem to stay off the higher elevations. Probably nothing up here for them to eat. Better to be as high up as possible when it gets dark. Do you think you can make it?"

"I'm all right," Diane said, and Howard nodded.

"Good," Guthrie said. "Let's move. We can be sure Banning will be after us as soon as morning comes. And he and his men will be moving fast."

It took them less than an hour to descend the ridge. As they came off the last of the ridge's little foothills, the shallow valleys seaming the ridge's slope degenerated into network of gullies that flattened out as they ran toward a broad dry wash winding across the lowlands a mile or more away. The deeper parts of the dry wash were choked with what seemed to be ragged masses of grayish, brambly looking vegetation, but the ground leveled out considerably to their left, and the vegetation thinned to sparse clumps then withered away altogether near a large circular depression in the sandy soil.

There might be water in the depression, Guthrie thought, but danger probably lurked there as well.

Ten minutes later, they reached the nearest of the swaths stretching across the countryside. Though its color was no different from the earth around, its surface was considerably smoother, something like rough, dull, and pitted glass.

"It almost looks volcanic," Diane said.

"I wonder how far down the melting goes," Guthrie said. He knelt and quickly dug through the sandy soil around the edge of the glassy encrustation, which, here, was brittle enough that he had to take care not to cut himself. He got his arm as deep as his elbow, but he still hadn't found the bottom edge, so he stopped groping through the dirt, got up, and dusted his hands. There'd been no moisture down there, either.

"You think this was left by Angra Mainyu?" he asked, and Howard nodded.

"I watched it leave that trail you saw in the first painting."

"But why...? How...?" Diane began then chuckled dryly. "I don't even know what question to ask."

"How can it leave something like this?" Howard supplied. He shook his head. "I don't know exactly, but it seems to me that Angra Mainyu doesn't consume food, at least not in the sense that we do, or even like the monsters. I think it consumes the organizational structure of reality in any form, maybe even all the way down to molecules."

"That's pretty wild," she said, shaking her head.

"Not really. All living things consume organization to live. They eat structure, break it down into usable components, and restructure it in their own bodies. Plants absorb nutrient structures from the soil to create larger and more sophisticated physical structures, herbivorous animals eat this structure, and carnivorous animals eat the even more organized structure of herbivores. Angra Mainyu isn't limited to absorbing specific forms of energy but can take advantage of any structural organization. It's something like an amoeba of energy—or maybe anti-energy—that envelops reality and consumes the energy that binds it into distinct forms. That's why its trails are like smooth pathways. It absorbs all the energy, leaving a less energetic, fused state in its wake."

"That also might explain why things closest to it warp the most, leaving behind a degraded form," Guthrie said. "Devolution. It makes sense—if something so insane could make sense."

Guthrie scanned the terrain in front of them and saw rough flats sparsely dotted with scrubby brush and trees and occasional clumps of tall, dried out grass. He didn't see anything that resembled a cactus, which was curious is so arid an environment. Maybe cacti hadn't developed on this world. Too bad. He knew that if he found a prickly pear, they'd at least be able to conserve their meager supply of water and food. But he wasn't going to chance eating or drinking anything that might poison them.

Angra Mainyu's trail cut diagonally across his field of vision. Guthrie knew its hard surface would make for easy walking as well as mask their footprints and their direction, but none of the visible swaths ran in the direction he and his friends needed to travel. And while the swaths would give Guthrie a greater range of view and there'd be fewer places for an ambush by one of the creatures, he and his friends would stand out on it like sore thumbs.

At first, keeping to the flats wasn't difficult, and they crossed the second of the melted-looking swaths without incident. Nothing at all grew on the swaths, but Guthrie noticed that the closer a plant was to one of them, the more deformed it was. Those right next to the trails were little more than pustulant blobs and puddles.

They were less than two hundred yards from the dry wash when the pterodactyl creature struck.

It wasn't either of the ones Guthrie had already seen, but its head was just as hideous, though instead of a slavering hole for a mouth, it had a wicked scimitar of a beak. Clumps of scruffy feathers clung to its purple and orange mottled hide, and it was a canny predator. They'd just emerged from a shallow gully, onto a broad hardpan that lead toward a dry wash when it came at them from an angle that wouldn't cast its shadow over them until the last moment. Only Guthrie's constant vigilance saved them.

"Down!" he yelled as the creature swooped low, crooked clutching talons barely missing Howard.

Guthrie fired a burst that tore a pattern in the creature's abdomen, then a second. The thing gave a raucous squawk, lurched to the side, and leaking black blood, banked away.

"Back into the gully!" Guthrie shouted.

They were there in seconds, cowering beneath the low wall as the pterodactyl made a second pass. Either the shots hadn't wounded it severely, or its hunger outweighed its caution. Guthrie figured that no wound would be severe enough to deter it. He only wished the thing would just go away. He'd already used up a third of one of his precious magazines on it, and he'd probably have to use the rest to bring it down. If he was lucky.

Then the thing was coming at them. It landed on top of the gully wall and craned over to grab one of them with its beak. Before Guthrie could react, Howard jerked up his shotgun and blew its head half off.

Amazingly, the thing kept moving, but all direction and purpose were gone. The humans scuttled out of the gully as the shuddering carcass crashed down where they'd just been.

Curious, Guthrie approached the still-jerking body. The creature was covered with a leathery skin that was mottled black and brown and dotted with irregular, cancerous-looking lumps. It stank like rotten flesh. Guthrie considered using his knife to cut out some of its meat for possible consumption, but the smell alone dissuaded him. Besides, there was nothing to make a cooking fire with, and he didn't think he could stomach raw diseased pterodactyl, even if it had smelled edible.

"Let's go," he said, and they hurried on.

35

THEY REACHED AND CROSSED THE dry wash without further incident. At first, Guthrie led them toward the large depression he'd seen from the slope of the ridge, wondering what it was. It didn't look natural. Maybe it was an artesian well of some sort. But as they neared its edge, he grew cautious. It was maybe eighty feet across and conical in shaped and almost looked engineered.

Guthrie peered over the edge and saw something very large shift in the sand at the bottom. Its outlines weren't visible, but when it heaved, the sand slid back from a section of jointed brown carapace tufted with thick clots of black bristles.

"I think we'd better keep moving," he said, noticing that the sandy soil beneath his feet was beginning to crumble. He quickly backed away as the little landslide careened down the slope, agitating whatever it was that lurked down at the bottom. He only hoped that it wouldn't crawl out of its pit and chase them.

The sun was only an hour above the horizon by the time they came to the base of the hill they'd spotted from the ridge. The hill was somewhat lower than the ridge, but it was rockier, and in places they had to climb and scramble toward the declivity that seamed its middle like a pass.

As they worked their way deeper into the pass, Guthrie scouted around for a place that might offer shelter, and at last his eyes lit on a shadowed overhang up the slope to their left where a rock face had come loose and scattered itself in a talus of scree. The cavity would help shield them from the cool wind that was rising as the sun descended, and from predators that might try to descend on them from above or behind.

"How you two holding up?" Guthrie asked after they'd reached the overhang and sipped a little water.

"Fine," Diane said. She didn't look it. Exhaustion seamed her face and her movements for the last hour had been sluggish. But she wasn't distraught, and that said a lot.

"Hungry," Howard said. "But fit enough."

He looked even worse than Diane. The effort and strain of creating the paintings had turned him into a rawboned shadow. Guthrie hoped he'd hold up long enough to reach the other gateway—hoped they all would.

"We'll stay here tonight," he said. "We're relatively protected and we have a good view."

The shallow valley that split the hill spread out below them, and through the gap back the way they'd come, they could see the ridge they'd first crossed lit brightly against the darkening sky by the rays of the setting sun. The crown of the hill hid their destination, but Guthrie took comfort in the facts that they were a day closer, they'd avoided confrontation with any of the monsters, and there was still no sign of pursuit.

Guthrie still had the three energy bars as well as about three-quarters of a canteen of water, and he broke one in half and gave the pieces to Diane and Graham.

"What about you?" she asked.

"I'll do. Banning fed me a big meal the night before he let me loose to be hunted. A meal fit for a condemned man." He gave a snorting laugh.

He did take a sip of water, though, before handing the canteen to Diane.

"Careful," he warned. "It's all we have."

"It's not enough," Graham said, shaking the canteen after Diane handed it to him. "We drank nearly half today."

"I'm just glad to have any at all," Diane said, brushing a straggle of hair out of her face.

"We're half way to the other painting," Guthrie said. "Maybe a little less. We have enough to get there, and after that, we'll either find it or we won't, and we'll deal with the situation then."

"All these monsters running around," Diane said. "They must be drinking somewhere."

"I'm not so sure," Graham said. "Nothing's natural here. Why should they have to drink?"

"They eat," Guthrie pointed out. "Drinking would seem to be a corollary."

Graham merely nodded.

"You two rest," Guthrie said. "I'm going to look around while there's still a little light."

"Do you have to, Clay?" Diane asked.

"I think it's better if I did. I won't be gone long. I'll call out when I come back. If anything else comes close, shoot it until it stops moving."

Then he slipped off into the growing gloom, trying not to disturb the scree as he made his way down into the valley they'd have to descend tomorrow. He kept the AR-15 ready. He wasn't worried about any of the flying monsters since they probably relied on sight for hunting and wouldn't be flying around after dusk, but there was no telling what sort of nocturnal creatures might be out there, even at this elevation.

He worked his way down to the desert floor without encountering anything that was alive except for several varieties of flora. The ones on the slopes were relatively normal, but as he descended, he suddenly found the ground beneath his feet smooth to the consistency of pavement. It was one of Angra Mainyu's trails, and strewn along its borders were a number of deformed plants, if it was possible to equate spiny creepers and pulsating blobs of slimy fungus, often sporting saw-toothed spikes jutting out at odd angles, with anything floral.

Curious, he stepped closer to one of the plants, but not too close. It appeared to be innocent enough, if disgusting, but even Earth had plants capable of trapping animals and consuming their flesh, and everything else in this place seemed inimical. The one he picked looked the least likely to do him harm.

A sour stench like old vomit assailed his nostrils, but otherwise, the plant made no move to assault him. Its body was roughly circular in shape, three or four feet across, and mounded about two feet high in the center. The general impression was of a gigantic and hideous fried egg. The "white" spreading out from the central mass was predominantly sienna and tan shading to aquamarine and gray at the fluted periphery. Instead of being relatively smooth like the white of an actual fried egg, though, the surface was rippled with convolutions teeming with shapes: some like patches of irregular craters, some like inert pill bugs, and others like a cross between veins and worms.

The central mass was even more arresting. Colored an irregular magenta mottled with blue, its surface was heavily warted and cratered in its middle by what appeared to be an oval mouth rimmed with a row of dark purple triangular shapes that looked like shark teeth. Inside the cavity pooled a clear gelatinous liquid, and suspended in the liquid was a knobby sphere the same mottled shades as the surface of the central mass. There didn't seem to be a throat, but the sphere blocked the bottom of the cavity, and Guthrie decided not to bend too close to examine it further.

Instead, he picked up a pebble and tossed it at the central cavity. The pebble never made it. The knobby sphere erupted, suddenly elongating like a frog's tongue striking. The tongue snatched the pebble out of the air and jerked it down into the mouth. There the charade ended as the plant—creature?—realized it hadn't snared a meal but a rock. With a spitting sound, it ejected the pebble, which landed a dozen feet away.

Guthrie straightened, backed away, and headed toward the overhang. He was gratified that he couldn't see Diane and Howard, although he could hear the sounds of their voices. He walked on, back the way they'd come, again encountering nothing that seemed like it might harm them.

At last, it was too dark to see much of anything, although the sky was filled with enough stars to cast a gentle glow. Guthrie hadn't been out of Houston's ambient glow for several years, but there appeared to be more stars than he'd ever seen.

As he approached the rock overhang, he called out softly and heard Graham's acknowledgement.

The artist was sitting with his back propped against the back wall of the overhang, the shotgun on one side, Diane, fast asleep, leaning against the other.

"You ought to get some sleep, too," Guthrie said, settling across from them.

"I can't. I haven't slept worth a shit since I started painting those godforsaken paintings. Bad dreams."

"Of this place?"

Howard nodded.

"You know, I've practically lived here—in my mind, at least— but I can't decide if this is another world entirely or some kind of alternate Earth."

"I think it must be an alternate Earth," Guthrie said. "The air is breathable, even if it does smell odd, and the sky is about the same blue. Also, I seem to weigh what I normally do. Besides, look."

He pointed to the ridge across the shallow valley. The sky there had been lightening for some time, and now the reason was apparent: The moon was rising. It was just peeking over the ragged ridge, but within a few minutes, it had cleared it enough for them to see it bore a familiar face.

"You're right," Howard said.

"This can't be our world," Guthrie said. "If it was, Angra Mainyu would be in the news. And it wouldn't need any kind of bridge."

"An alternate reality," Howard said musingly. "But we can figure this is what might happen to our world if Angra Mainyu gets loose there."

Howard was silent for several long moments.

"I had to paint the paintings to get the dreams out of my head," he said at last, "but I never thought it would come to this. I was greedy, I suppose. Not for money, you understand. I was after the ultimate technique. No, not technique, exactly. My technique was superlative, but even so, I knew that something was missing. Something that could take me beyond what anyone else had ever done."

"You were thinking of fame?"

"Not fame, really. Or, at least, not the cheap sort of celebrity everybody worships these days. Call it history. I didn't care if I was in *ArtForum*; I wanted to see myself in museums and history books. But I wasn't there, yet. Something was missing. I had an inkling of what, but I couldn't define the problem adequately enough to formulate a solution. It had to do with framing."

"Framing?"

"Yeah. Look. Every good picture has a point of reference from which the rest flows. This can be an obvious visual focal point in the picture or a more subtle psychological aspect that lends gravity to a given location within the frame and that may or may not be directly associated with the visual focal point. This locus of gravity is something most serious artists strive for, and I was no different. It not only gives meaning to the painting, it's what thins the space between the artwork and the viewer. There's a lot of art out there that is technically superior but completely devoid of psychological or emotional depth, and there's a lot that is technically average, or even mediocre, but that has true artistic value. The difference is the presence or absence of this locus of gravity. So the answer I sought wasn't in technique, even though I'd been chasing it with technique. The real problem was one of framing—where I placed the locus of gravity."

"And Adriana showed you where to put it."

Graham nodded.

"Most artists place it within the frame. I always had. But Adriana showed me that the locus didn't have to be within the frame. It could be off to the side or behind an architectural or geographic feature, hidden from the viewer. But it would be there, nonetheless, unseen but real and acting with a sort of psychic gravity that affects the viewer even though there's no obvious cause."

"But how could you do such a thing? If the viewer can't see it...."

"Exactly. The need to have a visual locus always kept me from seeing the truth. Adriana taught me something I already knew on an intellectual level but that hadn't really sunken into my artistic sensibility: that technique is merely a means, and any language might be invented to speak for an art form. And part of that was learning how to visualize a locus deeper within the normal frame, or even outside it. I can't really explain it. How I do it. It's a sort of mental shift. It's kind of spooky but exhilarating at the same time. Like a drug. The problem is, the locus of these Chinvat paintings doesn't thin the space between the artwork and the viewer; it somehow thins the space between our world and this one."

"So, what is the locus?"

Graham shrugged. "I don't know. But maybe the reason it isn't visible in the frame is because it seems to move around." Guthrie could dimly see him wave toward the darkness. "Out there, somewhere."

"Do you think it's Angra Mainyu?"

"Possibly."

"Anybody with sufficient technique could have painted the series?"

"Painting these pictures required a certain sophistication of technique because they had to be photo-realistic, but that's not the key to why they do what they do, just a necessary adjunct." Howard paused, staring into space, then went on. "Maybe that's part of the reason she chose me, and I was willing enough at the time. But I think she saw something else in me that I'd never recognized. I wanted to take a trip incredibly far into the center of the line separating art and reality. What happens when your art becomes so realistic that it ceases to be art?" He snorted derisively. "Well, here I am. And Diane and you."

"You said that Adriana offered you a deal. That implies you exchanged something for the ability she gave you."

"I already told you. I had to paint the larger painting right away and give it to her."

"I know there's more to it," Guthrie insisted. He couldn't see Graham clearly, but he felt the man slump.

"I don't...," Graham began, but Guthrie stopped him.

"You do," he said. "Tell me. It's the only way to feel clean."

"All right," Howard said with a shrug. "Adriana had two conditions. The painting was the first, and the second condition was that I had to spend the night—and one night only—with her daughter and have sex with her as many times as she wanted."

Graham lapsed into silence again.

"Melanie," Guthrie said to get Graham going again.

"Yes. It made no sense to me. There had never been any hint of sex between me and Adriana, and Melanie was just there. I mean, she was Adriana's daughter—my friend's daughter. My supposed friend. I couldn't figure it. Melanie had always been polite but distant, and I never thought she harbored any feelings of that sort for me. So I couldn't wrap my thoughts around this second condition. It was just too strange—a mother getting her friend to screw her daughter as payment for something.

"I resisted, but Adriana kept after me. It seemed like she wanted me to have sex with Melanie almost as much as I wanted to be able to paint as she suggested I could. Finally, thinking I had nothing to lose, I agreed. There's no point in going into the details. Melanie came to my studio, and I fulfilled the second condition. And that was that. Three days later, Adriana had me return to her shop to do whatever it was she did to me to enable me to paint this place."

"It fits with something Banning told me," Guthrie said, nodding. "Adriana's mother gave him the power to realize his dreams in exchange for a night of sex with Adriana."

"What?"

"That was a little more than twenty years ago, which would make Melanie...."

"She's Banning's daughter?"

"He told me last night." Now, Guthrie thought, looking at Graham. Let's see if you know the facts. "Have you seen Melanie since then?"

"No. I know she was at Banning's house while I painted, but I only saw Banning, Adriana, and the guards."

"Then you're not aware that Melanie is pregnant?"

Graham hissed then was silent for a long moment.

"Mine?" he asked at last.

"I'd say so."

"But I don't understand."

"I'd guess that's how the Lycorises perpetuate themselves."

"But why me?" Graham shivered. "I'm nothing like Banning."

"But you are. In one way, at least. You both are highly directed and devoted to your careers to the exclusion of personal relationships. You have your art, and that's been enough for you, just as Banning's love of pursuit—whether in business or for pleasure—is enough for him. I'd guess the Lycorises prize single-minded devotion over attachment as a positive trait to pass down and strengthen the line."

"God, I hate her."

"It's not too late," Guthrie said, laying a gentle hand on Howard's shoulder and nodding toward Diane's sleeping form.

Howard glanced quickly at her, but it was too dark for Guthrie to read his expression.

"I'm not sure I know how," he said, turning back to Guthrie.

"Do any of us?"

"I don't know. Are you married?"

"Was. Fucked it up irrevocably."

Howard snorted.

"You're a fine one to give advice, then."

"I just wish I had the chance you have right now. I'd grab it in an instant."

"Yeah."

"Get some sleep," Guthrie said. "We have a long day tomorrow."

"What about you?"

"I'll keep watch for a while then wake you."

"All right."

As Howard tried to settle into a more comfortable position without waking Diane, Guthrie crawled around a little outcropping of rock to a place where he could sit and watch the valley below, although in the darkness, he wasn't sure he'd be able to see anything before it was already upon him.

He must have slept for several hours, because his back was stiff when he felt a gentle shaking.

"Clay!" a voice hissed in his ear.

It was Diane. The sky was just beginning to lighten, and he could see her shape crouched next to him. Graham's dark form stood a few yards down the slope.

"What is it? One of the creatures?" He groped for the assault rifle.

"Look. Out there." She pointed down the valley, back the way they'd come.

Guthrie didn't have to stare long to see what she meant. Ten lights bobbled down the ridge they'd crossed the day before.

Banning's hunting party had gotten an early start.

36

GUTHRIE AND HIS FRIENDS WERE through the cleft that split the hill and descending into a basin of bluish-white soil before dawn fully broke. Almost immediately in front of them, across the basin, was a narrow, low ridge breached by a dry stream bed that entered the basin from around the foot of the hill to their right. Guthrie led them down into the stream bed and through the gap between the two parts of the ridge. Beyond the gap, the stream bed meandered across a low plain to the left, but in front of them, the land rose a hundred and fifty feet or so, the region of demarcation like a rank of huge, irregular toes.

As the three of them descended the hill, Guthrie scoped out a general route, and their way led up onto the higher land and across its rugged wrinkles. Apparently the land fell off after that because Guthrie couldn't tell what lay beyond, but Howard seemed to intuit the general direction they needed to take. The wrinkled terrain looked dishearteningly wide—half a day's walk, even under the best of conditions, and they were down to a quarter of a canteen and one energy bar. But Guthrie hoped that the roughness of the terrain would force Banning and his men to slow down, too.

Figuring there was no use in wasting time, Guthrie started up the incline between two of the toes, and in ten minutes, they set out across the uplift. What had appeared from a distance to be wrinkles were large, uneven slabs of rock protruding as high as three feet from a bed of hard-packed caliche. Even though it made the walking more difficult, Guthrie had them keep to the rock surfaces as much as possible to mask their trail. The air was warming a bit, and if the day was like the one before, at least it wouldn't get too hot.

At last, the uplift abruptly ended in a quick, crumbly slope that dipped to another dry stream bed. Beyond lay another playa that narrowed as it went between two rises Guthrie had seen from the hill, which now was a distant blur behind them. As they scrambled and slid to the bottom, Guthrie noticed a patch of dull-green plants sprouting from a cleft in the dun-colored hillside off to their left.

"I want to look over there," he said. "Looks like there might be some water."

"What about Banning and his men?" Diane asked. "Won't that give them time to catch up?"

"It'll take them a little while to pick up our trail over that last stretch. Besides, they'll definitely catch up if we're too dehydrated to keep ahead of them."

The cleft was around a long bend that marked the base of the uplift, and as they neared it, Guthrie thought he could smell water in the dry air. A few minutes later, the cleft came into view. It looked like there might be a spring leaking from the bowels of the uplift, although the cluster of brambly plants clogging the cleft made it impossible to tell for sure. Guthrie went closer, his companions on his heels, and stopped about fifty feet from the mass of plants, which trailed down from the cleft to the dry stream bed.

"There's water in there," he said. "Wait here. I'm going to take a closer look."

"Be careful, Clay," Howard warned.

Guthrie had no intention of being careless. He moved forward, assault rifle ready, scanning the surroundings and for any sign of a creature that might want to make a meal of them. As he neared, he could definitely smell water. And then he could see it: a pool about two feet across, lying just within the shaded precinct of the tangled brambles. It looked close enough that he might be able to reach it.

He pulled the canteen from its nylon sleeve and was about to lean into the bramble patch to try to dip some of the water, when the brambles rustled as if in the breeze. Except there was no breeze.

Guthrie took half a dozen steps back and stared at the bramble patch. There was something in there, waiting. He was sure of it.

He bent, picked up a rock, and threw it into the patch. Nothing. He threw another, this time at the water.

The entire bramble patch erupted the instant the stone splashed into the pool, lunging up and out, completely engulfing the pool and barely missing Guthrie, whose instinctive backward leap kept him from being snared by the thorny, out flung branches.

There hadn't been something in the brambles waiting for him to approach. It had been the brambles themselves.

"I think we're just going to have to make do with what water we've got," he told his friends as he walked over to them. Diane was ashen-faced, and Howard's knuckles were white against the shotgun's blued metal and dark wood. "Which way?" he asked Howard.

"There," the artist pointed. "Between that ridge and the hill next to it."

The ridge was on the far side of the plain, another couple of hours away. Guthrie would have rather have gone a different way because they'd be completely exposed out on its open expanse, and the soft, sandy soil would leave a clear trail behind them, pointing in the direction they'd gone. But if that was the way they had to go, there was no point in wasting time, so he set out, his friends following.

The wrinkled uplift they'd just descended had been free of any sort of life and showed no evidence of Angra Mainyu's presence, but the plain was littered with misshapen growths and was crisscrossed by a dozen of the fused-looking swaths.

About two miles farther on, the plain was split by a wide arroyo maybe a hundred feet deep and three hundred across. At the bottom snaked a narrow silvery stream.

"Water," Diane breathed. "No brambles."

"Wait," Howard said, putting a hand on her arm to keep her from rushing down the slope. "No plants at all."

"What?" she asked, but Guthrie already knew what the artist meant. There was no foliage, and there definitely would have been if the twisting silvery length below them was water.

"It's some kind of gigantic creature disguised as water," he said. "We'll have to go around.

They followed the rim of the arroyo toward the south. After a hundred yards, they passed the end of the silvery creature, but

Guthrie made them go another half mile before he led them across to the other side. As they topped the rim, Guthrie found that the sandy soil on the other side of the arroyo had been replaced on this side with hardpan littered with smooth gravel that looked like it had been seeded across the landscape. To the left, the plain was bordered by a long low ridge that marked the edge of an area of uplift. Farther out and to the right was a hill about as large as the one where they'd spent the previous night, but looking much more rugged, even from this distance. The plain funneled between the hill and the ridge.

"We're going straight through there," Howard pointed.

As they set out across the plain, the walking was relatively easy, but Guthrie was troubled by the lack of cover. He wasn't worried about Banning's hunting party yet. He'd kept looking back and had yet to spot it, so he hoped it was too far back to catch them here in the open. But there was no telling what was already out there, waiting for something tasty to cross its domain. From what Guthrie had seen so far, though, the creatures tended to stay in low areas, especially the dry water courses, which made a lot of sense in an arid region like this. It had to rain some time, and when it did, the dry washes would become rushing streams that would leave residual pools. As long as they stayed out of the stream beds, he figured they'd be okay.

A short while later, they came to a shallow gully. They scrambled through it, only to find another a few minutes farther on. And another.

Guthrie didn't like the situation. The gullies were getting progressively deeper, and not only were they slowing them down, they were perfect cover for an attack by one of the predatory creatures.

The attack came soon enough, appearing first in the form of a small creature with iridescent wings only a little larger than a hummingbird. Diane spotted it first as they came to the lip of a dry wash that was deeper than the other gullies they'd crossed.

"Look." She pointed at the sparrow-sized creature as it fluttered on the rim of the dry wash like an injured bird. "It's beautiful."

"The only beautiful thing we've seen in this place," Howard said.

"Yes," Guthrie said. "And that ought to make us afraid."

"Of that little thing?" Diane asked.

"Have you seen anything here that isn't dangerous?"

"No," she admitted. "But that doesn't mean there isn't."

"Just the same, we need to be cautious. Let's scout the gully before we go down. Howard, you go that way." Guthrie pointed to their right. "I'll go this way. Diane, you stay here and watch that little jewel. Let me know if it moves."

Graham started off in the direction Guthrie had indicated, and Guthrie called after him, "Be careful."

Howard waved back, and Guthrie turned his attention to the dry wash as he headed off in his own direction. So far, the wash looked like all the others they'd crossed, although there seemed to be more plants in this one.

"Clay!" Diane called out. "It's moving."

"Where?"

"Toward Howard."

Graham was a couple of hundred feet away, now, walking on the lip of the arroyo. Diane started walking toward him when he jerked up the shotgun and let it rip at something below Guthrie's level of sight. He pumped another shell into the chamber and shot again as he stumbled backward.

Guthrie ran toward him, and a moment later, he saw Diane recoil in horror as a mass of stringy brown tentacles boiled over the lip of the arroyo. She screamed then as one of the tentacles caught Howard's leg just above the calf and jerked him off balance. Diane rushed toward him as he fell backwards, dropping the shotgun. The tentacle started dragging him across the ground toward the edge of the wash.

She got there long before Guthrie. He saw her jack a shell into the chamber of her own shotgun and rush toward Howard. Ignoring the mass of tentacles looming over her, she aimed at the one pulling Howard and jerked the trigger. She was too close to miss, and the tentacle blew in half, splashing reddish-brown fluid. But another caught hold of Diane's shoulder and jerked her toward the arroyo. She tried to pull away and shot into the mass, which quaked, but the tentacle didn't release her. By now, Howard was on his feet, watching helplessly as the tentacle was joined by more, and Diane was drawn relentlessly toward the edge.

Guthrie started firing even before he arrived. Ignoring the tentacles, he sprayed a full magazine into the leathery blob from which they writhed. The .223 slugs drove more deeply into it than the shotgun pellets had been able to, and the thing seemed to hesitate just before it dragged Diane over the edge. Guthrie slammed another magazine into the AR-15 and leapt after her.

In a second, tentacles were all over him, too, and he was being drawn toward the middle of the mass and into a horrible stench. Down there, close to the body, was the carcass of some animal, half disintegrated and covered with slime. Guthrie wrenched the barrel of his rifle toward the center of the mass and emptied the magazine.

The thing quaked, and the tentacles clutching him released their grip enough for him to scramble toward Diane, grab her wrist, and roll them out onto open ground. He dragged her to her feet, and they dashed away from the thing, which was now clutching spasmodically in every direction with its tentacles. As the body of the thing heaved back and forth, Guthrie could see the carcass of a second animal that was even more disintegrated than the first.

"Hurry," he urged. "That way."

They stumbled down the arroyo, with Howard following them along the rim, calling out anxiously. They were nearing the first bend in the wash, when both of them tripped over a thin brown cable that lay along the ground, almost invisible against the soil of the arroyo floor.

"That bird thing," Howard yelled. "It just jerked down toward you. I think it's attached to that thing back there."

Guthrie helped Diane to her feet and put a fresh magazine into the assault rifle. He only had two more.

"I lost the shotgun," Diane said ruefully.

"Small enough payment," Guthrie said. "Come on."

They followed the cable, and sure enough, it was attached to the iridescent birdlike creature, although, as they came close, they could see it was little more than a collection of iridescent petals that now fluttered weakly.

"It's some kind of lure," Guthrie said.

Howard scrambled down to them and took Diane in his arms.

"I thought it had you," he said into her hair. "You saved me."

"Clay saved us both," she said. "God, I hope we don't meet another one of those."

"You all right, Howard?" Guthrie asked.

The artist nodded and said, "But maybe we should rest for a few minutes."

He was right. They all were exhausted as well as battered. But Guthrie knew they couldn't rest for long. Banning and his men, better fed and watered, couldn't be far behind.

Guthrie had Howard give his shotgun to Diane.

"Keep that pistol I gave you handy," he told the artist.

After a few minutes, they reluctantly rose and pressed on toward the gap between the hill and ridge. They'd gone about half the way to the gap when Guthrie's tattoo started itching. It wasn't much at first, but it increased steadily as they walked. He scanned the terrain but saw nothing unusual. But Howard noticed his increased vigilance.

"You feel it, too?" he asked.

"What?" Diane asked as Guthrie nodded.

"Angra Mainyu," Howard answered. "It's near. I think it senses I'm here."

"We'd better hurry," Guthrie urged.

Beyond the gap lay another flat plain, this one dotted with partially melted boulders and piles of rock and hatched by more of Angra Mainyu's trails. The plain was bordered about three miles away by another ridge.

"We need to go over that ridge," Howard said. I think we're close, and I'll be able to tell better when we get up there."

Guthrie could hear faint popping sounds come from behind them. He stared but could see nothing.

"Banning?" Diane asked.

"It sounds like they ran into something," Howard said.

"Whatever it is, it won't stop them for long," Guthrie said. "If their gunfire was close enough to hear, then they heard ours."

But as they went on, Guthrie wondered if they should. His talisman was itching more and more, and he had the sense that they were walking straight into the lion's den. Worse, he could feel madness and despair insinuate tendrils inside his mind. Howard's pace had become a shamble, and Diane also was reacting to the increasing but still unseen presence.

At last, they reached the ridge. They climbed it easily enough, but the scree on the other side was treacherous, and they slid down as much as walked. The earth at the bottom was more fused than before, often approaching a smooth glass, as if a tremendous heat had scorched wide swaths across the terrain. Perhaps Angra Mainyu had traveled multiple time across this ground.

More boulders and piles of rock and earth broke these flats than any they'd crossed previously, but all had a sagging, drippy look and were melded onto the hardpan like candles melted onto a tabletop. The surface was so rigid, that none of the plants they'd seen elsewhere were in evidence. Maybe any that had been here had been melted into the earth along with everything else.

Guthrie said something about it, and Howard nodded.

"I think Angra Mainyu has spent a lot of time around here," he said. "Probably drawn by the first painting."

At least the unyielding surface would leave few marks as a trail for Banning and his men to follow. But that might not matter if Banning reached the top of the ridge behind them soon enough. Surely he had binoculars and would quickly spot them in the open ground between the melted boulders and mounds.

They reached the base of the last ridge exhausted, but they didn't dare stop. Their pursuers had topped the ridge and were closing fast.

"Come on," Guthrie urged. "We have to go up."

Wordlessly, the others scrambled up the slope after him. At least there wasn't any loose rock here to slow them down. All the scree was just as fused as the boulders and mounds on the flats behind them, giving them good handholds as they climbed toward the top.

They were still thirty feet from the crest when bullets chipped the rocks around them and whined off into the still air. Banning and his men had caught up and were firing up at them from the bottom of the ridge. With no place to hide and nowhere to go but up, Guthrie kept scrambling, hoping none of them would be hit.

They managed to get over the top without being shot, partly because the range was so long and the pursuers were firing uphill.

After what seemed like an eternity, Guthrie flung himself down and peered over the crest.

Below, Banning and his men approached the base of the ridge. Taking careful aim, Guthrie shot at Banning. The range was still long, but Guthrie was firing downslope, and the bullet kicked up chips of stone near Banning's feet, and a second nearly got him. He and his men raced to the nearest rocks and took cover.

"That should keep them for a few minutes," he said. "Come. We don't have much time."

But as he rose to lead them down the other side of the ridge, something out on the fused plain to their right caught his eye.

"What the fuck?"

Diane and Howard turned to look at what appeared to be a hill about two hundred feet in diameter and slightly more than a mile away. A hill whose slopes were writhing and churning as if it were a living madness boiling from the ground. But it wasn't emerging. And it wasn't a hill. It was flowing across the terrain in their direction.

If Guthrie had to describe it, it looked like rodent trapped beneath a sheet, creating a mound that moved as it crawled around beneath the cloth. The hill moved, but not the earth that composed it. It was like a roughly circular wave that crept through the earth without moving the earth itself, as an ocean wave moves through the water without moving the water. The apparent writhing was the ground being uplifted and then falling in a melting cascading in the thing's wake.

"Angra Mainyu," Howard said, seeming to shrink within himself.

Guthrie's talisman was crawling beneath his navel. The thing was worse than madness. It was overpowering and intentional dissolution. Any feature of the terrain that it crawled through disintegrated into the glassy uniformity of the trail it left behind.

But instead of being featureless, itself, the thing's form was composed of a fantastical melange of images of plants, animals, and even buildings and people. They must be, Guthrie thought, memories of the world Angra Mainyu had consumed, surfacing as the substance of its body. Even more horrifying, the thing continually morphed through a range of humanlike features whose one similarity was a stark, alien insanity bedded deep in the eyes.

And then it turned those eyes upon them and began flowing in their direction.

"It's living madness," Diane breathed.

"More like an infection within tangible reality," Howard said. "We can't let it get close to us. It deforms anything that comes near."

Guthrie tore his eyes from the horrifying yet fascinating sight and stared toward Banning and his men. Apparently the hunters, being at a lower elevation than Guthrie and his friends, hadn't yet spotted Angra Mainyu. But certainly they'd soon feel its presence if they hadn't already.

"Come on," he urged. "We have to hurry."

"That way." Howard raised a heavy hand to indicate the left side of the hill that lay beyond the ridge. "It's on the other side of that hill, maybe as far away from the hill as we are now."

Two miles to the hill, Guthrie estimated. Four miles total. It would be close. With Guthrie and Diane following, Howard led the way down the slope. As soon as the mass of the ridge lay between them and Angra Mainyu, the feelings of madness in Guthrie's mind began to settle, and he scanned the ground ahead of them in the direction Howard was moving. It, like the other side of the ridge, was crisscrossed by glassy trails and littered with melted boulders and fused mounds of earth.

They traversed a mile of the boulder-strewn ground before Guthrie saw Banning's party come over the ridge behind them. It wouldn't take long for the hunters to catch up, and the exertion of the last couple of days and lack of food and water were taking their toll. Diane and Howard plodded along. Even Guthrie was moving sluggishly. He knew that the one mile separating them from Banning would all too quickly diminish.

He had to do something.

"You have to go on," he told them. "Find the other painting. I'm going to try to slow Banning down."

"You can't, Clay," Diane said. "They'll kill you. Or that thing will."

"They'll kill us all if they catch us. The only chance is to find the painting. If you can, go through and wait for me." He turned to Howard. "If Banning comes first, you'll have to destroy the painting."

"Even if you're not there?" the artist asked.

"No, Clay," Diane cried. "We won't let you."

"Yes," Guthrie said. "It's the only way."

"He's right, Diane," Howard said. "We have to find the gateway." To Guthrie, he said, "We'll wait as long as we can."

Guthrie turned and headed in the direction they'd come. He didn't look back.

37

GUTHRIE DIDN'T KNOW HOW FAR back Banning and his men were, but it wouldn't be far. Nor did he know exactly how many there were. He'd counted ten lights coming down the ridge that morning. A few would be Banning's men, the rest probably his safari friends, come to hunt in Hell. Knowing Banning, they'd all be experienced trackers and ruthless hunters, and on this strewn tableland, they could surprise Guthrie as easily as he could them. And with at least ten of them, he needed all the surprise on his side.

He found a tall boulder he could climb onto and cautiously scrambled to the top. He wanted it to be a lookout point, not a beacon to advertise his presence. It wasn't long before he spotted Porter and another man he didn't recognize edging around a fused mound of rock and earth about a hundred yards away and a little to his left. Almost simultaneously, Hayes and a second stranger showed up about the same distance away but to Guthrie's right. Porter vanished behind a boulder, but within a couple of minutes, the rest of Banning's party arrived, strung out in the space between the two pairs of flankers, Banning in the middle, with Spencer to his left and another stranger to his right. Spencer's arm was wrapped in a bandage, and he carried it gingerly. Four other men Guthrie had never seen were spaced behind Banning, all wearing what looked like expensive hunting clothes.

There were ten in all, not counting Stewart and Talbot. Guthrie hadn't spotted either of them yet, and while that didn't mean they weren't around somewhere, the two had never struck Guthrie as the safari sort. Just as likely, Banning had left them to guard the ranch.

Guthrie weighed his options. He could try to outmaneuver either group of flankers and ambush them. That would cut Banning's men by one or two, but the noise would quickly draw the others. Guthrie might be able to escape among the strewn boulders and melted mounds, but Banning would fan out his remaining men, and it would only be a matter of time before they targeted Guthrie and came after him in force.

Guthrie didn't like the odds. Besides, the whole reason he was here was to slow down Banning, not engage in a shoot out unless absolutely necessary. He waited for one of the flankers to reappear.

Hayes did, moments later. Guthrie took aim and squeezed off a shot. The bullet threw chips from the fused hardpan near the man's feet. Guthrie barely waited to see Hayes duck behind a boulder before he swung to the left, found the man with Porter, and shot at him, too.

This time, his aim was better, and the bullet took the man in the hip. He spun with a cry and fell a few yards behind Porter. Guthrie snapped off a shot at Porter but missed, and Porter dropped behind a boulder.

Banning and the others with him also had ducked behind cover when the shots sounded, but because the shots had come unexpectedly, none of the party had pinpointed Guthrie's location. But if he had to shoot again, it wouldn't be long before they'd know where he was.

He saw Banning incline his head slightly to a dark spot attached to his collar and his mouth move. Apparently Guthrie's adversaries were in radio communication. Guthrie couldn't hear the conversation, but he quickly figured out what had been said as Spencer cautiously eased out of hiding and crept forward. He didn't look too happy. He was the weakest man on Banning's team, and he knew that Banning had sent him out to be sacrificed.

Guthrie obliged. He aimed the AR-15 and squeezed the trigger.

Spencer, spun and fell, blood blossoming from the right side of his chest. He began to crawl painfully back toward cover, but Guthrie didn't wait. With another of their own down, Banning's party would be reluctant to move, and anyway, they probably were narrowing down Guthrie's location. He slid down the boulder, and keeping it between himself and the majority of Banning's party, he ran in a loping crouch toward a clump of boulders a hundred feet to his left.

He'd nearly made it when a string of bullets ripped the air around him. He fell behind the clump as another burst sent rock chips flying and lead whining into the air.

It was Porter, about forty yards away.

"Mr. Banning's paying fifty grand to the one who brings you down, Guthrie!" Porter yelled. "How do you like that? Payback and payday, all at once!"

Guthrie didn't bother answering. He wasn't sure if Banning or the rest of his men had seen him, but even if they hadn't, it wouldn't be long before they came.

Porter tried to ease around the side of the boulder, but Guthrie shot in his direction and he ducked back. Guthrie had hoped that caution would keep Banning and his men from proceeding too rapidly, but Guthrie couldn't indulge in caution. Crouching behind the clump that shielded him from Porter's bullets, he turned and ran.

More bullets whined off the glassy ground behind him, and he realized that Hayes and the man with him had nearly outflanked him. Banning's men may not have had much in the way of ethics, but they didn't lack guts or cunning. Guthrie had to stop after a few hundred feet to send more rounds at them. He was running dangerously low on ammo.

Suddenly, he heard a stealthy sound behind him, and he whirled, finger tensing on the trigger.

It was Howard.

"What the hell are you doing here?" Guthrie snapped.

"We found it. Quick!."

"It'll have to be quick," Guthrie said. "They're almost on us."

Several bursts from Banning and his men shattered against the rocks as Guthrie ran after the artist.

Three of the pterodactyl things circled in the sky ahead like gigantic leather vultures.

Howard had been running straight, but he suddenly changed course, angling off to the right.

"Some kind of huge worms," he yelled, pointing the open area they'd avoided.

Guthrie saw that the ground was crosshatched with long mounds six or so inches high, like large mole tunnels just under the surface. The hardpan's brittle surface lay on the mounds like panes of broken ice.

Howard went for a hundred yards before taking a tack that would lead them on in their former direction.

The maneuver had lost them some ground, though, and Hayes spotted them. His cries brought the others, who fired at the fleeing pair. The distance was too great for aim, though, and their bullets either went wide or spattered harmlessly short.

Guthrie hoped their pursuers would try to cross the worm-infested ground, but Banning spotted the tunnels and called his men to a halt. Seeing that Guthrie and Howard had gone around, he set off on the same detour, his men following.

As Guthrie ran after Howard, he saw more and more creatures. Most were hurrying in the same general direction as they were, but none of them seem interested in the two humans. They had a panicked look about them.

"It's like they're running from a forest fire," Guthrie said.

"Angra Mainyu," Howard gasped. "It's coming. Can't you feel it?"

Guthrie could, though in the excitement of the battle, he hadn't noticed. The air seemed murkier, and his visual field flattened, as if he'd lost some of his depth perception. Only the now-burning talisman beneath his navel kept him focused.

"Hurry," Howard urged. "It's just ahead."

Diane was crouched behind a boulder.

"Banning is right behind us," Guthrie said. "Where's the gate?"

"That way," Howard pointed.

At first, Guthrie didn't hear it, but then a sound like a faint, keening wail impinged on his consciousness. It seemed to be coming from inside his own head.

"What is that?" Diane asked, raising her hands to her ears. But she dropped them when she realized they couldn't block out the sound.

"It's Angra Mainyu," Howard pointed off to their right.

"Hurry!" Guthrie yelled.

As they raced forward, the sound grew louder, and their progress through the congealing atmosphere was more difficult. After a quarter of a mile, Guthrie felt almost as if he were swimming through air as thick as water, as thick as flesh.

"My god! Look!" Howard's pointed.

Guthrie turned with the rest of them and stared where Howard pointed. Out across the plain, only half a mile from where they stood, Angra Mainyu's huge, churning, rippling mass was coalescing. Like any predator sensing prey, it had followed them and their pursuers. The landscape around it seemed to glisten and melt like wax beneath the nozzle of a heat gun. One of the pterodactyls brushed through its upper reaches and twisted suddenly into a shape even more debased than before. It struggled to fly away, but its blunted wings couldn't support it, and it plunged to the ground with a distant thud.

Banning and his men were standing frozen, staring at the rippling mass. They were almost directly between the thing and where Guthrie and his friends stood

Suddenly, Angra Mainyu began to move toward them.

Banning, stepping as if through heavy mud, started moving away, followed by the rest of his men, as the squirming mound crept toward them. Spencer and the other man Guthrie had shot, weak from their wounds, weren't fast enough. The edges of the thing brushed against them, and Spencer's crawling form collapsed into a mound of squirming protoplasm ringing a blubbery mouth that sucked wetly at the air. The second man tried to hobble away on his ruined hip, but he fell to all fours, and his limbs turned to blocky stumps. He reared back his head and opened his mouth to scream, but instead of sound, a pair of tentacled appendages emerged and waved wildly toward the shimmering mass hovering over it.

"Come on," Guthrie urged. "We have to get to the painting."

Practically dragging Diane and Howard, he plodded heavily forward. The sound that wasn't a sound grew louder, and he could see the rippling thing moving toward them like a thunderhead of roiling insanity pushed by unfelt winds. The mounds and boulders it crossed directly over melted flat, and the second wounded man, also passed over by the shimmering mass, simply melted along with everything else into the glassy surface. Spencer's remains just lay where he'd fallen, puddled around the blubbering mouth.

Of Banning and the others, there was no sign. If the oilman was smart, he'd be on his way back to his own gateway.

The painting. Where the hell was it? The sound in his head was driving out all thought. Where the hell...?

As they rounded a boulder, Diane pointed to their right. "Over there," she said. "But why is it gray?"

Incongruously in the arid desolation, a gray rectangle hung in the air about four feet off the ground.

"It's face down on my garage floor," Guthrie said as he gestured to his companions. "Come on."

They followed him over to the rectangle, and Guthrie suddenly regretted having laid the painting on his garage floor. The same concrete that kept the monsters from going through now prevented them from escaping.

There wasn't much time. The edge of Angra Mainyu's writhing coagulation was less than two hundred yards away, and Guthrie could feel sickening forces tug at his mind and body.

"How are we going to get through?" Diane asked, panic in her voice. Howard looked practically catatonic.

How?

Then Guthrie had an idea. He jerked up his pants leg and pulled the knife from the makeshift sheath tied to his calf. He slipped the blade past the edge of the painting, laying it almost flat against the concrete, then he jammed it downward. The first two tries didn't work, but then the blade slipped between the painting and the floor, and he levered the knife's handle outward, prying the painting off the concrete. Howard, seeing what he was trying to do, roused himself and stuck his fingers into the gap far enough to grab the invisible stretcher frame hidden behind the canvas. In a second, the painting flipped over. The garage was dark, but light emanating from the painting lit the rafters.

"You first," Guthrie told Diane, and he and Howard boosted her through the small opening.

She squealed as she went through, but Guthrie wasn't paying much attention as he helped shove Howard after her. It was disconcerting to see them standing over the painting reaching downward to him when he was looking at the hole sideways. Then they grabbed his arms and dragged him through. He groaned as the difference in gravity between the painting's vertical orientation in this hellish world and its horizontal one on Earth played momentary tug-of-war with his body, and nausea twisted his gut. Then he was through and staring back into the other world.

With their limited view from the window of the painting, the three couldn't see much of what was happening out on the rugged plain behind the painting, but they could see that Angra Mainyu was still rolling toward them like a wind of corruption, twisting everything it touched into a perversion. Even the already-deformed creatures were further contorted, making Guthrie wonder what they'd been to begin with.

A momentary thought crossed his mind, and his gaze sought the boulder they'd just rounded. Sure enough, the eye that he'd spotted there before was staring back, and it seemed to be filled with a combination of fear and anticipation.

"Flip that switch," he told Diane, turning away from the sight and pointing. "And punch the button next to it."

She did, and the garage lights flared on and the roll-up door began to rise. Outside, it was nighttime. Just then, Guthrie heard a scream that came through the painting, where the landscape beyond was beginning to transform as it and everything on it deformed and fused. Angra Mainyu must have just rolled across another of Banning's party, but it had happened outside of the picture frame.

Guthrie spotted Banning, then, Hayes next to him, standing well beyond the far side of the shimmering force of dissolution. Before he had a chance to react, Banning aimed his powerful hunting rifle at Guthrie. Guthrie saw the muzzle flare and flinched, but there was no impact of the heavy bullet tearing through him. Like all else in this twisted, forsaken place, it could not survive Angra Mainyu intact.

Nor would they, Guthrie realized, if he didn't act quickly. He snatched up the painting, reversed it, and slashed the knife down its back. Slit open, the canvas lost its permeability, but the image in the ruined painting did not freeze. Guthrie wished it had. He and his companions watched in horror as Angra Mainyu oozed over the painting, warping and melting everything around it in a melange of insane images. Then the rectangle went black.

Guthrie grabbed a bottle of charcoal lighter fluid and a box of matches off a shelf, dashed out to the dark driveway, and flung the torn painting to the shell surface. In seconds, he'd set the damn thing on fire, and inside of a minute, all that was left was the smoldering stretcher frame.

38

"IN THE HOUSE," GUTHRIE URGED. "It's the safest place I know."

He led his friends around the house to the front door. As he was locating the spare key he kept hidden in the light fixture, Graham pointed to the calligraphic painting that Tereba had put on the door.

"What's that?" he asked.

"That's the watchdog I told you about," Guthrie said, sticking the key in the lock. "A protective talisman. You'll be safe here until this is all over."

He ushered them inside.

"What do you mean, until this is all over?" Diane asked as Guthrie shut the door. "We're safe now, aren't we?"

"Banning isn't going to let things rest if he makes it back to his gateway. It's only a matter of time before he comes after us. We don't want to spend the rest of our lives looking over our shoulders. Besides, Angra Mainyu will surely find its way to Adriana's gateway."

"He's right, Diane," Howard said. "We have to do something about Banning."

"Not we," Guthrie said. "Me."

"But what can you do?" Diane asked. "He has all those men. We barely escaped."

"I have an idea," Guthrie said. "And an advantage. But first, I have to get some sleep. Two or three hours. You two take the bedroom."

He showed them where it was then pulled a pillow and a couple of extra blankets from the bedroom closet. Since his phone was still back at Banning's ranch, he grabbed his alarm clock before bidding them good night. He shut the door and went into the living room, where he quickly made up the sofa then put the alarm clock on the end table, plugged it in, and set it. He was asleep almost the instant he lay down.

When the alarm startled him awake, he wasn't sure at first where he was. The house seemed almost too quiet. He got up, feeling groggy, but a hot shower got his blood flowing. When he stepped out of the bathroom, he saw a disheveled Diane moving around in the kitchen. The smell of coffee wafted into the hall.

"I heard you get up," she said. "The usual breakfast?" She smiled.

"I haven't eaten in a couple of days," he said, grinning back. "Better supersize mine. I'll be back in a little while. I have to get a few things ready. How's Howard?"

"Still asleep," she said. "He's exhausted from all this."

While she filled the air with the odor of frying bacon and cooking eggs, Guthrie gathered several items into a daypack and put the pack on the floor beside the back door. In the living room, he found Howard sitting on the sofa, a mug of coffee in his large hands. The artist didn't look any better than he had during the escape across the alien landscape, but the rock-hard tension was gone from his shoulders.

"I don't know what to say," Howard began, but Guthrie stopped him.

"Don't worry about that right now. Worry about Diane."

"Diane? After what I put her through?"

"Don't underestimate her. All you can do is give it a try."

Howard nodded.

"Food's ready," Diane called.

It tasted wonderful. When Guthrie was done, he told them to sit tight until he got back.

"Don't leave the house," he said. "Eat, bathe, sleep. Feel free to look around and find whatever you need. I'll be back by tomorrow night at the latest. If I'm not, there's a card on the fridge for Terry's Lawn Service. Call it and tell the person who answers what's happened."

If Guthrie couldn't deal with the situation, Tereba would just have to step in.

It was full daylight as he climbed the back fence into the apartment parking lot adjacent to his back yard, found his second car—his old Honda Civic wagon, which he'd registered to a false name and address—and headed toward the freeway. Of course, he had to contend with rush hour.

Why the hell not?

39

BANNING'S RANCH WAS A NEARLY six-hour drive from Houston. Guthrie didn't break any speed limits driving there. He didn't want to chance a cop catching him driving around with several loaded firearms, especially since he was driving a car that wasn't registered to him and he didn't have his driver's or concealed handgun licenses or his PI identification. Those were in his wallet, which, presumably, was somewhere in Banning's house.

But he didn't waste any time, either. Banning and his men had chased Guthrie and his friends across the face of that other world for something less than twenty hours, which meant that they probably could make it back to the gate in Banning's house in a little more than half that time. Maybe a little longer. They'd be tired, but desperate men can push themselves, and judging from the last glimpse Guthrie'd had of Banning, the oil man would be desperate. Banning had claimed he wanted to face the ultimate predator, but Guthrie didn't think he had in mind a boiling madness that deformed and corrupted everything it touched, including bullets.

But getting to Banning's ranch was just the beginning. Only three of Banning's men were with him on that other world, and he'd undoubtedly had left the others on guard. Neither Stewart nor Talbot had been with the hunting party, and there might be others.

Guthrie visualized the ranch's layout from his memory of the aerial photos and the time he'd spent at the place itself. He sure as hell couldn't go in the front gate. As far as anyone at the ranch was concerned, Guthrie and his friends already were Banning's first trophies from his new happy hunting ground. They'd all be watching the gateway to the other world, not their own front gate, but there still were the surveillance cameras. Maybe nobody was paying attention to the monitors, but Guthrie couldn't take the chance that a casual observation would give him away and spoil the one thing he did have in his favor: the element of surprise.

When Guthrie reached the ranch, he drove on past the pair of front gates, which still gaped open, and stopped where he had the first time he'd come here—out near the property's northeast corner. He quickly carried his weapons off toward the gully, then he came back and wiped down the car as best as he could. If he survived the next few hours, he'd think of a more permanent solution—maybe come back and torch the car, though he hated to lose it.

In the gully, he strapped on his full-size S&W .40, then he cinched on the tac vest he'd prepared, which held extra magazines for the .40 and the .380 he wore on his ankle. The vest also held extra ammo for the Remington .308 with a scope that he'd brought along. He'd never been hunting with the rifle. He'd bought it for target practice, and after he'd shot it a few times, it had resided in his closet, gathering dust. He wished he could have brought the AR-15 he'd been carrying, but it was out of ammo, and he didn't have any .223 rounds at home or time to buy any. The guns he had would have to do.

He slipped a small pack with extra ammo, a couple of bottles of water, and some other items onto his back. Then, slinging the rifle over his shoulder, he moved off slowly toward the spot where he'd ambushed the game wardens.

The bodies were gone, but there was plenty of blood soaked into the dry, rocky soil. It would be washed away by the next heavy rain.

A few minutes later, Guthrie came to the first fence. His work to undo the fence ties during his escape had been repaired, but that was nothing. He'd brought wire cutters, and he quickly snipped through the ties and pulled the wire patch aside. In another two minutes, he'd gone through the plastic pipe and under the second fence and was moving stealthily through the sparse woods.

During his escape, he hadn't noticed any surveillance cameras in the woods, and he suspected that there weren't any. If there had been, Banning would have had an easier time pursuing Guthrie, and he wouldn't have had to plant a tracking device in the canteen. But even if there weren't any cameras in the woods, Guthrie knew there were several around the compound. He also was extremely leery that the big cats might be loose on the grounds, but he suspected that wouldn't be the case. Not when there were important guests to entertain and no prisoners to guard. Besides, he'd busted all the gates wide open.

He finally arrived at the rim of trees surrounding the compound, having circled to the east so he'd come up from the rear. Carefully, he moved south through the trees, watching the buildings, until he could see the graveled area in front. In addition to Banning's car, Guthrie's Xterra, the white van, the green Suburban, and the ranch SUV, half a dozen expensive cars were parked there: a couple of Cadillacs, a Lincoln Navigator, and three sports cars Guthrie couldn't even begin to identify beyond their shimmering expense.

Banning's hunting party was, indeed, well-heeled.

Guthrie still hadn't seen any movement from the house, and he wondered how many were in there. Two at least, and maybe a few bodyguard types who might have come with the members of the hunting party. And the Lycori.

He sneaked around to the north side, watching the house for movement. There still was nothing, which meant there was nothing to do but wait. But he knew he couldn't do that for long. Whatever he had to do had to be done before Banning and the hunting party returned to the gateway, which they'd reach in just a few hours. He found a tree where he could sit and watch the front of the house.

Half an hour went by, and all Guthrie saw moving were a few birds and squirrels. He was getting impatient. He hadn't come all this way across two worlds to just sit here. Not to mention the fact that the hard ground was numbing his butt. He decided to give it another half hour before doing something. He didn't know what that something would be, but whatever it was, it would be better than sitting and waiting. Banning wouldn't just be waiting—he'd be moving as fast as he could back to the gate.

Not five minutes later, the front door opened, and a man wearing a shoulder holster and carrying a Kalashnikov stepped onto the front veranda. Guthrie didn't recognize him. He pulled the door shut, although, with its lock shot out, it wouldn't completely close. After slinging the assault rifle over his shoulder, he dug a pack of cigarettes from his shirt pocket and lit up. Leaning against one of the pillars, he stared across the parking area into the trees to the left of where Guthrie hid.

Guthrie snapped off the safety on the Remington and slowly raised it to his shoulder. He didn't dare stand for fear the man would spot him. As the man came into view in the scope, Guthrie had a pang of conscience. He'd killed before, but not counting Art, it had all been in the heat of battle. Well, even Art had been in the heat of battle, but that had been different. This was cold-blooded murder.

Cold-blooded murder of a man armed to the teeth who would shoot Guthrie down like a dog if he had the chance. Who, technically, was helping Banning and his hunting cronies hunt down Guthrie, Diane, and Howard to kill them. One of four or five equally dangerous men between Guthrie and the room where the painting hung. This might be Guthrie's only chance to whittle down their numbers before they knew he was here.

The man took another drag on his cigarette. He was almost done. Now or never.

Guthrie squeezed the trigger and felt the rifle buck into his shoulder. The man on the veranda tumbled back onto the slate, blood blooming from his chest.

As the gunshot's echoes vanished into the woods, Guthrie rose and pivoted behind the tree he'd been propped against. At first, there was no sign of movement from the house, then Guthrie saw a vague shadow move deep behind the living room windows.

He risked two shots, shattering the glass, figuring they wouldn't reveal his position. He knew he probably wouldn't hit whoever it was trying to look outside, but without the glass, the living room was a less inviting place for surveillance. Let them keep guessing and feeling less and less safe, he thought as he faded back into the forest.

He began a circuit of the compound, keeping a wary eye out for anyone who might be stationed in the woods. His first thought was to breach the fence along its left-hand periphery and make his way to the back of the little guesthouse where he'd been kept. The guest house and bunkhouse were only one story tall, which put their rooflines only a little higher than the chain-link fences blocking the gaps between them and the main house. If he could trim away the razor wire at the top with his wire cutters, he might be able to climb to the top of the fence and, from there, to one of the roofs.

But would he have sufficient time to do all that before he was spotted? There were cameras around the compound, and one or more of the men in the house might come out looking for him. Certainly Stewart and Talbot would know this side of the compound was more vulnerable to attack than the front. At least they didn't know who he was. Yet.

As he cautiously continued his circumnavigation of the fence line, he saw that he'd never get in that way. Talbot was hidden behind the little pump house, holding an AR. From where he crouched, he could survey the area behind the guest house and bunkhouse, and if Guthrie had tried that way, he wouldn't have made it as far as the fence.

Unfortunately, though he could glimpse Talbot through the trees and brush, Guthrie couldn't get a clean shot at him, so he kept moving, and soon he was rounding the back of the predator barn. If he could get inside, he might be able to get a better shot at the muscle man through the front door.

The back end of the barn was about twenty feet inside the perimeter fence, and about ten feet up, above the roll-up vehicle door and the personnel door in the wall, a camera kept watch over the two entrances. Nearby sat one of the Kawasakis with a small trailer attached to its rear. The cart was half full of animal manure, and a shovel leaned against its side.

Out of the camera's range, Guthrie clipped a slit in the fence, squeezed through, and darted to the Kawasaki's cart. There, he grabbed the shovel and leapt toward the door, keeping his face down. It didn't really matter if anyone saw him because they'd know soon enough that someone was back here. He just didn't want them to know who. With a swiping heave, he swung the shovel and axed the camera off the wall.

Even as it and the shovel clattered to the rocky drive, he was at the personnel door, reaching for the knob. A quick twist told him it was locked, but it readily yielded to his lock picks. He locked the door behind him after he entered. Even if they came to investigate, it would take them a few minutes to realize that he was inside the building.

His feline neighbors were still there, and their attitude toward him hadn't changed. The lion roared, and the tiger snarled and flung itself at the mesh. The rest of the animals grew agitated, too, but most remained silent, merely pacing nervously in their enclosures. He slung the rifle, pulled the .40, and ran down the line of cages toward the door that led to the front office space.

He came through the door with the pistol leveled, but the room was vacant. The office didn't have a window, so he had to crack the door a quarter of an inch to look out into the compound.

The door through which Guthrie peered gave him access to the compound, but it wouldn't do him much good. The hundred and fifty feet separating the barn from the backs of the bungalows was filled with scrubby trees and brush, but also the pump house where Talbot hid. Guthrie had hoped he'd be able to get a better angle on Talbot's position, but the scrub protected him from attack in just about any direction.

But he could see the gap between the side of the bunkhouse and the main house's left wing, and he watched Stewart edge around the corner with another man Guthrie had never seen, who carried an AR. Stewart pointed toward the barn then urged the other man forward.

"That's right," Guthrie muttered. "Go check it out."

He shut the door and ran toward the back of the building. There, he stood beside the personnel door, his right hand gripping his pistol, his left on the door knob. The man might check the doors to see if they'd been breached, but he'd find nothing but the surveillance camera lying on the gravel. And with the building's rear doors locked, he might not realize Guthrie was inside.

Two minutes later, cautious footsteps crunched on the gravel. They approached the fallen camera, paused, then crunched some more while remaining in position, as if the man was turning around to survey the woods behind the barn. Silence ensued for several long moments before the footsteps came up to the door, and the knob rattled. Then the footsteps turned and began to retreat back toward the corner of the barn, moving a little faster than they'd approached.

Before they'd gone ten paces, Guthrie eased the door open and stepped out.

"Drop it," he commanded.

The man whirled and tried to fire, but Guthrie's gun barked twice, and the man went down. Guthrie didn't know if he was dead, but it didn't matter. It was unlikely that Stewart would come after him or that anyone else would be foolish enough to check the back of the barn alone. Guthrie grabbed the AR and the two extra magazines from a pouch on the man's belt, then he went back inside and locked the door. Returning to the front room, he cracked the door again.

Stewart was still in the gap between the main house and the guesthouse, peering toward the barn. Guthrie hefted the hunting rifle and took shot at him. The round missed, and Stewart jerked back.

"Come on," Guthrie begged, sighting through the scope. "Try to lock the gate."

But Stewart was too experienced to expose himself. He pulled back, completely out of sight, leaving Guthrie in much the same position as he'd been before, although he'd managed to take out another of the opposition. How many more were there besides Stewart and Talbot? And where was Talbot now? Warned by the shots and watching the barn from the other side of the pump house? Or maneuvering to another position?

Guthrie exchanged the hunting rifle for the AR and raised it to his shoulder. Even if Talbot now hid on the other side of the pump house, the AR's powerful rounds would easily penetrate the tiny structure. Guthrie set the assault rifle to full auto and sprayed the pump house. He didn't know if he hit Talbot, but the big man rose from behind the pump house and raced in a zigzag pattern toward the central compound. Guthrie sent the last few rounds in the AR's magazine after him just to keep him moving but without any real hope of actually hitting him.

Guthrie glanced at his watch. Almost six. It would be dusk in less than two hours, and it had been about thirteen hours since he and his friends had emerged from Adriana's painting. Banning had to be getting close to the gate, and if he and his party got out....

With all the defenders now inside the central compound, Guthrie had more freedom of movement, and he concentrated on how he could get into the house. He figured the only way was to draw some of the opposition out and whittle them down. He also could blind them. He could forget the cameras on the fronts of the barns, but the area in front of the main house was observed by three. Two were on the house, pointing outward, and the third was mounted next to the gate that blocked the dirt road leading into the compound.

Guthrie shut the door and headed toward the back of the barn. They still didn't know who he was and how much knowledge he had of the compound, and that gave him the only advantage he had.

Before leaving the building, he went to the walk-in freezer in the back corner and opened the door. Inside, were stacked crates of supplies and 55-gallon drums whose labels said they contained ground beef and fish. In the aisles between the drums and crates lay the bodies of the two game wardens, Norris, and Brother Gregory.

"Cat food," Guthrie muttered as he closed the door and turned to leave the building.

He went out the back door, leaving it unlocked so he could easily get in the barn if he needed to. The man he'd shot lay motionless in a pool of blood. Guthrie turned away, slipped through the slit in the fence, and faded into the woods.

In a few minutes, he'd made his way to a position where he could target the three surveillance cameras through the Remington's scope. It was time to take them out before it got too dark to see and before that same darkness revealed his muzzle flashes. Moving from location to location to gain a clear field of fire, he shot out the cameras. Each took him several tries, but eventually all three were dangling junk.

Two minutes after the last camera had been eliminated, Guthrie found a tree where he could observe the front of the house without being seen. Sitting and leaning against the trunk, he opened his pack and pulled out an energy bar, dried fruit, and a bottle of water. He ate quickly and returned the trash to his pack. Then he waited for night to fall.

40

BY EIGHT, THE SUN WAS behind the distant hills and the air grown cooler. Half a dozen flood lights flared on, lighting the area. They proved easier targets than the cameras had been, and in a couple of minutes, he'd returned the compound to darkness. The lights in the houses remained off.

Guthrie slung the Remington over his shoulder and held the AR ready as he made his way back to the rear of the barn by the light of the quarter moon, praying that the door was still unlocked. The man he'd shot earlier still lay where he'd fallen. When he crept up to the door and tried the knob, he found it was still unlocked. That didn't make him any less wary, though he suspected that none of the defenders would be willing to follow him back here. But suppose they had found the door unlocked and left it that way to lure him inside where they could finish him off?

He propped the hunting rifle against the wall next to the door and hefted the AR. Crouching, he pushed the door open, half expecting a hail of bullets in response, but nothing happened. Leaping through the opening, AR sweeping the room, he darted to one side. Still nothing. The animals grew restless at his sudden intrusion, but that was all. In a minute, he'd retrieved the hunting rifle and dashed through the barn to the front door.

Now that it was nearly night and there was no light, he wished he'd brought a night-vision headset. The large, sparsely wooded area between the barn and the back of the guest house and bunkhouse was an impenetrable gloom that could conceal not only Talbot, but others as well. All of whom might be wearing night vision goggles. Guthrie wasn't about to mount a one-man frontal assault, but there still might be a way, he thought as he eyed the gap between the main house and the bunkhouse—the location from which Stewart had dispatched the man who now lay behind the barn.

Guthrie had counted six cars in the yard aside from Banning and Lycoris's vehicles and Guthrie's Xterra, which accounted for the six strangers Banning had taken into the otherworld to hunt Guthrie and his friends. Guthrie figured that each of the hunters might have brought along one man, which meant six at the most were guarding the house along with Stewart and Talbot. Two were dead, which left four. Stewart, at least, would be guarding Banning's vault and office, and now maybe Talbot, too. Guthrie couldn't imagine Talbot returning to the pump house and crouching there all night, especially if he didn't have night vision and couldn't see any better than Guthrie. Most likely, all the defenders were in the main house or guarding the courtyard.

But Guthrie had to make sure of that if he was going to approach the house. He propped the AR next to the door, shouldered the hunting rifle, and aimed where he thought the pump house might be. The rifle was nearly out of ammunition after he'd taken out the cameras and lights, and he might as well use the remaining rounds to make sure the pump house was clear. He squeezed off the rifle's last four rounds and was gratified to hear no return fire.

Almost certainly they were all guarding the house. Most likely, Stewart would have a man watching out the front windows, one out the back windows overlooking the courtyard, and one at the kitchen door. The fourth, if there was a fourth, could be anywhere, but Stewart probably had him helping guard the courtyard and the vulnerable gaps between the main house's wings and the two smaller houses at the rear.

To keep them guessing about his position, Guthrie went through the door and angled off to the right, then along the compound's north fence line until he was even with the kitchen. The defenders would have heard him firing the hunting rifle's last rounds from the direction of the barn, so their attention would be on that direction, and anyone inside the living room would be looking toward the front gate, not in this way. If there was a man in the kitchen, Guthrie would just have to deal with him when the time came.

He made it to the house free and clear then cautiously peered into one of the kitchen windows. Sure enough, a man was in there, half hidden behind the island, but he was watching the back door, not the windows, and hadn't seen Guthrie approach. Moving silently, Guthrie crept past the door to the corner just across the gap from the guest house. The gate was shut and padlocked. He knelt, drew a hooked dental mirror out of a pocket and poked it slowly around the edge of the wall. It took him several seconds to orient himself to what he could see in the small round glass, and when he had, all he could see was the back end of the pool and a clump of shrubbery at the far corner of the courtyard, just across the sidewalk from the front of the bunkhouse. He didn't immediately spot anyone, but he forced himself to remain still as he slowly angled the mirror so he could scan as much of the area as possible.

Still no one.

But the wings of the house and the shadowed shrubbery at the corner could easily conceal anyone waiting behind them. He concentrated on the shrubbery. It was a far distance to observe in the tiny area of the mirror, but after a few minutes, he was rewarded when a shape shifted in the shadow of a small ficus tree that stood a few feet back from the shrubbery.

If a man was there, surely one was concealed on this side, too. Stewart wouldn't have left either gap unguarded. But since Guthrie hadn't spotted him, he must be, like his partner, hanging back from the corner, waiting to ambush anybody who came through.

Guthrie slipped the mirror back into its pocket and shouldered the AR. Cautiously, he poked the muzzle around the corner and through the chain-link. The man across the pool was little more than a denser shadow within another shadow. Guthrie aimed into the center of the mass and squeezed off a three-round burst. He didn't know if all the bullets found their target, but at least one did. The man grunted and fell writhing to the ground.

Almost instantly, the second man, crouching low, appeared from around the corner of the nearer wing, pump shotgun in his hands belching fire and buckshot as he jacked round after round through its chamber.

Guthrie had ducked back as soon as the first man had fallen, and the shotgun pellets tore harmlessly along the stone-faced wall and scattered into the night. He blindly poked the barrel of the AR around the corner and sprayed an entire magazine into the gap.

Slamming his last magazine into the rifle, he risked a quick glance around the corner. He couldn't see the man, but he could hear the sound of him jamming more shells into the shotgun. He darted across the gap and headed toward the back corner of the guest house. There, he peered around the corner and down the back walls of the two bungalows. Seeing no one, he ducked around the corner and ran for the alley between the bungalows. This gate also was padlocked.

Sinking to one knee, he edged his face to the corner. From here, he couldn't see the gaps between the main house and the smaller houses, but he could see the remains of the plate glass windows and sliding glass doors that Stewart and Talbot had shot out when Guthrie and his friends had escaped into Banning's office. Though no one was visible in the darkness beyond, Guthrie was sure that someone lurked in the gloom.

"Lozano! Banks!" Stewart's voice barked out urgently. "You there?"

"I'm here," the man with the shotgun called out, his voice tight.

"Banks!"

"Yeah," came a more subdued voice from the man Guthrie had shot. "I'm fucked up. He got me twice."

"He?" Stewart hissed.

"I think there's only one," Lozano said.

"Where?"

"Out there. On my side."

"Fuck!" Stewart swore. "He could be anywhere, now. Banks, can you still fight?"

"I don't think so. My arm's fucked up. I'm bleeding bad. I need a doctor."

"Well, I ain't got no fucking doctor. But if you can get in here, I'll patch you up as best I can."

Guthrie heard Banks, grunting with pain and effort, get to his feet and stagger across the paving beside the pool. A second later, he came into view, shuffling toward the open door. Gritting his teeth, Guthrie shot him, and he fell heavily across the glass-strewn threshold. Even before his body hit, muzzle flares burst from the interior of the darkened room, and bullets gouged the stone wall near Guthrie's head before he managed to jerk back.

"Did you get him?" Lozano asked.

Guthrie replied by emptying the AR through the empty remains of the door and windows. He'd hoped to hit Stewart with the barrage, but he was disappointed.

"I don't know who the fuck you are," Stewart yelled as the AR's chatter fell silent, "but if you know what's good for you, you'll leave now while you've got a chance. We have reinforcements coming, and there'll be more than enough of us to take you, and you won't like it when we do."

But his words already were fading as Guthrie dashed around the back of the bunkhouse. Out of ammo for the AR, he dropped the rifle as he ran. There was still one man in the courtyard, but he'd be keeping back from the openings, hoping to ambush Guthrie if he came through any of them into the courtyard. The gate on this side would be out of his range of vision. Quickly climbing the chain link, Guthrie used the wire cutters to clip the razor wire at the top, then he scrambled onto the roof.

Directly in front of him was the south wing of the main house's second floor where Banning's rooms were. All the windows were dark and the curtains drawn. No sound drifted up from the courtyard below, and Guthrie didn't know if that was because the man down there hadn't heard the fence rattle or if he was just being silent.

Guthrie cautiously edged over the roof peak and peered into the dark courtyard. He hated to expose himself, but he had to see more of the courtyard. It took him nearly a minute to spot Lozano. He was standing in the middle of a clump of sago palms beside the kitchen wall. It was a good spot. He was well masked by the sagos and positioned so he could watch where all three gaps opened into the courtyard.

Guthrie glanced toward the shattered and gaping windows and sliding doors at the back of the house. The dead man still lay across the threshold. Was Stewart or Talbot— or even another man—inside? Probably, but he must be far enough back that he didn't have a view of the roof where Guthrie lay or there'd have been shots already.

Feeling like shit, Guthrie pulled his .40, aimed, and fired two rounds into Lozano, who pitched over sideways into one of the sagos then slid to the ground. Shots came from inside the house, but whoever was in there obviously hadn't seen Guthrie's muzzle flash and was just shooting. Not Stewart, Guthrie thought. Stewart would never shoot wildly. The gunfire stopped quickly enough, and a voice called out nervously.

"Lozano! Lozano!" The voice, inflected with a Latino accent, wasn't Stewart's.

Lozano wasn't going to answer, so Guthrie did, sending several bullets through the demolished door. There was no movement in the darkness beyond. Even Stewart would hesitate to investigate. Guthrie scuttled down to the eaves closest to Lozano and dropped into the courtyard. In a few seconds, he had Lozano's shotgun and a bandolier of shells. He blasted twice through the hole where the sliding doors had been then ran for the gate between the house and the bunkhouse. The .40 opened the padlock, and in another fifteen seconds, he was edging toward the shattered front windows, shotgun at port arms, being careful not to crunch broken glass beneath his feet. The man he'd first shot lay inert on the porch.

Guthrie paused alongside the window frame, which loomed darkly except for shards of glass clinging to the frame like so many ragged teeth, listening intently for any sound from within. As the pause lengthened, he thought he heard a faint rustling, as if someone inside was changing position, but he couldn't get an exact fix on the sound. Reaching into his pocket, he pulled out three of a handful of pebbles he'd picked up along the way and tossed them crossways through the window opening and into the room.

As they clattered across the floor, gunfire erupted, filling the room with the roar and muzzle flashes of an assault rifle. Guthrie swung around the corner, fired three blasts at the muzzle flashes, then quickly stepped back. Bullets from the assault rifle rode up the wall and across the ceiling, followed by a heavy thud.

Guthrie listened intently through the ringing in his ears for the sound of approaching footsteps, but all he heard was a groan. Then, a few moments later, Stewart's voice came.

"Gomez," Stewart hissed. "Gomez!"

Another groan answered then went silent.

"Shit," Stewart snarled. "You better keep out, you fucking bastard!" he yelled. "I'll blow your fucking head off!"

In reply, Guthrie stuck the shotgun around the window frame and fired at the sound of Stewart's voice. As the sound of footsteps retreated deeper into the house, Guthrie stooped as low as he could beneath the sills of the front windows and in a moment was beside the front door.

Guthrie nudged the door open with the muzzle of the shotgun, half expecting to be shot at. If his assumption that there were six new men was correct, one was still left in the house with Stewart and Talbot. Adriana and Melanie probably were somewhere inside, too, and Guthrie wouldn't put it past them to gun him down if they saw him.

But nothing happened. Maybe someone was inside waiting coolly across the foyer for Guthrie to show himself. Guthrie didn't want to take unnecessary risks, but he had to get inside, and that wasn't going to happen if he stood around here all night. The longer he waited, the worse his chances were.

He still had a few of the pebbles left, and he tossed them across the foyer floor.

No response.

There had to be a light switch just inside the door. He snaked his arm around the door casing, feeling for the switch, and his fingers touched three switches. One for the foyer, one for the porch, and one for...? Which one turned on the foyer light?

He settled on the one closest to the door, reasoning that that would be easiest to reach for anyone entering the house. He flipped the switch, and the foyer flooded with light as Guthrie quickly withdrew his arm.

No one took a shot at him, and he reluctantly stepped across the threshold. In a moment, he was at the doorway to the living room, and he listened for a moment, then edged an eye around the corner. There wasn't much light, but there was enough to reveal the prone form of a man lying in a dark pool, moving feebly but not making any sound. An AK-47 lay several feet away, its stock shredded by buckshot and stained with blood.

Maybe there were only five additional men, and this was the last. Or maybe a sixth was deeper in the house with Stewart and Talbot.

Guthrie padded across the foyer to the archway that opened onto the hall that led to the wing where Banning's office and trophy room were. And the vault with the painting. He listened intently for sounds from inside the house. All he could hear was the faint rustle of the wounded man in the living room, and even that stilled after a few minutes.

The hall was pitch black. Stewart or Talbot could be standing in the middle of the hallway and be completely invisible.

Guthrie reached carefully around the corner, felt two switches, and flipped them both. Bullets from two assault rifles tore the air, and one grazed his forearm before he could jerk his hand back. Without looking at the wound, he rammed the muzzle of his shotgun around the corner and fired.

That should let them know not to come investigate, he thought. He didn't think they would, anyway. They knew Banning would be back soon. They'd hold Guthrie off until the hunting party returned, then they'd counterattack in force.

For Guthrie, the only question was, how many of them were down the hall? Two? Three? Maybe five, counting Adriana and Melanie.

He glanced at his wound. The bullet had gouged a three-inch gash across his upper forearm, and it was bleeding steadily. Guthrie dug a compact first aid kit from a pocket on his vest, found a couple of squares of gauze, and wrapped them on with tape. The bandage didn't stop the bleeding, but it would have to do for now.

While he was tending the wound, either Stewart or the other man down the hall shot out the lights. Guthrie sent another blast in that direction, then slinging the shotgun across his shoulder, he hurried into the living room. The man in there had stopped moving. Ignoring him, Guthrie unplugged two end table lamps and carried them back to the foyer. He plugged them into a wall socket near the archway and set them on the floor where their light would partially illuminate the dark corridor without exposing them to gunfire. He shot once more down the hall, then hurried out the front door and turned left.

He went off the end of the front veranda, turned left again, and crept down the wall of the right wing. The vault holding the painting stuck out from the far end like a blocky appendage. Guthrie ducked under the windows for the den and another, small and set high in the wall. The hall bathroom for this wing. He paused at the fourth. The bathroom adjacent to Banning's office. Which made the next one the office. He peered around the lower corner of the sill but the room inside was pitch black except for a faint rectangular glow emanating from the far wall. The doorway. The light was from the lamps he'd set at the end of the hall.

He stood there, watching and letting his eyes adjust to the faint glow. Gradually, he became aware that two men were in the room. They were leaning against the wall on either side of the door, both bearing assault rifles. Guthrie couldn't see their features, but one was unmistakably Stewart. The other was as tall as Talbot, but he didn't have Talbot's bulk. The sixth man.

"I don't like it," the sixth man hissed loudly enough for his voice to carry through the glass. "This guy knows the layout of this place, and that ain't good."

"The fuck he does," Stewart snarled. "He's just lucky."

"Lucky, my ass. If I was you…."

"Well, you aren't. You just kill the motherfucker, and we won't have to worry. Or we just wait until Talbot brings Banning back. I'm going to the vault. Don't let him by."

Stewart went through the door to the vault and was gone. The sixth man stepped to the other side of the door and stared down the hall without exposing himself.

Straightening, Guthrie reared back and rammed the muzzle of the shotgun between the bars and through the glass and, almost simultaneously, fired once, twice, three times. The man's assault rifle chattered half a dozen rounds into the hall wall as he fell, torn and bloody, across the threshold.

Guthrie pumped another shell into the chamber and waited, but Stewart didn't reappear. Guthrie ran along the wall, turned onto the veranda, and in twenty seconds was leaning against the wall next to the door of the trophy room.

"You're the last, Stewart!" he yelled. "Give it up!"

41

"GUTHRIE!" STEWART SOUNDED INCREDULOUS. "HOW the fuck did you get here?" His voice came from behind the painting vault's cracked door.

"Maybe I know something Banning doesn't."

"Don't come any closer, you fucker, or we'll cut you to pieces!"

"You and who? Talbot? He's there with you?"

"Right here."

"Bullshit. You just told your dead friend here that he went out into that other world to get Banning. He shouldn't have bothered. Banning's already on his way back. But that's not going to help you any."

"Come on in, and let's see. This room is like a fortress. There's no way you can get to me."

Stewart was right, Guthrie realized. Guthrie might have access to a virtual armory in Banning's office, but there was nothing in there that could penetrate either the doors or the walls of the vault. On the other hand, Stewart had the vault door propped open for a reason. If it was shut, Guthrie could have locked it, but that wouldn't keep Banning locked out. The roll-up door would let out him and his gang any time they wanted.

The crack in the door was the key because, while the door itself was impenetrable, the crack wasn't. Bullets weren't going to do the trick, though. It had to be something else. Something that could go through the crack and give Guthrie an edge.

Smoke?

Guthrie didn't want to burn the house down. Besides, it was mostly stone, concrete, and glass, and he didn't think it would burn sufficiently. Also, he didn't want to destroy any evidence that the local police might discover to prove Banning's nefarious character. Like the human trophy heads.

Then he thought of something. After sending two shotgun blasts through the crack just to give Stewart something to think about, he hurried down the hall, Stewart's voice trailing him.

"No dice, Guthrie," Stewart taunted. "You'll have to come closer than that."

His voice faded as Guthrie turned off the hall into the room with the sliding glass doors that opened onto the courtyard. The man he'd shot still lay across the threshold. Guthrie stepped over the body and hurried around the pool to the storage room where the pool equipment was kept. He had to shove Lozano's body aside to open the door. Inside, he found a five-gallon bucket of chlorine tablets for the pool. He pried off the lid. It was half full. Sliding the lid back on, he grabbed the bucket's handle and went back into the house. A few turns took him to the kitchen, where he rummaged under the sink, collecting every cleaner that contained ammonia. He tossed the bottles into the bucket and carried everything back into the office. There, he took a couple of more shots at the crack in the vault door, just to let Stewart know it wasn't safe to come out and try to find him, then he went looking for a fan. He found one in one of the upstairs bedrooms—one that looked like it might be Adriana's.

Back in the office, he shot through the crack before setting the fan and bucket close to the vault door. He plugged the fan into a nearby outlet, turned it on, and aimed it toward the opening. He took the bottles of cleaner out of the bucket and set them on the floor before taking the bucket to the washroom attached to the office, where he filled it about one quarter full of water. The air quickly filled with the acrid odor of chlorine. He set the bucket in front of the fan then opened all the bottles and quickly dumped their contents into the chlorinated water. Even before he was done, choking fumes had replaced the acrid odor and were rising over the bucket's rim. He shot at the vault door again before thankfully retreating to the end of the hall, taking the bucket lid with him.

It didn't take long for Stewart to react to the fumes being blown through the crack. Guthrie heard him choking and, a moment later, saw him peer around the jamb to see what was causing the fumes. Guthrie beat him back with blasts from the shotgun.

"It's chlorine gas, Stewart!" Guthrie shouted. "Stay where you are, and it'll burn out your eyes and lungs!"

Then, all he could do was wait.

Within seconds, the sound of Stewart's choking retreated. As soon as it did, Guthrie, holding his breath, rushed forward and snapped the bucket's lid over the fuming stew inside. Eyes burning, he moved back behind the fan and gave it a few moments to clear the air before stepping quickly to the vault door.

Either Stewart had gone outside, into the other world, or he was hiding behind the door. In either case, he was waiting for Guthrie to make a move into the vault. Guthrie swung to the left side of the door, reached out with the barrel of the shotgun, and prodded the door open. Heavy as it was, it swung easily inward on its well-hung hinges. He risked a quick peek around the jamb. The room appeared to be empty, but Stewart could still be behind the door.

Without taking his eyes from the door and the room beyond, he backed up until his heels bumped into the bucket. He eased around it and the fan. Unplugging the fan, he carried it to the vault door and heaved it into the center of the room. The banging clatter brought an immediate response—not from behind the door but from the righthand side of the gateway to the other world—as Stewart sent a burst from his AR into the room before he realized he'd given himself away to a ruse. Guthrie fired the shotgun at the opening, but Stewart, too quick, pivoted behind the edge of the painting. From his position behind the gateway, he could be on either side in an instant.

Guthrie could have closed the vault door and locked it, and maybe jammed the roll-up door, but that wouldn't solve the problem of Angra Mainyu, who would just melt the door—the entire room—to slag before escaping into the Texas Hill Country. Guthrie had to get into the room and destroy the painting. That was the only sure way to end things.

And the only way to do that, apparently, was to confront Stewart head on. Guthrie knew he'd have to go through the gateway. That was the only option, but it didn't appeal to Guthrie because Stewart would be waiting for Guthrie to step out and expose himself. Guthrie would become instantly visible—and vulnerable—while Stewart would remain masked by the rectangle of the gateway. Stewart could even shoot Guthrie straight through the back of painting, which didn't exist where he stood, as soon as Guthrie stepped through.

Guthrie risked another glance into the room, and what he saw chilled him. Through the door into the other world, he could see the ridge up which he and Diane and Howard had escaped just two days earlier, and working its way down the cleft from the pass that went over the top was a figure. Even from this distance—maybe a mile—Guthrie recognized Talbot from his shape, the way he moved, and most of all by the loud Hawaiian shirt he wore. Then, a movement at the top of the pass above Talbot caught his attention. Four men appeared and started down the cleft, maybe ten minutes behind Talbot.

Banning and the remains of his party.

Guthrie's time had run out. He had to take care of Stewart, and quickly. Guthrie started to step into the room, willing to take a chance on bursting into the open and taking out Stewart before Stewart got him, but he suddenly halted.

Was Stewart still behind the gateway, waiting? If he was, there would be nothing he could do to prevent Guthrie from simply walking into the room and damaging the painting. On the other hand, he could be crouched in the gully where Guthrie and his friends had hidden when they'd first escaped into the otherworld. From there, he'd be covered and have a clear view of the room. No chance for an experienced shooter to miss at that range.

Guthrie peered around the lower left edge of the vault door frame. He couldn't see Stewart, but he saw something just as good. Stewart had made one miscalculation. Although he'd remained hidden behind the gateway, his shadow hadn't, and it crept across the ground ahead of him, warning Guthrie that he was standing beside the left hand side of the gateway.

Guthrie had to be smart, particularly since he was down to two shells for the shotgun. He retreated far enough into the office to grab the handle of the bucket of his seething toxic broth. Even though he'd tamped the lid on, noxious fumes were leaking around its edges, and Guthrie had to squint and hold his breath as he carried the bucket to the door. He ducked back for another moment to catch his breath, then holding it again, he unsnapped the bucket lid, stepped swiftly across the vault's floor, and slung the bucket through the left side of the gateway. It hit the ground at an angle and spewed its contents in Stewart's direction.

"Fuck!" Stewart bellowed. "You fucking bastard!"

Suddenly the man appeared. He'd stumbled through the back of the gateway. Fuming liquid streamed off his pants and his face was scrunched in a pained expression, but he was bringing the muzzle of his AR down as his eyes sought Guthrie's position, already firing. Only Guthrie was no longer in the middle of the vault but off to the right, half hidden by the open steel door, ready.

Before Stewart could alter the angle of his fire, Guthrie pulled the trigger of the shotgun. The blast took Stewart in his side and hip, and he spun and went down in the gateway, the AR skittering across the hardpan outside. To his credit, he tried to draw his .45, but Guthrie stepped up, shotgun aimed, and shook his head.

"Forget it, Stewart."

But Stewart couldn't. He jerked the .45 up, and Guthrie shot him in the chest before he could pull the trigger.

Guthrie tossed the empty shotgun aside and, trying not to look at the damage he'd done, stepped across the body, grabbed it beneath the armpits, and began hauling it out of the gateway. The bastard was heavy—heavier than Guthrie—and dragging his dead weight was hard and not made any easier by the fumes rising from Stewart's soaked pants and the awful stench reeking from the slimy pile of decay that had been the spiny creature Banning's men had shot to pieces. It was crawling with bugs and worms, but Guthrie didn't really want to peer more closely at them to see what they looked like. Nor did he have the time. A bullet whined by his head, and a second chipped the hardpan not two feet away.

With desperate effort, Guthrie heaved Stewart's legs out of the gateway, but he didn't have a chance to get back inside before another round sizzled the air near his head. All he could manage was to duck behind the gateway.

Here, he was completely masked by the gateway, but he could see through the space it occupied as if it wasn't there. And what he saw was Adriana and Melanie Lycoris scrambling out of the gully where Guthrie thought Stewart might be hiding, screaming and wildly firing pistols. But in their rage, they were oblivious to the fact that their rounds couldn't reach him, and they emptied their pistols into the vault, not him.

But Talbot wouldn't be so careless. He was running across the space between the foot of the ridge and the vault, chrome .357 glinting in the sunlight.

Guthrie checked the magazine of his .40. Only five rounds left. Plus one more full magazine. Seventeen rounds. Eight more nestled in the .380 strapped to his ankle, but that would be accurate only at close range. And he wasn't sure he could stop Talbot quickly enough with a .380 unless the shots were extremely well placed.

Talbot, knowing that his bullets couldn't reach Guthrie, held his fire and veered to his right, heading toward Adriana and Melanie, who'd retreated into the gully, only their heads peering above the rim. Obviously, he intended to lie low and keep Guthrie pinned behind the gateway until Banning and the others arrived. Shooting straight through the back of the gateway, Guthrie tried to hit Talbot, but the big man was dodging, and if any of Guthrie's rounds found their mark, it didn't show.

Guthrie had to get back inside the vault before he was outgunned. He ejected the now-spent magazine and slammed the last one into the gun's receiver. Waiting until Talbot had almost reached the gully, he emptied it at him, and was rewarded by a spray of blood as Talbot fell into the gully. Guthrie didn't know how badly he was hit, but it didn't matter. He'd gained the scant seconds he needed to spring through the back of the gateway and dive into the room.

There, pressed into the corner space between the edge of the gateway and the adjacent wall, he was momentarily safe. But he still had to remove the painting from its alcove, and to do that, he'd have to completely expose himself to fire from outside. He thought about trying to get into the house through the door at the far end of the vault to find something with which he could destroy the painting, but that would open him to Talbot's gunfire. And even if he did, it would leave the vault vulnerable for too many precious minutes.

He risked a quick glance through the gateway and saw that Banning's party had reached the base of the ridge. They'd be here in only a few minutes. Of Talbot, there was no sign. Maybe Guthrie's bullets had hurt him badly enough that he was out of the fight. Guthrie wondered if he dared step into the alcove to try to remove the painting, but thought better of it. Talbot might just be waiting for Guthrie to show himself. But Guthrie had to do something, and he didn't have long to figure out what that something might be.

He had to know Talbot's status. The empty shotgun lay within reach, and Guthrie retrieved it, removed his tac vest, and draped it over the barrel. Carefully, he extended the vest into the opening, only to have it torn off the shotgun's barrel by .357 rounds.

If Talbot was wounded, he wasn't showing it. Nor did he seem to be out of ammo.

As Guthrie leaned against the wall beside the door, reaching toward his ankle to draw the .380 and trying to decide what to do, the decision was made for him. The gateway darkened, and Talbot came in. Instead of the .357, his right hand grasped the hilt of a heavy combat knife. So, he's out of ammo, Guthrie thought just as Talbot lunged at him.

42

TALBOT'S BULKY MUSCLES WERE POWERFUL, but they also made him top-heavy and slower than he might have been otherwise. And he was wounded. Blood added a fresh blob of color to the right side of his Hawaiian shirt. Guthrie stepped to the left and, using a circular block up and outward with his left arm, diverted Talbot's knife hand. Talbot stopped short, and in an instant, Guthrie delivered a quick, sharp shove to his shoulder. Because Guthrie had hooked his right foot inside of Talbot's right foot, the big man was jolted over his own center of gravity, and he crashed into the corner of the vault near the gateway.

He was up almost as quickly as he fell, still holding the knife but now more wary. Guthrie saw him throw a glance through the gate to the other world and knew he was judging how long it would take Banning's party to arrive. Guthrie didn't bother. It was only a matter of minutes. Talbot knew that, too, and he simply stepped near the door, blocking it with his bulk. He didn't have to defeat Guthrie, only hold him off for a few more minutes.

Guthrie dashed to the end of the room nearest the door to the house and bent to draw the .380. As soon as he did, Talbot realized that he must be going for a gun and that holding steady wasn't going to work. Bellowing, he rushed Guthrie, who was pulling back the gun's slide as he straightened.

Talbot hit him before he could bring the gun to bear, and they slammed into the wall next to the vault door. Guthrie lost hold of the gun, and it skittered across the cement floor to the far side of the room. It was just as well. Talbot was incredibly powerful, and it took all of Guthrie's strength and concentration to twist enough to keep the knife from ripping out his guts. He batted the knife arm to the side, felt a searing along his ribs, and rammed the edge of his hand into the side of Talbot's neck, all in one circular movement. But the big man only grunted, and his left hand wrapped around Guthrie's throat in an iron grip as he reared back to ram the heavy blade into Guthrie's chest.

Clamping his chin down to keep Talbot's grip from crushing his larynx, Guthrie blocked the thrusting arm with his left, then snapped his right forearm up underneath Talbot's elbow. There was a crackling pop as Talbot's elbow gave way. It wasn't broken, only wrenched, but the knife clattered to the floor. Without hesitating, Guthrie followed up with a left palm strike that smashed into Talbot's face, shattering his front teeth and sending him falling back, blood fountaining from his ruined nose. He landed heavily, but he was back up more quickly than Guthrie expected, eyes inflamed in their mask of blood. But he didn't rush Guthrie. Instead, he took two quick steps and bent to retrieve Guthrie's fallen pistol.

At his first step, Guthrie knew what he was after, and he leapt toward him, scooping up the combat knife. As the big man lifted the pistol, Guthrie brought the knife up underhanded, slicing the blade across Talbot's inner arm. Blood gushed and Talbot's hand spasmed open, and before the gun hit the floor, Guthrie raked the blade back across Talbot's chest then drew it upward and rammed it halfway to the hilt in the left side of Talbot's head.

Talbot gasped and staggered, but he didn't seem to realize what had happened as he turned on Guthrie. But something had happened. As if the knife had severed some connection to Talbot's equilibrium, his rush veered sharply to the right, taking him several feet past Guthrie.

Grunting in surprise, he staggered to a stop, wheeled clumsily, and rushed again. Guthrie sidestepped Talbot's grasping arms, and the muscle man stumbled on for a few feet, stopped, bent forward, and shook his head.

"Fucking bastard," he mumbled. "Fucking bastard always plays that card. Can't have eggs without bacon. That's what Junior said. Junior! I'm over here!"

As if in a daze, Talbot waved his arms. Guthrie moved in, spun his bewildered opponent around, and shoved him through the gateway. Talbot stumbled outside and took a few faltering steps before he tripped over Stewart's body and fell to the ground. He struggled to his feet, and as he did, he spotted the pile of slimy, stinking remains of the spiny creature lying about ten feet from him. He looked like he might walk toward it, but the sound of shouts and gunfire attracted his attention. In the same instant, Guthrie heard a pair of angry hornets burn by his head.

Banning, out in front of his party, was shooting, and probably the only reason he'd missed was that he was running full tilt over the uneven playa as he fired. The rest of his party straggled out behind, and around them, several hideous creatures fled like animals before a forest fire. Banning and his men weren't just running toward the gateway. They were running from Angra Mainyu, whose boiling, twisting corruption crested the ridge and flowed down the pass, leaving fused earth in its wake.

Banning was leading it straight to the gateway.

Guthrie tried to remove the painting from its alcove, but all of Banning's men were shooting now, and bullets tore through the opening and smacked into the concrete walls around the vault door or embedded themselves in the steel roll-up door at the opposite end of the room. Guthrie ducked into the corner where he was protected. His fingers sought the edges of the painting's frame where it was fitted into the niche, but the gap was too narrow and the angle was wrong. He needed a tool—something flat, like a knife or screwdriver. But he had nothing.

Then his eyes fell on the .380 lying on the floor. He snatched it up, and shielding his eyes with his left hand, fired all eight rounds, concentrating on a single spot at the painting's edge where the panel was wedged against the concrete. Cement shards stung him. He didn't expect much, but he didn't need much. Dropping the smoking gun, he clawed his fingers into the shallow, rough grooves his bullets had made in the concrete edge. By now, the shooting from outside had stopped, and he could hear the pounding of footsteps not thirty feet away. His frantic fingers found the edge of the frame. It was ragged and splintered by his bullets, but there was just enough room to get his fingers behind it. He jerked, but the painting remained lodged in its niche. And in that instant, Banning's shadow loomed in the gateway.

Banning must have heard the shooting from inside the vault, because he didn't try to burst into the room. Instead, he dashed to the side, where he could spot Guthrie through the gateway. A tight grimace of triumph mixed with fear crossed his features as he raised his powerful hunting rifle and fired three rounds at Guthrie.

Guthrie barely had time to wince and start to duck—as if that could have done any good—but Banning's bullets didn't slam into him. Instead, they hit the gateway and, slowing drastically, practically oozed through like deadly drops of molasses. Two feet into the room, they lost their momentum entirely and fell with dull thuds to the floor.

By now, Adriana, Melanie, and two of the rest of Banning's party had arrived, and the men began shooting, too, with similar effect. Then Guthrie saw the reason. One of his bullets had gone through the painting's frame instead of just ricocheting through the gateway, and punched a hole through the back of the wooden panel, marring the painting from behind. Now it was less than perfect and no longer a true opening. Guthrie reached out and found that he could touch its surface, which felt greasy and yielding. He looked out at Banning.

"You fucking bastard!" Banning bellowed. He emptied his gun at the gateway, but with little effect. Then twin screams from Adriana and Melanie made him spin around.

Out on the playa, Angra Mainyu had overtaken one of the men Guthrie didn't know, and his body was twisting as forces beyond knowledge morphed him into something more akin to a deformed insect than a man.

Banning turned back to Guthrie, panic in his eyes.

"Let us in, Guthrie!" he yelled, his voice coming through as if from a distance. "You have to let us in!"

Guthrie couldn't have if he'd wanted to.

"Too late, Banning," Guthrie yelled back. "You wanted to hunt the ultimate predator. Now you're going to get the chance. There it is." He pointed out onto the playa, where Angra Mainyu was rapidly approaching the gateway.

Banning rushed to the gateway and threw himself against it in a futile attempt to enter the vault, but Guthrie ignored him. Instead, he went back into the house and out onto the front porch. The man he'd shot was still there. He'd been out there smoking, and Guthrie went through his pockets until he found his lighter. Then he crossed the compound to the predator barn where the Kawasaki four-wheelers were kept. Ignoring the roars, growls, and howls of the animals in the cages, he hefted a five-gallon gas can that felt full and returned to the house.

When he reentered the vault, Banning and the others were still there, trying to pry around the edges of the door with knives. Behind them stood Adriana and Melanie, bodies tense. Melanie had her hands to her ears, and her face was a grimace of pain. Beyond them, Talbot was stumbling around aimlessly, mouth moving as if he was talking to himself, though his words did not reach Guthrie's ears.

By now, Angra Mainyu was nearly at the room, melting rock and earth, marking the boundary of its influence. Oblivious, Talbot walked right into its roiling mass, and as it rolled across him, he froze, then collapsed and melted into the fused rocks.

Banning saw it happen, too, and he turned back to Guthrie.

"Let me in!"

"Please!" wailed Adriana.

"Better run," Guthrie advised them as he splashed gasoline around the sides of the painting. Those trapped in that other world watched him, horror on their faces, and when Guthrie pulled out the lighter, they turned from the door and scattered across the barren ground. Banning and two of the men made it to relative safety, but Adriana and Melanie froze in petrified terror, clutching at each other. And then Angra Mainyu's peripheral field touched them, and they began to fuse together, melting into a hideous, lumpen thing with three legs, tentacles, and six eyes that projected an eternity of hatred and pain.

Turning away in disgust and horror, Guthrie pushed the button to raise the door to give the fire plenty of oxygen, and as it lifted, he moved to the door to Banning's trophy room, dribbling the last of the gasoline in a trail. He lit the trail. Heat billowed, and choking smoke quickly filled the small room. Guthrie retreated into the house, shutting the vault door behind him. There, he busied himself erasing as much evidence of his presence and he could. He found his wallet and truck keys in Banning's desk, then he went upstairs to take care of the rooms where Diane and Howard had been kept.

By the time he was done, the flames in the vault had died along with the painting that fed them. Guthrie piled the charred remains in the center of the room, and burned them too. His final act before he went out to his truck was to thumb the switch that opened the trophy case of human heads.

"I got him," he told the heads. "Rest, now. Someone will be long soon enough."

A few minutes later, he left the ranch. At the blacktop, he turned left, and in a few minutes, reached his Honda. He pulled a five-gallon can of gas from the Xterra, doused his old Honda, and with regret, lit it on fire. He couldn't drive two vehicles back to Houston, anyway.

That should alert the authorities, he thought as he drove away, toward the little town to the north. Toward home.

43

GUTHRIE PRACTICALLY STAGGERED UP THE sidewalk to his front door. Before he could sort his front door key from the others on the key ring, the door opened.

"Thank God you're all right," Diane said as she stepped back to let him in.

"Is it over?" Howard asked anxiously.

"I burned the painting," Guthrie said.

"Adriana...?"

"Her, Banning, all the rest of them," Guthrie began, then he shrugged. "They're either one place or another, but none of them are here any more." He nodded toward the bedroom. "I think I need to lie down. For a long time."

He was out the instant his head hit the pillow.

When he woke, it was dark outside. He didn't bother to look at the clock. He hadn't when he'd laid down, so there was no way to tell how long he'd slept. He went to the bathroom and took a long, hot shower. He emerged to the smell of frying bacon.

"More of my limited cooking," Diane said, turning from the stove when he entered the kitchen twenty minutes later. She gave him a wry smile. "Hope you don't mind."

"I could get used to it," Guthrie said as he poured himself a cup of coffee. "What about you, Howard?"

The artist was perched on a stool, sipping from his own cup.

"Yes," Diane said before he could answer. "He can. Or we can eat out every night. Howard, why don't you show Clay his new acquisitions."

Howard gave Guthrie his own wry smile as Diane turned back to the stove, then nodded his head toward the living room. Guthrie followed.

"Diane and I borrowed your car while you slept," Howard said. "Hope you don't mind. I figured it was all right since you said the threat is eliminated."

By now, they'd reached the living room, and the artist simply nodded toward the wall where Guthrie had hung the collage he'd bought from Diane. That seemed like a long time ago. Hanging on either side were paintings by Howard, one a West Texas landscape, the other a scene from Central Texas.

"You don't have to keep them," Howard said. "You can sell them if you want."

"I think I'll keep them," Guthrie said. "I don't want to give up something precious." He gave Howard a meaningful look.

"Yes," Howard said. "There's precious little that is precious in life. I just hate that it took going through all this to realize how much Diane means to me."

"And painting? You don't plan on creating any more gateways, do you?"

"If I do, I'll choose an idyllic world next time. You'll be invited any time you want to escape with us."

"Do you think you still could, with Adriana out of the picture?"

"I don't know. I feel like my urge to paint that hideous world is wiped out, at least. But if I'm lucky, the technique will remain." He chuckled. "I'll just stop before that last brush stroke."

"It'll make you famous," Guthrie said.

"Even better, I'll have someone to share it with."

Yes, Guthrie thought with a pang. But he suppressed the feeling.

He'd been successful in his quest to save Howard and Diane, and he figured that was enough for now. At the moment, he was too drained to feel lonely, anyway.

They ate breakfast in a silence. That seemed odd after the whispered conversations of the past week, but it also felt normal for a change.

Afterward, with dawn just breaking, Diane and Howard left in Howard's car, which they'd retrieved when they'd brought the two paintings to Guthrie's house while he'd slept. Diane wanted to pay him, but Guthrie demurred.

"The two paintings are more than enough," he said.

"No," Howard said. "They're not."

"Then I guess you'll just have to invite me over for dinner sometime," Guthrie said with a smile.

When they were gone, Guthrie found his car keys and drove to the shopping center and Tereba's concealed door. The door was there, and Guthrie went through it.

"Mr. Guthrie," the old man said, looking up from his work behind the counter. He was grinding up some dried leaves with a mortar and pestle. "I am glad to see you hale and hearty."

"Hale and hearty, huh?" Guthrie snorted. "I thought I might come by to give you an update."

"That would be most welcome, though not entirely necessary," Tereba said with a smile. "I felt the flux return."

"The flux?"

"Yes. The fluid elasticity of reality. Gateways like those created by the Lycori, aided by Howard Graham's unwitting help, are places where the flux of two realities are cemented together. And like all such joints, they are as brittle as they are disruptively obtrusive. Such a condition can be sensed, and when it is released, the elasticity between the two realities returns. When you destroyed the paintings, I felt the anchor points slip free. Thank you."

"Well, I didn't feel much more than fear," Guthrie admitted.

"Fear of a flame is admirable, is it not, Mr. Guthrie?"

"It is, Master Tereba."

He watched the old man for a few seconds, the air silent except for the sound of the grinding mortar and pestle.

"What about the old woman?" he asked. "Adriana's mother?"

"Perhaps we should go check on her," Tereba answered.

"You have to be kidding. That evil old witch?"

"Deluded, perhaps, but evil? I don't know. You have looked upon evil, as have I. The Lycori were victims of the thing we're calling Angra Mainyu as much as Howard Graham, Diane Weston, or you. Adriana, Melanie, and even the old woman were guilty of using others to further their own ends, but that is unlike Karl Banning, who took pleasure in damaging and destroying."

"You're serious."

"I am always serious."

"Now?"

"No better time. You have your car, do you not?"

On the way to the Eternal Flame, Guthrie filled the old man in on the details of what had transpired since they'd last spoken. When they arrived at the Victorian house on Pequot, Guthrie told Tereba to wait.

"There's a guard inside. I probably ought to take care of him before you go in."

"Call me when you are ready," the old man said.

Guthrie got out of the car and went up the Eternal Flame's front steps. The glass he'd shattered on his last visit had been replaced, and the front door was locked. He went around to the back of the building, climbed the stairs to the apartment's back door, and knocked loudly. Bailey appeared a few moments later, and his eyes widened when he saw Guthrie through the window. He drew his gun and cautiously opened the door.

"You can put that away," Guthrie said. "I'm not here to zap you again."

"What for, then?"

"Adriana, Banning, and all the rest of them are dead. You are now out of a job."

"You kill them?" Bailey looked skeptical.

"Some of them. The rest were killed by their own folly. It would be smart of you not to follow in their footsteps. Time for you to go."

"What about the old Danae? I can't just leave her."

"Yes, you can. Go take care of your own mother."

"You do not have anything to worry about," came a voice from behind Guthrie. It was Tereba, who'd silently come up the stairs. "We will take care of her without harming her."

"And who are you?" Bailey demanded.

"The old Danae's new guardian."

Bailey hesitated for a few moments then holstered his gun.

"Go ahead," he said, resignation in his voice. "I hate the old bitch, anyway, and if there's nobody left to pay me, then I'm outta here." He let them in, and while they went to the old woman's bedroom, he gathered his possessions and left.

"Remember me?" Guthrie said as he entered the old woman's room. "The tool?"

The old woman sat up, snarling, then flinched back into her pillows, face stony, when Tereba entered the room behind Guthrie.

"At last we meet," Tereba said. "I've heard a lot about you."

"And I've heard nothing good about you, old man," she sneered.

"I suppose you wouldn't," he said. "My friend has something to tell you."

"Your daughter and granddaughter and her unborn child are all gone. They've crossed Chinvat Bridge, and they're never coming back."

"Crossed?" An expression of satisfaction took over the old woman's face. "I will miss them. But they will thrive with Angra Mainyu and haoma, and as soon as the child is born, I will join them."

"I think not," Tereba said. "Angra Mainyu transformed them into more of the horrible creatures that guard Hara Berezaiti."

"You lie."

"You will know soon enough that I don't. Delude yourself until then, if you choose, but know this: Your sisters are gone, and there is no one left but you, who are old and barren. You are the last of your line." There was sadness in his voice.

"And now you're here to finish me off?"

"We have won, have we not?" Tereba shrugged. "There is no sense in being overtly cruel to an aged woman in pain and despair."

"What, then? You leave me here to die in my own filth?"

"I have arranged for you to have a room in a private sanitarium. You will be taken care of in a pleasant environment for the rest of you life."

"I don't need your charity."

"I'd listen to him," Guthrie said. "He's being pretty generous considering you nearly helped to destroy the world."

"Angra Mainyu would not have...."

"Forget it," Guthrie snapped. "I saw that thing, and it destroyed Adriana and Melanie just as remorselessly as it did everyone and everything else it came into contact with. It laid waste to the world it inhabited. You called me a tool, but you were the real tool. I'd take Master Tereba's offer and be glad you're here and not on the other side of Chinvat Bridge."

He turned, drawing his gun, as he heard someone entering the apartment through the back door. But he holstered the weapon when he saw Li Wu come into the room, followed by a couple of orderlies in scrubs. Wu nodded pleasantly to Guthrie then gestured for the orderlies to take care of the old Danae.

"Careful," Guthrie warned. "She bites."

"I will ride back with Li Wu," Tereba said.

"Fine," Guthrie replied. "I missed my beauty sleep for the last few days. I'm going back to bed." He looked at Wu. "See you on Monday?"

"Nine sharp," the tai chi master affirmed with a smile.

Guthrie turned, left the apartment, drove home, and shut the door on the world.

Phosphene Publishing Company
publishes books and DVDs relating to literature,
history, the paranormal, film, spirituality, and the
martial arts.

For other great titles, visit
phosphenepublishing.com

www.ingramcontent.com/pod-product-compliance
Lightning Source LLC
Chambersburg PA
CBHW070531260626
47161CB00002B/337